NIGHTS WITH HIM

Book #4 in the Seductive Nights series

Lauren Blakely

Interior Layout by Jesse Gordon

TABLE OF CONTENTS

ALSO BY LAUREN BLAKELY

The Caught Up in Love Series

(Each book in this series follows a different couple so each book can be read separately, or enjoyed as a series since characters crossover)

Caught Up in Her (A short prequel novella to *Caught Up in Us*)
Caught Up In Us
Pretending He's Mine
Trophy Husband
Playing With Her Heart
Far Too Tempting (A spin-off, this book also ties into *Stars in Their Eyes*, since the hero is the brother of the *Stars in Their Eyes* hero)

Wrapped Up in Love

(A Caught Up in Love new adult spin-off series)

A Starstruck Kiss (A short prequel to introduce readers to the series and the start of William and Jess's love story)
Stars in Their Eyes (A full-length novel about William and Jess)
21 Kisses (A full-length new adult novel about Anaka's cousin, Kennedy, releases February 2015)
Stealing Her Love (A full-length novel starring Anaka and her love interest Jason, releases in summer 2015)
Untitled Novella (December 2015, a new adult novella starring *21 Kisses* characters)

The No Regrets Series

(These books should be read in order)

The Thrill of It
The Start of Us
Every Second With You

The Seductive Nights Series

(The first four books follow Julia and Clay and should be read in order)

First Night
Night After Night
After This Night
One More Night
One Night With Her (A short prequel novella about Michelle and Jack, this story is also included in the ebook of *Nights With Him*)
Nights With Him (A standalone novel about Michelle Milo and her lover Jack Sullivan)
Sweet, Sinful Nights (Brent's book, March 2015)

The Fighting Fire Series

Burn For Me (Smith and Jamie)
Melt for Him (Megan and Becker)

This book is dedicated to
Violet, Kim, Tanya, Gale, Kelley and CC.
Without them, this story would not exist. And, as
always, this book is for my friend Cynthia.

ONE NIGHT WITH HER

A prequel novella to Nights With Him

ABOUT ONE NIGHT WITH HER

First names only for one night of pleasure...

He's only at the hotel to close a business deal. Then he sees her, and his agenda for the evening shifts—woo her, win her, and make sure she never forgets who gave her the most exquisite pleasure she's ever had. Jack Sullivan, sex toy mogul, a billionaire, and one of New York City's most eligible bachelors is captivated by the brilliant and beautiful Michelle Milo.

From her witty mouth to her sinful body, she's his perfect fantasy. But there's more at play than the undeniable chemistry; they both might be exactly what the other needs.

As soon as he has her between the sheets, he knows one night with her will never be enough.

The trouble is, he's about to run into her tomorrow...in the last place he expects.

CHAPTER ONE
ONE NIGHT WITH HER
First Impressions

Pleasure, beyond her wildest fantasies.

"That's a helluva promise to make. Because some people have pretty wild fantasies," Jack said as he rattled off the tagline attached to the tall purple device that boasted twelve different settings designed to serve up "exquisite stimulation."

"That's exactly why we're making that promise," Casey replied as she hopped up on the edge of his desk and crossed her legs, absently kicking a high-heeled foot back and forth like a pendulum. "Because this bad boy can de-li-ver. Stories, I can tell you," she said, and Jack quickly held up a hand as a stop sign.

"I'll have to trust you on that."

She rolled her stormy blue eyes, the same shade as his. "Don't go all squeamish on me."

"Has nothing to do with squeamishness," he said, shaking his head. "You can just keep this on the list of things I never want to hear—stories about my little sister and our newest product."

"You don't have to trust me when it comes to The Wild One," she said, grasping the toy and cradling the newest vibrator in her hand, stroking it lovingly. "Trust our product testing group, otherwise known as The Happiest Ladies in the World."

"Do they walk around all blissed out, mouths open, eyes glazed?" Jack teased, hanging his jaw open in demonstration. Not mockingly, of course. He was a big fan of that deliciously sated look a woman wore after an orgasm. Usually multiple Os. At least, as far as he was concerned.

Casey snapped her fingers. "Allow me to quote some feedback from one of our testers. 'The Wild One is like a direct line to a pleasure palace I didn't even know existed inside of me.' Now that I think about it, we should rename this one The Wizard, because this is the closest anyone will ever come to real magic here." She stopped, took a beat. "Get it? Come?"

He nodded, a small smile tugging at his lips. "I do get it. Wasn't a hard one to wrap my head around," he said, tapping his temple.

"See? You've got the hang of the puns too. Hard one," she repeated.

"Been running this business with you for five years now, Casey. I'm well acquainted with your style. And with the magic we're peddling."

"Abracadabra," she said, miming waving a magic wand. "Joy delivered."

That's what the company they ran was called—Joy Delivered—and Jack had a meeting in an hour with one of the city's top purveyors of pleasure products, Eden. The classy shop on the Upper East Side, conveniently located above a private BDSM club Eden also ran, had been actively promoting another device, the Dancing Dolphin. That triple speed, nearly noiseless, terrifically thrilling pocket vibrator had developed a cult following among legions of erotic book club readers, who praised it as the perfect companion while they read one-handed, often about BDSM storylines, as it turned out. The dom-sub lifestyle wasn't Jack's personal cup of tea, but he was glad for whatever floated someone's boat enough to open the bedside drawer and grab a toy.

Yeah, business was good thanks to the erotica craze that had swept not just the country, but also the world, and had made it more acceptable to bring another party into the bedroom, even if the third party required batteries. Nothing wrong with self-love or with calling in backup between the sheets, Jack reasoned.

"Are you going to take this with you to your meeting tonight with Henry and Marquita?" Casey handed him The Wild One, but Jack quickly shook his head.

"They've already seen it. We're just finalizing the paperwork for the new shipment. We're beyond the giggle-at-the-dildo stage of conversation."

"But it's still nice to see the pleasure tools. Especially since they're going to that sexuality conference at The Pierson, right?"

"Right. He said he'd be attending some sessions in the afternoon. And yet, call me crazy," he said, stopping to scratch his chin, "I think I might prefer not to display a nine-inch fake schlong on the table at The Pierson Hotel. It's a classy joint."

"And all their guests are probably slipping plastic purple friends under those twelve-hundred thread count sheets at that classy joint. That's why you hear so many high-pitched screams at The Pierson," Casey said, rising from the desk, and slapping a palm on it to accentuate her punch line. With her other hand, she tossed him the newest toy, her blond hair swishing around her face from the throw. "Take it, Jack. Maybe he wants to bring a present home to his wife."

"Not one that's been manhandled already."

"That's what the toy cleaner is for," she said, reaching for a bottle of anti-bacterial cleaner from the edge of his desk and tossing it next. He caught it easily, snatching it out of the air.

"By the way, send Marquita my love. Tell her and Henry I say hi."

Casey sauntered out of his office and Jack grinned, *tsk*-ing her playfully under his breath. No way in hell was he bringing this device along, and it had nothing to do with being embarrassed, and everything to do with keeping it simple. He wasn't a bag man; he didn't want to tote his laptop to a meeting, along with a toy in the side pocket. A wallet, phone and keys were all he needed, so he left the rest behind as he stood up, pushed a hand roughly through his dark hair, and then jammed his phone into the pocket of his pants. He grabbed the cranberry-colored tie slung over the back of his chair and looped it around his neck, tying a neat knot. Best to look sharp for the team at Eden.

New York was still very much a suit-and-tie town, and so Jack wore the requisite uniform.

He was about to step out of his office when Casey popped back in, the look in her eyes now intense and serious. "Don't forget your appointment tomorrow at two."

He held out his hands wide, and grumbled, "I know."

She pointed at him and pursed her lips as she leaned in the doorway. "It's important."

"Yes, Mommy."

"Oh, ha, ha, ha. But you need it," she said, and she was right. Jack hadn't been the same since he'd lost his fiancée a year ago, and he needed to get his head screwed on right. *Correction.* His heart. He needed to get that annoying organ fixed.

If it were even possible.

That was the question.

But tonight, his mind was on business, plain and simple, so he headed off to The Pierson to finalize the deal.

* * *

Michelle Milo had sex on the brain.

Dirty, sweaty, slick sex. Limo sex. Office sex. Swanky-nightclub-bathroom sex.

Unfortunately, none of these were positive images, because they had nothing to do with her sex life, but instead her client's philandering husband.

And she was dying to shout, *leave him.*

She wanted to scream it, to slash it on the wall in orange paint, to get down on her knees and beg. But Shayla needed time to come to the realization on her own, even though it seemed patently fucking obvious that she should not only leave that cad of a husband, but kick him several times in the balls too.

"I just keep thinking about The Owl. It has these low lights, almost kind of a blue light, and the bathroom is all tiled in black, and I had such great memories about our time there," Shayla recounted, referring to a club in Los Angeles where her husband had been caught having sex with his assistant last month. "It was our place," she said, wiping a tear that had already streaked the mascara from her eyelashes, sending a black jagged line down one porcelain cheek. "Well, back when I used to want to have sex with him."

Michelle reached for a tissue from the box next to her, handed it to her twice-weekly client, and waited as she dabbed away the evidence of her sadness. Shayla sunk lower in the couch, framed behind her by abstract prints on the wall of the Lexington Avenue offices where Michelle ran her psychology practice. "What is it that bothers you most? Is it that he slept with another woman? Or that he slept with her someplace where you did in the past? Or is it something else?"

Shayla bit her lip and looked away, perhaps not wanting to deal with the *something else* possibility that had brought her here in the first place. Not that it was her fault that her husband had a dick that needed to be locked up and sent straight to jail for its one eye that wandered ALL. THE. TIME.

Shayla faced a different set of challenges, and that's what Michelle needed to help her with. She gently prodded her client, who sat frozen like a statue, her jaw set hard, as if she needed to hold all her fears inside. "Or is it because you think it's your fault that he isn't faithful?" Michelle asked cautiously.

"It is my fault," Shayla squeaked out, insistent. "I haven't wanted to have sex ever since we had kids."

"And you think that makes it your fault that he's cheating on you?"

"Isn't it?"

Michelle shook her head. "Of course it's not. He's responsible for his actions, and only you can decide if you want to hold him accountable for them. But we also need to keep getting at the root of the *why* for you. We spend a lot of time focusing on him and his actions, but we need to dive into why you don't want to have sex with him. Because you lost interest well before he started cheating on you," she said. That's why Shayla was here, to focus on her own intimacy issues, since that was Michelle's specialty—helping patients work through relationship challenges and fears of closeness. Shayla's were compounded because her husband was an ass. But first things first. There would be time to deal with him later.

"Let's talk about why . . ."

Forty-five minutes later, Michelle flashed a small smile at Shayla, pleased that her client was making a modicum of progress. Some days, progress was glacial, and sometimes it was cheetah fast. All that mattered was that Shayla seemed to be moving forward. Michelle said goodbye to her, then checked her schedule for tomorrow on her laptop. It would be another full day, with a new patient appointment, too. The evening ahead of her was packed as well—she had a presentation to give at a sexuality conference, sharing some of her findings with other psychotherapists on sex and love addiction. She had experience in that area, having helped guide several patients through the throes of addiction and into recovery, and the president of the New York Chapter of the Association of Intimate Relationship Psychologists had invited her. Carla Kimberly had been a mentor to her over the years, and had referred patients to Michelle, so it was a double honor to have been asked to speak tonight.

She smoothed a hand over her pencil skirt, adjusted the collar on her crisp white blouse, and changed from flats to her black pumps. She grabbed her work phone from the clutter of papers on her desk, but the battery was almost drained.

Crap.

Having two phones, an iPad and a laptop turned into a juggling act when it came to keeping them all charged. She forwarded the work phone to her personal cell in case her service called. On the way out, she stopped in the office bathroom to brush her teeth and touch up her lipstick.

There. Now she was ready for a quickie meeting at The Pierson.

She laughed to herself. *Quickie*. Too bad she wasn't having a quickie of another kind. It had been a while since she'd had one of those. She'd dated an actor for a few weeks in late spring, and she replayed some of her dates with Liam fondly. He'd been outgoing, gorgeous and quite capable with his hands, so they'd done plenty, but nothing close to a quickie.

The problem was even when she'd been pressed up against Liam, she'd been thinking of Clay. Her very good friend who also happened to be the man she'd been madly in love with for ten years. Clay, the gorgeous, sexy, smart entertainment lawyer, and best friend of her brother.

Oh, but there was one teeny, tiny little problem with that overflow of feelings she had for Clay. He didn't love her, and hadn't even known how she felt about him. To add insult to injury, he was happily in love with another woman. A month ago, he'd gone and married that woman in Vegas.

Yep, Michelle Milo, one of Manhattan's most sought-after shrinks, a true specialist in intimacy and well known for helping to heal heartache, was the poster child for unrequited love. Might as well slap a big *L* on her forehead. God, she was an idiot, and the definition of an oxymoron —she spent her days advising others, and her nights longing for someone she couldn't have.

She was doing her best to move on and push Clay far out of her heart. Like, ideally, into another galaxy. She'd been taking her medicine for the last few months, blasting loud anti-love songs in her apartment from her favorite musician Jane Black, trying out bowling with some of her colleagues, dabbling in Spanish lessons, and finally training for a 10K marathon she finished last month. She'd never been a fan of running, but it was growing on her solely because the relentless pound of her feet against concrete was starting to numb her feelings for her good friend.

The best method for moving on, though, was work, and she loved her job more than anything in the world. Burying herself in other people's woes was her deepest passion; the chance to help someone else change and become healthier her greatest joy. She headed off to the conference, eager to dive into work for the rest of the night as she shared some of her findings at the meeting.

The Pierson was only a few blocks away so she arrived ten minutes later at the swank hotel, one of those upscale establishments that doubled as a den for both sin and business with its lobby bar boasting blue neon lighting, its drinks in toweringly tall and thin glasses, and hip music playing in the background.

As she waited for the elevator she couldn't help but notice a smoking-hot man in the hotel bar, chatting animatedly with others at his table. She catalogued his features quickly—broad chest, dark hair with the slightest wave, crystal-blue eyes like the ocean, and a smile that was quite simply . . . beguiling.

Perhaps she lingered too long, or perhaps she lingered just the right amount of time, because he glanced across the open lobby bar, past the other tables, and his gaze seemed to land on her.

At least, she wanted to believe it had as she stepped inside the elevator and the doors closed. She'd try to remember his face for later. It could never hurt to put a face to a fantasy when one was alone in bed with her toys.

CHAPTER TWO
ONE NIGHT WITH HER
Favorite Parts

They hadn't asked to see The Wild One, but there'd been no need to see it.

Henry's partner in business and love, Marquita, had proudly boasted about the windows that had nearly shattered in her apartment building when she'd used The Wild One last week. Jack simply smiled and said, "I'm pleased that you were pleased."

"So pleased," she'd reiterated, then planted a kiss on Henry's cheek, one that suggested there'd be much more than kissing going on between them later tonight. That was one of the perks, so to speak, about working in this line of business. Not watching business associates lock lips, but rather, that the people he dealt with didn't have too many sexual hang-ups. Of course, he ran into plenty of over-sharers too. Some folks assumed if you peddled sex toys, it meant you wanted to hear about every single thing someone did with one, and Jack most decidedly did not want to be told about every escapade. But hey, it came with the territory. Besides, he was used to it with these two —they'd been business partners and friends since Jack and Casey had started Joy Delivered. They were like family.

"I'm glad you're feeling better, Marquita," Jack said, because she'd battled a serious illness most of last year.

"And The Wild One helps," Marquita said with a bright smile.

"And now there's something else we need to talk about," Henry began, steepling his fingers together, his tone shifting to serious as he motioned for someone to join them at the bar—a suited man with black hair, and a blue-and-red striped tie. Only politicians wore such ties. Jack tensed; politics was not his favorite playground.

"Jack, I want to introduce you to Marquita's brother, Paul Denkler. He's running for city councilman in our neck of the woods and he's been focused on safe streets, schools and a balanced budget. But somehow that message has been subverted by his opponent, who's decided to fight below the belt and attack our business. If Paul doesn't win, it could be very bad for business," Henry said, and Jack's ears pricked at the words *bad for business*. He didn't like those words. Not one bit. He preferred *good for business*, so if this fellow played on the good side, then he'd hear him out.

"Lay it on me," Jack said, and a meeting about selling The Wild One quickly became something else entirely.

* * *

The deal had been signed. The new product would have both prominent in-store and online placement, and Jack had promised an extra shipment for Marquita and Henry's personal stash. The undecided part? How he felt about Denkler. How he felt about getting involved in politics. He didn't have a thorny past with a politician; he didn't have a senator dad he detested. He simply followed the news, and knew that politics was a slimy, dirty battlefield. Jack had served his country for six years and that was about the extent of his interest in matters of state. This thing with Denkler, though—it wasn't a matter of state, so much as a matter of business, and a matter of personal business. Jack cared deeply about Henry; the man was a business partner, and had been through hell and back during the past year as his wife battled and beat breast cancer.

What pissed him off was the opponent's tactics, and how the other guy was going after Paul Denkler through his brother-in-law's business, which had nothing to do with the race. That was underhanded, and that didn't sit well with Jack.

But whatever he decided to do, he'd do it with Casey on board. The two were a team, and always had been, so he'd have to table Henry's request until he spoke with his sister and laid it all out for her. For now, he shoved thoughts of politics and campaigns and consequences aside. Henry and Marquita were off to a dinner meeting, and Jack was alone, so he settled in at the bar and ordered a vodka tonic, scrolling through his phone as he waited for his drink.

He'd been planning on having a drink with his good buddy Nate tonight, but Nate had to work late on a last-minute deal. They'd agreed to still meet tomorrow morning for a round of hoops before work. That meant Jack's agenda for the rest of the evening was simple—a quick drink, then he'd watch some of the Yankees game from the comfort of his living room. Those twin activities would help him crash later, because he sure could use a decent night's sleep before the appointment that Casey had arranged tomorrow at two. Just the thought of dealing then with the shit that was in his head gave him an ulcer, but he knew Casey would kick his ass if he didn't give it a shot.

She wanted him to start dating again. She'd told him the upcoming charity event they were sponsoring next month for breast cancer research would be the perfect time to get back on the market, or at the very least, to slough off all his regret from the past. As if that were possible. But Casey had her mind set. She seemed ready and eager to get him back on the scene, judging from the story link she'd just emailed him. The note was titled, *New York's Most Eligible Bachelors.*

Look! You're on the list! Sex-toy mogul Jack Sullivan tops this year's list of the city's most eligible bachelors in business. Don't you think he needs a new woman to mend his broken heart? Makes you just want to nab that man even more.

He rolled his eyes, and replied, *The depth of their insight never fails to astound me.*

He turned the damn thing to silent. He could do without the reminders tonight. Reminders of anything. Of the woman he'd lost, of the fascination the gossip rags seemed to have with his dating or non-dating status—as the case had been for the last year—and of the claws some women wanted to sink into him, thanks to the growth trajectory Joy Delivered had been on. While at dinner with Casey last week, he'd been propositioned by a young woman who'd said she was on the hunt for an eligible bachelor businessman.

Call him old-fashioned, but the next time he got involved, he'd like it to be with someone who actually gave a shit about him, rather than what he did for a living, the company he ran, or his prior love life.

Or with the absolutely stunning brunette who was walking past him and—hello, lucky stars—was now sitting at the other end of the bar. The same one who'd caught his eye when she'd stepped into the elevator earlier in the evening. Her hair was in a twist that showed off her neck. She had a fantastic pair of legs, strong and muscular, a nice trim waist, and she was rocking some kind of buttoned-up-on-the outside vibe with her blouse and pencil skirt that made him wonder if she was buttoned up on the inside too.

* * *

Michelle hadn't been expecting the barrage of questions, but what an eager bunch of counselors she'd encountered after her talk. She'd never felt so popular 'til tonight, when she was nearly mobbed by fellow psychotherapists as she attempted to walk away from the lectern. They fired off questions for her on treatment and guidance for love and sex addicts, and she happily answered all of them to the best of her ability. Then she gathered up her notes, and made her way down to the lobby. She adjusted her purse strap, and sighed deeply, pleased with her work for the evening. Sharing insights and learning was a true passion of hers, and she'd had the opportunity to do so tonight with colleagues.

Tonight. The word reverberated through her, and she felt the slightest pang when she stepped off the elevator and remembered it was a Thursday. She and Clay had often had drinks on a Thursday night. While they still did from time to time, along with her brother, Davis, the get-togethers had been curtailed since Julia moved in with him. Understandable; the man was committed, and now he was married. Julia hadn't cut them off; in fact, the redhead was lovely, and Michelle had visited Julia's bar a few times. But it was simply too hard for Michelle to see them together that often, so she'd kept them in her life, but put herself on a restricted Clay-and-Julia diet.

Keeping a distance was a necessity, but she missed those Thursday nights. And she missed the drinks, truth be told. She could *certainly* go for a little nightcap to finish off the day. She'd always been comfortable in her own skin and with her own company, so a quick solo stop at the bar was no big deal.

She followed the music and sat down at the tall, sleek metal bar, ordering a vodka tonic that arrived quickly, and taking out her iPad. There was a new Tumblr feed she wanted to peruse, but that would only happen from the privacy of home and bed since it was a terribly naughty one. She had an article she wanted to finish, and then a novel to dive into about a con artist, and she'd even downloaded a new app for practicing Spanish phrases, partly because the male voice on the app was so deliciously sexy. Perhaps better to listen to that in her apartment, she reasoned, as she lifted the cool glass to her lips and took the first sip. Raising her eyes, she noticed that same man she'd seen earlier. He was seated at the end of the bar, drinking what looked to be a vodka tonic too. The glass hit his lips at the exact same moment, his moves mirroring hers. His blue eyes seemed to sparkle, a hint of wicked delight in them.

Same drink, same time, same absolutely smoking-hot guy she'd spotted an hour before. One barstool away. When she set the glass down, she said, "Jinx."

"Jinx," he repeated.

"Does that mean you owe me a drink?" she asked, and then nearly clasped her hand over her mouth. But instead, she went with it. "Sorry, that's pretty much close to the cheesiest pick-up line ever."

His lips curved slightly into a grin. "Does that mean you're trying to pick me up?"

She laughed, and shook her head. The silvery metal surface of the bar revealed a rush of red racing to her cheeks as she answered. "No."

She wasn't, right? Those words had just tumbled out accidentally, not because she'd seen him earlier and memorized his face, and not because one quick glance at Mr. Cool, Calm and Collected had her adding him to an arsenal of possible late-night ammunition to feed her active fantasy life.

Very, very active, and she fed it regularly. With Tumblr, with toys, and with wild images of pleasure.

"That's too bad then," he said, and his voice was deep, with the slightest rasp to it, like velvet that had a rough edge. That edge in it sent goose bumps down her spine. Or maybe it was his words, the hint of possibility to them.

"Is it? Too bad?" she asked, tilting her head to the side, shifting her body language, one hundred percent aware that she was getting her flirt on.

"Not just too bad. It would be a travesty."

She brought her hand to her heart, playing along. "How sad. I'd hate to be responsible for a disaster of that degree."

"You could avert it, then," he said dryly, arching an eyebrow, then taking another swallow of his drink. The sight of his lips on the glass had her mind galloping off to a naughty land, because those lips looked delicious. Soft and kissable, while the rest of him looked hard and strong. She liked the way his tie was loosened, and his jacket draped over his chair. A businessman in repose.

"I could, couldn't I? If I were interested in avoiding such a sad turn of events."

"Are you, though? Interested?" he asked.

Michelle was almost certain a butterfly had taken off in her belly because her stomach flipped, and it was primed to flop again. "I'm getting there," she said playfully, enjoying the back and forth, the very fine layer of innuendo that lined this conversation like a cool evening mist after a hot day. She brought her glass to her lips and took another drink, hoping it would have the same effect on him that his sip had had on her.

"Excellent," he said, giving her a quick, appreciative nod. "So . . . are you having a good evening?"

"I am, as a matter of fact. Productive day, energetic evening, perhaps a satisfying night overall," she said, and he chuckled softly when she said *satisfying*.

"What would make your night satisfying?" he asked, his cool blue gaze pinned on her. Then he raked his eyes over her, and she couldn't deny that she enjoyed the possibility that he liked what he saw.

"I enjoy a satisfying conversation." She threw down the gauntlet. He seemed a good sparring partner.

"Let's satisfy you conversationally then," he said, picking up the challenge easily. "Now, I could ask you what you do for a living, but everyone does that. I could ask what brings you to this hotel, but that's also trite. Instead, why don't we talk about something that people don't usually discuss. For instance, what is your favorite body part?"

She burst into laugher at his out-of-left-field question and the completely deadpan manner he asked it in, but then quickly grabbed the baton of the conversation. "On me, I would have to say it's my elbows. I have absolutely amazing elbows," she said, crooking her arm and showing him her elbow.

"Wow. You're right. Those are glorious elbows. Smooth and soft, and yet pointy, too. And they make the arm move."

"Amazing, isn't it?" she said, demonstrating playfully. "And my second choice would be my right butt cheek."

"Not the left one?"

"Well, they both are pretty nice."

He raised his eyebrows appreciatively. "I bet they're spectacular," he said, that sexy gravel of his voice sending a charge through her.

"And you?" she asked, as her skin heated up. "Your favorite body part?"

"I've always been told I have great ears. It's weird, but women sometimes stop me on the street to comment on my ears," he said, shaking his head in faux wonderment as she laughed again.

"They are really nicely shaped," she said, pointing to his ears, then looking him in the eyes, before offering a true compliment, as he'd seemed to do for her. "But you have beautiful eyes."

He flashed her a quick smile. "Thank you. So do you. And legs. And arms. And lips. And eyes. Okay, here's another question," he said, after he moved through the sweet litany of compliments, as if he wanted to give them but was careful to not be more forward until he knew if she wanted it.

"Wait," she said. "You didn't research interesting questions to ask women at bars, did you?"

"What if I did?"

"Did you?"

"No." He held up his hands as if to say he was innocent.

"The favorite-body-part question just came naturally to you?"

"A lot of things come naturally to me," he said, with a confidence in his voice that bordered on cocky. She kind of liked it. More than she thought she would. He leaned back in the bar stool, his whole demeanor assured and relaxed, as if nothing could throw him off his game. She was willing to bet he was in a profession that valued this sort of mindset. She was also pretty sure this was an ideal mindset for random bar chatter.

"All right, then. Let's see how you do on the other side."

"Turn the tables on me."

"I will. Since we're not talking about professions, how about this one? If you had an extra thirty minutes free in the day for fun, what would you do with it?"

"Shoot hoops," he answered immediately. "You?"

"I'd spend more time on Tumblr," she said, and left it up to him to figure out what she did there. When he gave her an approving nod as he downed more of his vodka, she knew he understood what Tumblr was good for.

"Perhaps we should go back to that pick-up line, then?"

"The one where I buy you a drink?" she asked, as a mischievous look flitted past his blue eyes. Damn, they were gorgeous eyes. A pure and light blue, like the crystal waters off Fiji.

"Or I could buy you a drink," he offered, and this time the cool charm was gone, and his tone was direct. A direct line to her desire to spend more time with him, here at the bar.

There was a rustle of noise as the man grabbed his phone and his glass and stood up. Was he leaving? No, he moved a seat closer, and that brief few seconds of him standing gave Michelle the chance to look up, and admire his height. He had to be easily over six-feet tall. That height was a basic requirement for dating, she and her friend Sutton had joked. A man needed to be a "standard six" and then some, preferably.

He gestured to the stool next to her. "Is this seat taken?"

"When you sit down in it, it will be."

"Then I will gladly make sure it's taken, and that no one else can get it." He smiled at her, and extended a hand. "I'm Jack. Just Jack."

She shook his hand as he sat next to her. "Michelle with two *Ls*. I used to have one *L* in my name, but it always looked like it was spelled wrong, so I just decided to add the second *L*. Because I can."

"Hell yeah, you can. And it's a pleasure to meet you, Michelle who now has two *Ls*. I hope this isn't too forward of me, but you don't seem like a woman who's going to get offended easily. I noticed how hot you are when you walked into the hotel an hour ago."

Hot. He'd called her hot. Not pretty. Not beautiful. But hot. She'd take hot. She'd happily take being called hot, because hot was what she felt when he said it. Hot all over. Bothered in all the right places.

"How hot?" she asked, eager for more of his compliments.

He leaned in closer, and lowered his voice to a sexy whisper. "Fucking hot."

She shut her eyes for the briefest of moments, letting the words flare through her body, igniting something inside of her that usually was only lit up from her fantasy life. But now she was feeling something in real life, from a real person, who seemed to have real interest.

"I believe we could make a nice mutual admiration society then, because I noticed the same of you. Also about an hour ago."

He raised his glass and clinked it with hers. "To mutual admiration."

"And to another drink, and I will buy. Because it looks like we're ready for another one," she said, glancing at her nearly empty glass.

"I'm ready for more," he said, and brushed his hand against her shoulder. A fresh blast of sparks raced through her body as he traced a soft line along her collarbone. The tiny touch that started on her neck spread through her, like a golden comet, leaving heat in its wake. In the span of time, his touch was a blink, but it held the promise of so much more.

"I'd be up for more," she whispered.

"Much, much more," he said slowly, seductively, that deep, sexy voice threading its way through her, settling down between her legs, turning her on to the point where she was picturing reaching for that wine-red tie, tugging him close, and learning how that stubbly goodness on his jaw would feel against her. And how much more he could raise the heat inside her body with a kiss.

She ordered but when the bartender returned with the drinks and she reached for her purse, Jack placed a hand on top of hers. Firmly. "I was only joking about you paying."

"What if I want to pay?"

"I'm not going to let you pay, Michelle," he said in a determined tone, his bright blue eyes fixed on her.

She swallowed, looked down at his hand covering hers, and already her imagination revved into hyper-drive. Long, strong fingers. Big hands. Holding her down. Pinning her.

He seemed to sense where her mind had gone, or maybe he just felt the tension radiate from her body, because he didn't move away as he paid for the drinks. Before she knew it, his fingers were laced through hers, and he was holding her hand at the bar.

She'd never known holding hands would feel so erotic, but with the charge in the air between them, this was no kids' play. It was almost like . . . foreplay. Then, it most decidedly became the start of something when he stroked his thumb over her palm, tracing lazy circles on her skin, a promise of what he might be able to do with those hands. She nearly combusted from the spark he'd set off inside her body, like a fireworks twirler lit up and racing.

She shut her eyes briefly, breathed out, her body betraying her. There was no hiding the lust she felt radiating in the air. It was like heat in the desert, shimmering on the horizon. Undeniable.

He was a stranger who wasn't quite a stranger, and he was the only thing she was thinking about right now. Her mind was one hundred percent here, and nowhere near her past, nowhere close to anyone else, not lingering whatsoever on the man she had thought she loved for years. Nope. She was present, only present, and she enjoyed this moment so much that she hoped it lasted and knit itself into the rest of the evening.

Into sex with a stranger.

Because that was some of the best sex there ever was. No holds barred, no past, no future, no emotions or history to cloud the moment.

She knew what she wanted tonight. A night with him.

CHAPTER THREE
ONE NIGHT WITH HER
Wet Kisses

He was no virgin. He was no saint.

He'd had a quiet year by choice. Guilt had clawed at him, and though he'd had plenty of chances, and plenty of attempted set-ups from women in his office who wanted to introduce him to their sisters, or their best friends, or their cousins, Jack had kept his nose to the ground and his pants zipped. He was a mess in the head, and a fuck-up in the heart, and that had kept him out of the bedroom.

A self-imposed monkhood, his sister had called it.

But hell, he wasn't thinking of his sister right now.

He was thinking how much he'd like that dry spell to end tonight. Maybe even in the next hour. Because this woman was everything he wanted—sharp, clever, playful and hot as fuck in that blouse and skirt. She had the perfect body for that businesswoman look she had going on, with the skirt down to her knees that made him think of her in a boardroom, crossing her strong, sexy legs as she sat at the head of the table. She probably ran her own business, and that made her even sexier. He was drawn to the kind of confidence that a high-powered woman possessed. And he particularly liked that this high-powered woman had no clue he ran Joy Delivered, because that meant she was actually interested in the guy she'd met tonight, and not the label that sometimes lured others. With the years he'd spent in the military after college as an army intelligence officer before founding this company, he'd been labeled by the press as the Soldier-Turned-Sex-Toy-Mogul. It wasn't the sort of a title that could be bestowed very often, but it was part and parcel of who he was. Though it didn't bother him one bit, he also didn't mind *not* being that person tonight, along with the baggage attached. He could be himself again. Not a man with a past tethered to him, or a sandwich board slung on his chest.

And so the last half hour with Michelle with two *Ls* he'd been precisely that—himself. They'd polished off another round of drinks and he'd held her hand, touching her in a way he hoped was driving her wild, and enticing her as much as her sexy librarian look and smart conversation was luring him in. The business meeting with Henry and the councilman was in the rearview mirror; he no longer had politics or problems on his mind. He and Michelle had talked about baseball, and beaches they wanted to visit, and Jack had even admitted that he had a buddy who'd made it his mission to have unusual questions at the ready, should he meet an interesting woman. Michelle didn't seem bothered that he'd borrowed his friend's body part question.

"I like that you just confessed. It makes you seem like you're not just a smooth and polished James Bond lookalike, all dashing and debonair and able to fire off witty questions like that," she said, snapping her fingers.

"James Bond," he said, running his fingers down his tie. "I'll happily take that comparison. Dashing and debonair, too—I like that as well."

"Well, you are all of the above. So, Just Jack, what exactly is it that you just do?"

Uh-oh. The conversation he didn't want to have. "What do you think I do?" he fired back, hoping to deflect.

"Obviously something that requires you to wear a tie, so unless you're a gigolo," she said, and that drew a deep laugh from inside his chest, "I'm going with businessman, and you were here tonight working on a deal."

He breathed a quiet sigh of relief. Businessman. He could work with that.

"You are very good at putting clues together."

"That's kind of my job."

"Are you a detective?"

She shook her head and laughed. "Nope. But some days it can feel that way."

"So is this when I ask you what you do? Even though we're supposed to talk about far more interesting things?"

"But, see, I find what people do interesting and it says something about who they are," she said, her brown eyes hooked on him, her gaze confident and alluring.

"Then I'll tell you what I do, because I don't want you to walk away and say you didn't know anything about who I was," he said, figuring he could give her something without telling her everything. "I am a businessman. I sell things—usually online, sometimes in stores—that make people feel better."

"What sort of things?"

"Toys."

She laughed. "Toys," she said, amusement in her tone. "That is so damn cute."

"Cute. Not exactly what I want a gorgeous woman to call me."

"What do you want a gorgeous woman to call you?"

"*Oh, God,* at the top of her lungs," he said, watching her breath hitch with his words.

"You are naughty, Mr. Toy Salesman," she said, arching an eyebrow playfully. Fine, she thought he was a toy salesman. He didn't need to disabuse her of that notion. He did sell toys, but tonight, he didn't plan to use any because he was going to show her that this toy salesman wasn't dependent on his products. He could use the tools he came with. Tools to make her come, again and again. Before he could respond, she spoke again. "So you want me to call you *Oh, God, Jack,*" she said, her mouth falling open, her breath coming fast as she imitated an orgasmic cry.

Like a shot of adrenaline to his groin. He shifted in the chair, sure she could see his erection, and equally sure he didn't mind her knowing he was rock-hard for her. "As long as you're looking at me like that, you can call me anything you want," he said, watching her reaction as she pressed her lips together as if she were holding back. He didn't want her to hold back. He wanted her to let go.

"Well, *Oh, God, Jack,* we're in the same field. I also help people feel better."

She took another drink, and that seemed to be the end to the obligatory "what do you do" conversation. He was glad it was out of the way, that it had been handled without lies, and that they could move on to more interesting topics. He segued into something he'd wanted to ask all night. "Any chance you'd let me make you feel better, Michelle?"

"What makes you think I feel bad?" she countered.

"Nothing. But I think I could make you feel a little bit better if, say, I did this," he said, then brushed a loose strand of her hair away from her shoulder, and leaned in. It took five seconds for him to bend closer, and the air was charged, heated with possibility. Then he pressed his lips to her neck, barely there, brushing her soft, sweet skin that tasted faintly of honey and vanilla, something entirely alluring that made him both want to kiss her and rip her clothes off at the same time. A feminine scent, but a thoroughly suggestive one, too, that hinted at the way she might taste all over. "Mmm," he murmured against her skin, then pulled back to assess her response. The hazy look in her eyes told him all he needed. More. She wanted more.

She breathed out hard through pursed lips. "You know, I think, um, this spot," she said, tapping her neck on the other side, "might need to feel better too."

"I have a treatment plan for that," he said, leaning in close to kiss her neck. He groaned faintly, heat rising in his body because she tasted so good. The scent of her was beyond arousing, and he wanted to know how she tasted everywhere. Her hair, the back of her neck, her belly, her legs, between them . . . he wanted his mouth all over her.

"What about here?" he asked, brushing a fingertip across her bottom lip, watching her hitch in a breath. That quick gasp signaled that she was losing control, and that was how he wanted her to be. Lost in him.

She nodded. "Yes, my lips could stand to feel better," she said in a needy whisper.

"Then let me help you feel fantastic," he said, and he took his time, wanting to savor every single second of not only kissing her, but the time before, when he was *about* to kiss her. He ran his fingers over a few loose strands of her hair, so soft against his skin. He watched her, because he liked to watch, and because he liked to record a woman's reactions, and this woman had him wanting her badly. Her brown eyes were clouded with lust, and he was sure they matched the look in his. The only difference was he would lead the kiss. He would set the pace. He liked control, and he wanted to know how she felt melting against him. He traced a finger down her jaw, and her lips parted. Her breath was soft against his face, and then he pressed his lips to hers. She tasted faintly of lipstick and vodka, and it was one of his favorite taste combinations in the world. Running his tongue across the seam of her lips, he teased at first, priming her for how he wanted to kiss her properly. Hard, passionately, the kind of kiss that would make her weak in the knees, and foggy in the head, and leave her not only wanting, but desperately needing more.

A kiss that would make her wet.

She angled her body closer, her breasts pressed against his chest, and soon her hands had found their way to his hair. Their tongues tangled in a hot duet. The temperature rose, the volume shot way up, and they were practically clawing their way through the kiss, desperate for more.

Teeth, lips, mouth, tongue, all furious and fevered heat as her hands gripped his hair.

He needed to have her. Had to take her. She was hot as sin, smelled like lust, and radiated sexuality. Without her even saying it directly, he knew she was a woman who had no reservations about self-love. She'd pretty much admitted she had a bit of a porn habit, and he could see her alone in her bed, eyes fixed on filthy images online, spread out on a white comforter with her legs spread and her fingers wrapped around a red vibrator, thrusting in and out, bringing herself there.

Tonight, she didn't need to go it solo.

He broke the kiss, and traveled to her ear, whispering hotly, "If you were to go home right now, would you touch yourself?"

"Obviously."

"Why is it obvious?"

"Because I'm turned on as fuck, and it would be a fantastic orgasm."

"Would you think of me as you played with yourself?" he asked, then licked the shell of her ear. She shivered against him.

"You're giving me pretty good fodder, so I'd have to say that'd be a yes."

"What would you imagine?" he asked, so fucking eager to know what she wanted. He shifted back, looking at her gorgeous face, her brown eyes hazy with lust. He was curious if she'd say hands, lips, tongue, or cock. Dying to know what she wanted next if she were to have her way.

She shot him a stare, her eyes hooking into his. Something dark and naughty passed over her gaze.

"I would fantasize about you finishing what you just started."

His breath caught in his chest, and his heart stopped for a moment. The air around them was heavy, expectant, and suddenly it felt as if all the sound in the room had both stopped and been sharpened. Everything collided into this—the heavy pulsing sound of the music, the clink of glasses, the splash of liquor being poured, and then this—her breath, her chest rising and falling, and the heated look in her eyes that spelled unabashed lust.

He was going to fuck her good tonight.

CHAPTER FOUR
ONE NIGHT WITH HER
Stop, Don't Stop

Her reflection in the brass doors of the elevator would give her away. Her cheeks were rosy, her hair was slipping from its clip, and the collar of her blouse already needed readjusting. It was a look she hadn't worn in years, but it was one she found she liked on herself. The look of a woman about to have hot, dirty sex with a man she barely knew. Michelle Milo was getting some action tonight, and it wasn't the battery-operated kind.

A couple walked behind her. A man with slick black hair had his arm draped around a young blonde. They were wrapped up in each other, but seemed to check out Michelle before they turned the corner.

She stood alone outside the elevators, waiting for Jack to return from the front desk where he was getting a room, and she practically wanted to pump her first, maybe even high-five her own reflection.

But that would be premature, right? What if he was bad in bed? What if he had a small peter? Man, what a drag when that happened. You get all hot and bothered and raring to go, and everything is clicking on all cylinders from the conversation to the connection to the magical thing known as chemistry, then *bam*. Tiny revealed. She crossed her fingers and sent a silent prayer to the universe—or maybe just to the Patron Saint of Endowment, hoping that such a saint existed and if she didn't, she damn well should, because she'd have offerings of riches from women the world over—that Jack had the kind of package that would make her mouth water.

Then she chuckled to herself, almost shocked at the thoughts racing through her head. What happened to serious, focused, honest-to-a-fault Michelle who worked as a therapist and prided herself on being direct, upfront, and open? Of course, she wasn't always upfront. She'd never told her friend Clay how she felt about him all those years. Not that it would have made a difference. He didn't feel the same way, and who fucking cared anymore? What a welcome bit of luck that at least, for this moment in time, her mind was free of that unrequited love that had weighed her down like a heavy rusted anchor on the sea floor.

Because right now, she was living in the moment, and judging a man for the size of his cock. Or potential size, really. Hell, it felt wickedly good to let this side of her steer the ship. Far too often she was all-work-and-no-play Michelle. But she was her after-hours self now, and she hoped this man could match the ones in her fantasy. Or at the very least, the size of the phalluses in her nightstand drawer.

Jack—or Just Jack as she now thought of him—walked towards her, and he was the only one on her mind as she took him in, his tie loosened, his white shirt rumpled, his pants . . .

Her eyes had strayed there and she snapped them up quickly.

He brandished a key, flashing it at her with a knowing wink, then whispered in her ear, "Were you just checking me out?"

A flush splashed across her cheeks in a flurry. She nodded. "Caught red-handed."

"I like that you were looking."

"Really?"

"Yes," he said, and seconds later the elevator doors opened with a *swish*, then closed with a *swoosh*. Faint music played inside, a low beat, sexy and moody. The lighting was dim and silver walls flashed their faces back at them in a midnight-blue glow. Michelle was sure this hotel was rarely used for business.

"Are you sure you were here for a business deal?"

He raised an eyebrow. "Why?"

"Because this is a sex hotel. I think that's the only reason people come here."

"Then isn't it good that we met here?" he asked, but before she could answer, he spun her around, so she faced the wall of the elevator as the lift chugged upstairs. He crowded her in, and she gripped the bar as he pressed his body against her, his firm chest flush with her spine, and his erection against her lower back. The hard, full, thick length of it.

She sighed happily, and grinned at him in the reflection, then pushed back against him, letting him know she liked what she felt.

"I'm glad you approve," he said, in her ear, his voice low, raspy, and thoroughly intoxicating.

"Seems I do so far," she said, as lust washed through her.

As the elevator soared, he tugged her in closer, and the heat in her core shot up. He traveled from her ear to the back of her neck, leaving a trail of hot, wet kisses that made her belly clench and her thighs tighten. His hands roamed down her sides to her waist, her hips, her thighs, as he ground against her backside, giving her a hint of what was in store. "What do you want me to do to you when we get in that room?" he said, and then she gasped when she felt his hand on the back of her knee, brushing his fingertips against her bare flesh.

"What are my choices?"

"Here are some options. Lick you, finger you, or fuck you?"

Her eyes floated closed as a wave of sparks shot through her body like a flare gun. She licked her lips. "I'm hungry. Can I have the one, two and three, please?"

"As you wish." He moved his hand up her thigh, and she gripped the armrest harder because her legs felt wobbly from his touch. Then his palm was on her rear, and he teased at the lace of her panties with his fingers, trailing them along the edge, one finger hooking into the band. "You do have a fantastic fucking ass. Both cheeks are gorgeous," he said.

"Thank you," she said softly, loving his compliments.

The lift slowed as they neared the twenty-first floor.

"Almost there," he mused as he brushed his fingers along the edge of her ass. Instinctively, she shifted her stance, opening wider, giving him access even if they were only in this elevator for ten more seconds. She wanted to be touched so badly it felt like a madness. Like she'd go insane if he teased her more with those fingers that seemed to know the path around her body. He dipped his thumb under her panties, then edged closer to where she was molten for him.

"And you are so fucking wet already," he growled, lightly brushing his fingers over the damp scrap of fabric. Her back bowed, her body crying out for his touch. "Is this all from when I kissed you at the bar?"

"No. It's from you trying to fuck me in an elevator," she said, firing back. She wasn't some blushing virgin, or some innocent wide-eyed girl, who'd never seen the world nor heard a foul word from a man. She might have been terribly unlucky in love, but she knew plenty about sex, and she wasn't going to play the part of a sweet, shy thing. But he didn't seem to want her to, because he slipped his hand between her legs, sliding a finger through her slick flesh.

"Good, because I want to fuck you in the elevator. In the hallway. On the bed. In the shower. I have wanted to fuck you since I first saw you," he said as the elevator stopped and the doors opened. They spilled out and the hall was empty. Praise the Lord of One-Night Stands, because he pushed her up against the wall in seconds, grabbing her wrists and holding them at her sides, and kissing her so hard that she was sure she might melt into a puddle of simmering lust and heat. She was wanted. Desperately wanted. By someone she craved. She had no notion when she walked into The Pierson that she'd be doing anything but walking out an hour later when her talk was done. But her plan for the evening had been upended, turned and twisted inside out into something entirely unexpected. And something she didn't think she could stand going without. Her whole body pulsed for him, her blood thrumming through her veins to the rhythm of want, a pounding in her ears that blotted out everything but the feelings that charged through her.

She spent so much time in her head. So many moments of her life thinking, analyzing, considering.

Throwing that all out the door, she angled her hips as if she could pull him closer, even with her hands pinned. He responded with a press of his body. They were magnets tonight, crashing into their opposite charge, smashing, pushing, pulling.

His thumbs dug into her wrists as he held her tight, the pressure from them a new kind of sensation, hard against her bones. His lips smashed against hers, his mouth consuming her, taking her breath, taking her space, leaving nothing behind but hot need.

Now. That word echoed in her brain. She couldn't wait. She couldn't stop. She wanted him everywhere. Tongues, lips, mouth, fingers, but most of all she wanted him inside her. She ached with a deep throbbing desire that had to be quenched.

She managed to somehow separate her lips from his greedy ones that wanted to devour her.

"Jack," she breathed out in a voice that was feather-thin. She was barely able to form words. Language seemed a monumental task, akin to climbing a mountain right now.

Words were hazy, nebulous, but somehow she grabbed hold of the most important ones.

"I need you inside me. I can't wait for anything else."

"I can't wait to give you a much better orgasm than the one you were going to give yourself," he said, grabbing her hand, threading his fingers through hers and leading her around the bank of elevators and to the room. He slid the key into the slot and turned around, grabbing the waistband of her skirt, tugging her in close, and kissing her once more, as if he couldn't stop. As if he simply had to touch her and taste her. First her jawline, then her lips, then deep into her mouth, kissing her passionately and with so much fire that she was certain she was going to set off smoke detectors any second.

But even if she did, she wouldn't stop. Let them sound. Let them ring.

* * *

They didn't even make it to the bed.

There was no point.

Beds were for the next time. For all-night sessions. For lovers that had been together before. For this? The first time called for the wall, because they couldn't wait. He'd been hard since she sat down at the bar, that hot body taunting him in her sexy outfit that she didn't even realize was sexy. Or hell, maybe she did.

As the door clanged shut, he backed her up against the wall, reached his hand behind her head, and unclipped her hair. Her soft brown hair spilled onto her shoulders and over his fingers.

"Beautiful," he whispered, kissing her hair that smelled like jasmine. "Can I call you beautiful?"

She nodded. "Yes."

"Then stand with your feet spread, beautiful, and rock your sweet little body into my mouth," he told her, her eyes widening with both surprise and lust as he bent down, kneeling, and pushed up her skirt in seconds. "I have to taste you."

"Don't let me stop you," she said, her lips curling up, and he liked that she was so quick to talk back. A naughty one. A woman unafraid to speak her mind. He reached for her panties—black lace—and brought them down to her knees, then leaned in. He was dying to run his tongue along that enticing seam of her pussy lips. Spread them open and let her wetness flood his mouth. But first he wanted to inhale her scent, so he ran his nose along her thighs, feeling her quiver against his cheek.

"You smell so fucking good," he said roughly.

"Oh, God," she panted. He looked up and watched her as her head fell back against the wall. He hadn't even touched her yet, and she was already grasping for his hair, trying to draw him near. Heat tore through him at her reaction, and he buzzed his lips and nose closer to her delicious center, breathing in her sexiness, inhaling her arousal.

The scent of her desire shot through him like an earthquake rumbling across the land. He pressed one soft kiss against her swollen clit, and she gasped. "Please," she cried out, her voice ragged as it turned from sexy banter to bare need.

"Oh, beautiful, you make me want to tease you," he said, brushing his lips against her inner thighs, her wetness covering his stubbled jawline. Perfect. "You make me want to make you beg for it when you say that word."

"Please don't make me beg," she said, gripping his hair.

"I won't tonight, even though it drives me wild when you say *please*."

"Touch me. Just touch me," she said, panting now. The need from her was so intense it tore through him, lust spreading across every inch of his body.

But he couldn't resist the game. "Tell me what you want," he said, making it clear this was an order. "Say it. Tell me where you want my mouth right now."

"Please, Jack. Lick me, eat me, taste me, fuck me with your tongue."

He hissed out a breath. God, he loved that kind of mouth.

He licked her once, groaning from the intoxicating taste of her wet pussy. Flattening his tongue, he licked her again and she cried out. She let go of his hair, and brought her right hand to her chest. Touching herself, feeling her own breast. Fuck, that was hot.

"I need you to do something," he told her, looking up at her.

"Yes?" she said, her eyes hazy.

"Give me all of your pussy. Don't hold back."

That was all she needed. One piece of instruction, and she took it quickly. She started rocking her hips into his face as he kissed her delicious wetness, narrowing in on her clit, sucking it in his mouth as she arched into him. He glanced up again; her lips were parted, her mouth open, her breathing turning into erratic pants, signaling her need. She was so damn sensuous. She was like sex on fire.

She ran her other hand through her hair, gripping it hard, and in that instant he could picture her as she masturbated, threading a hand through her hair or fondling a breast as she took herself there. There was something about a sexy woman who liked to play with herself that brought him to his knees. Maybe it was why he did what he did for a living, but to find a woman this gorgeous who was so clearly in touch with her own need to come made his blood turn hotter than hell.

"Oh God, please stop," she called out.

He looked up at her, but didn't cease the attention he lavished on her swollen clit. He lapped her up, flicking his tongue against her, causing her to buck against his mouth. The thought of being covered in her juices stiffened his cock even further, straining against his zipper.

"Stop, you have to stop, you have to stop," she said, like a plea.

He relented, pulling back. "You okay?"

"Yes. I'm just going to come so soon, and I want to do it with you inside me."

As much as he wanted to press his hands on the inside of her thighs, spread her wider and ignore her request, he was also a gentleman, and if the lady wanted something different far be it from him to deny her wishes.

He rose, starting to unzip his pants. "I'm only stopping because you asked. But since you denied me the pleasure of tasting you come, I want to warn you that I fully intend to tease the ever-loving fuck out of your pussy the next time I'm down there."

His eyes were fixed on her, and he watched as she shivered, her shoulders shaking briefly as if his words had sent a wave of pleasure through her body. "I can live with that," she said, and in seconds she was unknotting his tie and unbuttoning his shirt in a flurry. She pressed her hands against his chest, and he hissed in a breath at the feel of her touch on his bare skin for the first time.

"Please tell me you have a condom," she said.

He nodded, grinned at her as she worked the final buttons. "I do, and it's kind of a funny story because I didn't have one when I walked into this hotel," he said, reciprocating with her shirt, stripping it off. "When I got the room, I asked the desk clerk if he happened to have a condom. He winked at me, slapped one in my palm, and said 'Always happy to help a dude out.'"

She laughed, the sound like a wind chime, and it dropped down in his heart for the briefest of moments. What the hell? This was a one-night stand. He wasn't supposed to feel anything anywhere except in his groin, so he focused on that, ignoring the fact that he'd had a fantastic time with her at the bar, and that one of the reasons he wanted her so badly was that he liked her mind as much as her body.

But her body . . . here before him . . . that's what he needed right now, and he had a mission—make her come once, twice, then a third time. A night like this, a woman like her, one time would never satisfy him.

He took the condom from his pocket. He guided her hand back to his briefs, and pressed her palm against his erection. She drew a sharp breath as she touched him for the first time, and her reaction sent a shiver down his spine. "I like," she whispered.

"Good," he said softly, moving her hands to the waistband. "Take them off."

She pushed his unzipped pants and his briefs down to his knees, then stared at his cock. She ran the tip of her tongue across her teeth and swallowed hard.

"I like it very, very much," she said, sounding mesmerized as she gazed at his hard length. She took him in her hand and stroked him several times, and he nearly growled from the pleasure that ricocheted through his body as she touched him. Quickly, he stilled her hand. "You made me stop, so now I'm going to make you stop."

He pressed the condom into her palm, and buzzed his lips along her neck up to her ear. "Put it on me," he said in a firm voice, giving her a command.

She opened the wrapper, tossing it to the floor, then slid it on him. She tugged his body closer, rubbing the head of his cock across her slippery wetness. A wave of heat licked his veins, scorching him. He welcomed it. *Fucking gladly.*

"Were you worried you couldn't come twice if I finished going down on you?"

"Yes."

"You know that only makes me want to prove you wrong," he said, then reached for her leg, gripped her thigh, and wrapped it around him. "Hold on tight, beautiful. I'm going to take you for a ride."

* * *

She'd be making an offering tomorrow to the Patron Saint of Endowment because Jack did not have a textbook cock. Not even close. He was long, thick, wide, and absolutely fucking perfect. But more than that, he knew what to do with this beautiful gift he'd been given. He entered her, and she moaned instantly as he filled her, stretching her in ways she hadn't been stretched in God only knew how long. He paused for a moment, letting her adjust to his size.

"I can handle it," she murmured.

He raised an eyebrow. "Good. Because I'm not going to take it easy. Not after you teased me when I was on my knees for you," he said, thrusting deeper into her. She grasped his shoulders, holding on tight. She wanted to run her hands all over his beautiful body, to explore his chest, to grab his hard ass, and run her fingers across it.

But all she could do was hold on as he pumped into her, giving her the fucking he'd promised. Taking her deep, and hard, and up against the wall. The room was dark, only a faint glow from the bathroom light illuminated them, but they would have made quite a picture. A silhouette of unbridled lust. His shirt open, his pants down to his knees, shoes still on. Half-undressed too, only her panties had made it off. Her shirt was undone, her bra still on, her skirt hiked up to her waist. He gripped her leg tight, his hands strong and unyielding as if he would never let go of her as he rolled his hips, sending his cock deeper into her, his hard length hitting her with just the perfect amount of friction.

"You tasted so good, Michelle. I don't like that you denied me," he said in a hot growl against her throat. "But it only makes me want you more."

"I just wanted you inside me. You feel so good inside me."

"Fucking you is perfection," he groaned, then reached his other hand to her ass, squeezing the cheek hard, unleashing a blast of pure heat through her body. She felt as if she were on fire, as if her body had become an inferno of pleasure as he drove into her. Words were no longer needed, not even their naughty back and forth, because they were reduced to pants and moans. His steely length filled her so completely that she was sure nothing else existed in the whole wide world. But *this*—the pure and absolute bliss of his glorious cock sliding in and out, harder, deeper, faster. His fingers playing against the soft flesh of her rear. Squeezing her cheeks.

The world around her was white with bright, hot stars exploding as he took her deeper.

He bent his head to her neck, all while gripping her, never letting go. Her belly clenched, and she felt the first surge of sensations, like a rocket engine starting to burn, rattling as it began to take off. He pressed his lips to her shoulder as he pumped into her. He bit down, his teeth sharp against her skin, sending a rush of fresh and sweet pain into her body. It was the key turned in the ignition, and in an instant there was liftoff. She shot into the sky, engulfed in pleasure that spread in a fury from her center all the way through to her fingertips.

Her moans escalated. Her words became a frenzied chorus of *I'm going to come, I'm going to come.* Then, finally, his name.

"*Oh God, Jack,*" she called out, not even recognizing her own voice anymore. Not even sure where it was coming from. She wasn't even here. She was in an opium den of bliss, a pleasure palace of his making as he thrust so deep and so hard that she swore her first orgasm rolled right into a second one. The next wave hit her unexpectedly, a shattering burst of bright light and gorgeous heat that pulsed through her in aftershocks. She didn't think she ever wanted to stop coming, even as he raced to join her on the other side, another bite into her shoulder setting him off.

He groaned, holding her tight as his brows scrunched, his groans turned primal, and he came too.

* * *

They lay tangled up in each other, clothes still half-on, having fallen into bed.

"If my calculations are correct, that was twice," he said, as he ran his fingers through her hair. He loved the feel of her hair against his skin.

"That has never happened to me before," she said, still dazed, and he wanted her to look like that again and again with him. As soon as he thought that, he realized he didn't want a one-night stand with her. He wanted two nights, three nights, more and more. To make her come again and again. To bring out that response.

"We can do it again," he said, offering in a tone that was both playful but truly sincere. He wanted her to know he meant it. He turned on his side, propping his head on his hand, running his fingers down her hipbone. "Michelle with two *Ls*, what would you think about another time?"

"Well, I should hope you're planning on another time in about, say," she stopped to look at her watch, "fifteen minutes."

He laughed lightly. "Yes, obviously this room is for multiples of multiple orgasms, and I fully intend on fucking you again in, say, ten minutes." Then he turned more serious, because he wanted her to know that this could be more than one night. Funny, how he hadn't expected that, and had figured a quick romp and then goodbye would be all that was needed. But even though he had no intention of anything serious happening, because he was no good at those type of relationships, he could go for dinner, and another night like this. Or just skip the meal and have her come over to his penthouse apartment, drink wine, and then enjoy some window sex in front of the full-length glass in his living room that overlooked the park. Yeah, he could go for either, both, any combo. "But I also would love to see you again. What are you doing this weekend?"

She paused, the corner of her lips quirking up in a half-smile. "Just Jack, are you asking me out on a date?"

He grinned, then leaned in for a quick kiss, brushing his lips against her bruised and red ones, the evidence of how she'd been kissed, and desired. His mark on her, this woman he wanted. "I suppose I am."

"Then you're going to need to be more than Just Jack. Want to cough up that last name now?" she said, making a *gimme* motion with her hands.

He parted his lips to answer, but was cut short when Beethoven's "Ode to Joy" started playing, a loud crescendo of the most famous part of the piece of music. Michelle twitched, her shoulders visibly tensing. She sprang out of bed, hunting for her purse, then fishing around in it for her phone as she buttoned her shirt. Possibilities flashed through his brain—was she married? Was this the Bat Call from a friend, saving her from a man she didn't want?

"Michelle here," she said in a crisp, business-like tone as she tucked her shirt into her skirt.

Maybe it was work. He didn't know what she did for a living.

Listening to the call, she nodded several times as she stuffed her feet back into her black pumps, then smoothed a hand down her shirt. "I understand. Please tell her I will call her in three minutes."

She hung up, and sighed heavily. "Jack. I'm so, so sorry. That was my service. A patient of mine needs me. But I swear I want to see you again, so please take my number and call me tomorrow, okay?"

He narrowed his eyes, not sure if he believed her. "If you just want a one-time thing, that's cool. Or if you're married and rushing home to your husband, maybe let me know that too so I can stay far away."

She walked quickly to the bed, bending down to drop a kiss on his lips. "I swear I'm not married, not even close. And I haven't been involved with anyone in ages, and I would really like to see you again, so give me your number and I'll call you right now so you have mine in your phone," she said, and she seemed so earnest and bullshit-free that he chose to believe her. He knew what she did now; she was a doctor, and that made sense since she'd said she made people feel better. Noble profession, and all. He rattled off his number, and she dialed it. His phone sounded from his pocket.

She arched an eyebrow. "You like Ravel?"

He nodded. "Classical music aficionado here."

"We have so much to talk about. Text me tomorrow. And, Jack?"

"Yeah?"

"Thanks for the two best orgasms of my life."

"Next time, we'll make it a double of a double."

"I'm going to hold you to it. And on that, I need to run," she said, slinging her purse higher on her shoulder then opening the door. It clanged loudly behind her when it shut, the sound of the night ending far too soon.

He shifted to his back, tucking his hands behind his bed, and staring at the ceiling. Too bad the room didn't have an hourly rate, because they'd only used it for thirty minutes.

The sound of a siren echoed in the distance, the noise of New York inserting itself into another moment. The room closed in on him, suddenly too small, too empty as he longed for both her company and her body.

CHAPTER FIVE
ONE NIGHT WITH HER

Your 2 p.m.

Jack wiped the slight sheen of sweat from his forehead and took aim, cleanly delivering the basketball through the net.

"Did you miss me last night?" Nate asked as he grabbed the ball.

Jack laughed. "Not one bit."

Nate raised an eyebrow as he dribbled the ball between his legs. "Does that mean what I think it means?"

His friend knew him too well. But then, any man would know what he meant, because that's where a man's mind was most of the time. Nate was no different. Besides, now that Nate's friend Bryan had settled down with Nate's sister, Jack was the one regularly quizzed about his late-night antics. He hadn't had much to say lately though, and he certainly hadn't shared details of his sex life with Aubrey back when they were together. Though his times with her had never been as exciting as only one night with Michelle.

It was okay that he was the quieter one when it came to the morning-after report. Nate usually had enough fodder for the both of them.

"Maybe it does," he said as Nate took his turn shooting.

"And does that mean you'll be the one canceling drinks next time?" Nate asked as Jack grabbed the ball.

"You know what? It just might mean that. But for a much better reason than working late on a deal."

"That deal is going to make my company a lot of money, though."

"That's a good thing then."

"Yeah, but not as good as other things."

He flashed back to last night. To Michelle's body, half-naked. He'd need to get the rest of her clothes off tonight.

"You're right. Definitely not as good as other things that I'm going to engage in again tonight," he said with a wicked grin.

"Lucky bastard," Nate whistled as the ball sailed through the net.

Maybe he was talking about the ball. Or maybe he was talking about the possibility of another time. The latter was a hell of a lot more exciting.

So exciting that he sent Michelle a text as soon as they finished shooting hoops that morning.

J: Are you still holding me to that foursome of orgasms tonight? Because I plan on delivering.

M: Four? Consider me game.

He texted her on and off throughout his day, until it was time for his appointment, and even then he kept up the volley on his walk to the Lexington Avenue building.

* * *

M: By the way, did I tell you that I woke up this morning thinking about what you did to me against the wall?

J: Did you touch yourself?

M: What do you think?

J: That you had that gorgeous sexy O *mouth going on this morning in your bed.*

M: Maybe I did

J: Would love to see that. Fingers or toys?

M: Both. And if you want to know more, you'll have to take me to dinner.

J: That can be arranged, but I'm going to need to eat food, and eat you.

M: How about you make arrangements for the former, and I do for the latter?

J: I'll make reservations at a restaurant. I might need to taste you first though. Not sure if I can wait. I'll text you later. I have a meeting in five min. Walking into the building now.

M: Mmm . . . I like the way you think . . . and I have an appt too. Can't wait to see you again.

J: Can't wait to see you.

Michelle grinned wickedly as she turned her personal phone to silent, then tucked it into a desk drawer. She always gave her clients supreme focus, and that included not only silencing the phone, but placing it completely out of sight. Besides, Jack was already front and center in her mind; she didn't need to clutter her thoughts with even more of him when she had to focus on her next patient. He was some kind of magic, though; he'd been the only man whose touch had made her forget Clay. She hadn't thought of her good friend once last night. Jack had been so overpowering, so dominant that there was no room for anyone but Jack in her head and heart.

He was a good drug, the kind who could wash away the bitter aftertaste of unrequitedness.

Now, here in the light of day, her mind tripped briefly back to Clay. She'd been in love with that man for ten years, and it sucked that he hadn't loved her back. She'd hoped that Liam, the charming actor she'd dated a few months ago, would blunt her feelings. But as she flipped open her laptop to check on her next appointment, Michelle knew there hadn't been enough of a spark with Liam—there wasn't a true light-up-the-night ignition that could erase the past.

It would take a once-in-a-century eclipse to blot out the ache she'd felt for Clay, who was now so happy with another woman. Longing had camped out in her heart for so many years it had squatter's rights. She wished someone had warned her that loving someone who doesn't love you is like a permanent sore in the mouth—painful, and you want to touch it all the time, to worry away at it. The ache had dulled in the last few months, but he was still in her heart and she had no clue how to fully erase him.

She clicked open her calendar, checking on the details of her next session. At least she had her work to focus on. Her clients and their challenges fed her, made her whole in a way that only her work as a psychologist could do. She scanned the notes from her office manager who'd arranged the appointment, though she knew very little about the man coming to see her. That was par for the course. She rarely knew much in advance, and her job was to get to know clients during their time together.

But she knew this much. No first name, but the last name was Sullivan. His sister had called to set up the appointment for him, citing *intimacy issues*. There was a line about "difficulty moving on from last relationship," and a reminder that discretion of the highest order was vital, since the patient was a prominent businessman.

Not a problem. Never a problem. Discreet was Michelle Milo's middle name. She hadn't even breathed Shayla's name out loud to Jack when she'd called her service late in the middle of the night to talk.

Well, let's see what we've got. She was ready to focus on this Sullivan fellow for the next hour.

When she heard a knock at two o'clock sharp, she opened the door to her office, and all thoughts rushed out of her brain but one.

One word. Blaring like a neon sign.

Smoldering.

This man was smoldering.

And she'd already met him last night.

NIGHTS WITH HIM

ABOUT NIGHTS WITH HIM

A sensual, sexy, standalone romance novel in the New York Times and USA Today Bestselling Seductive Nights Series by Lauren Blakely...

Jack Sullivan is a Sex Toy Mogul.

An extremely eligible bachelor in New York, he's the full package, right down to his full package. Hell, this man could be the model for one of the toys his company, Joy Delivered, peddles. Instead, he's the powerful and successful CEO and he's got commitment issues a mile-long after the tragic way his relationship with his fiancée ended.

He's looking for a way to erase the pain and that arrives in the form of Michelle Milo. From her pencil skirts to her high heels, she's his perfect fantasy, especially since she has no idea who he is the night they meet at a hotel bar. He doesn't have a clue either that she's the brilliant psychologist his sister has arranged for him to see to help him get over his past.

His touch helps her forget that other man.

When he shows up at her office door the next day, there's no way in hell she's going to treat him after they've slept together. Jack isn't willing to let go of the first woman he's felt anything for in years so he proposes a deal – share her nights with him for thirty days. At the end of one month of exquisite pleasure, they walk away, having helped each other move on from their haunted pasts.

But soon, all those nights threaten to turn into days as the lines between lust and matters of the heart start to blur. Can two people so terribly afraid of love truly fall head over heels?

CHAPTER ONE
Surprise

No way.

There was no way she was his shrink.

This was a cruel joke his sister was playing on him. Casey had to be setting him up, right? Or his buddy Nate, who loved to pull these sorts of pranks. Except Nate had no clue he was here. He hadn't given Nate a single meaningful detail about last night.

Maybe his mind was playing tricks on him and he was seeing Michelle everywhere. If he closed his eyes, counted to ten, and opened them again, perhaps the Dr. Milo his sister had booked his appointment with would turn out to be a school-marm type. A grandmotherly lady. Hell, how about a man?

Anyone fucking else, please.

Anyone but the absolutely enticing sex kitten he couldn't stop thinking of since last night's mind-blowing up-against-the-wall-in-a-dimly-lit-hotel-room sex. Not the owner of the hottest pair of legs, the most sinful mouth, and the wildest abandon he'd ever encountered.

He had plans for her. So many plans. Positions. Places.

Frozen still, they were two statues caught in shock. Jack gripped the doorframe and swallowed hard. Michelle's brown eyes were wide, etched with complete surprise as her hand remained wrapped around the doorknob, her knuckles white from the tight hold she had on it. The silence lasted, spinning from one second to the next to the next. As if this moment of sheer dumb bad luck would unspool if they did nothing. As if it would rewind into something that made sense. Finally, she went first.

"I suppose I have the answer now to the 'what's your last name' question," she said in a strained voice.

He nodded. "Sullivan. Jack Sullivan." Then, manners and protocol kicked in. He extended a hand. She stared at his hand as if it were an object acquired from a distant planet, a space rock she needed to study. But then, she took it, and the second they made contact, memories of her hands slammed into him.

He pictured them in his hair, grabbing his ass, trailing over his chest. Touching her own breasts.

Desire rolled through him, and he tried to tamp it down. To banish the thickening lust that was clouding his head as he flashed back to last night.

Was he supposed to tell her all his problems? All the troubles that gnawed at him? The guilt that liked to play hide-and-seek with his heart, reminding him when it peeked out from around the corner that Aubrey's death was something he'd unlikely ever come to peace with. That's why Casey had sent him here; Casey was the only one who knew precisely why the mythology the press had assigned to his newly-single status was horseshit. As if they could understand his heart, and his reasons. He hardly understood them himself.

He barely unloaded on his sister; he couldn't imagine telling Michelle what had brought him here.

Correction. *Dr. Milo. Doctor of Psychology,* as the diploma on her wall informed him.

"And you're Dr. Michelle Milo," he began. "Or Dr. Milo, which was the name I had on my schedule. I didn't know last night that my Michelle was the same Dr. Milo." She flinched when he said *my Michelle*. The words surprised him too; he shouldn't feel any sort of ownership for her, less than twenty-four hours after meeting. But hell, she was the first woman he'd felt a real thing for, a true fucking emotion, since Aubrey. Maybe that emotion was lust. Maybe it was lust plus possibility. He didn't know, but he'd enjoyed his time with Michelle in and out of the sheets. Even if it was too early, he was staking his claim to her. She didn't seem to want it, though, because she let go of his hand.

Crap. Did she think he'd scoped her out beforehand and tried to seduce her? That he'd pursued his shrink in advance, in some sort of clandestine operation? "I swear, I had no idea," he added, wanting to make sure they were crystal clear on that point.

She shook her head and shushed him, then grabbed his lapels, jerked him into her office and shut the door with a lightning kind of speed.

"I don't want anyone hearing us," she said, still in a whisper. She stepped away from him, walked to her couch, and pressed a button on a noise machine on an end table. A low hum filled the room. She turned around. "To preserve confidentiality," she said, waving her hand at the whirring machine.

"Of course." Was she talking about the two of them, or other patients?

She looked him straight in the eyes. Her gorgeous browns were steely. "First of all, there's no need to call me doctor. I'm not a medical doctor, so I don't use the title. Michelle is totally fine. Second, I can't see you."

The words hit hard in the chest. Like the sharp edge of a jagged rock.

"You mean tonight?" he asked, furrowing his brow.

She nodded, but seemed flustered now, too, fiddling with the collar on her blouse as she spoke. "I mean, now. I can't see you here. I can't treat you. It's 100 percent against the code of ethics. You can't sleep with your patients. It's the single biggest reason therapists lose their license," she said, and her voice rose. He could hear the frustration in it, but it was laced with self-loathing too. She was pissed at herself.

"All those stories about patients falling for shrinks are glamorized," she said. "It's wrong. It's just plain wrong."

"I wasn't your patient last night," he said, ready to absolve her of her guilt. He knew a thing or two about that awful emotion.

She clenched her hands at her sides, as if she were channeling all her feelings there. Frustration, perhaps? Annoyance? Or was there regret flowing through her veins too? "I had an appointment scheduled with you already."

"But I didn't know it was you. You didn't know it was me . . . did you?" he asked, then the possibility dawned on him. Had she known who he was? His brain was spinning now, and it wasn't making pretty kaleidoscopic images. Maybe she'd been the one scoping him out clandestinely.

"No!" She jammed her hands in her hair, and whatever she'd been keeping under the surface bubbled up. Her voice rose. "I never would have done that. Jack, I don't even know a thing about you, except you sell toys. I don't even know what kind of toys you sell. Do you sell Legos? Weeble Wobbles? Dolls?" She raised her eyebrows in question as she fired off options. "Do you run a toy store or something?"

He didn't even bother to contain the grin as he shook his head, laughing deeply. "I sell sex toys."

Her jaw went slack. She blinked several times, then swallowed. She sank down onto the couch, dropped her head between her legs and breathed out hard. For a second he thought she was having an anxiety attack, but she popped back up, grabbed his elbow, opened the door and escorted him out of the office. "You need to see someone else," she said, marching him down the hall to the stairs, and two flights down, then into another hallway. She walked him into another psychology practice, then mouthed *thank God* when she spotted a door open.

She tapped twice, then stepped inside. "Kana, hello. I think Friday at two is one of your free hours, right?"

"Yes," said the woman named Kana. Her long black hair was sleek and looped in a ponytail at the nape of her neck. She wore a long hippie skirt, a red shirt, and bangles on her arms. She looked young, perhaps late twenties.

"Is there any chance you could take my two p.m.? I have a conflict," Michelle said, then turned to him. "Jack, this is Kana Miyoshi. She works in another practice. I've referred other patients to her. She's excellent and you will be in good hands."

"Wait a second. Who said I just wanted to switch?" he asked, digging in his heels. His mental health wasn't a game of hot potato. This was his fucking messed-up life, and he wasn't some assignment to be passed around.

"Kana is great," Michelle said, in a too-professional tone. All the sexiness, all the teasing, and all the shock was gone, replaced only by a cool business-like demeanor.

"But Casey made the appointment to see you," Jack said pointedly.

"I assure you, Kana is one of the best in the field. She knows her stuff."

And he didn't care. He was masterful at shutting down. Hell, he'd been in the army for six years—he knew how to keep his thoughts locked up, with the key thrown away. If this was what therapy came down to—getting jerked around—he was ready to say goodbye.

He threw his hands up. "Hell, I'm more than happy to just leave and not do this at all. So thank you very much. Have a good day."

Michelle's grip on his arm tightened, and she met his gaze straight on. Her eyes softened. "*Please*," she whispered, and something about that one word on her lips said like a true plea, as if she couldn't have wanted anything more in this moment, or ever, than for him to relent, had him doing just that. She repeated it, her voice even lower this time, and that word worked its way into his heart. He wasn't sure why this was important to her, and he certainly wasn't sure why she was important to him after only one night. But he understood this much—it mattered deeply to her that she not harm her job. He got that. He respected that. If sitting down with Kana for fifty minutes would help Michelle in some way, he could do that much.

Thank you, she mouthed just to him, her sexy lips wrapping around those silent words.

She turned to her associate. "Jack is a friend. I didn't realize it was him when we set the appointment, and I don't want to leave him hanging. I know he'll be in good hands with you."

"Absolutely," said the other woman. "I've learned so much from Michelle, it'll almost be as if I'm channeling her."

Channeling her. The only way he wanted to channel Michelle was in the bedroom.

And there went his mind again. As he sat down on the couch, Michelle Milo turning on her heels, he feared it was going to be a painfully long fifty minutes.

* * *

She wasn't in the habit of Googling patients before their appointments. Nor was she in the habit of Googling them while she treated them. The Internet offered too much information, and her job was not based on hunting for details from Facebook profiles or corporate web sites. Her job was to talk to people, to help them understand and to overcome challenges in their lives.

The answers to those questions were never found on the Web.

But Jack was no longer a patient. She'd sliced off that possibility immediately so that it could never bite her in the ass. Getting involved with a patient sexually was grounds for losing her license, and Michelle's job was her world. She would never do anything to sacrifice her livelihood, nor would she ever willingly compromise the hearts and minds of her patients.

However, researching a lover was an entirely different matter. She'd known nothing about Jack the night before, and she'd relished the *Just Jack* mystery, the intrigue behind the toy salesman persona.

She scoffed to herself.

"Toy salesman, my ass," she muttered as she plugged his name into Google, and up popped a website for *Joy Delivered.*

Oh, my.

The man was the CEO of Joy Delivered? A thrill ran down her spine, electric and hot. She knew Joy Delivered, and it had delivered for her night after night. She had a drawer full of Joy Delivered goodies, and they were the Christian Louboutins of the sex toy world, as she and her friend Sutton liked to say. Everything else was Payless, and everything else paled in comparison. "Once you've gone Joy Delivered, you'll never leave your bedroom," Sutton had once said in her pretty British voice when the two of them had popped into Eden, a sex toy shop on the Upper East Side. Michelle vastly preferred the comfort of online shopping—you never knew in New York when you might run into a colleague, a patient, or a researcher you were submitting a paper to. But Sutton had insisted, and Michelle had gone along, acquiring one of many battery-operated boyfriends.

Her friend was right.

Michelle was Joy Delivered or bust now. A true brand loyalist, because the *O*s it had brought her were magnificent.

When she was tired and simply wanted to take the edge off before bed, she'd fire up some of her favorite naughty sites, grab the Fly Me to the Moon mini vibrator and take care of business in mere minutes. Other nights, she'd spent more than a round or two with The One—a delicious rabbit-styled vibrator that she swore had some kind of special homing device for finding her G-spot. Oh, she'd practically sung arias from the way that baby had her perform.

Her eyes fluttered closed as she flashed back to some of the orgasms his toys had wrought. Did he design them? Did he know what they did to women? Did he test them out on his lovers, making sure the butterflies, the bunnies, the fly-me-to-the-moons did the trick, and then some?

Would he try his latest products on her?

A burst of heat spread through her belly, settling between her legs. She dropped her hand under her skirt, brushing her fingertips against the cotton panel of her lace panties. Her breath caught as she pictured Jack watching her, telling her to spread her legs, offering to test his newest products on her, even though he hardly needed any help. The man's cock was divine. It should have a statue erected in its honor. A national holiday named for it. A parade to celebrate its length, width, and most of all, its *feel.*

Hot tingles raced through her body, causing a sweet ache between her thighs.

She sat up straight.

She did not need to get turned on in the office, and certainly not from perusing her lover's website.

Wait. Was he her lover? He wasn't. He couldn't be. He was a one-night stand, and she was simply a curious woman conducting the necessary post-mortem research.

She continued on the hunt for Jack Sullivan. One of the first results mentioned that his company was the gold sponsor for a charity gala supporting breast cancer research next month. The company even sold a small, pink pocket-sized vibrator called The Divine, and donated half of the proceeds from that product to breast cancer.

Damn. Not only was he fantastic in bed, he was good to women in important ways too.

One of the next results was an article in a business magazine headlined *Soldier-Turned-Sex-Toy-Mogul.*

She was almost ashamed at the way goose bumps rose across her arms and legs. She wasn't supposed to be stirred by such things, but holy fucking hell, the man had served his country, had been in uniform, had been stationed in Europe as an army intelligence officer. She didn't know much about the armed forces—she grew up surrounded by the arts, since her father had been a theater professor and her mother a choreographer—but she'd treated a few soldiers and a few officers too, and she'd learned enough about the work. An intelligence officer managed, analyzed and provided strategies for soldiers on the front line based on the intelligence gathered during missions. Many often went onto jobs in the corporate world after leaving the military.

And here was Jack, a sexy-as-sin CEO and a former soldier.

Yeah, that was hot as hell.

Emboldened by this candy trail, she continued on it, hunting out more details. She found an article from last night in a local news outlet.

New York's Most Eligible Bachelors

Sex toy mogul Jack Sullivan tops this year's list of the city's most eligible bachelors in business. Don't you think he needs a new woman to mend his broken heart? Makes you just want to nab that man even more.

Her heart fell when she read those words. She brushed aside her naughty thoughts, focusing instead on the man behind the headlines. A pang of concern took root inside her as she read on, clicking until she'd learned exactly why he'd come to see her.

Her heart lurched towards him. His fiancée, Aubrey Sheen, had been a former Olympic skier, who'd died on the slopes in a freak accident a little more than a year ago. Apparently, the pair of them had travelled to Breckenridge, Colorado for a ski weekend seven days before their wedding. On the last run of the day, she'd crashed into a tree on an intermediate trail that she held the speed record on. She'd died on impact, the reports said. Michelle's throat hitched as she read the stories, and the ones that followed it. Months later, the local press had started hounding the eligible-again bachelor about his status, and apparently being a *widower* had made him all the more appealing for those who cared about such things.

Michelle was not one of the people who cared about such things. Not one bit. She cared instead about the fact that somehow that man was hurting, and he wanted help for it.

She reminded herself that it wasn't her job to help him. It was Kana's now. She'd probably never see him again. Such a shame, since being with him was about the only thing that had made her feel it was possible to move on from heartache.

CHAPTER TWO

Improper

By the end of the session, Kana knew the basics, but not the truth. He wasn't going to pony that up to someone he hadn't even intended to spill a single word to. She was nice enough, a good listener, and asked questions that didn't make him want to squirm, as he'd suspected he'd feel being in a shrink's office for the first time.

But he'd be lying to the world if he said his mind was here between these four walls. He was elsewhere, trying to wrap himself around why it felt weird to want to see Michelle again. Or really, why it didn't feel weird. Maybe that's what was so off-kilter to him. Michelle didn't know the details of his reason for this visit, but she knew he needed help, and that *should* bother him. He was a private man. Sure, he had a public persona as the head of a company that had become something of a press darling by virtue of the type of products it peddled. But beyond the necessary appearances, Jack wasn't someone prone to sharing too much. That wasn't his thing. Growing up in a home that wasn't known for talking it out, or hugging it out either, he'd learned to deal with everything inside his head.

But oddly enough, it didn't bother him that Michelle knew he was seeing a shrink. And that was information only Casey was privy to.

Maybe that's why wanting more of Michelle didn't feel as strange as it should. She already knew he had crap to deal with; he didn't have to pretend with her that he was New York's most eligible bachelor.

He wasn't.

He had a hunch he didn't have to be that guy with her. He relished the freedom he'd felt last night in letting go of what everyone thought they knew about him. He had enjoyed being *Just Jack*. He wanted to be that guy again. He wanted to see her again. He wanted to get to know the woman behind the pencil skirt, the sharp blouse and the black high heels. The combo was like a straight shot of heat to his groin.

"So, do you think you'll want to keep going?"

Oh, crap. Kana wanted to know if he was game for more therapy. Hell if he knew. "Sure," he said.

After she said a quick goodbye and shut the door, he honed in on the stairwell, covered two flights, and headed to the first office he'd been in, knocking sharply on the wood.

In seconds, Michelle opened the door.

"Do you have an appointment right now?" he asked.

She shook her head.

"Good," he said, stepping inside, clicking the door shut, and locking it behind him.

* * *

"Do you like Italian?"

She scrunched up her brow at the question, but then she connected the dots as she sat down. The last text he'd sent her was about dinner.

"I do," she said, because it was the truth, and because it didn't commit her. She wasn't sure if she was going to continue this thing—whatever it was—with him. She wasn't sure about anything, except the fact that he looked good at three o'clock in the afternoon when his five o'clock shadow seemed to start. Add in that dark hair that had felt so luxurious in her fingers, the chiseled cheekbones and the slightly loosened tie, and she'd have to say he seemed like a man who'd stepped off the pages of a magazine.

He took another step closer. "I made a reservation."

"Where?" she asked, feeling a bit like they were having this conversation on another plane of reality. Then again, the last few hours had her feeling like she'd slipped into another world.

"There's a place near Madison Square Park. It has bocce ball and the best—"

"—Pasta primavera in all of New York."

He raised an eyebrow as she cut in, finishing his sentence.

"Restaurants are my thing," she said, by way of explanation. She loved researching New York's best eateries, both the newest shi-shi ones, the off-the-beaten-path spots, and the best-kept secrets in dining.

"Then you'll go with me to Gia's tonight," he said, and it wasn't a question. It was a statement, and the way his cool blue eyes held her gaze made it clear he wouldn't take no for an answer. She tilted her head, considering. The conundrum was this—Michelle wasn't a woman who was turned on by a lack of choices, but she was a woman turned on by *this* man. And she hadn't seen this *give-a-woman-an-order* side of him. Well, *of course* she hadn't seen this side of him. She'd only spent one night with him. There was no reason why she'd know that he had this kind of intensity, and such a commanding tone to his rich, deep voice that was like a note held long and lasting on a bass guitar. And it made her feel like this . . .

"Yes."

Because it turned out, she liked this side of him.

In his presence, she was keenly aware of her body. Of her physicality. She'd never been so aware of it before, but every bone, cell and nerve seemed to be on high alert near him.

He moved closer. She remained still, seated in her chair, facing him. He crossed the remaining distance and placed his palms on the arms of her chair, his chest inches from her, but not touching. The air between them was like an electrical storm in the summer. Charged, heated, and ready to crackle with a lightning strike in seconds.

"Did you think about me when I was with Kana?"

"Yes," she said, her voice bare and truthful.

"Did you look me up online?"

Another nod.

"What did you learn?" he asked, never looking away or breaking the gaze. The man radiated intensity. She could picture him in a boardroom, owning a negotiation. Winning all the points in his favor without breaking a sweat.

"What do you think I learned?" she tossed back.

"What the press says about me."

"I don't care what the press says," she said firmly, and his gaze drifted down to her throat. He stared at the exposed skin peeking above the top button of her silk blouse. "What do you care about, then?"

"I want to know how you can be a sex toy mogul and have intimacy issues," she said, reaching her hand to his chin and forcing him to look up again.

"Why should I tell you? I'm not your patient anymore," he said, and there was teasing now in his tone. The toughness was drifting away.

"But that's why you're here. In this office. Needing a therapist."

"And that's why I'm seeing another shrink. For my *intimacy issues*," he said with a scoff. "Besides, why does my job have any bearing on my life outside of the office? Are you the same person in here that you were with me last night? Or did you show me another side?" he said, and brushed the back of his fingers against her cheek.

Her eyes floated closed. Her breath fled, and one thing was clear. She wasn't the same person.

She was a different woman with him. A wanted woman. And it felt so good, especially as his breath ghosted over her neck and he whispered in her ear, "Did you touch yourself when I was in there?"

"No," she said.

"Not even a little?"

She shook her head, glad that her eyes were closed because surely they'd give away this lie. He reached for her hand, and brought it to his mouth, drawing her index finger between his lips. Her eyes snapped open.

"I bet this finger was between your legs," he whispered, disarming her.

Her lips parted, but no words came out.

"And I bet you didn't finish the job."

"I barely touched myself," she admitted defensively, her skin heating up all over.

His eyes darkened, and he groaned appreciatively. "When you *barely* touched yourself, were you thinking about me?"

"Yes."

"And were you thinking about me as your patient?"

She shook her head. "No."

"Were you thinking about me as New York's most eligible bachelor?" he asked, and she could hear the disdain in his tone. He didn't like those titles. She wouldn't like them either.

"No."

"Were you thinking of me as the man who wants to fuck you again?"

That was it. Her shoulders trembled, and lust took over. "Oh God," she gasped, and her body was not her own. It was his, and she desperately wanted some kind of relief from the way she ached everywhere, desire pounding inside her, ready to escape.

"Because that's who I want to be with you, Michelle with two *Ls*," he said, loosening his tie further. Then he moved his hands to her knees. Moaning the second he made contact, she was almost embarrassed that this simplest kind of touch had her pulse racing.

He dropped to his knees, pushed up her skirt, and spread her legs open. "I have unfinished business with your pussy," he growled, as he dragged a finger across the outside of her panties.

His blue eyes were hungry, and he looked as if he wanted to devour her. He lowered his head between her legs, buzzing a hot trail along a thigh. The temperature rose in her so high, she was sure she was giving off heat waves. He kissed the inside of her legs, teasing her as he slowly made his way closer to where she wanted him.

"*Jack*," she moaned.

"Yes?" he asked, as he continued taking her hormones hostage with his sinful mouth.

"You're teasing me."

"I know," he said, sounding wickedly pleased. "I told you I would, since you denied me last night."

"I'm not denying you now."

He moved his mouth from her leg to the wet panel of her panties, planting a kiss on the fabric that had her throbbing. "So many things I want to do to this beautiful pussy. So many ways I want to make you come," he mused and her skin sizzled from the way he talked to her.

"I want you to make me come," she said, spearing her fingers in his soft dark hair, pulling him closer to the place where he could soothe the ache.

He slid a finger underneath the fabric, touching her hot flesh at last. She cried out, then covered her mouth with her hand.

"Be quiet, Michelle. Even with the noise machine, I'm going to make you come so fucking hard that you might break the sound barrier," he said, and she was about to call him a cocky bastard until he yanked her panties aside and pressed his lips to her wetness. She couldn't say *cocky bas-*

tard, because she could no longer form words. She couldn't think. She could barely breathe. All she could do was *feel.* And she felt like she was flying, soaring into a new stratosphere of boundless pleasure as he swept his tongue through her wetness, groaning as he licked her.

"You taste so fucking good," he said, then returned to flicking his tongue against her clit.

"What do I taste like?" she asked, because no one had ever talked to her this way. No one had sung her praises like this man, and she was greedy. He was like dessert without the calories. He was cake and chocolate and everything delicious in the universe. She wanted more, and she had no problem asking for it.

"Like sex," he murmured. "You taste like hot sex."

She gasped, and shoved a hand through her hair, her head hitting the back of her chair as her body melted into him. She was completely losing herself to the way he touched her. To the intensity of his mouth. To the rhythm of his tongue. He slid his hands under her thighs, gently lifting her legs over his shoulders. She belonged to him like this, spread wide in her office, being licked and kissed and sucked by this man who knew exactly what to do to her.

This man, whose touch said he craved every inch of her. She was in ecstasy both from the sheer physical intensity of the moment, and from what it meant to her to be wanted like this.

He pulled back for a second to glance up at her. His eyes blazed darkly. He looked like a man who'd been feasting. "I want you to come on me," he said in a low, raspy voice. "Let me feel you all over my face. I can't get enough of you."

She was nearly there, and she began matching his movements, rocking faster into his mouth as he returned to her core, caressing her with his talented tongue, kissing her with his fantastic lips, and sending her to the brink as he cupped her ass tightly in his hands. His fingers dug into her soft flesh, gripping her cheeks. As if he couldn't get close enough to her. He went down on her like a man obsessed. As if he wanted to drink her in, to lap her up, to consume her.

She let herself be consumed by Jack as he took her over the edge.

She gave him everything. All of her pleasure. All of her body, as she did what he asked for, coming hard on his face.

* * *

"I trust that's a yes to Gia's?"

She breathed out hard. Her eyes were glassy. She looked so damn sexy that all he wanted was to bury his face between her legs again. But restraint was the most powerful aphrodisiac of all. And he knew how to use it. He knew how to play with denial. He planned to. But first, he needed to sort out tonight. She was the only woman he'd wanted to spend any time with since Aubrey had died. He needed to do this right.

"Meet me there at eight," he said as he tightened the knot in his tie.

"Yes."

"Oh, and you might want to straighten up before your next appointment. You look like a woman who's been fucked properly."

"But you didn't fuck me properly, Jack," she said, as she adjusted her skirt.

He buttoned one of the buttons on her blouse, savoring the soft feel of her skin beneath his fingertips, and the way she shivered from his touch. God, she was so utterly sensual. He wanted to do everything to her. He wanted to explore every inch of her body with his hands, his lips, his tongue, his cock, and with a whole treasure chest of toys. He wanted to give her every kind of orgasm imaginable. To bring her all the bliss in the universe.

"When I fuck you again, there will be nothing proper about it," he said in a low voice, leaving her with that hint of what he might do.

CHAPTER THREE

Pressure

Jack arrived at his high-rise midtown office, ready to dive into work for the next few hours. His time away from business for the afternoon had lasted longer than he'd anticipated, but he didn't regret the hour with Kana, and he definitely didn't regret the moments with Michelle.

When Casey finished her meeting with the marketing team—she oversaw the advertising and brand positioning for the company—she joined him in his office, plunking herself down on the eggplant-colored couch that she'd selected when she overhauled his office a year ago, declaring it too dull.

"A little splash of color makes everything better," she'd said as the movers lugged in the new couch, and then carried out the old beige one.

This morning, she'd been meeting with their ad agency, so this was his first chance to sit down with her and lay out the details of the Henry and Marquita issue with Eden. Last night, he'd met with one of their top retailers that boasted a storefront on the Upper East Side as well as a burgeoning online division. But the most profitable line of their business was the handful of under-the-radar BDSM clubs they ran in Manhattan. Those clubs were under threat because a rival politician had decided to play dirty.

"Here's the problem," Jack said as he joined her in the red chair opposite the purple couch. Yes, the red chair was her selection too. "We've got Marquita's brother, Paul Denkler, running for city councilman in District Four. There's a special election because of an unexpected vacancy."

Casey emitted a snoring sound and let her head loll to one side, her eyelids fluttering closed.

"Yes, I feel the same way about politics," Jack said, rolling his eyes as Casey 'woke up.' "But listen, his opponent is this guy, Jared Conroy, and he's a complete prick."

"Two of my least favorite words paired together," Casey said.

"Me too. Trouble is, he's a former litigator, and he fights below the belt."

"Below the belt is a pleasure-only zone," Casey said, gesturing to her skirt. "I don't approve of fighting there."

"Nor do I," he said with a laugh.

Casey twisted her blond hair into a knot and shoved a pencil through it. "So tell me the problem."

"The problem is, Conroy is hitting all the right notes the residents want to hear with his clean-up-the-neighborhood platform. And hey, who doesn't want to clean up New York? Nothing wrong with that. But he's twisted Denkler's schools-and-safe-streets campaign into a condemnation of Denkler's sister's business."

"How are the two even connected?" she asked, scrunching her brow.

Jack shook his head. "They aren't, of course. That's the issue. Conroy plays hard ball, and he's decided to make the campaign about the BDSM clubs. Conroy has deep pockets. With that money lining his pockets, he's promising to do a Times Square-style sweep of the—" Jack stopped to sketch air quotes "—tawdry elements. As if the BDSM clubs are causing problems in the area that necessitate a clean up. They're not, but he's making it seem like they are, and since the Times Square revamp was so popular, his message is resonating."

Casey bared her teeth and crinkled her nose. "Bastard. I hate him already. Nobody fucks with Henry and Marquita, especially after all that Marquita has been through."

"Couldn't agree more," Jack said. Not only were Henry and Marquita key business customers for Joy Delivered, they were like family. Jack had worked closely with the couple for years, and even donated half the proceeds from one of his company's products, a small pink pocket-sized vibrator, to breast cancer research, in honor of Marquita. Jack would go to battle with this guy and fight for him on a personal level alone. Add in the business ties they shared, and Jack was all in.

There was real cause for concern from the domino-like effect of a potential shut down. Henry and Marquita's reputation for carrying the best selection of vibrators was unrivaled. They were tastemakers in the business of pleasure. Where Henry and Marquita went, so went others. Many online retailers often stocked products based on what the Eden couple showcased and recommended. But on top of that, Jack didn't like that Conroy was going after one of his business partners with a scare tactic.

"Besides, Conroy's totally wrong with the whole the-clubs-are-seedy line. Henry runs the most prestigious BDSM clubs in New York. Have you seen the patrons?" Casey lowered her voice to a whisper, even though it was only the two of them. "They're all New York's elite. One of the state senators is a member. I bet Conroy has no clue that the good Senator likes to be whipped and flogged by pretty ladies."

Jack laughed. "Bondage and dominance is a God-given right. And so is battery-operated assistance. Anyway, I want to help them because it's the right thing to do for them, and because helping them helps us. Henry's backing his brother-in-law, of course, and he's asking if we can get behind him too."

Casey slammed a fist onto the arm of the purple couch. "I'll stage a march on anyone who dares to keep floggers and whips out of the bedroom."

"Or sex dungeons, as the case may be," Jack said dryly.

"That too," Casey said, her blue eyes wide and enraged. "You should be able to do whatever you want between consenting adults in a sex dungeon without politicians getting involved. Want me to make signs? Picket? Launch a PR campaign?"

Jack pushed his hands down, as if to say *let's take it slow.* "One step at a time. For now I think it's best if we stay off the radar, and Henry agrees. I think we should put up some money and see if that can help Denkler regain some traction with his schools-and-safe-streets campaigns. Get the focus off the clubs, since that's not what it's about, but in so doing, we protect them and Henry's business, and our business. And the real issues become important ones again."

She nodded. "Absolutely. I don't want anyone messing with our business, Jack," she said. While Joy Delivered was *their* company and he loved every second of running it, the partnership had started with his sister. She'd approached Jack about joining forces after she graduated from business school.

"You're going to think this is crazy, but I know what I want to be when I grow up," she'd said, her mortarboard in hand. Jack had just completed his service with the army, and after his time stationed in Europe, he was Stateside again. Eager for the "what's next in his life," he'd jumped on the chance to build a business from the ground up. His sister brought her natural passion; he brought his business mind. And, of course, an avid appreciation for the female body and all the ways that women could experience pleasure. He'd been a lucky man—lucky with the ladies, and lucky in business.

Until Aubrey, when luck ran out, and everything unraveled by his simple inability to tell her the truth.

The way things ended was a stone in his chest, heavy and unyielding.

"How did your appointment go today?"

Jack blinked, returning to the here and now, and the question Casey had asked.

"The one with Dr. Milo?" Casey said, rolling her hands, as if to jog his memory.

"It was fine, but I don't want to get into the details."

She parked her hands on her hips. "You're so closed off sometimes, Jack."

"Yes," he said, pointedly. "I know. It's called privacy. You should try it sometime."

"That did not compute. You must be speaking a foreign language."

He laughed and shook his head. His sister was relentless. She was also an open book. She always wanted to talk about things, to discuss them, to have them out in the open. The polar opposite of their parents. But he wasn't going to open up to her about the reason why Michelle wasn't his shrink.

"So, how was Dr. Milo? Was she as amazing as they say?"

"Yes," he said, keeping the smirk to himself as he gave the barest of answers, and yet one that was completely truthful. She was amazing, but in a different way than Casey was asking. Not only was Michelle clever and sharp, she was stunning. The woman was primed for passion, bathed in sensuality. She knew her way around her own body, clearly. She knew what brought her pleasure, and she was willing to give herself to him and let him take her there too.

No inhibitions, only openness. The things he could do with her.

"Well, I hope you and she start to dig into what's weighing you down up here," she said, tapping her skull as she stood. "And here too," she said, lowering her voice as she touched her heart. "I want you to be happy."

"I am happy," he said insistently.

"No. You're not happy. You're busy. Don't confuse the two," she said, then dropped a chaste kiss on his cheek, and sauntered out.

She was right, of course. She was always right. He was a man who filled his nights and days. If he didn't, the past would try to chain him up.

With Michelle, he hadn't felt chained. He hadn't felt guilty. He'd simply felt like one mistake didn't have to define him.

Like he could move on.

Whatever the hell that meant.

* * *

She wanted to shower. She wanted to shave her legs. She wanted to primp and prep and prime herself for Jack. But Shayla had another emergency, so Michelle was going to have less than thirty minutes to get ready for dinner once this appointment ended.

Shayla dropped her head into her hands, her shoulders shaking. "I don't know if I can do it. He's planning on it tonight. Expecting it. He told me he wants me to wear a red teddy."

Michelle nodded sympathetically, as much over the red teddy request—she preferred a matching set of bra and panties to any sort of teddy contraption—as for the latest demand from Shayla's straying husband.

"Are you going to?"

She shrugged helplessly. "He thinks that's how we're going to get our sexual mojo back," Shayla said, disdain lacing her words. "As if it's as simple as lingerie."

"The simpler answer would be for him to remain faithful. You might find that more alluring."

"Yes," Shayla said, holding out her hands to emphasize the obviousness of that answer. "Yes. I would."

"Perhaps he could even stop staring at other women as if he wants to undress them when you're together," Michelle added, reminding Shayla of something else she'd once told her about her husband that understandably bothered her.

"That too."

"Or," Michelle began, taking a pause, waiting to make sure that Shayla was completely focused. That she was hearing and listening. Because sooner or later, they were going to need to get to the heart of the matter. To the truth of Shayla's feelings for her husband. Or rather, her lack of feelings. "Or perhaps it doesn't matter what he does anymore."

"Because he cheated? I mean, I don't need a degree in psychology to know that," Shayla said sharply, speaking in an admonishing tone for one of the first times to Michelle. It didn't bother her. Sometimes, patients needed to lash out. She was a useful dartboard, and she willingly took the hits when needed.

"I'm not saying because he cheated," she said, in a gentle but firm voice, keeping her focus fixed on Shayla's brown eyes. They were sad, tinged with tears, and red with hurt. "I'm talking about how you felt long before he ever started straying."

"I felt fine," Shayla said quickly. Too quickly.

"*Shayla*."

Her client crossed her arms, looking away, her sharp nose in profile now. Shayla was dressed to perfection today, as always—decked out in crisp linen pants, leather heels, and a pretty peach silk top. Michelle had started to understand that her clothes were part of her uniform. The everything-is-together look.

Michelle began again. "Were you ever in love with your husband?"

The answer was instantaneous, like a viper hissing. "Of course," Shayla said, and Michelle swore she could see fumes.

The truth hurt though. The truth was like a wicked slap when you were least expecting it. But Shayla needed to start thinking hard about her heart, and whether she'd ever truly given it to that man. They'd talked about her lack of interest in sex, to how it stemmed from long ago. Michelle was willing to bet the house that Shayla had never truly felt any sort of spark for him.

She leaned forward, clasped her hands together, and tried again. "Tell me then what it felt like being in love with him."

Shayla sputtered and gasped, like a car engine rumbling, trying to turn over, but failing until finally she stopped running.

"I don't know," she whispered, and then they talked more, digging deep for the next fifty minutes.

At the session neared its end, she was still in tears, but they were starting to dry up.

"What do I do about the fact that I've never truly loved him?" Shayla asked.

"We'll have to deal with that next time," Michelle said. "But I promise you, we will deal with it. And we will figure out a way for you to navigate all the things you're learning."

"I'm scared," she said quietly.

"Of what this might mean?"

Shayla nodded. "And how he'll react. He gets unhinged at times. Paranoid, even."

Unhinged was not a good word.

"How is he paranoid?"

"He went through my email once when he thought I was cheating on him. I never was, but if he thinks something is up he might snoop."

Michelle nodded, glad for the warning. She'd dealt with this before with spouses. "I will help you through it all."

Shayla left first, mouthing a heartfelt *thank you*. As Michelle gathered her purse and started to shut down her laptop, a sense of calm washed through her. She'd done something positive for a long-time patient. She'd held her hand, metaphorically, and helped her walk into the dark, dangerous woods of the unknown. As she closed various browser windows, she spotted a few new emails that looked important, but she resisted the urge to check. That was why she had a phone. Well, two, really. Anything that had come in at seven o'clock on a Friday could be dealt with later. Once her computer was off, she locked the door and left, checking her work email in the elevator.

She scrolled through some notes from colleagues, answering a few brief ones on the ride down. As the elevator doors opened at the lobby, she clicked on the next note and nearly squealed for joy. One of the European journals she'd submitted her paper to loved her research and wanted to talk to her about the *next steps* for publishing it.

Michelle beamed, because this journal was the European equivalent of *Psychology Today*. To have an article run there had been a dream of hers, and would be a huge career high. She'd been wanting this, craving this, hoping for some sort of placement for her research. This could serve her quite well in her field, and earn her more recognition. But more importantly, this placement had the potential to spread her findings far and wide. Which, in turn, meant that more of her colleagues would be aware of how to better help patients struggling with love and sex addiction.

Equal parts pride and happiness filled her as she let those words echo through her body—*next steps*. Then she saw there was more to the note. She read on.

We are so excited about your research and findings that we want to introduce some of them at our upcoming conference. I know this is completely last minute, but one of our speakers fell through for our conference in three weeks. Perhaps the timing is fortuitous though. Would you be available to keynote? The conference is in Paris, France, and all expenses will be covered, as well as a stipend supplied.

Sincerely,
Julien

Excitement roared through her veins. And a tiny touch of nerves too. As she walked through the lobby, she re-read the email, and replied with the only answer there was, *yes*, when she smacked right into a tall man with dark hair in need of a cut, and square black glasses.

"Are you okay?" he asked, as if he were dreadfully concerned that he'd just walked into her.

"Yes, I'm fine," she said, even though she winced slightly from the bump. His hand was on her elbow, steadying her, and she stared at it.

"Oh," he said, and it registered. Time to stop touching. "I'm so sorry."

"No problem. Now if you'll excuse me," she said, gesturing to the noisy avenue where cars and cabs and buses were slogging along through the end of rush hour. She stood on the curb, thrust her hand in the air, and snagged a taxi in ten seconds. She might have been unlucky in love, but she was remarkably successful at snagging a cab. As she shut the door behind her, she noticed the guy with dark hair was still standing outside her building, eyes narrowed and fixed on some unseen point straight ahead. Something about him bothered her.

Then he snapped his head down to look at his phone.

Perhaps he'd simply been staring off into space, figuring out what to say on a Facebook status update, or contemplating a reply to a last-minute email, as she'd been doing. Yes, either option seemed reasonable. There was no need for her to consider anything more of him. Especially not when she had a date with a beautiful man who wanted her, and when she'd been invited to keynote a conference in Paris.

Just twenty-four hours ago she'd still been concentrating on letting go of her last residual feelings for Clay. Tonight, she felt different.

The tide was beginning to turn. True, nothing like love would come from a man like Jack Sullivan, and she certainly didn't expect it. He seemed tailor-made for a good time though, and she could use a little fun in her life. She'd take one more night with him and then she'd walk away. Because a man like that—no matter how stunning he was in bed, no matter how fascinating he was out of it—would never be good for this woman's heart. Michelle had given her heart stupidly and foolishly to a man who'd never returned her feelings. She was going to protect her heart much better now. She was going to keep it encased in steel.

But her body? She might as well own stock in Joy Delivered, since she'd bought so many products from them over the years. There would be no harm in one more time with the man behind those magic toys.

CHAPTER FOUR

Proposal

M: On my way. Had a last minute session that ran late.

J: Better not have been with a devilishly handsome CEO of a lingerie company or something like that

M: Jealous already, Jack? I assure you, you're the only devilishly handsome CEO I refuse to treat. If you know what I mean.

J: I do. Oh, I do. I'd like to make sure I'm the only one you refuse to treat.

M: That shouldn't be a problem. Incidentally, do you know any devilishly handsome CEOs who sell sexy lingerie? I'm in the market for a matching pair of white lace panties and a demi-cup bra.

J: I'd like to take you lingerie shopping.

M: For the white lace panties? Or do you have something else in mind?

J: The dressing room.

J: By the way, what color panties are you wearing tonight?

M: I would expect a man such as yourself would simply find out.

J: Oh, I will, Michelle. I will.

* * *

The red ball rolled along the sand and Michelle waited, waited, waited as tension and competitive hope coiled tight inside her. The ball slowed, and she clenched her fingers into her palms, willing the ball to pass the blue one of Jack's on the way to the small white ball. Closer, just a bit closer.

Then the red ball lazily turned once more until it nearly kissed the white one.

She raised her arms in the air victoriously, thrilled to have won this round of the lawn bowling game.

"You're on a roll today. First, your paper is accepted. Then you crush me at bocce ball," he said, flashing her a grin. She'd told him about the end-of-the-day email, and that had called for a celebratory round of drinks, which had then turned into a celebratory game of bocce ball, here on the makeshift court in the back of the restaurant. She was on some kind of high, and surely that had contributed to her victory. She'd called her brother, Davis, on the cab ride over to share the news, and he'd been thrilled. She'd also emailed Carla, her mentor, who'd replied with an all exclamation points email.

"It's my lucky day," she said, thinking it was more like a lucky night *and* day since it had started twenty-four hours ago when she'd met him.

Jack extended his hand as if they were gracious competitors and he was congratulating her winning game. But as he took her hand, he surprised her by tugging her in close, then planting a searing kiss on her lips. One that delivered a red-hot blast of lust right through her body, and sent all that winning glee whooshing out of her. In its place was a hot new wave of longing.

When he pulled away, she felt wobbly, and she was sure her lipstick had been erased by his lips. "Wow," she said. "Does losing at bocce ball bring out the beast in you?"

"Maybe it does. Maybe bowling does too. Maybe arcade games as well."

"In that case, I'm hiring a bocce ball tutor and a bowling expert so I can beat you every time," she said, with a wink and a sashay of the hips.

"You can beat me at any game any time, as long as I can kiss you like this."

"Does that mean you threw the game to get a little piece of me?"

"Never. But I'll take it," he said in a low, growly tone, then ran his hand along the back of her thigh, his fingertips darting near the hemline. She wore a simple, sleeveless black dress that fell to just above her knees. The material was soft cotton, and the skirt was flared, so the material allowed for easy access. Yes, Michelle was a planner, and this dress suggested possibilities. She wanted all those possibilities planted in his head.

"Purple?" he whispered in a question.

She shook her head. Every fifteen minutes or so he'd tried to guess the color of her lingerie. He'd been wrong. She loved that he kept guessing. She also loved that he couldn't seem to take his eyes off her, especially her legs. She'd worn her strappy black Louboutins. Four inches high, they made her legs look strong and toned. God bless heels and the natural enhancement they brought to a runner's calves. Even a temporary runner, such as herself.

"Rest assured I won't stop until I find out what color you have on," he said.

"I have no doubt."

"By the way, have I told you how sexy you look in this black dress?" He ran his hand along the small of her back. She arched into him, like a cat being pet. She might start purring any second. She wasn't used to someone wanting to have his hands on her the whole time. Jack seemed incapable of keeping his hands off her. She didn't mind that.

Not. One. Bit.

"No. Why don't you tell me?"

He raked his eyes over her, from her face, to her neck, to her breasts, to her waist. "It's perfect for you. For that whole sexy-librarian look you have going on."

She laughed deeply, his comment catching her off guard. "Shouldn't I have on glasses to complete that look?"

He raised an eyebrow, his lips curving up in a naughty grin. "Do you have some? And can you pin up your hair too?"

She had a hunch he'd like to see her dressed up in something terribly naughty. Engaged in role-play. Yeah, she could picture Jack getting into those kind of sexy games—the boss and the secretary, the teacher and the student, the delivery service.

"Are you sure you wouldn't prefer the French maid costume I have back at my apartment?" she posited.

He shook his head, and wrapped his arm around her waist. "I'm sure. Because that sexy librarian look of yours brings me to my knees," he said, his midnight-blue eyes blazing darkly at her.

She shivered against him, her body responding to every sensual, suggestive, and dirty thing he said. She ran her hand through his hair, savoring the soft slide through her fingers as she shifted her body closer. Who cared that they were on a makeshift bocce ball court in the back of an Italian restaurant? She didn't. "But maybe I want to get on my knees for you," she said in her best sexy voice.

His reaction was instantaneous. His breath caught in his chest. A low rumble sounded in his throat. Then, there was the press of his erection against her thigh. "I want to see that. You on your knees," he said.

She gripped his hair harder, moving her lips across the deliciously salty skin of his neck, traveling up to his ear, cataloging every second of his physical response to her. Playing into it. Feeding him the images he craved. "Imagine me with my black glasses, my hair pinned up, my pencil skirt on," she said into his ear, and he slammed her chest to him, crushing her. "Sucking you," she said, flicking her tongue against his earlobe, leaving him with that image firmly planted in his head.

She wrenched back, enjoying the look in his eyes. Hazy, wild, unrestrained.

"Later," she added, nodding to their table several feet away. The waitress had just set down their dishes.

* * *

"You have fans."

Jack looked up from the chicken parmigiana in front of him to see Michelle casting her eyes in the direction of the bar. He spotted a pair of young women wearing tops that revealed bare shoulders and holding glasses that held copious amounts of red wine. The redhead in the pair whispered to her friend when he looked up, the sort of conspiratorial *he's-seen-us* warning.

He shrugged as if to say *what can you do*. Whether from having been involved with somebody like Aubrey, a world-class athlete with sponsorships and Olympic medals to her credit, or from the job he held, he'd grown accustomed to being recognized from time to time.

"It doesn't bother me. Does it bother you?"

She laughed, and shook her head. "Not really. Honestly? I'm used to it. My brother's a well-known theater director and his wife is a Tony award-winning actress so I see it a lot with them."

"Good," he said, flashing her a grin that he hoped would melt her. "Then you won't be bothered by the stares as I take you out around town and romance you."

"You're presumptuous, aren't you?"

"You're the one who mentioned a bocce ball tutor."

"Maybe I've simply been hoping to improve my game."

He didn't give her a chance to answer. Instead, he cupped the back of her head and dropped his mouth to her lips, kissing away that first sexy gasp of surprise. Her lips were divine, soft and full and thoroughly delicious. He swept the tip of his tongue across the curve of her top lip, then nibbled on her bottom one. Her mouth was sweet and tasted of the white wine she'd been drinking. The scent of her jasmine shampoo filled his nostrils, and it was heady, and perfect for her, as all these scents collided in a kiss. He hardly wanted to break the kiss at all, but he was so tempted to explore more of her, to kiss her neck, her ear, to bite the soft flesh of her collarbone like he'd done last night. To hear all her sexy responses to every touch. Even the way she responded now, to a simple kiss, was intoxicating. She was a woman who relished kissing, who seemed to let go of herself in the moment from the way he touched her. He wanted more of her physical abandon.

He also didn't want to have a painful erection throughout the entire meal. He'd been hard the whole night sitting next to her. Then rock-hard when she'd teased him with her delicious blow-job imagery. But the more he consumed her lips, the more trouble he'd be in. Better stop now.

He pulled back, thrilling at the look on her face. Lips parted slightly, eyes closed. Then she shuddered and opened her eyes, as if she were dragging herself out of a trip down Unexpected Lust Lane.

"Who said you'd be romancing me?" she countered as she reached for her fork and dove into her plate of pasta primavera.

"I say it," he said, as he took a bite of his chicken.

"Maybe I'm only going on one date with you."

"I'll have to find a way to convince you for more then. I'll see if I have any tricks up my sleeve."

She took another bite, chewed, then set down her fork. Her expression turned serious. "Actually, I hate to be blunt, but I've learned a thing or two about being upfront, seeing as how I failed to be upfront about something really important for ten years."

"What do you mean?" he asked after he finished his bite and took a drink of his wine.

"What I mean is I'm not interested in getting involved with someone who has intimacy issues," she said in a direct tone of voice. She didn't mince words. She didn't pull punches. She simply told him. "I'm sorry if that sounds harsh. And I know I shouldn't be judgmental, given my job, but my reality is I was in love with a good friend of mine for ten years from a distance. From afar. I never said a word to him until he'd already fallen madly in love with someone else. He had no clue I had any feelings for him. Even if I had told him, it wouldn't have made a difference. He never saw me that way. He never thought of me romantically."

"That makes no sense to me," Jack said, speaking plainly. He could only see Michelle romantically. How any man could look at her and talk to her and not want to know her more confounded him.

She sighed, took another bite, and then continued on when she'd finished. "And that was three months ago, when it all came to a head. And it's fine. We're all good. But my point in bringing this up is I'm the poster child for unrequited love. And while I'm certainly not asking for love, the bottom line is, I don't think you'll be romancing me because I can't risk my heart again for someone who might be closed down," she said, and her words were like a heavy stone around his neck.

That described him perfectly. Closed down. Shut down. Battered and broken with guilt. "I'm not closed down," he muttered, denying the truth he knew inside himself.

She reached for his hand, and laid hers on top of it. "We don't have to bullshit, Jack. I'm not some blushing twenty-two year old who read in the paper that you were New

York's most eligible bachelor and wants to nab you. I have a business, a career, a respectable profession, a brother and sister-in-law I love dearly, and very close friends. I'm fine. But when you've been in love with someone who didn't love you, it really makes you protect your heart from anyone and everyone," she said, and those words stung him more than she could ever know. "We had a great time last night and I'm having a lovely time tonight. But this can't be anything. From what I can gather your heart is still with someone else."

He swallowed thickly. He was so tempted to tell her the truth that only Casey knew. "Why would you assume that?"

"I could be wrong, but your fiancée died a little more than a year ago. And you go see a therapist who specializes in intimacy. I don't think it takes a rocket scientist to figure out that's why your sister sent you to see me. To help you move on, right?"

"Yes," he said, and he clamped his lips shut so he wouldn't reveal the truth out loud. That he didn't need to move on in the way everyone thought. That he wasn't some poor widower. Yeah, he had commitment issues a mile long, but not because of what everyone thought about how things ended with Aubrey. Not because she died. But because of what he'd said before. Because of how it was all his fault.

He winced as the memories assaulted him.

High school sweethearts in Denver, Colorado where he grew up, Jack Sullivan and Aubrey Sheen were one of those couples. The couple everyone thought would be together forever. He was the school's star shortstop; she was captain of the ski team and an Olympic hopeful. It was first love. It was true love. It was as real as it could possibly be. She was bright and beautiful, ambitious and determined. They laughed together; they had fun together; they were going to be together always. But then they drifted apart, attending colleges with many miles between them, and the inevitable split set in. There were plenty of tears shed, but plenty unshed too. She was focused on her Olympic dreams; he was focused on school, and then on his time in the service.

Years later, when he returned from Germany and started Joy Delivered, they found themselves near each other again. With Aubrey living and working in New York, they reunited.

At first, it felt natural to be back with her. They fit. They made sense. On paper, they should have worked, and so he proposed. But at some point after that, one thing became painfully clear to him. He was living in the past with her. He wasn't the same person he had been when he was younger. She wasn't either. But their love had been borne of that time in their lives—young love. He'd mistaken that for forever love.

He hadn't realized that when he proposed. When he'd gotten down on one knee, he was sure it would be forever. But once the planning started, the sense that something was amiss kept tugging at him. Finally, he woke up one morning to the stark realization that he was about to walk down the aisle and say *I do* to a woman he cared deeply for. To a woman he admired. To a *friend.*

He was no longer in love with her. Marrying her would have been a mistake. Maybe it made him a jerk; maybe it made him an asshole. He was willing to be the punching bag for all those terms of un-endearment. Better to break it off before the wedding than after. Better to cause the hurt before they took those steps.

They went away for the weekend in Breckenridge. He knew Aubrey—she'd need to be near mountains to deal with his bombshell. Snow and slopes were her companions for the good and bad in her life. She processed everything through her sport.

He could still remember the look on her face when he'd told her he didn't want to marry her. Like he'd sliced her open with a knife. Her eyes had spilled tears. Her lips had quivered, and she'd given new meaning to the word *devastated.* Because of him. Then she wiped off her stream of tears, stood up and said what he'd expected her to say. "I need to go hit the mountains."

Twenty minutes later, Ski Patrol dragged her body down the blue square trail that she'd always owned and conquered, that she'd mastered at age six. This time, she'd slammed into a tree. Dead on impact.

That's how he became the *widower* a week before the wedding that he'd just called off, and no one knew the truth but his sister.

He wanted to tell all that to Michelle. Hell, if he hadn't slept with her last night, he might even have started to tell her his truth today. But there was no way he was going to unload on her right now. Not after she'd just revealed something painful about her past. That she'd felt unloved. That she'd been unwanted.

If she knew he was the kind of guy who'd called off a wedding, she'd run from him right now. He was everything she'd want to stay far away from. The guy who didn't love back. She was right to try to nip this in the bud.

But hell, he had no intention of letting a woman like her slip through his fingers. His greatest skill in business had been solving problems. He could always find new ways around the hurdles, and spot the routes others hadn't seen. The path to her was crystal clear to him. Because he wanted Michelle.

Badly. So very badly.

He might not be able to give her love, but he could show her what it would be like to be wanted.

He also didn't intend to start whatever this was with a lie. So he cast the truth in a new light as he answered her question. "You're right. I haven't moved on entirely, but not for the reasons you think. And since you're not my shrink, I'd rather not get into it. But I have another idea. Something that I think could meet both our needs. Want to hear my proposal?"

Her eyes blazed with curiosity.

* * *

She scoffed and laughed at the same time. "Thirty days? You want me to sign a contract or something?"

"Not unless it's one that requires you to use a safe word and call me sir, but somehow I doubt you're into dom/sub stuff," he said, his cool blue eyes twinkling, as if he'd just come up with the most brilliant plan ever.

Admittedly, it had some appeal.

"You read me right on that one, Jack," she said, and took another bite of her pasta, shaking her head in surprise. The food was good; she wasn't going to miss a chance to enjoy this delicious dish simply because he'd proposed something so ridiculous.

But he was undeterred. "So? What do you think?"

She finished her bite, set her fork down and clasped her hands together. "Jack, we had a great night, and I'd really like to sleep with you again because sex with you is spectacular, but suggesting we have a no-strings-attached affair for thirty days and then walk away is ludicrous."

"But why? Why is it ludicrous?" he asked in the tone of someone who was damn curious. As if he were asking a business partner why the terms in a contract didn't make sense. "You're not in a spot for a relationship. And you've already decided I'm not either. Let's not pretend it's ever going to be anything more. We're both mature, reasonable adults who had a fantastic night together. We're both looking to move on from hurt. Let's help each other do that."

"Through sex?"

"Yes. We can both be therapists," he said with a sexy glint in his eyes, and she laughed. "I'll give you the best kind of therapy there is. I'm very good at sex therapy," he added, his eyes looking so eager. So boyish for a moment. So young, like a kid at Christmas.

"I hardly even know you, though."

"What do you want to know? I'm thirty-four. I grew up in Colorado. My father taught at the Air Force Academy. I played baseball in high school, studied business in college at the University of Colorado, served in the army for six years, most of it in Europe. I speak German and French. I run a business. I play basketball for exercise with my friend Nate. I live on Fifth Avenue. I like classical music. I'd like to fuck you to Ravel."

She reined in the naughty grin that threatened to bloom across her face from the final statement. She could practically hear the rising crescendo of Ravel's "Bolero," the way the piece was sex in musical form. But now was not the time for picturing more orgasms from him.

"And you?" he asked.

"Thirty. Grew up in Westchester. My parents were in the arts—mom was a choreographer, dad a theater professor. They died in a car accident when I was seventeen."

"I'm so sorry," he said, tilting his head, his eyes on her, filled with compassion.

"It's okay. I mean, it wasn't okay. But it's okay now. My brother delayed college for a year to watch out for me when they were gone. Then we went to school together at Yale. I live off Park Avenue in Murray Hill. I've never done any sports. I like to go shoe shopping with my friend Sutton. I love wine and scotch and theater."

"And fucking to Ravel?" he asked in his deep, sexy tone, returning to his seductive side. The side that thrilled her.

"That's not fair. Now you're playing below the belt."

"That's where I'd like to be playing. So are we good then?" he asked, reaching for her hand, sliding his fingers through hers, as if he knew that contact would help win a yes.

"Jack," she said, with a sigh.

"Why not?" he asked in the barest of whispers, then bent his head to her neck. "You're beautiful, and captivating, and I loved every second of being inside you last night. The only thing better than fucking you was tasting you on my tongue this afternoon."

If he was going to play dirty like that she was going to lose. Because with those words, a heat wave rolled through her body, and she was aching for his touch again.

"Let me have more of you," he continued. "Let me have you for a month. Give me your body. I'll give you mine."

"I don't know," she said, but she could feel her resistance breaking down with his lips on her neck, buzzing a path to her ear. She lingered in the moment, considering. Was his plan so crazy?

"I haven't been with anyone since Aubrey, and last night with you blew my mind. I could sit here and try to break it down, and try to analyze it and understand it, but I'm not a shrink. I'm only a man who wants a woman. I want you. Badly. Let me have you; let me give you the exquisite pleasure you deserve."

She burned inside for him. Flames licked her body from head to toe, turning her into an inferno of desire. She'd come to dinner wanting only one more night; and now he was asking for thirty nights with him.

Thirty nights of pleasure. Thirty nights of bliss. Thirty nights of being wanted in ways she hadn't ever been wanted.

She didn't know how she could say no. She was about to say yes when he spoke again.

"Let me give you a taste of what I can do to you. If I don't give you the best orgasm of your life within the next hour, I won't ask again."

She tossed her napkin on the table. She was dying to know how he planned to top this afternoon.

"Check, please."

CHAPTER FIVE
After Hours

She expected they'd catch a cab to his place, that he'd own some swank high-rise apartment overlooking the park. But that's not where he took her. They were in the elevator at the Met Life Tower, shooting up nearly fifty flights. He had a friend who owned the company that was converting the landmark skyscraper into a new hotel. The friend had called security, and security had waved them in.

Overlooking Madison Square Park, the building was eerie and shadowy at night, shrouded in secrets of the city after hours. She was about to become part of that after hours New York. When they reached the top floor, the elevator doors whooshed open.

Jack rested his hand on her lower back as they walked through the hall. The sizzling warmth from his palm spread through her body. Even the simplest touch from him melted her.

"You must think the Empire State Building is so passé, when you have a friend who owns this building," she quipped as they neared the balcony.

"No. I'm thinking the balcony here is private, and you can see all of Manhattan when you come."

She had no retort.

Hot sparks tore through her, lighting her up with more desire than she'd ever known. While she'd dated and had lovers over the years, none had spoken to her like this. None had talked to her as if *her* pleasure was vital to their happiness. That's how she felt with Jack. Hard to imagine he was a stranger twenty-four hours ago, yet now, he was a lover on a quest to bring her the best climax of her life.

The balcony circled the peak of the Met Life Tower with a spire above them, a clock right below them. A high fence surrounded the perimeter, and the view of Manhattan was endless, stretching to the rivers and the towns that lay far beyond the city that never slept.

Michelle felt a rush of tingles in her belly that had nothing to do with him at the moment, and everything to do with being this high above her city. She wrapped her hands around the railing at the edge of the balcony, drinking in the view of Manhattan. The headlights from the distant streets below streaked across the dark night; the sounds of horns and music and madness morphed into a quiet radio station din. The dirt and grime was gone, and New York was aerial and beautiful—a darkly gorgeous nocturnal creature, lit up against the night sky.

Jack dropped his hands to her waist, his thumbs rubbing circles against the fabric of her dress at her hips. She murmured something unintelligible, leaning her head back against him, stretching her neck. But then he was gone—he was on his knees behind her, kissing the back of her bare legs, starting at her calves.

"Stay here. Like this," he told her.

"I'm not going anywhere," she managed to say.

"Don't close your eyes. Watch the city as I touch you."

No wonder he did what he did. He was a man in tune with pleasure. A man thoroughly connected to his senses, which was all the more unusual, given his background as a numbers and logic guy. But he also had some intuitive sense of the physical.

Or simply the physical of her. His tongue flicked against the back of her knee, and she felt her legs wobble. He steadied her, his strong hands tight on her thighs as he kissed his way up her legs, pressing his lips against the back of her thighs now. First one leg. Then the other. Higher and higher still, the fabric of her skirt rose in his hands as he exposed her flesh for him. Soon he'd pushed her skirt above her butt, and his sinful mouth was leaving a hot, wet trail of kisses against the crease where her ass met her legs.

"Light blue," he murmured as he slid his finger under the edge of her lacy panties. "Gorgeous, sexy, perfect sky blue."

"Yes. You like?"

"So much I want to keep them," he said as he returned his mouth to her skin.

Pleasure pulsed through her veins. She gripped the railing tighter as the sensations spread, starting deep in her belly, radiating to her fingertips, her toes, the ends of her hair, as he brushed those soft lips against her body. He kissed her with a kind of reverence, with a deep appreciation for her body. He kissed her as if she were the most sensual person he'd ever touched. As if she were made for passion, for pleasure, for this kind of bold desire that ran rampant through her cells.

Because everything he'd done so far had been a slice of heaven. A heaven for lovers of the flesh.

He ran his nose across her upper thigh, then pressed a kiss between her legs, his lips grazing the soaked panel of her panties. Useless thing. A completely useless piece of fabric, since the way he'd touched her had turned them hot and damp.

"Take them off," he said roughly.

She obliged, sliding her panties down her legs, then lifting them over her ankles as she stepped out of them.

"Give them to me."

She handed them to him, and he stuffed them into his pocket.

"You can have them back later. Or not," he said with a glint in his blue eyes.

"That will probably be a not."

He stood and gently placed his hand on her chin, turning her gaze back to the sky. "Watch the city," he told her, as he pressed his chest against her back, his long, tall body aligned with hers.

Anticipation built between them, the tantalizing wonder of what would come next. Only he knew. She was placing her pleasure in his hands, and that's exactly where she wanted it to be.

A soft hum whirred through the air. At first, she wasn't sure what it was. Then she recognized the noise. The way it signaled a response in her body. How the sound tapped into her deepest core, a reminder of something she loved.

Assistance.

One hand gripped her hip, and the other slid down her belly, dipping between her legs as he tugged her closer. Her breath fled her chest. The thrill of not knowing ignited her more, and she felt a rush of heat between her legs. She wanted him to feel it too. To know what he was doing to her. She was After Hours Michelle with him, so she let go of her other self, allowing herself to fully be the sexy, alluring woman who appeared when Jack Sullivan was inches away. "Touch me," she said.

She felt *it*. The first press against her throbbing clit. The slide through her wet folds. The pressure from something that wasn't his finger. Something that had been *made*. That had been created to bring her bliss.

"What is it?" she asked in between staccato breaths.

"It's The Lola," he said in a hot, husky voice, whispering in her ear as he rubbed a small toy against her aching pussy. She looked down—he held a sleek circular device between two fingers, one finger through a silver hole in the middle. The toy was like a large ring, made of the same soft material the world's best pleasure toys came in. Only this one didn't just stimulate her with vibrations. Somehow, the toy felt like a tongue against her. Like fast, intense flicks from the most wonderful, amazing, fantastic tongue she'd ever felt. Like Jack today. Times ten.

It was that good.

"I don't have this one," she said, in between gasps and moans.

"I know. It's new. They say it feels fantastic against the skin," he said, rubbing the vibrator against her. "Tell me if it does."

She cried out. "Oh, yes."

She felt as if her body belonged to this toy, to the intensity of the pleasure strumming through her blood and bones. It owned her.

"Does it make you want more of me?"

"So much more," she moaned.

"This part," he said, slowing only to press the soft middle section to her clit, the beads beneath the surface rotating against her, simulating the intoxicating sensations of a tongue flicking against her. "Does that feel like the way I licked your pussy earlier today?" he asked in a whisper, his breath hot against her skin.

"Yes. Oh, God. Yes."

"I can make this feel like a soft swirl, or like I'm fucking you with my tongue," he said, and began cycling through the levels of vibration. Her vision blurred from the sweet intensity. She wasn't sure how she was still standing. "I can show you worlds of pleasure."

"I want it," she said, now begging because this was a new land of desire he'd taken her to, and she didn't ever want to leave.

Working the toy expertly between her legs, he yanked her body closer, his erection hitting her backside. His voice was low and dirty as he growled in her ear. "This is what I can do to you for thirty nights."

"I want it all. I want you," she said in between pants and moans, her body arching into the toy.

"This is how you'll be mine," he said, gliding the toy across her clit that was so swollen she ached with the need to come. She felt desperate in every pore of her body. The intense need to climax was bearing down on her. Her world narrowed to this hot neon need as pleasure took over, spinning wildly out of control, blissfully into chaos as she leaned back into his chest, his arms holding her in place, his finger working her over and over with his toy as she shattered into endless erotic bliss, crying out his name above Manhattan.

Minutes later she turned around, looping her arms around his neck. "You win. That was the best orgasm of my life. I'm yours for thirty nights."

* * *

He was right. He didn't fuck her properly. Not one bit. Everything about the way he lifted her skirt and pressed a strong hand on her back, pushing her forward and forcing her to grasp the railing even harder, was thoroughly improper.

Rough. Demanding. Confident.

So was the slap on her ass and the bite on her shoulder blade—oh, the sweet sting of that bite, sure to leave marks. Then there was the way he shifted gears, running his hands down her back, layering kisses along her spine. As if he relished the transition from rough to tender.

"Now that I've won you, I'm going to have you," he said in a hungry voice.

He palmed her ass, digging his thumbs into her cheeks and spreading her open. For the briefest of moments, she tensed. He wasn't going to do that now, was he?

"Like that," he said, his voice a rumble against her ear. "I want you like that. Nice and open for me."

A shot of worry torqued through her. How far would he go? How much did he want from her? But the worry was less about him, and more about her. Everything he'd done so far was like a sensual reawakening. A reminder of the kind of sex she wanted to have. Earth-shattering. Mind-blowing. Pleasure beyond her fantasies. As she bowed her back, her hips high in the air, she couldn't have felt more exposed even though she was half-dressed.

"Close your eyes," he told her, and she trembled, but obeyed.

"They're closed," she whispered. She heard him open a condom, then there was a pause as he rolled it on. Off in the distance, a horn honked, and a car somewhere slammed on its brakes. A night breeze gusted by, kicking up her skirt even higher. She shivered from the momentary chill. Everything sounded and felt more intense with her eyes closed.

Especially the anticipation.

She waited for him.

For his next move.

His next touch.

His next order.

Then, she felt him, rubbing the head of his cock between her legs.

The first touch undid her. Like an unraveling. She wanted him so badly, so much, that her body was a beacon for him. She was aching to be filled. Mercilessly, he refused her wishes, her attempts to draw him in. He teased her. Taunted her. Giving her the barest taste of what his fantastic length would do this time. She couldn't bear to wait any longer.

"Please," she said, her voice a beg, and she didn't fucking care.

"Please what?"

"Please fuck me."

"How? How do you want me to fuck you?" he asked, buzzing his soft lips over her shoulder blade, as his hand moved up to her throat. He ran his thumb across her collarbone. Heat blasted through her. Like a powerful force of nature, swallowing her up, enveloping her in nothing but raw, unabated desire. He rubbed his steely length along her sex, hitting her clit once more. The world around her was black and fuzzy, noise and haze. There was only *this*. Pure physicality. Unadulterated need. "How?" he asked again, demanding an answer.

"Fuck me improperly," she said, arching her back for him. "Fuck me now."

"That's right," he said, his voice hot against her ear. "That's exactly how I'm going to do it."

Her breath caught in her chest and that moment felt like a stitch in time. As if everything in her life would be marked before or after. That was silly, she knew, to think of one night of sex as so goddamn monumental. But then, all thoughts drained away in one single thrust.

She inhaled sharply, and panted hard as he filled her so completely she wanted to sing out. She wanted to cry from the sheer ecstasy of the way he stretched her, driving deep inside her, opening her body to him.

"Give yourself to me."

Instinctually, she knew what he wanted. *Control.* Complete control of her body, so she raised her ass higher, flattened her back more and handed over the keys to him. He thrust deeper and harder, and she cried out in pleasure. Soon, she could feel that tightening in her body, that climax just within reach.

Then he surprised her with his next words. "Don't come," he growled.

"What?" she asked, her body begging as she pushed back on him.

"Don't come until I tell you I'm ready to let you," he instructed, all while sliding deeper into her.

"But," she protested, and her words were cut off by a hand over her mouth, a slowing of his rhythm, and his voice in her ear. Soft. A sharp contrast to how he held her. Imprisoned. "Let me take you there," he whispered, his tongue flicking across her neck, punctuating his words. "I promise I'll get you there. Just hold back."

She breathed out hard, full of longing and untamed desire. But she chose to trust him. Though this kind of submission was foreign to her, she was willing. How could she be anything but willing, seeing as how she was fifty stories above Manhattan with her skirt hiked up her spine, and his hand over her mouth?

He slowed down, gliding into her in one long, torturously delicious thrust. Inch by inch, she felt his cock filling her all the way. Her walls clenched around him, hot and tight. She tried to wriggle against him but he shook his head, lowering his hand to her neck.

"No. Not yet," he told her. "Tell me you can wait."

"I can try."

"Tell me you can do it." His voice was rougher this time. There was no room for trying. There was only doing.

"I can."

Another breath released, another shudder as he moved out, nearly leaving her pussy, where she desperately wanted him.

She moaned and reached her hand behind her, trying to gain some sort of control, to hold onto him. His hip. His leg. Anything. But he grasped her hand, clutching it tight as he drove into her yet again. Deeply, so deeply that she saw the edge of her climax coming into view. There. Close. So fucking close. If only he'd let her have it.

"Hold back," he told her, as he fucked her harder, gripping her hand, as if the force with which he held her would keep her desperate orgasm at bay. "Don't come yet."

She couldn't speak, could only whimper as she concentrated so fiercely on denying the quivering in her core, the molten heat coursing through her veins from the absolutely overwhelming way he took her. From the way he fucked her into such a state of wildness. "Please," she begged as he took his hand from her throat and moved his fingers up the back of her neck, threading them through her hair.

Grabbing her hair. Pulling it. Keeping her immobile.

He thrust into her, sending shock waves of pleasure from her center all the way through her body.

"Please what?"

"Please let me come."

He lowered his mouth to her shoulder, kissing her so hard he'd leave marks. When he let go, he whispered, "Are you ready?"

"Yes."

"Give yourself to me," he said and she knew what he wanted. All of her body. All of her pleasure. Nothing for her to do but be consumed by him. He wanted to give her everything, and to take nothing from her as he fucked her relentlessly.

She let her head fall forward, her shoulders go slack. She held onto the railing, but the rest was up to him. He dropped his hands to her hips, gripping her tightly, and so fucking possessively that if he didn't let her come right now she was sure she would die from wanting to climax.

"Don't hold back anymore," he commanded, and his tone made it clear—he owned this orgasm. He controlled her body. He was driving this train and she was not only along for the ride. She *was* the ride.

"Oh, God," she shouted.

"Tell me you're coming," he growled. "Say it."

She shuddered as the world around her shattered. "I'm coming, Jack. I'm coming now," she cried out, as her orgasm crashed through her body like a goddamn force of nature. It was better, stronger, more powerful than the last one.

"Yes, you are," he said, his voice rough and dirty as he fucked her hard and ferociously, giving her everything as he took her. His fingers dug into her flesh, gripping her, driving into her with a fierceness that felt like ownership as he came inside her with a loud, deep groan. As he began to slow his pace, he bent over her back, his chest on her, one hand gently looping around her belly, sensing she needed him to keep her from falling. He held her close as he slowed to a leisurely pace, rocking inside her, like a wave rolling back out to sea.

But even as her orgasm ebbed, she was marked. By his teeth, by his fingers, by his beautiful cock still deep and hard inside her.

By his voice.

And by his control.

He was right about everything. He wanted her badly. He'd shown her how much.

"*Michelle*," he whispered, in a voice that was both savage and tender. And she understood then completely what he'd done. He hadn't merely won her over. He'd claimed her as his own.

CHAPTER SIX

Addictive

When she hung up the phone after taking a quick call from her brother, Jack pulled the beautiful woman who'd spent Friday and Saturday night with him back onto the couch.

"Why is 'Ode to Joy' your ringtone?" he asked, as he tugged her against him. She'd come home with him on Friday, but then left after midnight. She'd returned on Saturday, but left late that night too. Maybe it was self-protection; maybe his mattress wasn't her favorite. But he hoped to convince her soon enough to stay the night. He liked having access to her. Being near her eased the ache of guilt that surrounded him. Hell, it did more than ease it. It erased it. It blotted it out. With Michelle, he felt strangely free of that clawing sense of self-condemnation that surrounded him like a bad cologne. The scent of regret.

"Because it's a happy piece of music," she answered as he ran his fingertips along her waist. It was Sunday evening now, and he planned to have her one more time before she left. But for now, he wanted to talk.

"So's Jack Johnson. But he's not your ringtone," he countered.

"Are you saying this cigar isn't just a cigar?"

He laughed. "Shrink humor?"

"Of course."

"And yes, what I'm saying is most people don't pick something like Beethoven's Ninth unless it means something to them. I want to know what it means to you," he said, running his hand along the fabric of her skirt as it fell on her hip. She'd worn nothing but skirts whenever he'd seen her, and he was ready to build an altar to the absence of those pesky wardrobe items like pants and jeans. Never had he been more grateful to be with a woman in a skirt.

She pressed a hand against his chest. "I thought this was just sex," she said, and her tone was playful, but he sensed she was covering something up.

He brought her hand to his lip and pressed a soft kiss. "Forgive me for asking a question that doesn't involve your magnificent ability to climax multiple times with me."

She swatted him playfully. "You are a cocky bastard. Trying to use all those orgasms against me."

"I would never use an orgasm against you. I only use orgasms for good. In fact, I think more orgasms could bring about world peace."

"The more you come, the less you fight."

He nodded knowingly. "Exactly. Anyway," he said, returning undeterred to the topic, "your ringtone. What's the story? Is it because of that guy you liked? Is that why you're avoiding answering the question?"

Her eyes widened. Perhaps he was right. Perhaps she was still in love with him. A kernel of jealousy rooted into his chest. He hadn't expected to feel that so soon. He'd have to fuck the in-love-with-another-man problem right out of her too.

"No." She shook her head. "I swear, it's not because of him." She sighed, and ran her hand through her hair, still messy from sex. "My parents liked classical music."

Just like that, he felt like a heel. Jealousy, guilt, putting his foot in his mouth—they'd become too familiar to him. He'd like to rid them all from his repertoire of emotions, limited though that repertoire was.

"Ah. I'm sorry I suggested it was something else," he said softly, brushing his fingertips gently across her cheek. "I didn't mean to bring up something that might be hard for you."

"It's okay. You didn't know. We don't know each other, so we're just guessing at things. It's better to ask. And it's not that hard anymore. It was thirteen years ago."

"Was 'Ode to Joy' special to them?"

"That was the song they got married to," she said softly. But her voice wasn't sad. Maybe wistful. Or perhaps it was the tone of someone who was simply used to missing. Used to longing.

"That's beautiful. Was it their favorite song?" he asked, and he was enjoying getting to know her better, liking that she shared some things so easily. So many women he'd dated had played coy, had been flirty all the time. There was something refreshing about her frankness. Maybe it was refreshing too because he'd kept so much of the truth about his last relationship bottled up. Even Nate didn't know the full truth. Sure, his friend knew he hadn't been in love with Aubrey, and he and Nate had even talked about the possibility of calling off the wedding, but Nate was traveling for business a lot that fateful year, so he didn't know the finer details of that weekend in Colorado beyond what everyone else knew.

Michelle nodded. "They used to play it a lot. My dad would turn up the CD player—back in the day—and pull her in close, and they'd dance. Funny, because it's not typical dancing music, you know?" she said, her gaze hooking into his and he nodded. "But even so, they'd laugh and dance, and I always felt as if they were remembering their wedding. He'd twirl her around, and they were like some postcard, like a happy black-and-white postcard of two people still in love. And who were still happy about it years later."

He smiled against the back of her neck. His parents weren't like that at all. His memories were of snippy comments, bitter moments, barbs and cut-downs. No happy times. No dancing. He wasn't envious though. How could he be? Hers were gone. His were simply miserable when he was younger, and happily divorced now. They'd filed for divorce two days after Casey graduated from high school. "And you love it now? The music?"

"I do," she said, her lips curving up. "I think it's beautiful. I could see why they'd get married to it. It is a joyful piece of music. It makes you want to celebrate." She placed her phone on the coffee table and relaxed back into him. "What about you? Why is a Ravel sonata your ringtone?"

Here they were, curled up on his couch, the view of Central Park and its lush green trees greeting them through the floor-to-ceiling windows, and they were discussing their phones, for Christ's sake. But they also *weren't* discussing their phones. They were talking about something that seemed to matter.

"I listened to classical music a lot when I was stationed overseas."

"You did?" she asked, quirking her eyebrows in curiosity. "Why?"

"It reminded me of home. It reminded me of the world beyond the battle. Even if I wasn't one of the guys on the front lines, I was studying them. Helping our boys to understand them, to navigate what was going on."

"What were you working on? Or is that classified or something?"

"We provided the intelligence support for some of the operations in Afghanistan and Iraq."

"I can't even imagine what that's like," she said, shaking her head, perhaps in some kind of admiration. "Playing a role in something so big."

"It was our job to make sure they had the right information to act on. Sometimes, when I was studying the reports coming in, I would listen to Ravel or Brahms or Mozart. It helped me sort it out. I found it strangely calming."

"I can picture that," she said, and this time she reached out, running her hand down his arm. "I can see how that would help."

He liked that they both had reasons for their ringtones that were deeper than just randomness of the universe. That it was about music, and the way music mattered to them both. It mattered differently, but it was equally important. A cigar wasn't always a cigar.

"Stay the night," he said, trying again with her. He wanted more of her. He liked himself better when she was near.

She shook her head.

"Please. I like the way you feel next to me, even just like this."

"No. I need to be in my own bed."

"But you look so good on mine."

"I feel good in it. But I need to go home."

"First things first," he said, then dropped his mouth to hers and kissed her deeply, the way she liked, the way that made her wriggle underneath him in seconds, and wrap her legs around his waist. The way that turned her on in a heartbeat. Made her wet and hot and needy for him. He'd learned her body quickly, studied her cues, and knew how to turn her on in record time. It was as if he alone possessed the secret code to unlock her desire.

He pulled off her panties, rolled on a condom and entered her. Within seconds she was moaning, her head back, her arms wrapped tight around him, her legs gripping him. It was a quick fuck, a goodbye-and-see-you-tomorrow one. It was a promise that this wasn't the last time, that there would be many more.

And that they both just needed one more moment of connection before she left without staying the night.

* * *

from: justjack@gmail.com
to: michellewithtwols@gmail.com
date: Sept 10, 10:32 AM
subject: Your email address

Been meaning to ask this—I take it there are no devilishly handsome CEOs of lingerie companies who have access to this email? That you set it up just for me?

from: michellewithtwols@gmail.com
to: justjack@gmail.com
date: Sept 10, 10:55 AM
subject: Spotting it from across town

You have a bit of a jealous streak, don't you? And I assure you, there are no other devilishly handsome CEOs that I know at all, lingerie or otherwise, and they certainly wouldn't be emailing me here, seeing as I just set it up for you. But I have often thought the handyman in my building is quite cute.

from: michellewithtwols@gmail.com
to: justjack@gmail.com
date: Sept 10, 10:56 AM
subject: Couldn't resist

I'm just kidding. He's not that cute. OK, maybe a tad cute.

from: michellewithtwols@gmail.com
to: justjack@gmail.com
date: Sept 10, 10:57 AM
subject: Couldn't resist either

Not as cute as you though, when you're jealous.

from: justjack@gmail.com
to: michellewithtwols@gmail.com
date: Sept 10, 11:01 AM
subject: A mile wide

My jealous streak knows no bounds. Especially not after this weekend. Not after the hallway. Not after the couch. Not after the shower. Hell, not after what you did to me on the Met Life Tower.

from: michellewithtwols@gmail.com
to: justjack@gmail.com
date: Sept 10, 11:03 AM
subject: WHAT I DID TO YOU?

I think it was the other way around.

from: justjack@gmail.com
to: michellewithtwols@gmail.com
date: Sept 10, 11:11 AM
subject: YES

No. It was not. What you did to me was make me want more of you. I have a large appetite when it comes to you.

from: michellewithtwols@gmail.com
to: justjack@gmail.com
date: Sept 10, 12:01 PM
subject: I have to ask

Why?

from: justjack@gmail.com
to: michellewithtwols@gmail.com
date: Sept 10, 12:18 PM
subject: I have to answer

Why do I want you? Because you are smart. Because you are beautiful. Because you make me laugh. Because you are sensual and passionate and the way you give me your body drives me absolutely fucking wild, and now I am rock-hard again for you. There. Satisfied?

from: michellewithtwols@gmail.com
to: justjack@gmail.com
date: Sept 10, 12:56 PM
subject: With you? Always satisfied . . .

Thank you. That was very nice of you.

from: justjack@gmail.com
to: michellewithtwols@gmail.com
date: Sept 10, 1:08 PM
subject: Nice is a bad word

It wasn't nice. There was nothing nice about that. It was true, is what it was. Which is why I set up this email just for you. Why aren't you here working in the same fucking building? I want you, Michelle.

Because if she were in the same building she'd get nothing done. She'd keep popping up to his office to visit him. Better that he worked across town. Besides, she had a packed schedule, and another new client in ten minutes, so she clicked out of her email and skipped over to her patient notes from the office manager. Another scant set of details, as was expected. The only info she had on the man named Clark Davidson was two words long—*marital challenges*.

She closed her eyes, took several deep breaths, and let her mind clear of Jack. The last thing she needed demanding space in her frontal lobe was that sexy, naughty, dangerously addictive man. She scoffed quietly to herself. *Addictive*. Funny that she'd used that term. She'd treated so many patients who had struggled with sex and love addiction; she'd helped them find their way to the other side. To peace. To sanity. To calm. To real love.

Here she was, using that word as if it were a good thing that Jack was addictive.

Addictions were bad. Addictions were trouble. If Jack felt addicting, that could only mean one thing—it was damn good their relationship had an expiration date. They'd spent three nights together now, and each time she'd left around midnight. "I turn into a pumpkin," she'd say, then tell him how busy she was the next day. That was all true—well, perhaps not the pumpkin part. But the busy part. There was another side to the coin though, and that was the side where sleepovers unfurled into intimacy. They translated into vulnerability. Closeness. Cuddling and snuggling while deep in REM, then waking up next to someone in the broad light of day with the hope that the person would still like you was too risky. That's why she preferred to meet at his place. If he came to hers too often, then he might fall asleep there. It was easier to be the one to leave than to kick someone else out. Meeting at his apartment gave her a small semblance of control.

She didn't need Jack to have any questions about her. He viewed her as a sexual creature, a sensuous woman, and that's all he needed to see of her. Any more would ruin the point of them. To help each other move on.

Right?

Right.

Once more, she pushed Jack from her brain. No. That was wrong. She gave him a massive shove, then kicked him under the carpet, because she needed to focus. Soon, she opened the door for her new patient, and said hello to the dark-haired Clark Davidson. He had deep brown eyes, a square jaw and a close-cropped cut.

"Good to meet you," he said, and shook her hand. He was unusually confident for a first-time patient. Interesting.

"And you as well. Please, come in," she said, holding open the door.

"Thank you," he said, and his eyes lingered on her a tad longer than she would have liked.

Fifty minutes later, she had the oddest feeling that he'd been studying her the entire time. That even as he unspooled bits and pieces of his challenges with his wife, he was cataloging her.

From her hair to her lips to her breasts to her shoes.

She wished he'd look her in the eyes.

* * *

The next evening, she mentioned the session to the consultation group of other therapists that she met with every week to share best practices. There were five of them, all other women who specialized in intimate relationship psychotherapy. Carla Kimberly led the group; she was Michelle's mentor and the president of the New York chapter of the Association of Intimate Relationship Psychologists.

"I had a strange appointment today," Michelle began, then gave a brief overview of the session, and how his behavior and wandering eyes had made her uncomfortable. "Am I reading too much into things?"

Carla adjusted the gauzy blue scarf around her neck. "Only you know if you're picking up on a vibe. But the key is always to refocus the patient, if this becomes an issue," she said in her warm and friendly voice. She was a pro. She'd been doing this for many years, and Michelle was lucky for her support and her insight.

"Right. Of course," Michelle said, since she certainly understood how to handle matters if a patient were ever attracted to her. Refocus the patient on the inner emotional experience and the therapy work. That was the rule of thumb. "It just seemed that something else was at play," she added.

"Maybe he recognized you," Jennifer said with a smile. She was a newer therapist to the group.

Michelle cocked her head. "What do you mean?"

"Maybe he's seen you out and about around town? Do you ever think about that?" Jennifer asked the crew.

Carla nodded, tucking a strand of her dark brown hair neatly behind her ear. "I do. You could run into anyone anywhere. I think it's strange for patients to bump into their therapists in a public setting, but it's inevitable. It's happened to me a few times at the grocery store or movies, and then all of a sudden, the person you are trying to treat knows you buy Trader Joe's Vanilla Almond Crunch cereal."

"Well, that's just a good cereal," Michelle said with a smile.

"Or they know you went to see *It's Raining Men*," Carla added, lowering her voice to a conspiratorial whisper.

Michelle's eyes widened. "No way. Did you run into a patient at the stripper movie?"

Carla nodded sheepishly, and covered her face with her fingers. "I did. It was so embarrassing. It's as if we're not supposed to have a life outside our offices, but I did love that movie."

Michelle laughed, and this was one of the many reasons why she adored Carla. The woman could shift from stripper movies to serious talk in the snap of a finger.

Jennifer jumped in. "I agree. So how do we find the balance between going to see a stripper movie and being able to guide a patient through their challenges with love?"

"I think it's fine for a therapist to behave like a human being. To kiss your husband in public; to pick up a celebrity magazine at the store. To see a sexy movie. You just have to know the lines not to cross," Michelle said. Lines like getting involved with a patient, and she'd made damn sure that hadn't happened.

At the end of their meeting, Carla pulled her aside. "Your talk last week at The Pierson was well-received," she said, and Michelle was filled with an odd cocktail of feelings—professional pride chased with the slightest dash of cat-who-ate-the-canary syndrome. That talk on new treatment strategies for love and sex addiction had set her on a collision course with Jack Sullivan and the best sex of her life. If she'd only slept with him one time, she'd still consider herself a lucky bitch. As it was, she'd had more than a baker's dozen of times with Jack in the last several days, each one better than the last. "We've gotten a lot of great feedback from attendees," Carla added.

"I'm so happy to hear that. It was an honor to have been asked."

"I hope it'll be an honor when I ask you for something else too," Carla said, flashing a quick smile.

"Anything."

"We have a workshop with other psychotherapists coming up on learning to love again. It will look at love after infidelity, grief, divorce and so on. And, I was hoping you could lead it."

Michelle's answer was instant. "Of course. I'd love to. Just let me know the details."

"Absolutely. I'll email them to you this weekend. I also have a referral to send your way. Are you still taking new patients?"

She glanced away briefly to hide her smirk. "Yes. I have an opening on Fridays at two."

* * *

from: justjack@gmail.com
to: michellewithtwols@gmail.com
date: Sept 12, 6:18 PM
subject: Therapy

Looking forward to another "therapy" session with you this evening.

from: michellewithtwols@gmail.com
to: justjack@gmail.com
date: Sept 12, 6:20 PM
subject: Healing aids?

Will you be bringing any battery-operated friends?

from: justjack@gmail.com
to: michellewithtwols@gmail.com
date: Sept 12, 6:23 PM
subject: Therapy

I have many toys slated for our time slot. Though I should warn you—I need more than the standard fifty minutes. Much more.

from: michellewithtwols@gmail.com
to: justjack@gmail.com
date: Sept 12, 6:27 PM
subject: A few hours works for me

I look forward to being in your hands.

from: justjack@gmail.com
to: michellewithtwols@gmail.com
date: Sept 12, 6:32 PM
subject: Soon . . .

By the way, I told the doorman I'd be expecting someone at nine p.m.

from: michellewithtwols@gmail.com
to: justjack@gmail.com
date: Sept 12, 6:46 PM
subject: Very soon . . .

So you want me out of there by 9?

from: justjack@gmail.com
to: michellewithtwols@gmail.com
date: Sept 12, 6:52 PM
subject: Open invitation to spend the night

No, beautiful. It's you, I'm expecting.

from: michellewithtwols@gmail.com
to: justjack@gmail.com
date: Sept 12, 7:03 PM
subject: Maybe someday

Presumptuous.

from: justjack@gmail.com
to: michellewithtwols@gmail.com
date: Sept 12, 7:09 PM
subject: Someday very soon

Ravenous.

from: michellewithtwols@gmail.com
to: justjack@gmail.com
date: Sept 12, 7:32 PM
subject: After last night

I can barely walk today.

from: justjack@gmail.com
to: michellewithtwols@gmail.com
date: Sept 12, 7:46 PM
subject: That's what I like to hear

I should feel bad about that, but I can't find it in me.

from: michellewithtwols@gmail.com
to: justjack@gmail.com
date: Sept 12, 7:55 PM
subject: No guilt needed

Beating your chest instead?

from: justjack@gmail.com
to: michellewithtwols@gmail.com
date: Sept 12, 8:02 PM
subject: Like a caveman

Yes. Fucking you senseless has a way of making me feel damn good about myself. I'd like to see you bent over my kitchen counter in about an hour.

CHAPTER SEVEN
Services

The next several nights passed in a haze of sex, food, and conversation. In a fantastic blur of 69s, and town cars, and swank bathroom stalls at shi-shi restaurants—including a new sushi spot near the Chrysler Building—and Chinese food ordered in. In late-night chats curled up on his couch, talking about college, or his time in the army, or her days in grad school, and the crazy role-playing she'd had to do with other shrinks as a part of her training. He'd lie back on a pillow, an arm wrapped around her, and listen to her stories, her hair fanned out across his chest as he ran his fingers absently through it. Or they'd find their way to her place in Murray Hill, and after a hard and fast session in the shower, or a long and lingering one on her ottoman, or an endlessly wet one—pun intended—in the bathtub, she'd be the one listening to his reminisces about the early days of Joy Delivered with his sister, and how they'd run the company out of a windowless one-room office in Queens before they hit it big.

She was easy to talk to. No surprise, though, given what she did for a living. Maybe what was so surprising, if he only studied the surface, was how that openness extended to the bedroom. She didn't hold back in bed. She turned over her body to him every night, and every time he had her he found himself wanting more of her. Wanting that sexy vulnerability he saw in her eyes. That gorgeous desperation he felt in her body. That dirty mouth that begged for him to fuck her to yet another release.

During the day, they'd text and email. He looked forward to her notes in between work and meetings and product launches, and the damn updates on Denkler's campaign that was still struggling. At the end of a long day, there was her. She was his letting go.

But every night ended the same. With a goodnight kiss at her door, at a town car, at the curb.

Like a shopkeeper slamming down the gates after midnight. That was Michelle. She had a closing time, and he understood why. Protecting her heart, and all.

She'd erected the sturdiest walls, but he wanted to knock them down.

* * *

Ten nights of Jack Sullivan was like some kind of voodoo magic. If the first third of these thirty nights was anything to go on, she'd be living in a bubble of bliss for the rest of the month of September and on into October. Her body seemed to be 100 percent okay with that kind of cocoon. Her mind seemed amenable, too. Because Jack was stimulating on all fronts. She'd just finished updating him on the details of her Paris trip later next week. Her flight had been booked, her hotel reserved, and the conference organizers had even sent her a box of French chocolate to say thank you. She'd brought them over to share, and she popped a raspberry-filled dark chocolate square in her mouth.

"Good thing I have a business trip to California that week to distract me from not being able to have you while you're in Paris," he said.

"Yes. Thank God. I'd hate for you to miss me."

"Oh, I'll miss you. Have you been to Paris before?"

She nodded as she chewed. "A few times."

"Do you speak the language?" Jack asked and held up the bottle of wine, offering her another glass as she smoothed her skirt and adjusted the buttons on her shirt. They were in his kitchen, his gorgeous, brick and wood kitchen in his penthouse apartment, though he admitted the shiny Miele appliances were rarely used. He was takeout all the way, he'd said. She shook her head at the offer of the wine.

"No to French?"

"No to another glass of wine."

"Damn. I was hoping to loosen you up enough to discuss something I want to do with you," he said and raised his eyebrows suggestively.

She rolled her eyes in response. "You don't need to get me drunk to discuss something you want to do to me. And to answer your question, I speak French. I studied it in school."

He looped an arm around her waist, then whispered something in her ear in French.

"Perhaps someday," she said suggestively in answer.

"Someday soon, I hope," he said, squeezing her butt, then shifting gears. "What do you love most about Paris?"

"This chocolate is pretty good," she said, then reached for another one and handed it him. "For you."

He took the chocolate and rolled his eyes in pleasure. "That is pretty damn good. But I know it's not what you love most about Paris. What is?"

"That's not a fair question," she countered, running her fingers through her hair. She'd have to keep a brush here, but then that also would be too intimate. She didn't plan to leave any evidence of all these nights with him. Evidence led to memories, and memories led to closeness. That's what they both desperately needed to avoid. True intimacy. "It's impossible to pick one thing."

"I like impossible choices, though," he said, flashing her a wicked grin.

She placed a hand on his chest, moving in close. "Why?"

"Because they force people to show who they really are. I thought you'd appreciate that, being a shrink."

"Fine. I'll answer," she said, counting off the potential options on her fingers. "What I love most about Paris isn't even in Paris. It's Monet's Gardens, but that's outside of the city. So if we're talking purely Paris, I might choose the food. I might choose the museums. I might even say the cobblestoned streets, or the rich history, or the way the French don't care if you like them. But if you really want me to choose, my favorite thing about Paris is the beauty. And the way the French love beauty for its own sake."

A smile tugged at his lips as she continued. "I love the beauty in the every day. I love the glow from the streetlamps. I love that you'll find a store in Montmartre that sells glass perfume bottles with gorgeous designs on them, and they're things no one needs, but they exist solely because they're pretty. I saw a sapphire one once that I wanted, but the store was closed that day. So I just stared longingly through the window. Because that's the other thing—even the shop windows are beautiful, and full of gorgeous displays, whether of cakes or candies or jewelry or clothes. Doesn't matter. The French find beauty in the magnificent and in the seemingly mundane."

"They do. And now I'm picturing the city perfectly, from the glass displays of a cake shop to the towering spires of Notre Dame. I love that answer. I love that you respond to beauty."

"Why?"

"Because I do too," he said, and raked his eyes over her in a way that made her skin heat up. The compliment was loud and clear in his gaze.

"Who are you then, Jack? What are your impossible choices?"

In an instant, his smile erased itself, as if it had been bleached away. He said nothing for one moment that stretched into many moments, and felt far too long. The expression in his beautiful eyes looked pained, haunted even. In that span of silence, she sensed all the reasons why he'd come to see her in the first place. Self-loathing, maybe even guilt was written in his eyes. She wanted to ask him more, to try to help ease his burden. She was tempted, even as he swallowed and looked away.

"I don't know how to talk about them," he said in a ragged whisper.

Her heart staggered to him. "It can be hard to give voice to certain things."

When he turned back to her, he parted his lips to speak more.

But she wasn't ready. Wasn't ready for knowing why she'd seen guilt edging in on him. She wasn't his shrink and she wasn't his girlfriend, and the more she knew of his inner truths, the more she put her own heart at risk.

Her heart was too fragile. It was made of glass, and could shatter if dropped.

Something else held her back too. She didn't want to press him to share too much, too soon. Whatever he had to say, he'd say when the time was right for him. She leaned in to him, brushed her lips against his, using closeness as a way to absolve him from speaking. "It's okay," she said softly. "We don't have to go there. Besides. I need to leave. I have some early appointments."

"Okay," he said, as if it had ten syllables, and they all tumbled awkwardly over his tongue. Then he ran his hand through her hair, and the gesture, maybe even the movement, felt sad. But she tried not to read too much into it; she had to be careful on that account.

The matter was helped by him spinning her around, so her back was flush against the edge of his counter. Like a door closing, and another one opening, he'd erased that momentary anguish, that brief hint of pain. He replaced it with raw heat as his eyes blazed at her.

"I need to give you something for the road. Stay like that," he said harshly. He walked across his hardwood floors to the bedroom she'd come to know so well in such a short amount of time. He returned with a mischievous grin on his face and his fist closed.

"Another toy surprise?"

He nodded, and uncurled his palm, revealing a small blue vibrator. Slim, with a wide head, this was the kind of vibrator that sent you off into a good night's sleep. "It's called The Dream. I want to watch you come one more time before you go," he said, his eyes dark, his tone that commanding one that thrilled her. Heat scorched a path through her body.

"Do everything I say," he said, his rough voice hot on her skin.

"I will."

"Lift your skirt," he told her, and she did, tugging it up to her hips.

"Pull down your panties," he said, and she pushed them down to her knees.

"Run your finger through your pussy and let me suck your finger," he said, and she gasped, but did as instructed, sliding her finger across her wet lips, then bringing it to his mouth. He drew her finger in deeply and sucked hard, making the most satisfied sound. His eyes floated closed as he moaned, like a chef tasting his favorite dish.

"Now spread that delicious pussy open for me," he said as he opened his eyes, and she lowered her fingers between her legs again, gliding through the slick evidence of her desire for him, her unabated desire that had no end in sight. It was ceaseless.

"Like that?" she asked, opening herself wide for him.

He nodded. "Leave them there," he said, and she kept her hand in place as he pressed his thumb against the on-switch for the toy. He lowered the vibrator to her already aching clit, and rubbed gently at first. She cried out in pleasure.

"This will serve as a reminder that if you'd stay I could do this to you in the middle of the night or the morning or whenever you fucking wanted," he said as her breathing turned erratic, and she trembled from his touch. The vibrations worked quickly, and she felt herself turning loose and hot, and close to the edge.

"Tell me what you pictured the morning after I fucked you for the first time. When you masturbated to me alone in your bed."

Her back bowed, and her lips fell open. "I thought about sucking your dick."

"Were you on your knees?"

She shook her head. "No. You straddled my face. You fucked my mouth like that," she said breathlessly, as she rubbed herself against the toy.

He hissed in his breath. His teeth pressed into his lips, his eyes dark and wild. "Did you come like that?"

"Yes," she said on a pant. "I called out your name. I came tasting you."

His chest rose and fell, as if he were exercising every ounce of self-restraint right now to concentrate on her orgasm. "I jacked off to you that morning too. To making you come. Do you want to know how I made you come?"

"Yes."

"Rock into this and I'll show you," he whispered harshly, and she moved with him, riding the vibrator as he dropped his other hand between her legs, sliding his fingers across her, then thrusting one into her, and another he slowly pushed into her rear.

She cried out, first in shock, then in pleasure, as the twin—no, the triple—sensations shot through her. A burn, like the first taste of whiskey, then pure, unabashed ecstasy from the vibrator on her clit, and then his fingers playing her insides like a fucking pro, her whole body beholden to the sheer prowess of his hands as he drew another shattering orgasm out of her.

She called out his name, gripping his shoulder and clawing her nails into his skin as her climax rocketed through her.

When she finally could focus again, he spoke first. "I fucking love watching you come. I love what I do to you."

"Me too," she said, and for some reason it felt like an intensely vulnerable admission. As if there was more going on than him showing her pleasure. It was as if he needed to do this to her after their brief conversation. He'd revealed the tiniest bit of himself minutes before, and that was probably hard for him. So he'd needed to chase that with sex, mix it with pleasure, so he could watch her give in to his hand, to his toys, to his tricks.

She gladly gave into him. He made her feel so many things.

It was her turn to make him feel. To keep up her end of the deal. She wasn't going to enact her morning-after solo fantasy right now. That might be too intimate for where they were. But she had no problem dropping to her knees, freeing his erection, and taking him deep into her throat until her name became some kind of chant as he lost control, just the way she wanted him to.

A few minutes later, after they'd both straightened up, she grabbed her purse to leave.

With a hand on her back—he always seemed to place a hand on her back, a possessive gesture and one she enjoyed—they walked down the plush carpeted hallway from his penthouse apartment to the elevators.

"Do you have a busy day tomorrow?" he asked.

She nodded. "Always. You?"

He laughed lightly. "Yes. The same. Meeting after meeting, including far too many about politics."

"Politics? In your line of work?" she asked curiously.

He shook his head, a look of disdain flashing across his cool blue eyes. "I hate politics. What's on your agenda?"

"Oh, you know, just planning my trip to Paris to keynote a conference. That's all," she said, giving him a saucy sashay of her hips. His palm landed hard on her ass as he pressed the *down* button to the elevator.

Her eyes widened, inviting more slapping.

"If you tempt me like that, beautiful, I will insist on you staying the night so I can spend more time with you and your gorgeous ass," he said, back to his playful self.

"I better not tempt you then, since we're both so busy."

"How ever will you fit me in tomorrow?" he asked, raising an eyebrow as they stepped into the lift.

Reaching for the collar of his shirt, she tugged him close, and lowered her voice to its sexiest purr. "The same way I fit you in this week. All that wetness," she said, grabbing his hand, and placing it between her legs as she lifted up her skirt, savoring the reaction her words elicited from him. Another groan. Another press of his body against her. She removed his hand as the elevator shot down. "But I'd hate to tempt you anymore."

"I'd hate it if you didn't tempt me," he growled, and then lifted her up against the elevator wall, wrapped her legs around his hips, and gave her a tease of what would likely happen the next night.

She expected him to continue on like this for the whole ride down, but instead he gently lowered her to the floor, and leaned in to her neck, whispering in her ear. "I'm having a great time with you. I can't wait to see you again."

Instinct told her to toss out a witty comeback, to say, *Presumptuous, are you?* But tomorrow sounded damn good to her. So she simply said, "Me too."

When they reached the lobby, he took her hand. As his fingers laced through hers, she felt a rush of something else entirely. Not the heat that had been spreading through her body all week, but a softness, a sweetness that this man seemed to possess. He held her hand as they crossed the marble floor and passed the doorman, out onto Fifth Avenue. A town car idled. A chauffeur in a black cap popped out, and opened the door.

"Your chariot," Jack said, with a grin.

The first night he'd done this she'd said, "You didn't have to. I would have been fine with a cab," because she was used to taking care of herself. Now she was used to the service from him. She liked all the services he provided, come to think of it.

"By the way, do you like the symphony?"

"I haven't been in ages."

"Would you like to rectify that on Saturday night?"

The symphony sounded less like thirty nights of sex and more like a path to romance. Even so, she said yes.

CHAPTER EIGHT
Surface Scratching

Kana crossed her legs, waiting for him to answer the question of why he was annoyed today.

Because the regret was suffocating. He was tired of regret. Because he was tired of thinking he deserved to *not* feel regret. Absolution wasn't coming through therapy. How could it? Jack's world was eminently logical, and he believed in one plus one equaling two. How could he see anything but the mathematical relationship between the events?

One, he told Aubrey he didn't want to marry her, and two, twenty minutes later, she died.

Aubrey didn't crash into trees. Aubrey flew down the slopes, but she did it with control.

Except for that time.

He was the trigger. His lack of love the loaded gun. An impossible choice. He'd picked wrong. Hadn't he?

"This woman I'm seeing asked me about impossible choices," he offered as he crossed his arms over his chest.

"And how did that make you feel?" Kana asked during their third session; this one had been moved to late morning because he had a lunch meeting. Jack wasn't sure if they were making progress. He didn't know what progress would look or feel like. Or how he was supposed to feel.

"Like shit," he said, spitting out the words.

"Why? Did it touch a nerve?"

He nodded. She paused, tilted her head, waited. Shrinks were good at waiting. Waiting for you to cough up answers. He didn't have any to serve.

"Are you going to tell me about these impossible choices that have brought you here?"

He shrugged. "I don't know."

He didn't know why the hell he needed to open up to anyone. Casey knew. Why did anyone else need to know?

"How do you feel keeping it all to yourself?" she asked.

The same way he'd felt for a year. The same way he'd felt since the Ski Patrol carted Aubrey's body down the mountain. Like hell. Like he was cloaked in the guilt that clawed away at him. The only thing that made it go away was Michelle. Being with her, being close with her, fucking her into the fantastic bliss that only sex could bring. Yeah, that was the kind of therapy he needed.

"Fine," he muttered, his mind on Michelle; the nights with her were doing a far better job blanking out this mangled stew of emotions in his gut.

Hell, it wasn't only the sex. It was the before, during and after. It was all of it. It was *her*. She was sexy and she was guileless. She was naughty and she was direct.

She was two floors away from him right now. He wanted to see her. Wanted to touch her, taste her, hear her laugh, watch her raise an eyebrow at some comment he made. Then take her.

When he was through with Kana, he pushed open the door to the stairwell, ready to head up the steps to her office. But he stopped himself. She had a job to do. He couldn't go barging in.

from: justjack@gmail.com
to: michellewithtwols@gmail.com
date: Sept 19, 12:02 PM
subject: Could you sense my masculine intensity just two floors down?

Was so tempted to stop by your office a few minutes ago.

from: michellewithtwols@gmail.com
to: justjack@gmail.com
date: Sept 19, 12:04 PM
subject: Ah, that was the heady scent wafting into my office

Just finished with a session. Too bad I missed a potential "session" with you. I'd have happily let you eat me out again.

from: justjack@gmail.com
to: michellewithtwols@gmail.com
date: Sept 19, 12:09 PM
subject: Starving now

You little fucking naughty dirty vixen.

from: michellewithtwols@gmail.com
to: justjack@gmail.com
date: Sept 19, 12:12 PM
subject: Only scratched the surface of dirty

That's how you like me.

from: justjack@gmail.com
to: michellewithtwols@gmail.com
date: Sept 19, 12:15 PM
subject: As dirty as you want to get. That's how far I'll scratch.

God, I love it when you say dirty things. Do dirty things. Spread your legs for me right now, and tell me what you'd say to me if I had walked into your office.

from: michellewithtwols@gmail.com
to: justjack@gmail.com
date: Sept 19, 12:16 PM
subject: This.

Fuck me with your tongue.

from: justjack@gmail.com
to: michellewithtwols@gmail.com
date: Sept 19, 12:18 PM
subject: I want that.

I need to be drenched in your pussy tonight. I need to eat you and fuck you and lick you all over. I need to have my fingers in you.

from: michellewithtwols@gmail.com
to: justjack@gmail.com
date: Sept 19, 12:19 PM
subject: All of that and more

You should test some of your new toys on me. I'm very willing to be your research project.

from: justjack@gmail.com
to: michellewithtwols@gmail.com
date: Sept 19, 12:21 PM
subject: I am a very thorough researcher

I am going to research the fuck out of your beautiful body. Prepare to be ravaged tonight. That is a promise. I have to go into a meeting. This is going to be the most painful meeting of my life. Where can I meet you when it's over? I need to see you.

Tugging at his white button-down shirt, as if that would sap the heat from his body, Jack powered down his phone a few blocks from his destination. Michelle was still on his mind, and the effect of even that one email exchange was abundantly evident in his body right now. He didn't need an erection this demanding knocking on his fly at a lunch meeting, so he tried to force his brain to let go of the images tearing through his skull. Potent pictures of all that had transpired over the last two weeks wouldn't leave his head; the time on his couch; the time in his shower; the time in the hallway; the time in front of the window. Each time was better than the last.

And then there were the images of all the times he intended to have with her. The things he wanted to do to her. The adventures he wanted to have with her willing mind and body. She was such a passionate lover, such a sensual woman, whose body responded to his every touch. She gave herself freely; he could only imagine the paths they could continue to explore.

He stopped at the red light on the corner of Fifth Avenue. A mannequin in the window of a lingerie shop down the street beckoned to him, her barely-there lacy pink bra and panties like a goddamn magnetic force calling out to him.

"Fuck," he seethed as the September sun beat down. These images were not helping the case one bit, nor was that strategically placed shop. As if it were there to tempt him. Taunt him. He needed to think of baseball players or bunnies, not of how enticing Michelle would look in that bra and panty set. Because of course she would. That was a given.

Focus, Jack. Get your mind out of the gutter.

He grappled at topics that were boner killers.

The Yankees were playing tonight. They were down by a game and a half, which meant they'd need to win tonight and then again tomorrow. Jack computed batting averages and RBIs and statistical likelihoods of no-hitters, given that there had already been two so far this season. By the time he reached the next block, weaving around a bicycle deliveryman riding on the sidewalk, Jack was a man on a mission.

Today's mission? Politics. Henry had called this meeting with his brother-in-law, the city council candidate they were throwing gobs of support behind. Jack hated politics and was still outraged that Henry's brother-in-law was being attacked because Henry and Marquita owned BDSM clubs. Jack would be surprised if Paul Denkler had ever been to a BDSM club. He seemed to be straight-laced, and trying to do some good things for the city.

He reached McCoy's in mid-town, a favorite spot for late afternoon power lunches. A shot of air-conditioning blasted him as he opened the door. The cooler inside air was a relief. He joined Henry, Marquita, Paul Denkler and Casey at a plush red booth in the back, cloth linen napkins spread across laps, silver utensils gleaming.

After orders were placed, Henry clasped his hands together. "We have a problem."

Jack nodded. "I figured as much. Unplanned lunch meetings usually stem from problems."

Paul cleared his throat and opened his tablet, clicking open a news article from a prominent NY blog site. *Conroy Blasts Denkler for East Side Fire.*

Casey's jaw twitched and her eyes burned. "Now you're responsible for a fire?" she said, narrowing her eyes as she bent closer to Denkler to read the post.

After a fire broke out last night on 88th and Madison in the basement of an apartment building that had been hosting a sex-themed bondage party, former litigator and city councilman candidate Jared Conroy called anew for closures of all the BDSM private clubs that have sprung up on the Upper East Side.

While the small blaze was quickly snuffed by the local fire department, a few attendees suffered smoke inhalation. "This is a classic example of why we need to shut down these establishments. Not only do they bring an untoward element to our neighborhoods, they are clearly dangerous. I shudder at the thought of the type of damage the fire could have wrought had the fire department not been nearby," Casey said, reading on, the frustration deep in her voice.

Jack blew out a long stream of air after she'd finished.

"What are we going to do about this? This is a whole new wrinkle. How are you going to finesse this?" Jack said to Henry.

"We don't have to finesse it," he said. "Because the facts are wrong. This isn't one of our clubs."

Casey's eyes lit up. "This is perfect. This shows exactly why it's better to have regulated clubs run in a reputable fashion."

Jack beamed at his sister. "Look at you. Already toeing the party line."

Denkler laughed. "We'll send her to Nevada next. Talk up keeping prostitution legal."

"Well," Casey said insistently as she turned to Henry, "that's the point, right? You don't have any problems at your club like this. You have regular inspections. You adhere to the fire code. You have a liquor license. You follow laws."

"Exactly," Henry said with a nod, and Marquita dropped a hand over his, a look of pride on her face as her husband spoke. "We afford a safe place for these activities. If the regulated clubs are shut down, there will be more incidents like this."

"The question is, how hard do you want to hit this message?" Jack asked, turning to Denkler. "How bad is this killing you in the polls?"

"It's pretty bad. No one wants to hear about schools and safe streets anymore, now that Conroy has made everyone think the clubs are bringing down the neighborhood," Denkler admitted, his voice that of a man nearing the end of his rope, as he pushed a hand through his hair. He seemed like a classic heart-of-gold guy. He'd clearly gotten involved in politics because he wanted to make a change for the better, but his platform had been turned upside down by a bastard who went for the jugular.

"You need to get preemptive," Jack said firmly, reflecting back on his days with the army. "You don't let the enemy walk all over you. You have to understand the enemy. Understand the problem. Act on it."

Denkler nodded enthusiastically. "We've tried refocusing back to the core message, but my PR manager doesn't think that will work until we explain openly why we're *not* opposed to the clubs, like Conroy is. He thinks we need to talk about why the neighborhood doesn't need a Times Square style sweep of the clubs. Come at it from an education point of view."

Henry jumped in. "We should be more vocal in our support too. I think we need to talk more to the press about why Eden and the clubs support Paul, and not simply because he's my lovely wife's brother," he said, squeezing his wife's hand.

"And by extension, why Joy Delivered does too?" Casey asked.

Henry nodded.

Jack sighed, but didn't say no. "I don't know, guys. A lot of people from all walks of life and political persuasions like a little assistance in the bedroom. I don't want to be a company that takes sides."

"We don't have to take sides," Casey said, piping in. "We just have to explain the facts."

"We're backing Paul. We're already taking sides," he pointed out.

"But the side we're on is the side we're already on. We promote pleasure. That's our side," she said insistently. "Besides, it's okay for us to take sides. We sell sex products. We're not teachers. We're not cops. We want consenting adults to be free to do what they want so long as they're safe. And no one runs a safer club than Henry. Safe for the people who go, but also for those who don't go."

Paul's eyes lit up, and he snapped a finger. "Exactly."

Jack leaned back in his chair as the waitress brought over iced teas and waters. "There's your slogan. Safe for those who go, and those who don't."

The politician nodded and smiled broadly, as if all the problems had been solved. "That is indeed a great slogan."

Jack gestured to his sister. "She needs to be more involved. She's the idea woman. She'd be a great strategist on this."

Casey smiled, and waved a hand as if to say this was all nothing.

"You have great ideas," Paul said.

"She does," Jack added.

The problem hadn't been solved though. Jack knew why Denkler was swimming upstream. His opponent fought dirty, but he didn't know how to get muddy. Denkler was a good guy, but he was *too* good.

"Listen," Jack began, his tone commanding, the same one he'd used when he talked to his men back in Europe on how to proceed. "I get that politics is a battleground, and you're losing right now, Paul. You've got a sneaky opponent who knows how to twist some serious shit." He parked his elbows on the table. "But you need to get on the offensive. You're standing here like a goddamn punching bag, taking his blows. You need to get a handle on what you're up against. Why do you not have some dirt on Conroy?"

"We've been looking into him," Paul said, but the red flush on his cheeks made it clear they'd found nothing.

"Yeah?" Jack raised an eyebrow in question. "What have you found?"

"We're still looking."

Jack nodded. Held up a hand. "You need to run some serious counterintelligence on him. Everyone has skeletons in the closet. Every single person has something they don't want the opposition to know. My job in the military was to find that out. Everything was findable. Everything was obtainable. You need to get your intelligence men working harder, and figure out what Conroy has in his closet so you can fight this battle."

Paul gulped and nodded, and Jack couldn't deny it felt good to give some kind of order again.

* * *

Jack walked back to the office with his sister, unknotting his tie on the way.

"I hate having to tell a good guy like that to dig up dirt," he muttered, as he dropped his shades over his eyes to block out the afternoon sun.

"I bet I could find something on Conroy," Casey mused, and Jack shot his baby sister an inquisitive look.

"I know I could. Since when are you a spy?"

"I grew up with you. I learned how to find things out," she said with an impish grin as they walked past a group of construction workers whose heads all turned to stare at his sister. Instinct kicked in, and he turned to the crew, his eyes flared with anger. That was enough for them to focus on their jobs.

"Look at you. Running a little espionage."

"I just don't want someone messing with our business. I love Joy Delivered. I'll fight for it," she said as they walked past a Duane Reade on the corner, bustling with mid-day shoppers. What would he fight for? He'd fight for this company, and he did every day, especially now, with the Conroy onslaught. He'd fight for his sister, of course. But beyond that? What did he love madly? He'd like to know because he hadn't loved his fiancée enough. That had been the big fucking problem.

"Speaking of fighting, you were ornery at lunch. Was it only over the campaign?" she asked, stopping in her tracks when they reached the red light at Madison. She parked her hands on her hips and stared at him, her blue eyes refusing to let him get away with anything. She'd always been like this. Firm, strong, passionate. Take no prisoners. This was one of the reasons he was so close with his sister —she was fiery and full of emotion, and yet their parents were so . . . dispassionate. They rarely held hands with each other, and hardly ever kissed, even a peck on the cheek. That lack of affection had extended far and wide. Jack could remember riding his bike in the summers as a kid, then running inside, sweaty, but wanting to give his mom a hug. She'd always refuse, saying it was too hot for hugging. That was her modus operandi. There was often a distance with her, as if she didn't want to get too close.

Maybe that was his problem. Maybe he'd inherited it like a congenital disease—a lack of the ability to love. If he couldn't love Aubrey, what the hell was wrong with him? That's what he'd really like to figure out. He bet Michelle would know. He was sure Michelle would have all the answers as to what ailed him.

But it wasn't as if he could ask her those questions. Not now. Not for so many reasons.

"I just saw the shrink," he said in answer to the ornery question.

"Ah. Then all that talking has got you pissed off."

"Hardly any talking from me. More like the questions she asked."

"So how is it going?"

He heaved a sigh as the light changed, and the cars squealed to their stops at the red. Casey started to walk, but a cab careened by, not bothering to stop. Grabbing her quickly at the waist, he tugged her back.

"Careful," he said, his heart galloping.

She looked up at him with wide, fearful eyes. "They're crazy here."

"Everyone's crazy. Just watch out, Case."

"Anyway, so how is Dr. Milo?"

"Here's the thing," he said in a clipped voice. While his sister didn't need to know he was sleeping with his almost-shrink, he didn't like lying to her. He could skirt the details. "It didn't work out with her so I'm seeing someone else. A few floors down."

"Oh," she said, sounding surprised. "Is the new one good?"

He shrugged.

"*Jack*," she said, like a plea.

"I'm trying, but I don't know that anything is going to make a difference. It happened. I said what I said to Aubrey and she's dead, and there's nothing that I can ever say or do to unwind things."

She grabbed his shirt collar and shot him a rueful look. "Don't say that. Besides, you need to work on this. You need to fix your head. We have a business to run and a big charity event coming up soon," she said, her words a reminder of the gala they were supporting to fund breast cancer research. "I got a call from a reporter at the *New York Press*. She does lifestyle pieces, and she wants to do one on you, a year later."

Jack rolled his eyes. "I don't want to do a piece on me a year later."

"I know. But it would be good for business. The press loves you. And this isn't *Page Six*. *New York Press* does classy pieces. I think it would be good for business, and good for you. You're the Soldier-Turned-Sex-Toy-Mogul, and one of NYC's most eligible bachelors, so get your butt in gear and stop all this self-loathing."

"I don't hate myself," he said, then tapped his breastbone as they neared their office building. "Something in here doesn't work properly. No shrink is ever going fix it."

Besides, everyone was better off if he didn't try again. If he didn't get close to anyone, he wouldn't have the power to wound her. If he didn't love a woman, he would never hurt that woman by breaking her heart.

She rolled her eyes. "You are going to fix yourself. Because it's time to move on."

His phone buzzed with a text from Michelle.

M: I'm going shopping right now.

J: For?

He tucked his phone away, but was eager for her answer.

CHAPTER NINE
Disguises

She was surrounded by fake schlongs.

"Explain this to me," her friend said in her crisp, British accent. "How large does a vagina need to be to accommodate this?" Sutton's eyes sparkled as she held a monster-sized vibrator that might have been as long as her arm.

"You need a jumbo size vagina for that," Michelle answered, tapping a fingernail against the fleshy dildo that could likely double as a truck.

Sutton set the toy that neither woman would be buying back on its shelf. "Seriously, I do not want to feel as if I'm fucking a truck when Reeve is away on shoots," Sutton said. She had freely admitted to spending more time with her toys while her actor husband was shooting a new movie in Canada. "Anyway, we're not here for me. We're here for you."

They wandered away from the alien-size dildos at Eden on the Upper East Side to a classier section of the still-quite-classy shop. Michelle had scanned the sidewalk up and down before they'd entered the store, then had been careful to survey the shop itself to make sure the coast was clear. Sure, a patient could walk in at any given moment, but she was taking her chances anyway because she didn't want to wait for an online delivery.

A flurry of tingles rushed down Michelle's spine as she spotted The One. Jack hadn't used that toy on her, but still, just knowing that he'd played a role in its creation excited her. Then again, most things he did thrilled her. Their first two weeks together had been nothing short of spectacular. It was everything he'd promised when he'd made his most unusual proposition. Nights of bliss. Nights of pleasure. Nights with him were that and *only* that. They'd laughed, and teased, and flirted, and then they'd fucked. Every time, she'd felt as if he were fucking the hurt and the longing away. The ache inside of her from the last several unwanted years was being erased. Jack Sullivan was a crash course in learning to heal.

She had something in mind for him. He'd had a busy week, so she wanted to surprise him with a treat. She and Sutton perused a section of the store with smaller toys.

"What does one get for the man who makes these things?" Sutton mused.

"It is quite a quandary, isn't it?"

"I mean, it's not as if you're going to peg him."

Michelle cracked up, one hand on her belly reining in a huge laugh. "I'm absolutely not ever going to peg him, or another man. I like my men to be men. And I like their assholes to remain virgins," she said in a whisper as she draped an arm around her friend.

Sutton raised an imaginary glass. "To virgin assholes. May they always remain un-penetrated."

"I'll drink to that."

Michelle spotted the gift that she wanted for Jack. She snatched it off the shelf, marched to the counter, purchased it, and then left with Sutton.

"How are things with you?" Michelle asked. "Do you miss Reeve, with him in Vancouver right now?"

"Terribly," Sutton said, clutching her heart. "I should be used to it, but I'm not."

Sutton and Reeve had been together for two years, married for one. A powerful casting director, she'd helped him earn his first big break, but once he nabbed the role in *Escorted Lives*, his career took off like a shot.

"It's hard, isn't it? All the missing," Michelle said, and while she'd never known the kind of love Sutton and Reeve had, she knew a thing or two about those pangs of longing. She'd experienced it in the deep heart-wrenching way that only death can bring when her parents had died. And she'd felt it for Clay for years, though in a vastly different way, of course.

Even so, it was a far-too familiar emotion—the empty ache she'd felt for years for her friend who she'd hoped would become something more. In college, at the height of all that loneliness, he'd come into her life. Beautiful and handsome, kind and smart, he was best friends with her brother. That made him forbidden, in a way, even though they'd had only one drunken kiss during her sophomore year. That kiss had done a number on her vulnerable heart. It became the match that lit the fire she'd been building on the kindling of her very own raw and untended emotions.

Now, years later, she understood enough about emotions to figure out there'd been a transference going on, a displacement of grief into unrequited love. In retrospect, she should have let go of the unrequitedness years ago. She should have known better. Perhaps she'd clung on to it to protect herself from more hurt. Perhaps believing that Clay was the one had kept her heart in that safe zone where it couldn't be broken again, like it had the night her family fractured.

Now that she knew that, and truly understood it, she had started to move on from Clay.

Or maybe it was so much simpler. Maybe it was the birds and the bees. Perhaps it was Jack that made Clay start to feel more and more like a distant memory.

Great sex had a way of erasing the past.

"Missing is the hardest thing," Sutton said.

"It truly is," Michelle echoed, linking elbows with her friend as they walked down the street, two New York women, out on a quick late afternoon shopping break and talking about their hearts, and their men.

Not that Jack was hers.

Not at all.

"By the way, did you see that picture of you with Mr. Sex Toy Mogul?" Sutton asked in an offhand way.

"What?" Michelle stopped in her tracks.

"I saw it on Twitter. Someone was sharing it, and I was searching to check for Joy Delivered products. I think it was you in the picture. You were the *gorgeous brunette he was spotted having dinner with at Gia's*, I trust?'

Michelle blushed, flashing back to Carla's comments about public lives. At least she hadn't been named. No one knew her. No one needed to know her. She flew under the radar, unlike Jack. She'd been right, though, about Jack being recognized by those women that night. They must have taken his picture. Hers too.

It was an unsettling feeling, having her picture taken without permission. Having it taken and posted online was even odder. But then she reminded herself it wasn't a big deal. She'd simply had dinner. There was nothing wrong with that. It wasn't as if she'd been filmed having sex on top of the Met Life Tower.

They resumed their walk, passing a drugstore.

"Oh, Sutton," Michelle said. "I forgot. I need to pop into the store and get a pair of cheaters."

"Since when do you need reading glasses?"

"I don't need them for reading," Michelle said suggestively.

"You dirty bitch." Sutton said, her eyes lighting up. "Let's go get you some cheaters."

* * *

He'd said hello to the receptionist then headed straight to his corner office and shut the door, a clear sign he wanted to be left alone. His only companion was the view of Manhattan from the windows. He could see New York. No one could see him. His phone buzzed, and he was tempted to ignore it. But the possibility that it might be her again had him grabbing it from his pocket.

M: Remember that time you knocked on my office door after your first appointment?

J: Yes.

M: You told me you had unfinished business with my pussy.

J: I did. I still do. Only because I fucking love your pussy, so I'm always going to want to do business with it, to it, for it, and in it.

M: I have unfinished business with your fabulous fucking cock.

J: Now you've done it again. Why do you torture me like this?

M: It's only torture if I'm going to leave you blue-balled.

J: Well, what's your plan, beautiful? Because my dick is hard, and I have no intention of jacking off in my office, and I have two more hours of work to get through.

He waited, and waited, and waited. But no reply came.

"Fuck it," he muttered, because it was time to focus.

He tossed the phone on his desk. He needed to take care of a few thorny issues with suppliers before the weekend, but all he wanted was to rid his body and mind of the residual tension from the day. The meeting with Denkler combined with the time at the shrink's, in addition to all those jumbled feelings of fuck-uppery with Aubrey had him on edge.

Michelle was nowhere to be seen to take that edge off.

He fired up the computer screen when his office phone beeped with the receptionist. He stabbed the answer button. "Hey, Christine. How are you?"

"Good afternoon, Mr. Sullivan. There is someone here for you with a delivery from the library. She wants me to send her back," the receptionist said, lowering her voice.

"The library?"

"She said you ordered some books for personal delivery," Christine said, sounding thoroughly flummoxed. He was, too. Until, some neuron fired and he had the sneaking suspicion the edge was about to come off. "Send her back," he said, and then hung up as his cell phone rattled once more.

M: I hope it's not work that involves other people.

J: Why not?

M: Because I wouldn't want them to see what I'm about to do to you.

CHAPTER TEN

It is Certain

"Come in," he said, as the brown door slowly opened.

The first thing he saw was a pair of strong legs. Then, black pumps, with a strap across the top of her feet. Then the owner of those gorgeous legs stepped inside, and he dropped the paper in his hand.

Holy sex of his fantasies.

He raked his eyes up and down, not even sure where to stop or where to linger because the whole package was a dream. Bare legs, black pencil skirt, tight as sin, her gorgeous brown hair pinned up on her head. Then there were the glasses.

Sexy cat's eye glasses.

Peering over the top of them seductively, she shrugged off the black belted jacket she wore, tossing it on the purple couch. She had on a white blouse, unbuttoned to her cleavage. In her hand, she held a library book. She thumped it against her palm and gave him a stern look as she shut the door. "I believe you have some overdue library books, Mr. Library Patron."

"Is that so? What sort of fines am I looking at?" He licked his lips, never once taking his eyes off the stunning woman who owned this moment as she walked across the carpet in his office as if she'd been designed for this kind of play. She made her way to his desk, and hopped up on the corner of it.

"You could be looking at some hard time," she said, her eyes twinkling with naughtiness, her voice laced with innuendo. God, her mouth looked superb as she said *hard.* Her perfect red lips were so fuckable.

His gaze dropped to his hard-on, tenting his pants. Her eyes followed his. "Very hard time," she added, as she crossed those legs that he wanted to lick from her ankles all the way up. He could spend all day between her legs.

"Would you like to collect that overdue fine?"

"I might," she said, leaving the book on his desk, then removing something from the breast pocket of her blouse. Lipstick. She opened the tube, and slicked some across her lips, turning them redder. He hissed in a breath at the sight in front of him. Michelle. Perched on his desk. Applying lipstick. He wanted to pin her down and ravage his sexy librarian.

But he knew how to read women. And he knew this woman was running the show right now. This was her surprise for him, and hell if he was going to do a damn thing right now but take whatever she wanted to give. He only hoped she'd be giving it to him soon, because all the blood in his body had rushed to one organ. His cock throbbed.

She tucked the lipstick between her breasts, and he groaned.

"I'm jealous of your lipstick," he said, his eyes straying longingly to her shirt. "Why don't you unbutton that shirt a bit and let me see your tits?"

"You should be very jealous of my lipstick," she said, raising one hand to deftly undo a few buttons, exposing the swell of her full breasts.

A low rumble worked its way up his chest. "Let me suck on them."

She shook her head, and wagged a finger. "No. That won't pay the fine on your overdue books."

"What will then?" he asked, his fingers gripping the arms of his chair.

In a blur, she dropped to her knees, and he was ready to sing halle-fucking-lujah. Michelle on her knees was his perfect Friday afternoon.

"Do you like payback, Jack?" she asked with a perfect pout on her cherry-red lips, her quick hands reaching for his fly, and mercifully unzipping it.

"If it involves your lips wrapped around my dick, then I do," he said.

"You came into my office and had your way with me in my chair. Now it's my turn to finish you off," she said, and quickly tugged down his briefs.

His cock sprang free, and she wrapped her hand around him.

"Fuck," he hissed out, that first touch some kind of temporary relief from the throbbing. She stroked him, and he watched her, savoring the way her eyes turned hazy as she stared at him, like she was mesmerized by his dick. She dropped her lips to the head, and he groaned loudly at that first dizzying feel of her soft lips wrapped around him.

A tremor rolled down his spine, and he speared his hands through her hair that was still up in some kind of twist on her head. "Fuck, Michelle. Your lips are fucking perfect on me," he said, moving her up and down as he watched.

She glanced up at him, flashing him some kind of knowing look with those brown eyes.

"Look at you. Look at how good you look with my dick in your mouth," he said, and relished the way her lips curved up while she sucked up and down. His fingers dug deeper into her hair. "I'm messing up your hair, but I don't think you'll be bothered."

She shook her head, then his balls drew up as her lips tightened around him. More friction, more suction, and he closed his eyes briefly, relaxing into the pleasure bursting through him with every stroke of her tongue, every suck of her lips. She tugged on his balls, rolling them between her fingers as she worked him over with her lips. All his frustration from the afternoon, all the tension from his session, it all melted away with the glide of her lips and the pressure of her hands.

He groaned loudly as she dropped him from her lips, only to take his balls into her mouth and suck. He opened his eyes, not wanting to miss the sight.

"You look so hot and dirty," he told her.

She let him fall momentarily from her lips. "Just you wait, Jack," she said, then licked him back into her mouth, and he felt her throat relaxing as he rocked into her. He began moving his hips in synch with her, setting up a perfect rhythm.

Then he heard a faint buzzing, just enough for him to open his eyes. He drew a deep, sharp breath as he felt a hum against the base of his cock. A hum he'd recognize nearly anywhere. Then a vibration sent waves of pleasure through him.

"You are a naughty girl," he gritted out as his blood pulsed. He gripped her head tighter, staring down to see what he suspected. Her lipstick was a vibrator, and she was rubbing it against his shaft. The twin sensations—her lips and the vibrations in his body—sent him closer to the brink.

"I want to fuck your mouth so badly right now," he bit out.

She let go of him momentarily to whisper hotly. "Do it."

She turned up the toy, sending waves of pleasure through him, like an annihilation of the senses, and there was nothing else in existence but the sinful press of her mouth. His lungs tightened. His vision turned blurry. The rattle and hum of the lipstick sent mini tremors through his bones. Release was in sight, so close, and he curled his hands around her skull and pumped into her mouth, watching her as she took his cock all the way in. Her mouth was like a miracle, her body was divine, and she was built for the most sinful kind of sex he wanted to have.

Hot, rough, adventurous.

This wasn't the first time he'd been privy to her talented mouth sucking him, but there was something about this moment that sent a molten thrill through him. It was the way this blowjob was a fait accompli. She'd strutted into his office with one thing in mind. Being his fantasy.

"I'm going to come so hard and I want you to take it all," he said. "I need to fuck your mouth hard."

She squeezed his cock in her hand as an answer and drew the orgasm out of him in one long deep powerful suck.

"Fuck," he cried out, his hands wrapped around her head, her hair spilling all over his fingers as he gave her everything inside of him and she took it. She took every last drop as she slowed her pace, and he moved with her until finally, he let go of his hold on her, his dick dropping from her mouth.

He exhaled deeply. A satisfied sound. She wiped her hand across her lips, her eyes lit up and her smile devilish.

"Come here," he whispered, and pulled her up in his lap. "You're so beautiful when you do that to me."

"You like the way I look with you in my mouth?"

"I love all the different looks you have. I love the way you look naked. I love the way you look with your legs spread. I love how you look in this seductive outfit. I love how you look when you come," he said, lowering his voice as he traced her lips with his fingertip.

"Were you surprised to see me?"

He nodded. "Surprised and happy," he said, edging her cheek with soft kisses that made her tremble against him and sigh sexily. Soon, soon he'd take his turn with her.

He smoothed away her hair that had fallen in a wild tumble around her face. Some strands were still in the clip, but the rest had fallen free. Reaching up to the back of her head, he opened the clip and let the rest fall out.

"Nice glasses, by the way. Do they help you see better?" he teased.

"They make large objects appear even larger," she said with a naughty grin. He laughed deeply, looping one arm around her shoulders, the other around her waist, and holding her close.

"Thank you for making my Friday go from being annoying as fuck to hot as hell."

"Why was it annoying?" she asked, gentle concern in her tone. She ran her fingers through his hair. Softly. Ever so softly, and that small, tender gesture somehow undid him, loosening the remaining tangles of annoyance in his chest. He sighed heavily. He didn't want to revisit the frustrations now that they'd started to dissipate, but here she was on his lap, and she'd done something that stripped all the tension from his body, and also somehow peeled away another layer from around the steel cage of his heart.

"Remember when I said I hate politics?"

"Yes."

He scrubbed a hand across his jaw. "I had to have a meeting about some political race today," he said, then shared more of the details about the race and the clubs.

She arched an eyebrow. "I've never been to a BDSM club," she said.

"Do you want to go?"

She shook her head. "Not at all. It's not my thing. And don't say how do you know if you haven't gone."

He laughed, leaning back in his chair, holding her tighter. "It's okay. Even though I like fucking you into submission, we don't need to play dom-sub games to do that."

She laughed too. "No, we definitely don't. You can fuck me pretty much any way you want, but any submission on my part will be in the moment, not because of a need for roles. However," she said, and he could sense she'd shifted to some sort of professional stance now, "I do think it's ridiculous that Conroy wants to try to close those clubs and has somehow made that a rallying cry in a campaign."

"I know, me too."

"Consenting adults should be free to do what they want in the bedroom. Or the club, as the case may be."

"Which is only one of the reasons why I'd rather not have to deal with this situation."

"I take it you didn't get into this business thinking you'd have to work with politics," she said.

"I'd rather just run the business. That's what I like. I like the business side of it. Figuring out what works. How to make different lines more profitable, more successful." He looked at the stunning view of Manhattan from his window, a reminder of how well Joy Delivered was faring. "Starting this business was my sister's idea. We went in together because she brings the passion, and I bring the business side."

"You're the numbers man. The logic guy. But Jack, that's what you're passionate about, right?"

He nodded, liking that she'd understood him so quickly. "Exactly. And with this problem, I get why it's important, but I wish I didn't have to bother with it."

"That could be said about a lot of things though, right?"

He raised an eyebrow in question. "What do you mean?"

"Well, no one wants to have to deal with the problems that get in the way of our everyday lives, but yet it's part of everyday life, right?"

"True."

"You just have to think about it as another problem to solve. Because that's what you like doing. You like finding the clues. Putting them together until you reach the answer, right?"

"Yes," he said with a small smile. She was getting him.

"Look at this the same way. Don't look at it as getting involved in something seedy, like politics. Look at it as a —" She stopped, stared at the ceiling as if she were hunting for the right word, then continued, "—as if a new vibrator was stimulating the labia rather than the clitoris, and you have to fix it."

He laughed so hard he had to grab her hips so she wouldn't fall off him from the chuckling. "I would never make a vibrator that stimulated the slit, not the clit," he said, being deliberately crass, and it was her turn to laugh. "But that's good advice. Just treat it as yet another challenge in the business day."

"Exactly," she said with a crisp nod, and it hit him. Like a blast of light blaring through the room at dawn.

"You just gave me advice," he said, kind of awestruck. "Like a shrink." He quirked up his lips.

"That's what I do," she said playfully.

And it didn't bother me. And I was able to talk to you.

"Sometimes, I can't help myself," she added.

"I liked it," he said, and he wondered what it would have been like if he hadn't met her at The Pierson. If he'd simply shown up for his appointment two weeks ago. He was quiet for a moment, drifting off to that notion.

"Are you thinking about what it would be like if we were working together? In therapy?" she asked in a soft, quiet voice.

"Are you a mind reader?"

She smiled. "I am, actually. It was part of my coursework. I'm certified not only in intimate relationship psychology but also in mind reading. As well as tarot. Shall I read your cards?"

"Oh, please do. Though I'd honestly feel a tad better if you relied on an 8-Ball. Are you certified in that too?"

She mimed shaking an 8-Ball. "What would you like to ask it?"

He stroked his chin, pretending to be deep in thought. But when he spoke, the question was borderline serious. "Would Michelle still have been attracted to me if we first met at her office?"

Her lips parted as if she were taken aback by the question. Then she peered at the pretend glass window in the makeshift 8-Ball. "Without a doubt," she said, and he watched her. The way she swallowed as if nervous. How her eyes stayed fixed on him. The clarity with which she spoke.

He ran his fingers across her wrist. "Would you have fought it?"

She let go of the pretend toy. "It is certain," she said, giving another 8-Ball answer, but one that seemed truly serious.

"Then I'm glad we met the night before. I don't know what I would have done sitting across from you in your office, trying to talk to you as my shrink when I want to do bad things to you," he said, toying with the hem on her skirt.

"But you're talking to me now as my lover, and I presume you'll still do bad things to me later."

"I will absolutely do them," he said, then shifted gears because he liked getting to know her better. "Did you always want to be a shrink?"

"It was my fallback option."

"What was your first choice?"

"I thought I wanted to be a Broadway star."

"Yeah? What happened there?"

"Only three things got in the way of that dream. One—I can't sing. Two—I can't dance. Three—I can't act," she said and he cracked up, shaking from the laughter that rang through his body.

"That was really fucking funny," he said through a wide smile, and he could hardly believe that this woman could make him think, make him laugh, and make him hard. She was a triple threat, and the more time he spent with her, the more time he wanted to spend with her.

"Why, thank you. I've been working on that for a while now. Decided to test it out on you."

"So, let's answer the question now. Have you always known you wanted to be a psychologist?"

Her lips curved up as if she were thinking of the answer. "I don't think I had it on my list in high school. But I always liked helping. I think I always enjoyed being someone my friends could turn to for advice, even with simple things when I was younger like what to wear on the first day of school, and then when I was older on things like what to say to their parents when they got in trouble, or what should they do about this teacher, or that boy, or this problem."

"You were a natural," he said.

She shrugged, as if blowing off the compliment. "Maybe. But it wasn't until my parents died, and I had a tough time of it for a while in college that I started to try therapy myself for a few months, to deal with all the residual sadness. It made a difference for me so I realized it was the perfect marriage for me professionally."

"I bet you're good at," he said, stroking her collarbone absently. Her skin was so soft, and he loved touching her, loved the feel of her beneath his fingertips.

"You missed your chance. That ship has sailed for you, sir."

"I can't say I regret it. Because I like this arrangement we have going on."

"Me too. Is the sex therapy working for you, Jack? Helping you heal that wounded heart?" she asked, tracing a heart shape on his chest. He tensed momentarily at the suggestion of why he was a damaged man. He almost wanted her to know the truth. That he wasn't hurting; he was besieged by guilt. But they weren't dredging up the past now. They were focused on the present.

"It's working immensely," he said, and that was true—he felt lighter, freer with her. "And you? Are we getting that guy out of the rearview mirror?"

She leaned closer, pressed a soft kiss on his cheek. "How could I think of anyone else while I'm sitting on your lap like this?"

"I like you on my lap," he said, glancing down at her and the way her gorgeous body molded to his. How her ass felt on his thighs. How her back rested gently against his arms. How her legs felt draped on him.

"Funny, but you don't really seem like a lap person," she said, playing with the collar on his shirt, then his tie, running her fingers along it.

"Why not?" he asked, wrenching back as if she'd offended him.

"Don't know. It just seems sort of warm and cuddly."

He rolled his yes. "This from the woman who won't spend the night. This from the woman who keeps me at arm's length."

"Isn't that the length you prefer?"

He shook his head. He didn't know why, but the guilt that normally clawed at him was absent right now. It had slinked off, like smoke curling away. He felt stripped bare, but he didn't mind her knowing how he felt, because somehow she was working her way past all those barriers he'd built to protect people from himself, and she wasn't even trying to knock them down. She simply did it by being herself. By talking. By asking. By wanting to know him.

Their conversation today seemed to be a stepping stone to something more. To closeness. It should have scared him. Should have sent him into preservation mode, both for his sake and for hers. But it didn't. It only made him want more of her. He hoped this feeling wouldn't lead to an impossible choice down the road. Or even in two weeks, when their thirty nights ran out.

He didn't want to focus on that, though. He wanted to exist in the moment with her.

"With you, I don't mind less than arm's length," he whispered, then brushed his lips against her hair, burying his face in the soft strands and bringing her even closer.

"And I want you to spend the night with me. I want to see you in the mornings too."

She pulled back. "I don't know."

"Is that you protecting your heart again?"

"Yes," she said, and he liked that she didn't hide the truth. She simply admitted it.

"But I make amazing scrambled eggs."

"Well, in that case," she teased, as she finally unknotted his tie, "I'll take it under advisement."

He looked down his nose at her handiwork, her hands tap dancing on his chest.

"If I didn't know better, I'd think you were trying to get me naked."

"Maybe I am," she purred.

"But I'm working," he said in a playful voice, as her fingers undid his buttons. The afternoon was shot. He didn't care anymore. He had other things on his mind.

"I think work is over for you today."

"Do you want me to do bad things to you?"

"What do you think?"

He nodded. "All signs point to yes," he said, giving her an 8-Ball answer. He didn't need a fortuneteller or tarot cards to tell him she was going to enjoy all the bad things he'd do. Her body made it clear.

He reached for her hips, lifted her off him and set her down on the edge of his desk. He stood up, zipped his pants and held her face in his hands, and moved in to plant a bruising kiss on her lips. She gasped the second he made contact and he kissed the sound away, feasting on her lips, turning everything playful into something hot and hungry once more.

CHAPTER ELEVEN

Dirty Inquisition

The moment shifted in a nanosecond. She'd held the power when she'd sauntered into his office, costume on, plan in hand. Now he had the reins and she was quivering with want from the way he devoured her lips, as he spread her legs easily with a strong nudge of his thighs.

His tongue swirled against hers, his lips crushing her mouth, her head gripped tight in his strong hands. She held on to the edge of his desk. If she didn't, she might topple backwards. When he broke the kiss, she was dazed. But maybe that was the point. Jack might be content with a little role-playing, but his favorite role was dominating her.

"Stay like that," he said. Turning around, he reached for a shelf behind his desk, and grabbed a black box with the letter *J* embossed in silver on the front. She shivered; just the look of the box was arousing.

"Open your shirt," he said, his voice husky, laden with power.

She steadied herself, and began unbuttoning her blouse down to her waist, his eyes staying on her the whole time as she spread open the fabric. She wore a black lace push-up bra.

He drew a sharp breath, and ran his tongue over his teeth as he opened the box. "Don't take the bra off. Just push it down, and free your tits," he told her.

She did as she was told, her breasts tumbling free, resting on the underwire, framed by the lace. Heat spread fast through her body, whipping through her veins as he opened the box, and dipped his fingers inside. He lifted out something that looked like earrings. Each had a gold chain and red hearts on the end.

"What's that?" she asked because she knew they weren't earrings.

Pressing one hand on the desk, he cupped a breast with his other hand, palming her. A moan escaped her lips as he rolled her nipple between his fingers. "Nipple clamps. May I?"

It was the *may* that led to her yes. It was his ask that brought the permission. The manners in the midst of this intense moment led her to give in to try. "Yes."

He carefully clamped one on. She gasped, biting back a small *ouch*.

"Does it hurt?" he asked, concerned.

"Yes, and no," she said, shooting him the tiniest smile.

"Sounds like it's working then," he said, and moved to her other breast, clamping it down and giving a quick tug. The sensation was like a bite. The sharp, sweet sting of pain mingled with pleasure. "I'm not done with you, Michelle," he whispered hotly in her ear, his voice like a hard warning. "You don't come to my office and blow me and not get fucked."

"I would hope to get fucked," she countered, letting him know she might play these games, but she wasn't a woman who'd ever roll over. She'd spar verbally even as he flicked the red heart on her breasts, sending an agonizingly delicious zing from her breasts straight to her core. Perhaps she might meet that elusive nipple orgasm today. She doubted it existed, but with the way heat pooled between her legs, she might start believing.

"I need you to understand me, beautiful," he said, gripping her thigh. "This is my company. My office. My desk. I make the rules, and you tried to subvert them. Now I'll show you how I run things here when a woman like you tears me away from work."

"Show me," she said, daring him. Taunting him.

He took another box off his shelf, then opened it, showing her a purple vibrator. "The Wild One. It's new. You'll be my personal focus group of one. The walls in my office are very thick, so be as loud as you need to."

She eyed it suspiciously. "You're not going to use that on me, are you? Has anyone touched it?"

He laughed, breaking his dominant character for a moment. "It's never been used. I'll clean it too," he said, and stepped into the restroom attached to his office. She heard the water running, then the faucets being turned off. She leaned forward, peering into the bathroom to see him wiping down the toy. She smiled to herself. He was a good man to make sure it was clean.

He returned, and stood between her legs again, pushing them open wider.

"Put your feet up on my desk. Show me how far you can spread your legs."

She lifted her heeled feet onto the edge of his desk. Not once did she think about how she looked. She knew she looked hot to him. She knew he wanted her badly as she sat perched on his desk, wide open, nipple clamps dangling, underwear soaked from her desire.

He stared between her legs at her wet panties. "We have a problem."

"What's the problem?"

"I don't want you to move from this position. But I need to get those the fuck off," he said, and stretched across her and reached for a pencil holder on his desk, grasping a pair of scissors.

Her eyes widened in fear.

"Don't move. I won't hurt you."

He pulled the side of her black lace panties, tugging them away from her leg. "Tomorrow I'm taking you lingerie shopping. That's a promise," he said, and then sliced the panties neatly, and tugged the ripped fabric to the side, exposing her wet pussy to him. She followed his gaze downward.

She was glistening for him.

He shut his eyes briefly and rubbed the outline of his cock in his pants. She ached. Watching him touch himself after he came moments ago thrilled her. This might just be sex, they might only be playmates, but hell, she *had* him. He was aroused to no end by her, and that knowledge turned her into an inferno. Her skin sizzled and she dipped a hand between her legs.

He opened his eyes, and they blazed darkly at her.

"Are you going to fuck me now?"

He shook his head. "No," he said, and handed her the toy. "Fuck yourself. I want to watch you masturbate on my desk. I want to see the sexiest woman I've ever known make herself come on the desk where I approved this product," he said, hitting the *on* switch, rubbing the head once through her wet lips, and then handing it to her.

"*Jack*," she moaned.

"Are you embarrassed to show me how you fuck yourself?"

She shook her head. "No," she said, her voice strong. "I would never be embarrassed. I love to masturbate."

He breathed out hard, and she saw the outline of his dick grow. "God, that's so fucking hot. I want to see you love yourself. Show me how you love your own body with something I made," he commanded, and she rubbed the purple head against her damp, throbbing center. Her breath fled her chest. The intensity of the vibration spread quickly, rippling through her body from the rabbit.

"No, I want it in you. Put it all the way in. Rub your clit. Fuck your pussy. Show me how it works on the woman I want," he said, pressing his palms on the desk, his body next to hers as she rubbed the rabbit's ears against her clitoris, then in one slick motion, slid the shaft inside her. Her inner walls clenched against the device, and her eyes floated closed as she began to work it inside her. She heard him panting, and groaning, and then out of nowhere came a sharp sting as he tugged on the nipple clamps, both at the same time. The pain shot through her, careening through her bloodstream, but instead of hurting, it hurt so good. It was like wildfire, raging and out of control as it ran rampant in her body. In and out, she thrust The Wild One, the shaft filling her, the head of it touching her deep inside her pussy, the rabbit's ears vibrating her into the fevered frenzy she often sought.

"Do you love fucking yourself?" he asked, flicking on the red hearts on her nipples.

"Yes," she panted.

"Do you watch porn when you do it?"

"Usually."

"What do you watch? Do you watch beautiful women in stockings and heels fucking themselves with their fingers?"

"Sometimes," she admitted.

"What else?" he asked, demanding answers. Answers she was too happy to give.

"I watch it all," she said in a breathless rush.

"Do you watch women licking each other's pussies?"

She nodded on a harsh breath.

"And women sucking off men?"

"Yes," she cried out.

"Do you watch men fucking men?"

"Sometimes."

"And men fucking women, and coming all over their beautiful fucking bellies and tits?"

"Yes, yes, yes."

"And what about this?" he asked, spreading her ass and flicking his finger against her rear. A tease. A hint. "Do you like to watch ass play? Fingers, toys, cocks?"

"Oh God, yes."

He groaned loudly, and no more words came from him. No more questions. Just primal sounds of pleasure.

She was vaguely aware of the moans and groans, and it took a few seconds for her to connect all those sounds to her. She was making them. She was spread on his desk, heels hooked on the edge, legs wide open and vulnerable, head thrown back, hair spilling out, fucking herself with his toy as she cried out.

She concentrated fiercely on the orgasm she felt cresting. She swore she could see it rising up on the edge of a far cliff, like a swirl of pleasure, like a drug-induced opium haze. Jack's voice cut through her cries.

"Stop." His voice was firm. One word. That was all. A command.

"I don't want to," she protested.

"Do it anyway," he said, and she somehow found the strength to slow the pace, her chest convulsing, her pussy twitching with the desperate need to come.

He wasn't a sadist. He surely didn't believe in torture. He was a man of pleasure. A man constructed and outfitted, whether it was his passion or his business, to deliver endless joy to a woman. Because when she looked up through hazy, lust-filled eyes, she was greeted with the most beautiful sight. He'd unzipped his pants, pushed down his briefs, and was rolling a condom onto his long, thick, beautifully erect cock.

She removed the toy, dropped it on his desk, and two seconds later, he yanked her by the hips, positioned himself at her entrance, and shoved into her. His breath hissed out as he filled her to the hilt. She wrapped her arms around his chest, and murmured his name. "*Jack*."

"*Michelle*," he said, sliding out, then back in her. "You feel so fucking good." His eyes were glassy with desire. "I love how you made your pussy so fucking perfectly ready for me."

"I'm so ready for you," she said, reaching up to his face, cupping his cheeks, his stubble rough against her hands.

"Are you ready to come?" he asked, never looking away as he thrust into her, sending a flurry of white-hot sparks through her body.

"So ready. Please make me come."

He pumped into her, fast and then faster, and every part of her felt him. Her breasts were full and on high alert, swelling with sensations, her legs were wide open for him. Her pussy was drawing him in as deep as he could possibly be, and all the while she held his face in her hands, and watched him. Watched his eyes, those cool blue eyes that didn't seem to want to look away either. He didn't want to break the gaze. He stayed with her, fucking her forcefully and relentlessly on his desk as she reached the edge. "That's right. Come on my desk," he instructed. "Come so fucking hard that I'll never think of anything but you when I'm trying to work here."

She didn't know if one orgasm would ruin his work ethic for life. She didn't care. All she knew was that her body was shattering, sensations rolling through her in some sort of sinful chaos of bliss and beauty. Crashing, rising, falling, exploding. And all that noise. All that shouting. His name. Her name. God's name. Swearing. A cacophony of sounds of sex, flesh on flesh, slaps and moans and groans as she came undone for him. And the deepness. Oh, the terribly wonderful deepness as he pushed further into her, still driving, still thrusting, hard and then even harder until he collapsed onto her, his weight on her body, his loud grunts landing on her ears like a manifesto of his pleasure.

She panted. He groaned. They didn't move. They lay there, spent, exhausted, their breaths harsh in the silent office, sated beyond words in a heap on his desk, turning work and the business of pleasure obsolete that Friday evening.

When at last he separated from her, he brushed his fingertips along her face. "So beautiful," he murmured, then bent his head to her neck, layering kisses all the way to her ear. She shivered from his tender touch. "I love being with you."

She tensed at the words, but then relaxed into his embrace. Try as she might to hold back, to resist, she loved being with him too. He asked her for her body, but the more he took of it, the more it was a package deal.

Which meant she was speeding straight into heartbreak. Only she didn't have the will to press the brakes.

She should find it. She really ought to find it. But it was nowhere nearby as he gently scooped her up from his desk, held her in his arms, and kissed her face.

CHAPTER TWELVE
Fit

Work was out of the question, it seemed.

After straightening up his desk, he knotted his tie, and handed Michelle her jacket.

"I'm famished. Do you want to get something to eat?" he asked as he held the coat for her.

"Yes, and I'll just carry my jacket," she said. She didn't need it for the weather; she'd worn it for the costume. "I only had it on for the effect."

"I'd say it worked. So long as the intended effect was a spectacular orgasm. For both of us," he added.

She shot him a smile. "Yes."

He placed his hand on her back and led her out of the office, now bathed in the twilight glow of a building coasting into evening. Most of his employees had left for the day, and he waved quick goodbyes to the few remaining, hunched over laptops in their cubicles.

Perhaps she should have been embarrassed to be seen leaving with the CEO, knowing what they'd just done in his office. She wasn't, though. Maybe because she believed him when he'd said his office was soundproofed, or maybe because she was still glowing from that earth-shattering orgasm he'd delivered. Honestly, she wouldn't have been surprised to hear a news report that one of the planet's tectonic plates had shifted. It had been that powerful a climax. Unbidden, she shuddered, the sweet, memory washing over her.

"Chinese? Thai? Indian?" he asked as they walked past the gleaming white reception desk with the letter J embossed in silver on the wall behind it. Joy Delivered was the Louis Vuitton of sex toys.

An image of a Thai fusion restaurant on the Upper East Side flashed in front of her eyes. She'd been researching cool new eateries, so she mentioned the name, and some of the dishes on the menu. "I've been wanting to try it. Tonight seems a perfect opportunity," she said, and he dusted her lips with a kiss saying *yes*.

"Do you want to walk there? It's not too far away."

"I'd love to."

When they reached the lobby, he laced his fingers through hers, and squeezed. A private little gesture. A silent moment. Sending a message just to her that he liked holding her hand in public. Tingles skipped through her bloodstream, so happily and so quickly that she barely noticed a familiar face a few shops down, watching her from the fruit stands outside a bodega.

When it registered why the dark hair and thick glasses felt so familiar—like the man who'd bumped into her then held her elbow too long—he was gone. Worry shot through her bloodstream, but she quickly tamped it down. This was Manhattan, an endless island of people and faces.

It was the land of the unknown, but when you live in close quarters with millions, the city has a way of fooling you. Tricking you into believing you know everyone.

Even so, she peered into the doorway of the bodega as they walked past, but the view inside only confirmed her theory. New York was jam-packed with people. He was nobody she knew, just like last time.

"You okay?"

She smiled. "Totally. I just thought I saw someone who looked familiar. This guy with glasses." She returned to far more pleasant topics. Their hands together. "I never would have pegged you as a guy who likes to hold hands in public."

"Why? Do I seem like an asshole who doesn't want to have his hands all over his woman?"

She laughed, but thrilled inside—against her better judgment—at the use of *his*. She wasn't his woman. She had no plans on being his woman. But she was his woman for another fourteen days. *Happily.*

"I just would never have thought you were that type of guy."

"You didn't think I wanted to have you in my lap, either. But yet I did," he said, stopping to bring their clasped hands to his mouth for a quick kiss as they passed a florist, the front of the shop teeming with flowers in bright orange and yellows—late summer shades. "How else am I surprising you?"

How else?

In so many ways. He was not what she would have expected from the first night, or from what she suspected people saw on the surface—his gorgeous chiseled good looks, his sharp well-dressed style, his cool blue eyes, both warm and distant at the same damn time.

He had more contradictions than she'd ever have suspected, and she was someone who trafficked in contradictions. Who was accustomed to them. Who had come to expect them. But Jack was tender and sweet when he could have been removed; he was removed when he could have been calloused; he was self-protective when he could have been cruel.

"Well?" he asked, prompting her as they darted past a group of teenage girls hanging onto each other and their phones outside a yogurt shop. The girls clearly weren't going to move. And Jack clearly wanted her opinion. "How am I different than what you expected?"

She parted her lips to speak, her natural instinct, her professional desire to speak the truth plainly kicking in. "You're sweeter, kinder, and more affectionate than I would have thought, given why you were in my office," she said, looking him square in the eyes.

He stopped in his tracks, forcing her to stop too. "You didn't think I could be affectionate?"

"Well," she said as if the answer were obvious.

"I *so* can," he said, and wrapped his arms around her waist, and tugged her close, dropping his forehead to hers. They stood in the middle of the crowded sidewalk. Men and women in suits and clickety-clack heels with determined looks on their faces, rushing to catch trains and buses and cabs home, were forced to walk around them. "With the right woman . . ." he said and brushed his lips ever so gently against hers so that all thoughts tumbled out of her skull, leaving her with nothing but feelings. The fresh bloom of feelings for this man.

"Who's the right woman?" she asked when he pulled away.

"You," he whispered, in a voice that was clear and direct.

And cut straight through the walls. He couldn't possibly be suggesting there was more to them? Could he? They were nighttime. They were deadlines. They were the city after hours. They weren't *more*. They weren't a couple. Whatever affection he felt for her was clearly borne of sex. So she turned the conversation in that much less frightening direction as they resumed their walk uptown.

"By the way, Jack, I've noticed that filthy mouth of yours was much more refined the first night I met you."

He raised an eyebrow. "Is that so?"

She nodded. "Yes. Now the way you talk to me is blunter. Rougher," she said, and she'd seen the slight changes the more they were together. He seemed to let go more with that dirty mouth, using words he hadn't used the night they'd met, asking rougher questions, demanding answers.

"Maybe it's part of my plan to woo you," he joked. "Is it working?"

"I don't know. What do you think?"

He leaned closer, brushed her hair away from her shoulder, and whispered hotly in her ear, "I think you're a very dirty girl beneath that good-girl exterior."

His words sent a rush through her. He was right. He was so right.

She tilted her face to him, and answered with a curve of her lips. "And you like it that way."

"I *love* it that way," he said in a husky voice that gave away his desire.

She tensed, wondering if he'd been like this with Aubrey. If he'd thrown her down on his desk, if he'd demanded answers about her dirty fantasies. She wished terribly that the thought had not touched down in her head, but now that it was there, it worried away at her. There was no way she'd ask him if he'd been like that with other women. That was too personal. Besides, it was a rude question. Michelle Milo aspired not to be rude.

Instead, she simply sighed.

"Hey, what's wrong?" he asked, as they turned the corner onto a quieter street lined with trees and a mix of pretty brownstones, some white, some brick, all beautiful.

"Nothing," she said, putting her game face back on.

"I don't believe that. And you're too damn smart to think you can get away with that kind of answer."

"What kind of answer?"

"The kind that's a lie. There is something wrong, and I bet I know what it is."

"Okay. Try me," she said and they were treading in dangerous territory, but then this was her stock-in-trade. Surely, she could handle it with him.

"You wanted to know if I'm like this with other women I've been with, don't you?"

She gasped in surprise, and they stopped walking. She backed up to stand near the brown stoop of a building with planters in the first floor windows.

"I'm like this with you," he added, his eyes locked on hers as he held her hand tighter.

"You are?" she asked carefully.

He nodded. "Of course I like the way we fuck. I love the way we have sex. Does that mean every other woman wanted it this way?" he asked, and a part of her hoped and prayed he wouldn't answer. He didn't. Thankfully. "It means *we* fit."

Her heart jumped at those words, and she wasn't entirely sure why. She wanted to swat it back into place. Hell, they were talking about sex, not matters of the heart, so why on earth should that annoying organ be doing a pitter-patter? But as he gazed at her, his blue eyes never wavering, she saw a flash of something *more* in his expression. He wasn't just talking about how they fit in the bedroom.

"I think so too," she said quietly, as they delved into territory she usually only started to explore in a therapy session with a patient, but here they were on the streets of New York having a frank conversation about how they liked to fuck. And yet it was a conversation about *more* than sex too.

"It means you're perfect for me. And I can be myself with you," he said, grasping her hand tighter, as he moved in closer. Heat radiated off of him.

Oh God, her heart thumped hard now. And she couldn't take it. She couldn't take all this beating in her chest, this heat, this stretching and expanding inside. "So you can be the dirty guy who likes a good girl on the outside but with a filthy mind?" she countered, arching an eyebrow, and somehow successfully deflecting the deeper meaning of this conversation, even though she wanted to clasp it and hold it close.

He threw his head back and laughed. "Come on. Let's get that stomach fed, so I can have more of that filthy mind and hot body later."

* * *

"Do you miss her still?"

He crinkled his brow at the question she asked over dinner. "Hmm? What do you mean?"

"Aubrey."

Oh. Right. The reason he'd gone to see Michelle in the first place. "Honestly?"

She nodded, and laughed once as she lifted her wine glass. "Yes," she said emphatically. "Of course I'm asking you honestly. We talked about it at Gia's. It must be hard for you. I mean, that's why you came to see me. I don't expect you to be over her in just a few sessions with Kana, and I'm not asking you to tell me about them. I'm just asking if you miss her."

There was one answer. The truth. He could give her that right now. "No. I don't miss her. Sorry if that makes me seem callous. But it's the truth."

"Hey. The truth is okay. It's okay not to miss anymore. Or even just not today," she said, then took a drink and set down the glass.

"And honestly, being with you helps. I like being with you."

"I like that you're with me."

Later, he sent her home in a town car. Her choice. Not his. Someday, someday soon, he wanted her to stay the night. When he returned to his own bed, alone, he missed Michelle more than he'd ever expected to.

CHAPTER THIRTEEN
Sooner or Later

The ball slammed the backboard and wobbled once on the rim before sinking through the net.

"I won!" Nate declared, thrusting his arms high in the air as the sun rose higher in the morning sky.

"Right," Jack said, shaking his head as he laughed, since the two of them never really kept score. He grabbed the ball and tucked it under his arm as they headed out of the court and onto the street. New York was already bustling. Families were out pushing strollers and grabbing bagels, and twenty-somethings were spilled over small tables at cafes, nursing lattes and wearing sunglasses.

"I scored Yankees tickets from a client. Third baseline. Two rows up," Nate said as a cab screeched to the curb to pick up a fare. "You up for it?"

Jack's ears pricked. He was always up for the Yankees. "When?"

"Tonight. Game's against Boston. It will be epic," Nate said. The Yankees were down by two games in the division, and the pennant race was on. But none of that mattered.

"Can't. I have plans," Jack said, as they neared the avenue.

Nate rubbed his knuckle against his ear. "What's that? I didn't hear you. Sounded like you said you had plans."

"Can't go. But thanks."

Nate held up his finger, his brow crinkling. "You never turn down Yankees tickets. You must really like this woman."

Jack slowed his pace, the observation Nate had made dawning on him. His friend was right. The Yankees were sacrosanct. You didn't mess with a chance to go to the temple of baseball. And yet, he had no interest in the game. Time was limited with Michelle. The clock was ticking, the second hand racing by faster than he'd like. It was a Saturday morning now, two weeks after their night on the Met Life Tower when they'd agreed to a start and a finish. He could already see the end in sight, and he wanted to make the most of every second with her, especially since she'd be in Paris for some of their thirty days.

"You never even turned down Yankees tickets when you were with Aubrey," Nate added, and the reminder was like a slap in the face.

"Yeah, well. It's not like I was some role model for how to be a great fiancé," Jack muttered.

Nate clapped him on the back. "Don't be so hard on yourself, man. Nothing that happened was your fault."

That's where Nate was wrong. Everything was his fault. Completely and absolutely, and he was ready to linger on that reminder, let it gnaw its way through him like a daily exercise, when he heard a familiar voice.

"Jack fucking Sullivan."

His eyes snapped up. His sister was marching up to him, slapping her smartphone against her palm, her lips set in a tight line, her nostrils flaring. She wore a short skirt and high-heeled boots. Jack noticed Nate checking out her legs before he too looked up at Casey, her blond hair bouncing high in a ponytail.

Nate raised an eyebrow. "Looks like someone is in trouble with his little sister."

"What else is new," Jack mumbled.

When she stopped, she stabbed him in the chest. "Why didn't you tell me?"

Jack gave her a confused look. "Tell you what?"

"Yeah. Tell him what?" Nate chimed in, staring at Jack and playing along with Casey's indignation.

"Oh hi, Nate," she said in a normal tone, shooting a friendly smile to his buddy.

"Hey, Case. Good to see you."

When she turned back to Jack, her eyes narrowed again, and he swore he could see smoke billowing out of her ears.

Nate must have too. He cleared his throat and clapped Jack on the back. "Looks like you two have lots of catching up to do," he said then tipped an imaginary hat to Casey, whose expression softened once more for Nate as he said goodbye and turned the corner. Casey glared at Jack.

"What do you want to chew me out for, Case?" he asked, holding his hands out wide. He had no idea what her deal was.

Stabbing her finger at her phone, she said, "Why didn't you tell me you were screwing your shrink?"

His jaw dropped and his eyes widened. He couldn't have been more surprised if she'd said she was joining the circus. "What?"

"Right here. It's on *Page Six*." She pointed to the phone once more, brandishing it like a weapon. He peered at the screen to see a post on a NY tabloid paper.

"Allow me," Casey continued. *"One of NYC's most eligible bachelors, Jack Sullivan, was spotted having dinner with a lovely brunette at Sushi Den near the Chrysler Building. The brunette was later identified as Michelle Milo, and a quick Google tells us she's a psychologist who specializes in intimate relationships. Can you hear the weeping and gnashing of teeth of all the single women in New York? Is she catering to your intimate pleasures, Jack? If she doesn't, we will!"*

He seethed. He'd never been bothered by the things the press said. He'd never cared. Not about himself, and not about Aubrey. They were both used to it. They didn't even notice. But Michelle belonged to him, not the public eye. He hated that she'd been thrust there without her permission.

"Jack," Casey said in a measured voice, "This was not the plan when I made that appointment. How did this happen?"

"Oh, right," he said addressing his sister's concerns. "She's not my shrink. I told you that. Weirdly enough, I met her before the appointment and neither one of us knew who the other was, and then when I realized who she was the next day, we agreed I'd see someone else."

"But you're seeing her?" she asked skeptically.

"Yes."

"Romantically?"

Sexually, he wanted to add. But somehow, *romantically* fit too.

"I suppose you could call it that."

"And you like her?"

"Well, yeah," he admitted.

Then Casey squealed, her expression shifting instantly, and she jumped up and down. She threw her arms around Jack. "I can't believe you met someone you like. I'm so happy."

He hugged her back. "Let's not get too excited."

"I am, though. I am." She pulled back. "I want you to be happy."

He was finding that he was with Michelle. Which meant he was sure to fuck it up sooner or later. Knowing himself, he'd be betting on sooner.

* * *

Casey had become a stalker. Later that afternoon she trekked to Conroy's block to conduct some recon. By three-thirty, she'd paced up and down his street too many times to count. Found nothing. The door to his brownstone had remained closed. She'd snapped a few photos and sent them to her brother with silly captions.

But even if Conroy had emerged, what did she hope to learn? That he wore red pumps on a Saturday afternoon? That he had a mistress he was stupid enough to screw at his own house? She wasn't a private detective and snooping had never been her forte. She'd tracked down everything interesting she could find online and that had still amounted to a whole lot of nothing.

Besides, Denkler's people had access to the same Internet and they'd found nothing either.

She left, shaking her head at herself, annoyed that she was coming up short as she tried to gumshoe it on her own. It made her crazy that somehow this politician had decided to go after the clubs they supplied, turning sexual pleasures into the bogeyman of the election. She walked up Third Avenue, yanking out the ponytail holder in her hair then redoing it.

Maybe she didn't know how to run counterintelligence like her brother did. But Joy Delivered was her baby too, and she'd find a way to protect her business somehow. Fine, in the grand scheme of things, she wasn't saving the whales or solving world hunger. She was damn skilled, though, at selling pleasure, because she was a big believer in the power of intimacy, and its potential to do good. The world was a nasty, violent place, and if she could bring about happiness through more orgasms, then that was her small contribution. More pleasure instead of more cruelty. More bliss to blot out the urge to do harm. The world would be a better place if people made love, not war.

That's why this battle mattered to her.

She headed in the direction of Henry and Marquita's clubs. For a sliver of a second, she hoped she'd see Conroy, or maybe even his campaign manager, slipping out through the black unmarked door, furtively glancing side to side, trying desperately not to get caught having indulged in that particular predilection on a Saturday afternoon.

She laughed privately at that image. How fitting would that be? Also, how convenient. Life didn't work that way.

She wasn't going to catch Conroy with his pants down and a whip in his hand. No, that'd be too easy. That'd be the answer out of a TV script. Not real life.

As she walked away, she spotted a campaign flyer resting atop a trashcan. *For a better Upper East Side*. She stuck out her tongue at it, but then as she boarded a subway to head to her downtown apartment, an idea sparked.

This guy was all about the marketing. Maybe she couldn't dig up the dirt, but she could go toe to toe with anyone when it came to marketing.

* * *

"Are you sure I can't interest you two in a Long-Distance Lover?"

Julia directed the question to Michelle's brother and his wife, Jill.

"Because I'll need it to get through the next few weeks?" Davis asked.

"Of course. Think of it as sublimation for when your wife leaves town for a month," Julia said, that familiar playful tone in her voice as she handed him a scotch.

Michelle was at Speakeasy, the bar in midtown that Julia was part-owner of. Michelle didn't come around here too often, but her brother had asked her to join in a send-off round of drinks for Jill on Saturday afternoon. She was headed to London to rehearse for a limited run in a production of *A Streetcar Named Desire*, and Davis was staying behind to finish up his work directing a new Broadway show.

"If a drink can get me through that, I'll take ten," he said, then planted a long and lingering kiss on Jill's lips.

"Make that a double for me," Jill said when he pulled apart.

"The drink or the kiss?" Michelle asked, doing her best to fit in and be a part of the celebration. That task was all the more challenging since Clay was there too, looking as handsome as ever. He had on his Saturday attire—jeans, a button-down shirt, and an unshaven jaw. She winced, some part of her hurting for knowing these details, especially since his eyes were on Julia the whole time as she mixed another one of her signature cocktails for him. Michelle could still remember the night Julia first whipped up the Long-Distance Lover here at Speakeasy before it opened, during a late-night poker game. That was back before Julia had moved to New York from San Francisco, back when Michelle was dating Liam, back when she was still madly in love with Clay.

He hadn't even known how she felt about him. Julia had been the one to figure it out. That had made it all the more embarrassing.

Julia set down the drink for him, whispered something in his ear, then laughed, and gave the drink to Jill instead, who promptly declared it delicious.

"And what will you be serving me tonight?" Clay asked his wife.

She leaned in closer, and mouthed the word *myself.*

He raised an eyebrow appreciatively. "My favorite drink."

"But for now, a scotch," she said and poured the amber liquid in a glass for her husband.

Michelle waited for that familiar stabbing pain that came from watching them and their innuendo. A wince inside. An ache in her chest that hurt. But none of those feelings arrived on the scene. She felt nothing at all. *Thankfully.* That realization—of the lack of pain their interaction caused—was a rather lovely one.

Julia turned to Michelle, holding up the bottle in question. "Scotch for you, Michelle?"

"That'd be great," she said. Julia remembered her favorite drink too. She shouldn't be surprised. The woman was a bartender. It was her job to remember drinks. Still, Michelle was touched.

Julia handed her the drink, and said in a voice just for her, "I'm glad you're here. And incidentally, you have some kind of glow about you, so if you're using some new moisturizer, I need to know what it is. Your skin looks gorgeous."

Michelle smiled, then blushed. "Thank you," she said, and even though she hadn't seen Jack yet today, she knew exactly what Julia was referring to. Sex—great sex—was good for the complexion.

As she took her first drink, savoring the familiar burn of the scotch, she pictured Jack here with her. Would he fit in with her brother and his wife, with Clay and Julia? Would she even want him to? They'd only spent time alone together, never with anyone else. Their relationship—if you could even call it that—existed in a bubble of privacy and secrets. Of nights together and days apart. Would they even play well together with friends? With family? What did he wear on a Saturday afternoon? She imagined Jack sitting casually on the stool next to her, looking sexy as sin in a pullover shirt that showed off the slightest bit of his strong arms and jeans that fit him delectably. He'd drape an arm around her, unable to resist touching her, because he was like that. He'd chat with her brother about the theater and musical composers, he'd talk with Clay about his latest deal, he'd ask Jill if she'd always wanted to play Blanche, he'd ask Julia for a drink recommendation, and then he'd happily take what she served, his eyes on Michelle the entire time.

He'd fit in, she decided, and he'd be with her. Only her.

As she looked at her friends, she could see him there—part of the crew, but yet entirely *hers*.

A few minutes later, her phone buzzed.

J: How's your Saturday? Are you having a good day?

M: Great. Just hanging out with friends and family, having a drink.

J: Enjoy yourself, beautiful. Missing you. Will I see you soon?

M: Yes. Very soon.

She tucked her phone back into her purse.

"What have you been up to lately?" Jill asked her. "We haven't seen you around much."

The corner of Michelle's lips quirked up, but she tried to rein in her secret grin. "Oh, this and that," she said, and then the conversation turned again to London, and to Jill's show, and that was fine with Michelle as she listened to them chat.

When her eyes landed briefly on Clay, she saw him anew. She saw him as he was when she'd first met him. A friend. While she could certainly recognize he was good-looking, empirically so, he was no longer the man she pined after. She was seeing him, but she wasn't seeing *only* him anymore.

Somewhere inside of her, a heavy brick had been moved. A weight had been shifted. Her heart was no longer pinned down and foolishly handed over to someone who didn't care for all she had to give. It felt like hers again. And she could do with it what she wanted.

CHAPTER FOURTEEN

Peaches and Lace

The words dissolved on his tongue the second he saw her.

Page Six and the snarky comments were erased from his brain when he spotted her walking up Madison, big sunglasses over her eyes, a few strands of her brown hair whipping across her cheek from the late afternoon breeze. She moved her hand to brush them away, and the sight of her was breathtaking. She wasn't wearing a sexy outfit like yesterday at his office, when she'd arrived in heels, a pencil skirt, and a tight shirt. No, today she simply wore jeans, and a short-sleeved shirt, but she stunned him nonetheless. Everyone around him could have vanished—she was all he saw.

Walking toward him.

Waving.

Smiling.

Happy.

God, he didn't want to let her down.

He didn't want to let her go. He was a selfish bastard for wanting to keep her even when he could never give her what she deserved.

She stopped outside the store, her hand reaching toward him, fingering a bit of fabric from his pullover shirt. "Is this what you wore today?"

He eyed her curiously. "Yeah. It's not only what I wore, it's also what I'm wearing."

"It's what I pictured you in," she said, her lips curving up.

"You were thinking of me?" he asked, and his heart thumped harder.

"Yes," she said, nodding to the lingerie store where they'd met up. "Now buy me some panties to replace the ones you ruined yesterday."

Just hearing the word *panties* on her lips made him hard. He growled and tugged her in for a quick, searing kiss, her lips parting, her mouth opening as he made contact. He'd never tire of the way she responded to him. Then it hit him. *Never.* Why the hell was he thinking in absolutes?

He broke the kiss, clasped her hand, and led her into the store. Hetty's Secret Closet was a high-end lingerie store he'd walked past yesterday. Once inside, Manhattan disappeared, and they were in a pink and white boutique surrounded by silks, satins, and chiffons, by reds, blacks and peaches, and by a lavender scent that was overwhelmingly feminine. Soft music that sounded like Sade or some other sexy songstress piped overhead, and the air-conditioning hummed low, keeping the store cool, not too chilly.

Michelle perused the racks of camisoles, casting sexy eyes at him as she held up different items. He clenched his fists so he wouldn't pounce on her. He wanted her so much.

A saleswoman walked across the carpet, her steps so soft it was as if she was gliding. She was young, blond and pretty, and he didn't give a shit how she looked, because his arm was around Michelle's waist, and she was the only woman he wanted to see *in* a bra and panties, and *out* of a bra and panties.

"May I help you find something?" the saleswoman asked.

He didn't look away from Michelle as he answered. "I want something for this stunning woman I can't take my eyes off of," he said, and watched as a red flush spread across Michelle's cheeks.

"*Jack*," she whispered.

"It's true."

"A cami? A teddy? A lingerie set?"

"The last one," Jack said.

"Any particular color?"

He flashed back to the black pair he'd sliced off. The color truly didn't matter. He wanted to devour her in any color. He wanted to lick her from head to toe, to eat her, to taste every inch of her, whether she wore stripes or polka dots or solids.

"Anything," he said.

Soon, the saleswoman had selected a white demi-cup bra with matching panties, as well as one in peach, and one in dark blue.

"If you'd like to wait by the dressing rooms, we have a very comfortable chair outside them," the saleswoman said as she guided them to the back of the store. She unlocked one of the two rooms, holding open the beige scalloped door, and hanging the items on a hook. There was a full-length mirror in a gilded frame on the wall. "I'll check back in a few minutes and see if you need anything," she said, and then returned to the front of the boutique.

"Don't worry. I'll show you how it looks. Be a good boy and sit and wait," Michelle said, gesturing to the chair before she shut the door.

"Waiting is hard," he said in a low voice as he sank down into the soft cushiony chair.

"I bet it's hard," he heard her say from the dressing room, and she was so right. His dick was like steel, knocking against his fly, eager to be freed. He ached with wanting her; his mouth watered as he imagined her skimming off her jeans, tugging off her top, sliding on the lacy underthings.

He drew a deep breath, his lungs burning with desire for her.

The door creaked, and she peeked out. "Come see," she whispered, and in an instant, he was standing, walking, stepping into the tiny dressing room with a cushioned stool in the corner. She was hidden behind the door, and when she shut it, closing them into the small space, his heart tripped over itself.

She was so fucking beautiful. Peach lace hugged her curves, the tops of those luscious breasts luring him in like beacons of desire. He wanted to look everywhere at once, to touch all of her, to slam her against the wall and take her.

To savor her.

His eyes roamed her, landing on the underwear. A small section of white peeked out on the side. She must have left on a thong as she tried on the peach panties. "I had a feeling I'd be getting wet, so I left these on," she said, tugging at the side.

"Are you? Wet?"

She nodded as she licked her lips. "I am. With the way you look at me."

"I can't stop looking at you," he whispered, moving closer, running a hand down her bare arm, feeling goose bumps rise on her flesh. She gasped as he touched her. "Do you have any idea how beautiful you are?"

She shook her head as his fingers made their way to the soft flesh of her belly.

"You're so gorgeous. So stunning. I couldn't stop thinking of you today."

"What were you thinking?" she asked, her breath shallow as his hands moved down to her legs, mapping her thighs, both soft and strong.

"Everything. How much I love being with you. How beautiful you are. How much I'm looking forward to taking you to the symphony. Your ass. Your tits. Your belly. Your lips. How much I missed you, even though I knew I'd see you soon," he whispered, as he dropped down to his knees. "I find myself looking forward to the time with you and then missing you when you're not here."

She laughed softly. "You are dirty, and you are sophisticated at the same time. I've never known a man to say tits and ass and symphony in the same sentence," she said, and then he heard a sharp intake of breath as he pressed a kiss to her new underwear. He could smell her through the fabric, even through the layers. He wanted to bury his face in her, his lips, his tongue, his cock. He wanted to inhale her scent, to taste her arousal, to feel her flood his tongue. He kissed her harder through her panties, and in seconds her hands were in his hair, gripping strands. Her legs shook. Her nails cut into his skull. He groaned as he kissed her panties a final time, biting her gently through the material, drawing out a sharp gasp from her. Somehow he found the strength to stand up. He pressed his hands against the dressing room wall, caging her in. "Obviously, I'm getting these for you."

"Obviously."

"You're killing me," he said, as he looped a finger into the waistband, tracing his fingertips across her. "You're fucking killing me, and I love it."

"Me too," she said, her voice feathery and barely there. But he heard every sound in it. The sound of her desire that matched his.

"You've become a habit," he said as he moved to her neck, leaving a soft kiss against the hollow of her throat. He could feel her heart beating fast under her skin. As fast as his. "One I don't want to break."

"I don't want to either," she said, and he pulled back to look her in the eyes. They were vulnerable, so open to him, like the rest of her. It was so hard for him to hold back. So hard to protect her from him when he wanted her this much. He refocused on the sex. The part of them that was undeniable.

He turned her around so she was looking in the mirror, then looped his arm around her belly, and dipped his hand inside her panties. Her chest rose and fell and her eyes went hazy. "You have no idea how much I want to fuck you with my fingers right now," he said roughly in her ear, nibbling on her earlobe with his teeth as he glided his fingers across her wet pussy. "I want to slide my fingers inside you and watch your reflection as you come in this dressing room."

She met his gaze in the mirror, her lips parting on a muffled moan.

Then he stopped, removing his hand from her panties, a task that felt monumental given the way his dick was dying to break free. "But I want to wait. I want to see you at Lincoln Center in a fancy dress, knowing you have on this underwear, and I want to be tortured all night being next to you, thinking about how much I want to be making you come, so by the time I finally do it will be the only thing either of us wants in the world."

"It's all I want now already," she said.

He turned her around and devoured her lips, as he unhooked her bra, slid off the peach panties, and then told her he'd meet her at the front of the store.

He left the dressing room, but before the door closed, he pushed it open wider. "Oh, and Michelle?"

"Yes?"

"Don't touch yourself right now. I know you want to, but just don't."

She nodded. "I won't."

"Don't when you go home to change either," he told her, his voice firm. "Promise me you won't."

"I won't."

"And don't when you put on the gift I left for you with your doorman."

Her eyes widened. "You left a gift for me?"

"Yes. Wear it tonight."

CHAPTER FIFTEEN
Misbehave

The car waited at the curb outside her building.

In a crisp black suit and a matching cap, the driver held open the door. She slid into the backseat alone. The car was cool, the air-conditioning whirring softly. She needed the chill because of the warm September evening, and because she was sure she'd be burning up soon enough. Good thing she was meeting Jack at Lincoln Center. If he were in the car with her right now, she'd surely be pushing the partition button, rolling it up, and causing all sorts of trouble.

As delicious as that sounded, she wanted to arrive calm and still put together, rather than already in a fevered frenzy. Especially given what she was wearing. Under her cranberry-red dress, a silky number that hugged her curves, she wore the peach lingerie and Jack's gift.

When she'd opened the pretty black shopping bag at her apartment she wasn't surprised to find a white box with the silver J embossed on it. Still, the possibilities of what it might be thrilled her. She'd held the bag close in the elevator, holding onto her naughty secret, then tighter still as she walked down her hall until she reached 7E, where she lived. Once inside, she'd opened it with eager fingers, so damn curious and admittedly, already turned on, to see what he'd given her.

After showering, blow-drying her hair, and applying make-up, she'd put on the gift underneath her panties.

She'd never felt so sexy in her life, knowing he wanted her to wear it on their date.

Now, anticipation threaded through her, like a plume of smoke from a genie's lamp. A promise of wishes coming true. Of pleasure enveloping her. The driver pulled up at Lincoln Center and her gaze landed on the gorgeous fountain in the middle of the plaza, water shooting up in arcs, lit up like fireworks as the sprays cascaded. She'd been here many times for shows and events, but the fountain always awed her with its beauty.

The driver opened her door, and she grabbed her clutch purse, then she thanked him before he drove off. She gathered a bit of fabric from the dress in her hand so she could walk up the steps more easily, even as the toy rubbed against her from inside her panties. Her Louboutins clicked against the stones as she joined the sea of art lovers —men in tuxes and suits, women in formal dresses and gowns, milling about on a warm evening, waiting to see the ballet, to watch a play, to listen to the New York Philharmonic play a Brahms symphony.

She scanned the crowds for Jack, hunting out his dark hair, his chiseled jawline, his dark blue eyes, and his strong body. She'd know him anywhere, the feel of him, the shape of him, the cut of his shoulders, the trim lines of his waist. How his suits and shirts and pants hung on him so well.

But he was nowhere to be seen. She turned in a circle, laughing to herself because her twirl was timed to a string quartet playing several feet away. An older couple ambled past her, the woman with her hand clasped around the man's forearm. Across the plaza, couples and families made their way into the Vivian Beaumont Theater to see a Sondheim revival. On the other side of the fountain, a young woman in a form-fitting dress sat with a man in a suit who was making her laugh.

Michelle looked once more for Jack, checking her watch. He said to meet her at 7:50 at the fountain, and it was 7:51. Jack was an on-time kind of guy. Most military, active or not, were pretty damn punctual, so she was surprised.

Then her breath hitched, and she clasped her hands over her belly, as if that would somehow hide her reaction. She did her best to stay still even as the silent vibrations sped up ever so briefly between her legs. Holy hell, this wearable butterfly was stronger than she'd expected.

As quickly as it started, the sensation stopped, fading away in an instant.

Michelle surveyed the plaza again, making a quick lap around the fountain, but Jack was still not in sight. She wanted to see him and wanted him to know that one quick burst of pleasure from the remote control was already working, ratcheting up her longing for him. But she could only wait until he appeared or did it again. She walked through the crowds to the middle of the plaza, weaving through the throngs of people when the rattling began anew. She nearly stopped in her tracks because the pleasure was so intense, the quick hit of buzzing on her most sensitive spot from the butterfly inside her panties.

A flurry of tingles ignited in her belly, spreading rapidly through her chest.

The buzzing grew stronger, and the intensity of the vibration was centered completely on her clitoris. She drew another sharp, silent breath, swallowed and turned around, coming face to face with a wickedly grinning Jack Sullivan. The man was beautiful—so stunning in a tailored suit that fit him like a dream, a crisp white shirt, and a thin black tie that she wanted to grab, and use to tug him close to her. But she didn't dare move. He was a man who cherished control, and since he did so many amazing things to her with it, she'd let him keep having it. That was the bargain, and it was a fair trade, because she trusted him with her pleasure. He loved to give it, but he also loved to control it. She could handle her half of that deal.

He held up his right hand, pressed on something with his thumb and flashed a satisfied smile. As soon as he hit the device in his hand, the buzzing stopped. She missed it; she wanted to grab hold of the remote, and bring that feeling back before it escaped her.

"I'm so sorry to have made you wait," he murmured, dusting her cheek with his lips. He barely left an imprint; it was the softest, faintest kiss he'd ever given her and it made her crave so much more. It was a teaser kiss, a hint of what was to come.

"I didn't mind waiting," she said, raising an eyebrow, letting him know she could play along.

"Good. The philharmonic is going to start soon, but they have this great string quartet that plays rock songs in the plaza before the symphony begins. Dance with me."

"Of course," she said, placing her hands on his shoulders as he brought her in close. His right hand was curled in a fist over her shoulder. The string quartet began playing "We Are Young" by Fun, and the upbeat anthem was in stark contrast to how she felt inside—like a torch-song was being sung by her body. A song of longing.

"You look stunning. Are you wearing the peach panties?"

"Yes.

"Anything else?"

"What do you think?" she countered, her blood still racing with the anticipation of when he'd hit the remote again and send a fresh rush of hot, fast vibration between her legs. He gave new meaning to the term "having the keys to her body."

"What do you think about this September weather we're having?" he asked, and it began again. The humming was faint this time. A low pulse, a flickering against her, like a teasing promise.

The pop song grew louder, nearing the chorus. She was grateful for the background noise. Perhaps it masked all she felt in her body. "It is quite hot for late September," she said, and they weren't talking about the weather.

"Fall is one of my favorite times of year in Manhattan," he said, in a casual, offhand voice, as if he were musing on the vagaries of the sun and moon and stars.

"Me too," she said, keeping her voice as steady as she possibly could, even as the pressure increased. She hadn't realized he'd turned it up, so subtle was his touch against the tiny remote in his hand.

"And fall colors? The red, and gold and oranges," he said, as he spun her in a circle, holding only her right hand. She felt terribly vulnerable, as if the world around her, the fancy crowds, the rich patrons, and the glitterati of Manhattan knew what he was doing to her. But they couldn't, could they? She kept her face stony even as she wanted to unleash a guttural moan of primal pleasure. "They'll be coming soon," he added, returning her to his arms.

"Will they?" she asked in a ragged voice. Her bones felt liquid. Her body was electric as the vibrator thrummed against her wet, hot center. She wasn't far off now. She was dying to throw her arms around him, to rub up against him, to yank him into a dark corner and let him have his way completely.

"Or maybe they won't. Maybe they'll come later," he said, a devilish glint in his eyes, as he pressed down in his hand.

The vibrations stopped, and she nearly stumbled into him. Michelle wanted to curse him. She'd been so close. She was hovering now, but she wasn't going over the edge.

She grabbed his jacket. "You cruel bastard," she said, through narrowed eyes. She didn't mean it as an insult.

He reached for her hand, threaded his fingers through hers, and guided her inside Avery Fisher Hall, the bells inside sounding that it was time for audience to find their seats.

"Did you enjoy 'We are Young'?" Jack asked, as he led her to the balcony seats on the right side of the expansive auditorium. The hall was a rich, warm brown with soft lights that cast an inviting feel across the seats, almost creating an afternoon glow. What sounded like Mozart piped overhead as patrons took their places.

"I did. Very clever to play pop songs like that."

As she sat down, Jack planted a kiss on her cheek. "I'm terribly cruel, I know," he whispered, addressing her earlier comment.

"You are the worst."

"You're not going to leave me, are you?" he said, flashing his winning smile.

Eventually, she wanted to say. *Isn't that the plan after thirty nights? To leave each other?* Instead, she kept up the game. "Not yet."

His expression turned serious as he ran his finger down her cheek, as if he was unable to resist touching her. "By the way, I wanted to let you know you were mentioned on *Page Six* with me," he said, and she shot him a curious look. He dug his phone from his pocket and showed her an item from the tabloid, citing her by name. She read it, taking her time as she let the commentary about their "intimate pleasures" sink in. It was oddly surreal, and a bit disconnected. But then, that made perfect sense—she was being written about without being truly known.

"Wow. I think the only other time I've been in the papers is when I attended the Tonys with my brother a few years ago," she said, still a bit shell-shocked to be thrust into the limelight like this.

"I'm sorry. I hate that they made some sort of insinuation," he said, seeming contrite.

She flashed back to her conversation at her consulting group with Carla, who'd been spotted seeing *It's Raining Men*, then to her own comments about having a life. "Look, it's not as if we were caught on-camera fucking," Michelle said in a whisper.

He laughed. "And there were plenty of chances to catch that."

"We just need to be careful," shc added. She wanted to believe that she was allowed to have a life, to date, to even be seen out and about with a man in the public eye. She was a human being. She couldn't live in a bubble, and it made no sense to pretend she had no life. "I'm not a nun. I'm simply a shrink. It's fine. I'm allowed to date. Besides, we aren't a secret. Our affair might be private, but we were never sneaking around. We've always gone to dinner and to bars and for walks. We're adults, living in Manhattan. Remember the first night we had dinner?"

"Yes."

"A picture showed up on Twitter a few days later. My friend Sutton noticed it."

"When you said I had fans?"

"Yes. I guess the fact is there are a lot of women in this city who want to fuck you, Jack Sullivan," she said with a wink, tugging on his tie and pulling him closer.

"But there's only one who is. And there's only one I want to fuck," he said, his voice low and husky in her ear.

"Good. I like it that way."

"That's the only way for me," he said, then pulled back to look her in the eyes. "Are you sure it doesn't bother you?" he asked, serious once more.

She shrugged. "It's not that bad a piece. We were only at dinner, and the rest is the columnist making a joke. So truly, I can't let it get to me." If she stopped buying cereal at Trader Joe's, or going out to dinner, or skipping the theater, she'd be less human. And to do her job—which was her passion, her love, her soul—she needed and wanted to be fully involved in the world around her. To be a part of it. To live. To love. To feel.

He smiled and fingered a strand of her hair. "Do you have any idea how nice it is to be involved with a shrink? You don't overreact to things."

She laughed. "I still have emotions, Jack. Being a psychologist doesn't mean I'm devoid of them, or that I can manage them properly all the time. Sometimes, I can misbehave horribly."

Just then the lights flashed, and the orchestra took the stage, the virtuoso musicians settling into their chairs, ready to launch into Brahms *Fourth Symphony.*

"I can misbehave too," he said, mischief skipping across his blue eyes.

She drew a sharp breath, expecting him to brandish his remote and send pleasure shooting straight into her core.

But he didn't. Instead, he took her hand, and turned his attention to the stage to watch, and listen. She enjoyed the music too, feeling it wrap its way around her, slink into her mind and body as the sound of the flutes soared through the cavernous hall. But she was waiting, too, tense, hoping to feel that pleasure again.

As the violinists picked up their bows, her eyes widened, and she gripped the arm of her chair. He'd turned it back on, and he'd turned it to high. She held her breath as she let herself adjust to the intensity of the vibrations between her legs, but soon he lowered the pressure, letting it buzz against her at the lowest level, a faint but still-present sensation, as if he were gently rubbing his fingertip against her clit. Like they were lying on her couch, watching a movie, and he'd decided to dip a hand inside her panties and absently stroke her while staring at the screen.

That was how it felt. Enough pleasure to send her body into a heightened awareness, a craving for more. But not enough to satiate her. Not enough at all. She wanted more, and as the bassoons joined in she was about to beg for it, to tap him on the shoulder and ask him to turn it up and get her all the way off. But this man could read her perfectly. He glanced over, and she was sure he was taking in her expression as she tried valiantly to not show the world that she wanted him to make her come in her panties at Avery Fisher Hall.

He dialed it up once more, and she crossed her legs, the pressure from her thighs intensifying the feelings flooding her. He eyed her with a pleased look, nodding at her crossed legs as if to say *smart thinking*. The Allegro non troppo crested, more instruments joining in, playing, building, mirroring the pulsing in her body. Jack grabbed her hand, brought it to his mouth and kissed her as if he had to touch her while he was doing this.

She gasped, and her noise of pleasure made landfall at a brief pause in the score. She was sure someone had heard her, and she dropped her gaze down, embarrassed momentarily. Here she was, seated in the balcony of a concert hall, desperate for an orgasm.

He leaned in. "No one heard you. Tell me if you want me to let you come."

"Yes."

"Are you sure? Do you want to wait until I can fuck you in bed? So you can scream and moan like you want to?"

"I want that," she whispered in a barren voice. "But I want to come now."

"You're so turned on, aren't you?"

He sounded as if he wanted to pounce on her.

"Yes. I'm unbelievably turned on," she whispered, her voice sounding like she might very well cry if he didn't take care of her.

"You must be so wet."

"I am."

"You should hold back. Can you hold back until later?"

She clenched her teeth. She knew what he was doing now. He was playing her. He wanted her to be strong. To say she could handle it. If she used reverse psychology and told him she could wait, then he'd probably let her come. As a reward. But the game was exhausting her right now. She wanted him. Without games. For real. She told him the full truth. "No. I can't wait."

"But I want you to," he whispered. "I want you to wait for me."

He turned off the toy, and she wanted to wither. To die. She thought she might claw her way out of her own skin right now. To climb the walls of Avery Fisher Hall. Anything to release this desire from her body. She hated that she was encased in it. That she'd been reduced to nothing but *this*.

It was so base. So animalistic. But at the moment, she was no longer a professional, no longer an evolved being. She was a fucking animal, and she wanted to be satisfied. And the bastard wasn't letting her. She inhaled quietly. The orchestra played, shifting to the second movement. Everyone listened. The minutes ticked by. Jack's fingers uncurled. He no longer had a tight grip on the remote. He was focused on the stage, and he was nodding his head, keeping in time to the music. He stuffed the remote in his pocket, then returned his hands to his lap. He wasn't even touching her. He wasn't even thinking of her. He'd asked her to wear a goddamn butterfly to the symphony and she'd done it for him. She'd let him turn her up and turn her down wherever and however he pleased. And now he was bored with her. Interested in something else. She was nothing but a plaything, and the worst part was she was still aroused.

She was mad, too. She didn't want to play this game right now. It had gone far enough.

She tapped him on the shoulder. "I'm going to go. Good night."

She stood up, and walked out quickly, pushing on the door that led out of the auditorium and into the quiet hallway.

In seconds, he'd followed her, catching up to her. Only an usher at the far end of the hallway noticed them.

"Michelle," he said, grasping for her wrist. "Are you okay?"

"No," she said, not bothering to mask it or hide it. "I'm not okay."

"What's wrong?" His brow furrowed, the look in his eyes one of confusion.

She parked her hands on her hips. "Sometimes games work, and sometimes they don't. It didn't this time." She held up a hand. "Don't turn it on again."

"I won't," he said, like a boy scolded.

She stepped closer, speaking in a low voice for only him. They'd had their picture in the paper. She didn't need anyone to hear this conversation. "You know I love what you do to me. But you took it too far in there."

"Because it's public?"

"No."

"Then why?"

"Because I wanted you to finish," she seethed. "I don't care if that makes me petty or foolish or stupid. I don't care if that makes me greedy. I didn't want to play. And then you stopped, and I was just squirming in my fucking seat. You were wrapped up in the music, and it was like you'd forgotten what you'd done to me. And I'm sorry if I sound like a selfish horny bitch for wanting you to have finished me. But that's what I wanted."

The corner of his lips quirked up for a second, but then he stopped, adopting a serious look when she narrowed her eyes at him. "I thought it was all part of the fun we were having," he said.

"It is fun. To a point. And then it stops being fun when you don't even realize the effect you have on me. Physically. Mentally. Every way. You asked me if I could wait, and I said no. I was completely honest with you, and you just toyed with me," she said through gritted teeth, grabbing his tie, pulling him close. "Don't you get it? You turn me on and you build me up and you control me and I let you. Because I love it, too. Because I love what you do to me. But sometimes I don't want to be toyed with. I want to be taken care of. Even if it's in the symphony."

His chest rose and fell. He breathed out hard. He didn't speak. Maybe she'd gone too far. But she was okay with that. She knew how to live alone. To survive alone. If she lost Jack because of this, then she'd be fine with it.

CHAPTER SIXTEEN
Fall Apart

He was certain.

He'd never been more stripped bare or turned on in his life. He'd never had a woman call him on something like this, and forcefully tell him to not toy with her. To be blunt and direct and to say *make me come*. Maybe he had pushed it. Maybe he'd gone too far with the game. He was going to go all the way right now.

He grabbed her and crushed her mouth to his, and she resisted at first, pushing her fists into his chest, trying to shove him away. But he wasn't going to let her go. He kissed her harder until she gave in, melding into him, her lips fused with his, their bodies sealed tight. Kissing in a mad frenzy of anger and frustration until he pulled apart. "Screw Brahms. I need to take care of you right now."

Fifteen minutes later, they were at his building. They were grappling at clothes in the elevator. His shirt was unbuttoned, untucked, and his tie was simply gone. Hell, maybe it was on the floor of the elevator. Maybe it was in the cab. He didn't care. Her dress was at her waist, and he yanked down her panties, then ripped off the butterfly. He'd already fingered her to orgasm in the cab. He owed her so much more.

"I'm sorry," he muttered harshly. "I'm sorry I didn't let you come. I need to make you come all night to make up for it."

"You do," she said, as he balled up the panties in one hand. "The cab wasn't enough to satisfy me."

The elevator slowed at the top floor, the doors spreading open. They spilled out, and he grabbed at her, pushing up her dress higher, as they stumbled down the hall, drunk on desire. Clutching at his shirt collar, she pulled him in, kissing him hard and deeply, biting his lip. He groaned, letting her know he wanted that kind of touch from her.

"When can I fuck you without a condom? I'm clean," he said when they reached his door.

"Me too. I'm on the pill."

"Let's get inside," he told her, fumbling in his pocket for his key and unlocking his door. Once inside he dropped her panties and the butterfly. Then he scooped her up, carried her to the couch in front of the floor-to-ceiling windows, and gently placed her on the cushion. The softness stopped then as he spread her legs roughly, opening them wide. He felt like his entire body was on fire as he stared hungrily at her. Her cunt was a sight to behold. So ready for him in every way. He thrust a finger inside her tight, wet heat. She shrieked and threw her head back.

"That's right. Now you can be as loud as you want. Let it out. Tell me how much you hated it when I made you wait."

"I hated it," she cried out as he added another finger, the wetness coating him instantly. He took a deep fueling breath as he crooked his finger inside her, hitting the spot within her that drove her wild. Made her writhe. Widen her legs.

"And me. You hated me for toying with you," he added, dropping down to his knees.

"So much," she moaned, her breathing harsh and heavy.

"You'll forgive me now. I've made you so wet, haven't I?"

"Yes. God, yes," she said, opening her eyes and grabbing his face hard with one hand. Rough. Grasping his chin. Making him stare in her eyes as he finger-fucked her. "You turn me on so much. Don't you understand? Sometimes I just need to be touched. I need you, Jack. I need you to touch me, and taste me, and fuck me," she said, and she was firm but so damn open and honest at the same time. Laying out her wants. Making everything clear. There was no uncertainty in how she spoke to him, and he absolutely loved her directness.

"You're a fucking wet mess and I love it," he said, then he spread her legs and dived in, lapping her up, licking, tasting and kissing her like a hungry man, like it would be the last time he'd taste her in his life.

Instantly, she gripped his hair and arched into him. "You better not stop now, Jack Sullivan," she said on a moan. "I mean it."

She arched and writhed into him, rocking into his face, grabbing his hair, moaning and groaning and panting with every touch. His dick throbbed in his pants, and his own want thundered through him forcefully, like a hurricane. My God, she was divine. She was the embodiment of passion, the manifestation of pure sensuality. Never had a woman taken such fierce ownership of her own sexuality in front of him before, and it allured him like nothing ever had. Everything about her was an elixir, from the delicious taste of her, sexy and musky, to the sounds she made, to her sharp nails digging into his skull. She curled her hands around his head, grasping him, so there was no room between his face and her pussy. He didn't need any room. He wanted to bury his face in her. He didn't even need to use hands or fingers or a toy because seconds after he'd started, her hips were shooting off the couch, her hands gripping the edge of the furniture, and she was bucking into his face.

"I'm coming so fucking hard," she screamed, as he licked her mercilessly, not stopping, not wanting to, as her orgasm flooded his tongue and he tasted her heat. He gripped her ass, pulling her even tighter as he kissed her until she wriggled, so sensitive from the orgasm ebbing away.

When he looked up, her hand was flung over her face, her chest rising and falling heavily, and her dress was twisted in a bunch at her belly.

"I'm not done eating you," he said, as he rose, reaching for her dress, tugging it over her head, revealing the peach bra he'd bought for her. The material was nearly see-through. Her nipples were hard diamond points pushing against the fabric. Reaching behind her back, he unhooked the bra, letting it fall to the couch. She was naked now, except for those shoes. Those black pumps that made her look like pure sex. As he stripped she stood, rising up only to push him down on his back once he was naked.

His whole body groaned with need for her. He held her perfect ass in his hands, running his fingers along her cheeks as she ground her pussy into his face. He could barely breathe and he savored it, the feel of her rocking into him once more as she went to town on his cock. She didn't tease, she didn't toy, she took him all the way in and lavished her tongue all over him, as heat scorched a path through his chest. All the blood rushed to his cock, thick in her mouth. She rode his face, and he drove into her mouth, and they were nothing but animals now. Powered only by the need to get off, the need to please and be pleased, to fuck and to come, to have it rough and hard and fast. She drew him in deeper, the head of his dick hitting the base of her throat, and a blast of heat roared through his veins. He could feel his body hit that point, like an engine turning over. Soon, he'd be seconds away from the point of no return.

That wouldn't do.

He pushed her off him and it pained him when her mouth broke contact with his erection. "Window. Now. Your hands up against the glass."

She nodded, her eyes as wild as his, her breath fast, a bead of sweat sliding between her gorgeous breasts.

She moved to the window that overlooked Central Park, bathed in the dark of nighttime and shadows, the treetops barely visible. Down below, Fifth Avenue snaked by, a strip of cabs and sleek cars, and across the street he saw other New Yorkers enjoying the night.

But not as much as he was.

He spread her cheeks, ran his fingers through her slick pussy, and then shoved into her. No waiting. He needed her as much as she needed him. She felt amazing like this, skin against skin.

He palmed her breasts as he thrust into her. "Michelle," he moaned, the pleasure prowling through him. "You feel so fucking good like this."

"I love this," she said, arching her back in an invitation for him to sink his teeth into her shoulder. She yelped, but didn't pull away.

He pumped deeper, harder. "I want to come inside you so badly."

"Do it."

He shook his head, grabbing a breast harder in his hand, then sliding his other between her legs. "No. You need to come again. I've barely started with you. Don't hold back. Don't stop. Come whenever you feel like it."

"I'm so glad I have your permission," she said with a laugh, and he loved that she'd made a joke in the middle of this heated moment.

He rubbed her clit faster, feeling it swell more under his fingers, feeling her grow hotter against his dick as he pushed into her. "Everything about you," he said, his breath coming hard and fast. "Everything about you is perfect for me."

She moaned his name, and nothing had ever turned him on more than this woman, and how she was with him. Their chemistry staggered him. It stole his breath and threatened to annihilate his heart. She was designed for him; and he was made for her. They were meant to be together like this. To connect in this primal and beautiful way. To share in this kind of intimacy.

"God, I love it when you come. I love making you feel good. I love when you fall apart for me," he said.

"Then tell me how much you want me," she said.

Blood pounded in his head. Breath ripped out of his lungs. He gripped her tighter. "I can't stop thinking about you. I think about you all the time," he said, driving in farther.

"Yes. That," she panted, and rolled her hips back into him, her movements telling him she wanted everything he gave her.

"I can't get enough of you. The more I have of you, the more I want."

"Oh God," she said, crying out, throwing her head back, and shouting that she was there.

And as she screamed her pleasure louder than he'd ever heard her, he pumped through it, until his orgasm plowed through his body, obliterating everything else in its path, but the intensity of coming inside her. No barriers, nothing held back. Nothing but him with the woman he needed.

And wanted.

And craved.

His words from moments ago echoed in his mind. *Fall apart for me.* If he didn't watch out, he'd be the one falling apart for her. In every way.

CHAPTER SEVENTEEN
Perceptions

Shayla could barely meet her eyes. She kept snickering and looking away. She'd been like this for the whole session, and Michelle was getting frustrated. Normally, Shayla was a challenge only because she struggled to see her own role in her troubled marriage. But never because she was a laughing bean.

Michelle decided it was time to refocus her patient on the serious nature of the hurdles she was trying to overcome. In the last few sessions, Shayla had finally begun coming to terms with the possibility that she was going to leave her husband. She'd even started talking to an attorney quietly, being cautious to make sure her husband didn't know she was making plans. While it wasn't Michelle's job to advise her on divorce proceedings, it was very much her role to help Shayla out of the marriage with her sanity and her soul intact.

"Are you still feeling that you're on the right track with the potential separation?"

"I think so," Shayla said, but then stared pointedly at her silver Tiffany bracelet and began fidgeting with it. She'd never been a fidgeter.

"Are you sure? Are you having second thoughts?" If she wasn't ready to leave him, then Michelle didn't want to push her.

Shayla shook her head, her curls bouncing with the movement. But she didn't look up.

Enough.

Michelle cleared her throat. "Is there a reason you won't look me in the eyes?"

Shayla snapped up her gaze. "Because all I can see is The Lola now," she blurted out.

The Lola?

Then it hit her, and her head felt like it was swimming, and her vision went blurry. *Please no. Please God no.* She'd hoped there weren't pictures of him using that on her. They'd been on top of the Met Life Tower. Alone. Had his friend at the hotel tipped someone off? But that was weeks ago. There was no way someone had seen or caught that on camera, right?

"What do you mean?" she asked carefully.

Shayla shook her head and took a deep breath, then words spilled out in a wild rush. "I'm so sorry, but you've taught me to be direct, you've taught me to speak my mind, and I can't hold back anymore. I know this is personal, but all I can think about now is how he must use all these toys on you. The One, The Dream, The Lola. I have them all. I'm in a loveless marriage; I need my BOBs. And now you're dating him. It's all I can see when I look at you now, and if I don't acknowledge it, it's all I will ever see. So

I just have to get it out there," Shayla said, her eyes wide with her confessional, her hands slicing the air.

Michelle felt as if she'd been walloped. Smacked with a pillowcase full of bricks. She nodded curtly, accepting all that Shayla had dropped in her lap. Lines were being crossed left and right, up and down, as her personal and professional life collided in an unexpected zigzag. She'd counseled patients through emotional crises, through breakdowns, through divorce, death and love unreturned. But knowing what to say next and how to handle Shayla's TMI about *her* was one of the toughest challenges she'd ever faced.

She latched onto Carla's words about refocusing the patient. She flashed back to all her coursework on how to manage over-interest in the therapist. But this was such a messy stew.

Even so, she had to wade through it. Step by step. First, address the issue professionally.

"I take it you're referring to the *Page Six* item over the weekend about the man that I'm dating?" she asked, deliberately not using his name. A patient didn't need to refer to her lover by his name, after all.

"Well. Yeah. And that picture of you guys dancing at Lincoln Center that showed up this morning on *Page Six*."

That was news to her.

Michelle dug her fingers into her palms, and told herself it was all going to be fine. She'd been in sessions all day and prepping for Paris. She hadn't been online, and hadn't checked her work or her personal email either. And while she felt a small ounce of relief that the photo that had appeared was one of them dancing outside, rather than of them inside on the balcony, she was still bothered that the gossip rags were following them at all. Weren't there far more interesting people to photograph than her and Jack, even if he'd been deemed New York's most eligible bachelor?

"And does it bother you to see my photo online?" Michelle managed to ask, concentrating on her client, not on her own reaction to being in the tabloids.

"It's weird," Shayla said loudly. "It's completely bizarre. Honestly, I've always thought of you as a blank slate. Someone who existed in the little framework of this office." She gestured to the four walls.

"And now you realize I'm both a therapist and a human being."

Shayla nodded. "Yep."

Michelle took a breath, clasped her hands, and addressed the elephant in the room once more. "So, here's the deal. I'm a human being. I date. I see plays and movies. I have a brother, and I have good friends. I like to go out to dinner. I like to try new restaurants. I enjoy fall in New York City, and I'd like to have a dog someday. There you go. That's me. I'm not a blank slate. I've never been a blank slate," she said, pausing to gauge Shayla's reaction. Her client's eyes were fixed firmly on Michelle. Good. "But the time we spend together is not about me. It's about you. And I'm not going to address any specifics of my dating life. I do, however, want to keep working with you and helping you sort out the matters that are most important to you," she said, her voice clear and direct. This was how things would be done. Take it or leave it. "Can you keep doing that?"

Shayla gulped and nodded. Red bloomed across her cheeks, and her eyes turned watery. "Yes," she squeaked out. Then, she chased it with a choppy, "I'm sorry."

"It's okay," Michelle said softly. "Truly, it's fine. I'm here to help you, though, and I want nothing more than to do just that."

"Thank you. I'm just so scattered and emotional with the divorce pending," she said, and they returned to what mattered most during the fifty minutes they had together.

Later that morning, Clark Davidson arrived for his appointment, dressed sharply in a suit. Michelle suspected he was a high-powered businessman, fitting this in during his day. Quickly, they dived into the marital challenges that had brought him here.

"It's as if any true intimacy has died. My wife and I don't have that authentic connection anymore," he said, and his words made the hair on her arms stand on end. She'd written a paper for a journal that used those terms. *True intimacy* and *authentic connection*. They weren't trademarked or coined by her, nor were they unusual words. But they weren't often used by her patients. It was as if he was quoting her back to her. "I read that in one of your papers," he added, flashing her a grin.

She breathed a sigh of relief and smiled that he was so open about it. It all made sense. "I hope it was useful."

"Very much so. I hope you don't mind, but I read a bit of your research before I made the appointment. That's my field. I'm a market researcher, so it's sort of a natural habit for me. And I was impressed, so that's why I had wanted to see you," he said, fiddling with the wedding band on his left finger.

"And I'm glad you found me," she said, and privately she was grateful that all he seemed to care about were her professional credentials, not her personal track record in bed. "Let's talk some about why you feel true intimacy has died. Can you give me an example?"

He nodded several times and exhaled heavily, as if what he was about to say would be hard. "I feel like Sarah doesn't want to have sex anymore. The other night I was —"

He hacked sharply. A loud, bark of a cough. Then came another. His hand flew to cover his mouth, and he coughed once more, like a wheezing trombone. His cheeks began turning red.

Michelle sprang up. "Let me get you some water," she said, and quickly headed to the door, then down the hall to the small kitchen tucked in a corner of the office suite. She opened the fridge to grab a water bottle, but it was empty. Crap. They'd need to replenish the supply. She swiveled around, spotted a clean mug from the cupboard, filled it from the tap, and returned to her office, the sound of wheezing like a homing beacon guiding her back. She handed him the cup, and he gulped most of the water down greedily. Then he took a deep breath, and finished it off.

"You okay now?" she asked gently.

He nodded.

"Do you want more?"

He peered in the cup and tossed the rest of it back. "I think I'm better now. That was embarrassing. I'm so sorry."

"Please don't apologize for coughing. Shall we go back to your concerns about true intimacy?"

They chatted more, and as he shared his concerns about the lack of sex with his wife, she felt a strange sense of déjà vu. She flashed back to her last session with Shayla. The problems mirrored Shayla's challenges. Shayla had even said before that her husband had a paranoid side. Could he be so worried about trying to keep her that he was infiltrating her therapist to try to learn what sort of advice Shayla was getting? Could this man actually be Shayla's husband? With a fake name?

No, she sharply admonished herself. Plenty of couples had marital woes and there was no need for her to jump to any conclusions, and assume Shayla's hubby was here under false pretenses.

She had no true evidence that he was a fraud, so she mentally talked herself down. For now she had to treat him as she would anyone else. Besides, he seemed open to some of her suggestions about reconnecting with his wife, so she recommended a book for him that she thought might be helpful. "I don't have a copy to loan you, but perhaps you could check it out on Amazon or your bookstore," she said, and he grabbed a pen and small notebook from inside his jacket.

He spread the notebook open on the ottoman in front of him, then dipped his hand into his pocket once more and pushed on a pair of glasses. "Can't see a damn thing up close without these on," he said, then wrote down the name she gave him, folded up the paper and removed his glasses once more. She caught the briefest glimpse of him with the glasses on—thick and black—and it was as if she'd been shot back to the night she went to Gia's with Jack. The man she'd bumped into outside her building had worn glasses like that—thick and black. He'd had dark hair too, but it was longer, wasn't it? The memory was far too fuzzy, and that's all she could latch onto. It had been such a lightning-fast encounter that more than two weeks later she couldn't recall any more details.

And really, what were the chances that this man was the same guy? Even if she had bumped into Clark, maybe he'd just been doing his research and scoping out the building before the appointment, to get the lay of the land. A lot of patients did that. That was normal. Plus, he'd said he was a market researcher, so it would make sense that he'd checked things out in advance.

But after he left, she couldn't shake the feeling that something was amiss. Perhaps it was simply this day. Perhaps it was a side effect of Shayla's nosiness. Lately, she'd been feeling like others knew things about her before she learned them. And she didn't like being in that position.

She didn't have another session for an hour, so she locked her door. She never locked her door. But then, she was about to do something she rarely did. She was going to Google a patient. She'd made it a point not to search out her patients online—what mattered was what they shared in her time with them. Still, Clark Davidson had left her feeling unsettled, no matter how hard she tried to apply logic to the situation. She flipped open her laptop, and plugged his name into Google.

She found a Clark Davidson who was a realtor. A Clark Davidson who was a sales manager at an advertising technology company. And a Clark Davidson who was a lawyer. But none were market researchers. And none of the images that returned matched the man who'd been in her office.

She dropped Shayla's name into Google next, but very little turned up about her that Michelle didn't already know. Where she went to college. Her brief time working at an art gallery. Some of her charitable donations. She moved onto Facebook next, even though she didn't have a Facebook profile for herself, and had never felt any need to. Dropping Shayla's name into the search bar on the social site made her feel dirty. She felt even seedier when she spotted the icon for *photos* on Shayla's profile. But they were set to private.

Michelle closed the browser, disgusted with herself, and grateful that she'd been stopped from going too far. The tabloids were already invading her personal life; she didn't need to start doing that to a client. It would simply be wrong.

Perhaps Clark was just a troubled man who needed help. Not someone who'd studied up on her more than she would have liked. She hopped over to her work email, and smiled broadly when she read a note from her Paris contact, Julien, about how much they were looking forward to her talk.

She was excited for the trip too. The only problem was she'd miss Jack terribly during those five days she'd be away. Especially after she took her phone from the desk drawer and clicked open a new note from him.

from: justjack@gmail.com
to: michellewithtwols@gmail.com
date: Sept 22, 11:47 AM
subject: You

Hi. You might have seen the picture of us dancing at Lincoln Center. We're online again on *Page Six*. I know this is probably more than you bargained for the night we met. I guess I'm just used to it now. The press has been fascinated with my dating, or non-dating, as the case was until I met you. I suspect it will all blow over soon, and they'll move on to someone else in this city. I hope you don't mind, though, when I say that I can't stop looking at this picture of you in my arms. It captured that moment so perfectly and everything I see when I look at you—you are so beautiful and in this photo you look simply incandescent. I am going to miss you when I go to California later this week.

She closed her eyes and let that gorgeous word wash over her. *Incandescent.* Who said things like that? Who used that kind of an adjective? Only a man like Jack. A man who loved the symphony, and who loved her ass. A man who was refined on the outside, and filthy on the inside. Her lips curved up in a naughty grin as she lingered on her dirty, sexy, sophisticated man. When she opened her eyes, she searched out the photo of the two of them, quickly reading the caption. *Sob, sob. Looks like things are getting serious with the sex toy mogul and the shrink. They were spotted dancing outside Lincoln Center Saturday night. They look so happy together we want to cry. Don't tell us you're off the market, Jack!*

She beamed in spite of being in the public eye once more. She beamed because Jack was right. She did look incandescent. Because she was looking at him. She didn't see what everyone else saw. She didn't see a sex toy mogul and a shrink. She saw a man and a woman, dancing, gazing, holding.

That's what she saw.

Surely, that's all anyone could see.

* * *

But her good mood from Jack's letter didn't last. Because there was a knock on her door later that afternoon, and Kana popped in.

"Hey. How's it going?" Michelle asked.

"Great. May I sit down?"

She gestured to the couch. "Lie down and tell me about your mother," she joked, and Kana laughed, but the laughter quickly faded.

"So, you're seeing that guy you sent to me?"

"Whoa," Michelle said, holding up her hands. "Does everyone read *Page Six*?"

Kana crinkled her brow. "Um. Yeah. I love that site. I'm addicted, like half of Manhattan," she said, brushing her black hair away from her face. "Anyway, I just wanted to make sure he was never your patient. You said he was a friend the day you referred him to me."

She shook her head. "He was never my client."

"Good. Because you're one of the best, and I just want to make sure you weren't leaving yourself open to an ethics investigation."

"No. God, no. I swear," she said, and dropped her head in her hands in frustration. Then she lifted her head and met Kana's gaze straight on. Her colleague was simply concerned, that was all. And Michelle owed her the facts, given that Kana was involved, in a way, now. "I met him the night before. I didn't know he was scheduled to see me. We hit it off and as soon as we both realized he had an appointment, I marched him down to see you. I haven't crossed any professional lines."

"Good. I'm just looking out for you. Besides, I wouldn't want to have to report you," Kana said in a deadpan voice. But when Michelle stared at her without cracking a smile, Kana quickly added, "I'm kidding. I'm totally kidding," then laughed to emphasize her point.

But Michelle didn't reciprocate. Even though she knew she was 100 percent above board on that count, the notion that someone else might question her ethics sickened her.

* * *

She arrived early to the consulting group that afternoon, and snagged some one-on-one time with Carla, updating her on Shayla's session, then Clark Davidson, then the photo from Lincoln Center.

Carla listened, and was quick to answer. "I don't think we need to freak out, but this is a good reminder to be careful."

She hadn't expected that. She'd assumed Carla would reassure her. "What do you mean?"

"You're dating a man who's in the public eye. Who the press adores, and fawns over. That man *also* runs a sex toy company that is well known for supplying to BDSM clubs, and for better or for worse, some people find those clubs seedy. That's just reality, and you can't change that. That's why you need to be more cautious than if you were dating a cop, or a teacher, or even the CEO of a dishwasher detergent company. Do you know what I mean?"

"Sure," Michelle said with a crisp nod. Carla had always given her smart advice.

"He doesn't have to worry about boundaries and public or private lives in the same way you do. You're an intimate relationship therapist, and you have to be cautious, in the same way that a teacher or police officer would be. Society has certain expectations about different professions, and we're in one of those professions where we have to be circumspect. The reality is there are bound to be speculations about your sex life now," she said, giving new meaning to the word blunt.

"So that's it? This is not an *It's Raining Men* situation?"

Carla laughed. "No. But I'm not saying you shouldn't date him. If you enjoy his company and he's good to you, then by all means, have some fun. What I'm saying is be aware of these eagle eyes that can't seem to stop looking at him, and now at you. For better or for worse, the man is a magnet for the cameras."

Michelle nodded, agreeing with her mentor. "I don't think I realized just how much. We started dating a few weeks ago, and no one noticed. No one cared. And now, in the last few days, *Page Six* has taken an avid interest. And it was so uncomfortable when my patient asked about him. She just kind of word-vomited up this whole thing about whether we used his sex toys. Talk about boundaries," she said, shaking her head in frustration.

Carla gave her a sympathetic smile. "Look, you won't be the first psychotherapist to deal with dating someone in the public eye. It's not as if you're forbidden from it. The key is to manage it properly. That's why I said to be careful. You don't want your patients or colleagues to start seeing you in a particular light, and seeing you only as this man's lover. That won't help. And if that keeps happening, I would have to stop referring patients to you."

Michelle's stomach dropped at that prospect. She valued Carla's referrals dearly, as well as the chance she was giving her to lead the upcoming workshop. "I don't want that to happen. I want to keep growing in my career."

"I know," Carla said matter-of-factly. "So let's take steps now to protect your career. And as frustrating as it may be, you need to operate under the assumption that you're dating a celebrity. And until it becomes serious, and you're engaged or married—not that I'm saying that will happen," Carla said, holding up a hand when Michelle's eyes threatened to pop out of her head because clearly she and Jack were never getting married, let alone going to date beyond thirty days, "—you simply need to be chaste in public, but behind closed doors," Carla said, lowering her voice to a conspiratorial whisper, even though it was only the two of them in her office, "feel free to have some fabulous sex."

"Carla!" Michelle pretended to be taken aback.

Carla wiggled her eyebrows. "Is it fantastic? Is that why you've been glowing lately?"

She brought her hand to her cheek, as if she could discover this so-called glow everyone kept noticing. "Am I glowing?"

Carla laughed. "No. But you seem happy. Truly happy, and I hope you are. And I also hope you're having great sex. Because everyone should. Besides, isn't great sex something to strive for in an intimate relationship?"

"I suppose it is," she said, and she and Jack certainly had great sex in spades. They also had an intimate relationship. Which was a weirder thought because where she came from intimate relationships were more than just great sex. And that's what she and Jack *had* to be about. The sex; only the sex. Nothing more.

Besides, these problems would all end in a few more days. The clock was ticking, unspooling minutes and seconds until their thirty days expired in a little more than one week. She fast-forwarded over the next ten days. She'd be spending half of them abroad. Without him. Which would suck royally because their plan was working, at least for her. Her heart was healing. Clay was in the rearview mirror. She felt like herself again. Like she could breathe and live and feel without the weight of all that urequitedness yanking her down.

She didn't want to miss a single second of her time with Jack. And she wanted to let him know how much she would miss him while she was away. When she walked back into her office fifteen minutes before her last appointment of the day, she returned a few quick calls to colleagues, then dialed Jack.

CHAPTER EIGHTEEN

Too Far Gone

"I don't want to fuck this one up."

Jack tossed a Nerf basketball up in the air, catching it easily on the way down. He lay on his purple couch, feet crossed on the armrest, an afternoon coffee on the table. Casey lounged on the chair with her cinnamon dolce latte and an iPad, as they reviewed their plans for the upcoming charity gala. He also needed to talk to her about his meeting later this week in Los Angeles with the CEO of one of their online retail partners.

She shot him an inquisitive look, tilting her head to the side. "The charity gala? 'Cause you're good at fucking up a lot of things, but I don't even know how you could mess that up," she said, then the corner of her lips twitched playfully.

He threw the ball at her, but she caught it quickly. "Ha. Now I have your weapon."

"To answer your question, no, not the gala. But things with Michelle."

"Ah," Casey said, and set down the iPad. "So you like her a lot?"

He took a deep breath, nodded several times and sat up. This was not a conversation to be had lying down. "I do. I really do. She's . . .." He started, but let his voice trail off. He shared more with his sister than anyone, but could he really say all the things that were forming on the tip of his tongue? *Amazing, smart, beautiful, direct, open, lovely, funny, and absolutely perfect for him.* "She's great," he said, and it seemed wholly inadequate, but when Casey flashed her winning smile he knew she understood all that was unspoken.

Casey drummed her hands on the coffee table in excitement. "You should bring her to the gala next month," she suggested.

Jack narrowed his eyes. "It's not like that."

"What? How is it not like that?"

While he might run a sex-centric company with his sister, he didn't want to dive into the finer details of his sex arrangement with Michelle. So he deflected. "That event will be crawling with photogs. She's a prominent psychologist. I sell dildos. I should do my best to keep her out of the limelight."

Casey laughed, then tossed him the ball. "Well, when you put it like that, you are kind of Captain of the Dildos."

He caught it easily in one hand. "And you're Queen of the Dongs."

"I wear that title with pride," she said. "So when do I get to meet the Princess of the Weiner Dealer?"

Jack cracked up, a deep, rumbling belly laugh. After his shoulders stopped shaking, he threw a question back at his sister. "Why are you so focused on my love life?"

She shot him a look, like he was crazy for asking. "Because I don't want you to wind up like Mom and Dad," she said, as if the answer were obvious, and when she phrased it that way, it was. "The last four years when you were already in college and I was still home were the worst. Dinners were painful. I'm just glad you were in school nearby."

Their parents had met in college, married soon after, and then proceeded to drift apart for the next twenty-one years they were together. He swore they kept a calendar and marked with an *X* each day until they neared Casey's high school graduation. Bitter, snippy, unhappy people, they simply didn't want to be together anymore, but they clearly felt it was their duty to do so until they got Casey out the door. Jack had tried to come home on weekends as often as he could, to rescue Casey, take her to the movies, attend her swim meets, help her with homework and then college apps. As soon as graduation came, their dad walked out the door happily swinging his suitcase, and their mom threw a party.

Never had two people been so excited to sign dissolution of marriage papers.

"I'm glad I was nearby too. And I'd rather not end up like them either, but I think we're safe in that regard, seeing as I have no plans to get married, or get serious, or anything like that."

She rolled her eyes, huffing at him. "You're already too far gone."

"What do you mean?"

"You just said you didn't want to fuck this up. She's not just someone you're dating. She's someone you care deeply about."

He didn't want his sister's observation to register, even though somewhere inside, it resonated, hitting a part of him he'd thought was broken irreparably. Michelle awakened feelings in him he'd thought were missing from his very DNA. Her vulnerability, her strength, her humor, and most of all, her openness with him on everything floored him, and had worked its way into his heart, that stupid organ that barely worked. He didn't know how to handle all he felt for her—but his desire for her went much deeper than the physical.

"And that's another reason why you should do the story with my friend," Casey added. He arched an eyebrow in question. "The one at the *New York Press*. I mentioned it before. It would be good for you."

He shook his head. "Moving on. Let's talk about the campaign," he said, tapping the newspaper spread out on his coffee table. "The metro section says our guy is still getting clobbered. You said you were going to do some digging on Conroy. Did you find anything?"

Casey's lips quirked up. "As a matter of fact, I did."

"I knew I wasn't the only spy in the family. What did you find?"

"Actually, I didn't dig up any dirt. You saw the picture I sent you of the door. But I don't think we need to go that way. The people in their district are really responding to Conroy's message about cleaning up the area, right? Even if it's not based on the truth, he's touching a nerve that everyone can agree with. Everyone wants a cleaner, better neighborhood."

Jack nodded. "Sure."

"At its heart, that's a positive message. He might have subverted it with his focus on the clubs, but he's doing well with that message. And my theory is Denkler's just backed into a corner now, trying to fight back, and it's not working. Conroy made the campaign about something else and now Denkler's on the defensive."

The cogs in his head started turning. Slowly at first, then more quickly, and soon the train was racing down the path. "He needs to go on the offensive and change the conversation. That's what we need to do. This isn't about digging up dirt. This has to be about something better than dirt," he said, snapping his fingers as the ideas whirring in his head came fully into focus. The data points, the bits and pieces, the clues all came together, and he assembled them quickly into a strategy. "I know exactly how to do it," he said, then laid out his plan for his sister.

Her eyes sparkled with excitement as he shared his thoughts.

"I love it," she said.

"Can you work on it while I'm in California? I fly out in two days."

She shook her head. "You didn't hear?"

"Hear what?"

"She went into labor. Danielle Paige. You were meeting with Danielle, right?"

"Yes."

"I was talking to her marketing VP earlier today. She said all of Danielle's meetings this week are being postponed."

"That does sound like a reasonable excuse," Jack said dryly.

After Casey left a few minutes later, his cell phone buzzed, and it was Michelle on the other line. His damn heart thundered just from hearing her voice. Her sexy, pretty voice that he loved to listen to.

"Hey. I have a session in a few minutes," she said. "But I just wanted to tell you I'm going to miss you a lot when you're in California and I'm in Paris, and you better be able to handle that nine-hour time-zone difference because I'm going to require *a lot* of phone sex with you."

Lust swamped his body, and he was hard instantly. This woman affected him like no one ever had. A dirty word, a sexy line, and he was at attention. "It'll only be a six-hour time difference. My trip to California was cancelled," he said, and then the rational part of his brain bounded forward, knocking on his skull. His schedule was clear. But just as he was about to speak and suggest they *not* have phone sex, she beat him to the punch.

"Jack, do you want to spend the night with me? Or really, five nights?"

It went against everything they were supposed to be. But then, his time with her was already turning into more than he'd bargained for. He said the only thing he could say. The only thing that was completely true. No questions, no concerns, no second-guessing. Besides, it was everything he wanted from her.

"Yes. God, yes. So fucking much."

CHAPTER NINETEEN

Illusions

"Are you going to tell the truth now?" he asked, as he ran his finger against the top of Michelle's hand. The plane soared away from New York, the sparkling lights of the city he called home growing more distant. He wouldn't miss it one bit, since he was with her.

She pulled her gaze away from the window and raised an eyebrow. "The truth about what?

"You might not even have to tell me. I guess I might see when we land at seven a.m."

She shot him another confused look. "What are you talking about?"

"Well, this is the first time I'll have seen you in the morning. You turn into a monster, right? You have dragon breath, or seven toes?"

She turned her fingers into claws, then bared her pretend fangs. "Thirteen toes, actually."

"I knew it. That's why you've been afraid of spending the night."

"Absolutely. I'm hideous, and you'll go running for the hills when you see me when the sun is all the way up."

He leaned in close. "What if I want to fuck you in the morning?"

"We'll just have to see if I let you," she said.

"I'll take my chances."

"Was it tough to get away from the office at the last minute?" she asked, shifting gears.

He shook his head. "Not when you run the company," he said, flashing her a confident grin.

She rolled her eyes.

"Besides, I was supposed to be away this week in California anyway."

"I'm sure you'll be working the whole time too in Paris."

"Not while I'm fucking you."

"You have a one-track mind, Jack Sullivan."

"No, it's two tracks. Fucking you, and thinking about fucking you."

"You know that only makes me want to tease you this whole flight," she said, her eyes sparkling. "Sort of like what you said to me the night we met."

"Payback is a bitch," he said, grabbing her shoulder and planting a quick kiss on her delicious lips that tasted of the champagne the flight attendants had handed out in the first-class cabin during boarding. Surely, they wouldn't be the only couple locking lips on this flight. The cabin appeared rife with lovers, boyfriends and girlfriends, husbands and wives, and of course, solo businessmen, and women, too. Even though he'd only had a day's notice, he'd snagged the last seat in first class, and the airline had found two first class seats together. Being next to her for a seven-hour flight and unable to touch her the way he wanted was hell, but he'd happily suffer that kind of torture. He found he preferred the time with her to the time without her.

"But to answer your question, no, it wasn't that hard to get away. My sister pretty much pushed me out the door."

"She knows about us, right?"

He nodded. "She wants me to date again," he said, the words coming out easily. Everything was becoming increasingly easy to say to her. Maybe it was her warmth, her lack of judgment, her kindness that made talking to her simple. Even about things he didn't usually share.

"Because of Aubrey?"

Like this topic. "Yeah."

"I think that's common with widowers. The family *always* wants to set the man up with a new woman not too long after and vice versa. There's a whole subset of the romance novel genre with widower heroes."

He cringed inside, gritting his teeth. Okay, maybe it wasn't so easy when he hadn't come clean with all the details. When she still operated under the illusion the rest of the world had about him. "Yup. I know all about that."

"Remember when you told me at dinner that you don't really miss her anymore? Is that why you came to me in the first place? To be able to move on and let go of all that missing?" she asked, her voice quiet to keep the conversation private. The low hum of the airplane flying through the night was like a shield; their words were just for them.

But how could he answer her without lying? He was tired of being weighed down with guilt, and with the public's misperceptions about his emotional state, or lack thereof. Obviously, he'd been devastated by Aubrey's death. He wasn't a cruel asshole who had no feelings. He was broken when it happened, and in the days and months that followed, he missed her in the way you miss a close friend. But he wasn't grieving a lost love, a significant other.

He didn't want to waste a single ounce of energy with Michelle on anything but the truth. He couldn't lie to her, not when she was so patently open with him about so many things. He shook his head. "No."

She raised an eyebrow. "No?"

"It's not missing that I came to you for. It was other feelings. Guilt. Regret," he said, biting out the honest words.

She shot him a sympathetic smile, cupped his cheek in one hand. "It's normal to feel all that as well. I hope you're starting to let go of that too," she said, then ran her thumb across his lips, almost as if she were wiping away the rest of the conversation, exonerating him of the need to expand on what he'd said. He'd managed not to lie; but he hadn't revealed the whole truth. That would have to do for now. It was a step. A small one, but it brought him closer to this woman who always seemed able to share her whole self.

Well, except overnight.

"Besides, it's hard for me to think of anyone but you," he said, and it was freeing to say something that was incontrovertibly true. He kept his gaze on her the whole time, searching her eyes for her reaction. The expression in them matched the one in his, making his heart thump harder against his chest.

"I feel the same," she whispered, and it was as if a layer of the ice he'd encased his heart in split wide open, letting loose what lay beneath. He could feel that damn organ trying to wriggle free from the chill he'd wrapped it in.

"That guy you mentioned the first night we went to dinner?" he asked, and she nodded, so he kept going. "Do you still think about him? You said you were in love with him for ten years." Maybe he was playing the shrink now, asking her questions about her past. But it wasn't a question borne from a game, or pretend therapy. He was asking as the man who wanted her all to himself. Who didn't want to share space in her head or her heart with anyone else. The more he had of her, the more he wanted. And he wanted it all.

She shook her head, her lips curving up in a smile. "You're the only one I think about now, Jack."

He cupped the back of her head, pulled her close, his lips brushing hers. "I want you so much. I don't know how to go this whole flight without being inside you."

She laughed. "You are a two-track man."

He laughed too. "I told you so."

"But aren't you the one who taught me about holding back?"

"Yes. Ignore all I've ever said on that."

"Just think about how amazing it will be when we finally make it to the hotel," she said in a sexy purr.

A low rumble worked its way up his chest as he pictured her naked, spread out on white sheets for him. "I want to walk into a hotel room and find you with your hand between your legs."

"That might happen. But there's something else I want to do while we're in Paris," she said, taking time with each word then pulling back to meet his eyes. Her teeth were pressed into her lower lip, the only sign she was nervous.

His eyes widened with anticipation. "What is it?" he asked, heat roaring through his body with ideas, images of what his sexy, naughty woman might want.

"This is going to be kind of dirty," she said, her mouth falling open in an *O*, her eyes wild. Blood pounded in his head. He hoped she was going to say the very thing he wanted, the thing he'd been planning to ask her for in bed. Tension rolled through his bones.

"I like dirty," he growled.

She moved closer. They were face-to-face, inches apart in their cushy, leather first-class seats with more than three hundred other passengers, not to mention pilots and flight attendants on this jet with them. But she was all he saw.

She reached for his collar, played with the edge of the fabric in her fingers, her eyes still on him. "You know how I like it when you play with my ass?"

Lust thundered in him. He was engulfed by hot, raw desire for her. "Yes."

"I want more."

He swallowed thickly. He wasn't sure he could speak right now. He knew he couldn't move. He was so fucking hard it hurt. "Oh God," he groaned.

"I never have before, and I want to. With you. Do you want to?" she asked, her pretty voice so straightforward. He'd never been asked before. He'd never encountered anyone so blunt with her wishes.

He threaded his hand through her hair, gripping the back of her head as the strands fell like silk waterfalls across his fingers. "I dream about your perfect little ass. I fantasize about how it would feel. You have no fucking idea how much I want that."

She shivered against him, a sexy little movement that revealed how utterly in synch they were in the bedroom. She was his perfect fantasy. She was his perfect reality. She was everything he'd ever wanted, even if she'd never asked for this. But she had asked for it, and he was going to do everything he could to make it perfect for her.

"We have to wait 'til after my keynote though," she said, her voice a soft warning.

He laughed lightly. "Yes. Of course. I do want you to be able to walk."

"But after that, you can have me."

"I wish your keynote were ending this very second," he said, and dropped his mouth to hers, consuming her in a hot, wet kiss that would have turned into so much more if they weren't on this goddamn plane.

CHAPTER TWENTY
Mais Oui

She was radiant in the gaslight from the streetlamps along the Seine.

The soft glow illuminated her, a faint golden light at night that made her all the more breathtaking. She wore heels and a skirt, her strong legs on display for him, always for him, and a pretty top that was falling off her shoulder. He'd already had her twice today. The second, the very nanosecond they'd arrived at the hotel room, he took her. The door had fallen shut and he'd thrown her on the bed, stripped off her jeans and his, and entered her. It was a hard, fast fuck, but after that red-eye flight it was what they both desperately required. It wasn't enough to quench his desire, though, and after a nap, he'd put her on all fours, and made her cry out his name once more.

Then they'd behaved, spending the afternoon working. She'd practiced her talk alone in the room at the Sofitel Hotel in the 8th arrondissement, near the Champs-Elysées and the Louvre, while he'd gone to a cafe around the block and worked on his laptop. He'd drunk espresso at a sidewalk table, and watched the Parisians stroll by as he dealt with business matters related to vibrators, bullets, and butterflies. It seemed quite fitting to work on Joy Delivered business in a city like this, where anything goes and everything went, where the residents embraced sex and sexuality. Hell, the politicians here often had mistresses. Paris was a city that celebrated passion.

Judging by the P&L numbers his chief financial officer had just sent over, there were plenty of Americans and Upper East Siders, as the demographic data told him, who enjoyed the full range of Joy Delivered products, from basic massagers to butt plugs to leather floggers. But yet, there was such a vocal outcry to shut down the damn BDSM clubs, even though Denkler's campaign had tried the whole "safer for everyone" route. Admittedly, it was working the tiniest bit, based on the new numbers Henry had sent over earlier today. That gave Jack a needed boost of confidence that turning the tide was possible. It wouldn't be easy, but it seemed doable, even though time was running out on the campaign.

The whole situation had left Jack with a bad taste in his mouth. Politics and sex were terrible bedfellows. Ironic too, because there was so much demonizing of the clubs on the outside, but he bet some of those same opponents had red marks on their asses from using toys behind closed doors.

But here? Even when he'd had his laptop screen open to a photo of a prototype of a new double-headed dildo, neither the waiter nor the gray-haired woman who'd been sitting next to him, holding a teacup poodle in her lap as she drank a coffee and dragged on a cigarette, seemed to care.

The woman had even leaned closer and whispered, "looks like fun," to which he'd responded "*mais oui.*"

He'd always enjoyed the pace of life here in Paris, and the conversations he overheard revealed the city's true nature—discussions about movies, art, an Yves St Laurent exhibit at the Grand Palais, a music festival on the steps of the Musee d'Orsay, even a debate about religion. Very few conversations were about business.

It was a different way of life in the City of Love.

Now, he and Michelle had finished dinner at a small bistro on a cobblestoned street, and were wandering along the river, buzzed on the bottle of wine they'd drunk. The Eiffel Tower beckoned in the distance, lit up like it was covered in diamonds, its nighttime jewels glittering across the night. The Seine cut a ribbon through the city, and he held Michelle's hand as they threaded their way along a grassy path by the water, still-green trees forming a canopy overhead. They stopped several times to kiss. A small green cab scurried by, its horn bleating loudly. They were surrounded by other lovers on this path, tangled up together on benches, under the trees, on the stone wall.

"Think anyone is taking our picture now?" he joked when they broke the kiss as a young hip couple walked past them, looking at a photo on their cell phone. Even from a few feet away, he could tell the picture was of a dog.

She laughed and shook her head. "Hate to break it to you, big shot, but I don't think anyone here cares about who Mr. NYC Eligible Bachelor is involved with."

"God, I love the French."

"No one knows we're here, either," she said.

"No one?"

She jutted up a shoulder. "Well, my brother knows, and Sutton knows. But I didn't tell my clients where I was going. I only told them I was going to be away on business, and then arranged for a backup therapist. They don't know where I am, and I like the privacy. I had a new client the last few weeks who just kept throwing me off-kilter."

He quirked up his eyebrows in question. "What do you mean?" he asked, his shoulders tensing.

"It was weird," she said, looking at the sky as if she were remembering. "He just seemed to be checking me out during one session, then in the next one he knew too much about me. And when he put his dark black glasses on, he reminded me of someone I'd bumped into once outside the office."

Now his hackles were raised. He clenched his fists, immediately hating this guy, and he wasn't entirely sure why. Except he didn't want anyone making the woman he cared for uncomfortable. "What does he look like?"

She shrugged. "Standard businessman, I guess. Short dark hair, dark eyes. Why? Are you going to go all Army Intelligence on me and track him down?" she asked, shifting to a playful tone.

"If I have to, I will," he said, wrapping his arm around her waist. He would protect her if need be, though he doubted this dude was anything but a man who couldn't keep his eyes off a beautiful woman.

"Well, I like that the Paris tabloids don't care about you."

He nodded in agreement, grateful that *Page Six*'s obsession with him didn't extend overseas. Besides, only Casey and Nate knew where he was. "I'm nobody here," he said.

"Then let's get back to the hotel, Mr. Nobody." She looped her arms around his neck as a soft night breeze blew by, kicking up her skirt. He copped a peek. "Pervert," she teased.

"You love it."

"I do. You could even grab my ass here and no one would care," she said, egging him on. Like he was going to back down from that dare. He pushed her up against the stone wall at the river's edge, reached his hands under her skirt and cupped her cheeks, squeezing them, then smacking her rear once. Hard. So hard it probably stung. Her eyes lit up.

He grabbed her hand, and they strolled away from the river and along the streets of the left bank.

"Are you ready for tomorrow's keynote?" he asked as they walked.

She nodded. "I think so. I'm as prepared as I can be, and the conference organizers have been amazing at making me feel welcome."

"You're going to be incredible. Standing ovation, I bet."

She laughed, throwing her head back. "You're such a flatterer."

"No, it's the truth! Not that I have a clue about love and sex addiction, except I think I'm addicted to making you come. Does that count?" he said, dropping a hand to her back as a breeze blew by again, smelling like rain this time.

"I encourage that addiction."

They turned a corner onto a narrow street with apartment buildings all boasting flower planters in the windows of the flats. They walked in comfortable silence for a few more blocks, the sounds of Paris at night their companions, faint music floating from open windows, the clink of glasses and dishes at still-open cafes, the din of an ambulance siren somewhere in the distance, such a different wail than those in New York. The clouds swelled, turning heavy with the promise of a late September storm. The air sang of rain; the heavy earthy scent trailing along with it. The hotel wasn't far and they both picked up the pace.

But soon he spotted the Palais Royal nearby. He raised an eyebrow. "I think we got turned around. We're a little farther away from the hotel than I thought."

She stopped and turned in a circle, then pointed toward the avenue at the end of the next block. "I think we go that way to get back on track."

The first drops fell then, and within seconds the skies were unleashed. Michelle laughed, brushing the droplets off her face, unfazed. She tipped her chin to an archway at the end of the block. "I think that's one of the passages," she said, referring to the dozen or so covered walkways scattered throughout the city.

Ten seconds later, they ducked into the Passage Vivienne, stepping through the tall stone archway that soared high above them. They were inside a shopping arcade, stuffed with a bookshop, an old-fashioned toy shop, a store selling all sorts of hats, and more. Their footsteps echoed across the mosaic-patterned floor. The passage was lined with tall plants, and half-moon windows high above. Michelle craned her neck to look skyward. The curved ceiling was made of latticework windows, dark with the rain pounding out its steady drumbeat. All the stores were closed except for a cafe at the far end, still bustling with patrons drinking wine and chatting into the night.

Michelle gasped, and he followed her gaze. She was pointing at a shop. The windows were lined with glass perfume bottles in all sorts of colors—rich emerald green, bright vibrant gold, and sapphire blue. "Remember I told you about the perfume shop in Montmartre? This is just like it. I wonder if the store moved here?"

He shrugged, not knowing the answer, but remembering the conversation in his apartment perfectly. "*They exist solely because they're pretty,*" he said, repeating her words from their chat in his kitchen..

She beamed at him, her smile so inviting, then she tugged him into the stone doorway of the shop. Off in the distance, he heard the click of shoes on the marble floor fading. Someone must have left the cafe and headed out the other end of the passage.

"Admit it. You're still trying to avoid spending the night with me, aren't you?" he teased.

"No," she said, shaking her head, looking him in the eyes. "I want to so much."

His heart beat faster. "Why were you so resistant then?"

"Because I needed to stay separate from you," she said, her fingers threading their way through his hair. God, he loved the way she touched him. "To protect my heart."

He circled his arms around her waist. "And now you no longer need to protect it?"

"I *can't* protect it anymore," she said, tilting her chin up at him, keeping her gaze on his. "It's too late. I can't fight this any longer."

He should be terrified; he should shut down. But he did none of those things. He feathered his hand across her back, sneaking it under her shirt. She arched into him.

"Don't fight it," he told her.

"*Jack*," she murmured, worry in her tone.

"Don't protect it. I'll protect it. I want to," he said, moving even closer to her, spreading his palm across her smooth skin.

"I don't know that you can."

"I don't either. But I want the chance. I want you. I want all of you," he said, never looking away. He couldn't. He was too far gone. His heart thudded painfully, beating out a new rhythm. He half wanted to shout at it to stay cool, but he wanted to embrace it as well. To revel in all that he felt for her. This living, breathing mix of everything he never expected to feel, but was powerless to stop. She had stolen into his life in a random coincidence, and now he was driven with need for her.

"Don't you realize? You have all of me. I am yours. Completely," she said, taking her time with every word, and each of them landed deeper and deeper inside him. Hooking into him.

He moved his hands to her cheeks. He held her face and stared into her brown eyes. They were so inviting, so trusting, and he could barely hold back anymore. He felt so much for her. It was bubbling up, overwhelming him, threatening to spill out.

"Michelle," he whispered, his voice as ragged as the beating of his heart. "I love everything about being with you."

"I love being with you."

"I don't want to think about not being with you." He brushed her cheek with his calloused fingertips; her skin was still wet from the rain. He pressed his groin against her, grinding as he kissed her, pushing her hard against the stone wall of the doorway, where they were concealed from any patrons at the café. His mind was on one thing—getting her back to the hotel room as quickly as possible. But she was faster. Her hands were on his zipper.

"Make love to me now," she said to him, a soft but oh-so-clear command.

Like a straight shot of desire, his body thrummed with need from her heated request. Lust took over, even as he glanced down the hallway. They were all alone, but the risk was palpable. They could be caught, seen, spotted. Or they could be seen and ignored. The more likely option. But as his zipper came undone and she reached into his boxers, wrapping those soft, talented fingers around him, nothing else mattered.

He didn't care about anything but her. He couldn't care. His need for her was all he felt. Not having her now felt like the bigger risk.

He reached under her skirt, palming her. "Your panties are drenched," he said, yanking them to the side, revealing her, so wet and ready for him. He hitched up her thigh, wrapped her leg around his waist, and guided his cock into her. She drew a sharp breath and moaned loudly.

Instantly, he covered her mouth with his hand. "I'm going to fuck you in public, and you're going to be quiet. Nod if you understand."

She nodded, and he kept his hand over her lips as he thrust into her. Her wet heat coated his cock. "Oh, beautiful, your pussy is soaking wet. You love Paris, don't you?"

A muffled yes.

"And you love being able to fuck me in public, don't you?"

Another nod as she grabbed his hip bones, holding on tight.

"And you love needing me so badly that you can't even wait for the hotel, don't you?" he said, releasing his hold ever so briefly to let her speak.

"Yes," she moaned.

"Quiet," he warned, covering her mouth once more. With his other hand, he held tight to her hip, his thumb digging into her flesh as he pumped. "You love that I want to fuck you anywhere. That I want to be inside your beautiful body everywhere. That I can't ever get enough of you."

She bit down on his palm, and he yanked his hand back. "I love needing you," she said on a pant, her erratic breaths telling him she was so close to coming. She dug her nails into his skin. He could feel them deeply, like daggers, starting to draw blood. The possibility that she was going to come so hard she'd break his skin made his dick throb harder inside her.

"Come on me," he whispered harshly. "Come on me in public. Mark me with your nails."

He felt her tighten around his erection, clenching against him, her body drawing him deep into her. She shuddered, and trembled violently, then shuddered again and again, her cries muffled by his hand.

While still covering her mouth, he dropped his face into her neck, tasting the slightest bit of sweat, mixed with rain. He drove into her, the pressure in his body building, his balls drawing up as his climax started to overtake him.

"*Michelle*," he said on a groan as his orgasm plowed through him relentlessly. Crashing through him, pulling him under.

He gripped her body harder, probably breaking skin too, needing to be as fucking close as he possibly could as he released himself in her, biting back his own groans of pleasure. He collapsed against her, and he was vaguely aware that he might be crushing her against the wall. He managed to slide away an inch so he wouldn't hurt her. She looked more beautiful than she had earlier.

Finally, he released his hold on her mouth. "I need you so much," he said, and it was the barest truth. He had to be with her.

"I need you too, Jack," she whispered, looking up at his eyes. Never breaking the hold. "I'm falling in love with you."

The second the words made landfall, he tensed. Like a coil, tightening inside him, locking him up. A warning bell that this was the moment he needed to prevent. This was the line in the sand that neither one of them should even come remotely near.

A little voice told him to bolt, to run, to get the fuck away. Because saying those words could change everything.

But then just as quickly, he quieted that fear. He'd come far. He'd made progress, hadn't he? He had to let go of the grip the past had on him. He had to let go of anything but his deep and absolute need for this woman who gave herself to him so completely.

He could give her what she'd given him.

Surely, he could.

He parted his lips to speak, but an invisible hand gripped his throat. Came down hard on his mouth. The dark cloak of regret was like a silencer that choked all the words he wanted to say, turning them into dust on his tongue. The old familiar standby had resurfaced inside him, wormed his way through his conscious with the reminders of where words could lead. Right words, wrong time. Wrong words, wrong time. They were one and the same, and held too much possibility for pain.

He wanted to tell her everything. He wanted to tell her he was so afraid of saying the wrong thing, of hurting the right person, of loving the wrong way. Most of all, he was terrified of not loving enough. He wanted her to know all that was true and dark and painful inside of him.

But he didn't know how to give voice to that without causing more hurt. So he bottled it up. He tried to contain all that he felt for her in a small space so that it was manageable, so that it never could slither out and wound her.

The last thing he wanted was to hurt her, even though her words both scared him and thrilled him.

He took the easy way out. He brushed his lips softly against her cheek. Then kissed her neck. Then her ear.

"I can't ever get enough of you," he said, whispering words that were wholly inadequate. But when he returned to her mouth, he hoped she knew in the soft press of his lips all the things he couldn't say. He hoped that *this*—the physical—would be enough to assure her.

But he knew deep down it would never be sufficient. Not for a woman like her. Not for anyone who felt the way she did.

* * *

As the sun peeked through the windows early the next morning, she stretched in bed, reaching her arms over her head, then casting her gaze at him. He was gorgeous next to her, still sound asleep on his side, breathing the slow rhythmic breath of a deep sleeper. She was tempted to run a hand down his bare arm, his muscles so strong. Then to his trim waist, his hips exposed above the sheets.

But she turned away, slid out of bed, and headed to the bathroom to brush her teeth and wash her face.

She was safer by herself.

Perhaps Paris had been a bad idea.

Maybe they should have gotten separate rooms. Because here she was, exactly where she didn't want to be. She didn't want to share a bed, a night, a morning with someone who didn't feel the same.

The night before had been magic; it had been stitched from a dream—the rain, the doorway, the perfume bottles. *Him.* All the things he'd said until that moment. She was sure he'd felt the same.

But then, she hadn't said she was falling in love with him to get it in return.

She'd said it because it was unequivocally true. Because it was impossible to keep it inside her any longer. She'd held back with him for so long. She'd been so protective, erected arbitrary boundaries to seal herself off from falling. She'd tried valiantly to keep him at arm's length, but he'd been so insistent, burrowing his way into her life, her heart, and her head. Such a passionate man, and such a caring one, too. He was the ultimate lover, that sinful mouth and smoldering body a staggering combination. There was so much more, too. His tender side; his funny side; his warmth. She was willing to bet he relished the appearance of Mr. Cool, Calm and Collected, but beneath that veneer he was passionate and fiery, dirty and loving, and, unexpectedly, he was needy. In exactly the way she wanted him to be. He needed her.

Or so it had seemed, she reasoned as she brushed her teeth, erasing the taste of the night.

After ten years of longing, after a whole damn decade of her heart being a goddamn one-way mirror, she thought there were iron gates around it, and it would take moving heaven and earth to knock them down. It hadn't. It had taken one man less than thirty nights.

But once more, she was back where she'd always been. Loving too much. Feeling too much. The only one of them who felt this way. Putting herself out there to be met with a black hole in return.

She spat out the toothpaste and filled a glass of water, rinsing her mouth.

Soon, her rational side took hold, stuffing her emotional self back into the trunk where that side belonged.

This was all her fault. Jack had never pretended this was for love. He'd laid the cards on the table that night at Gia's. She'd agreed. Willingly. She hadn't wanted to risk her heart either. She didn't have to keep risking it, she reminded herself. Hell, if she'd managed to wash away Clay and the feelings she'd had for him, she could damn well do the same with Jack. All she had to do was suck it down. To swallow up that annoying emotion of love, and replace it properly with desire.

She was a smart woman. She knew how to manage emotions. She and Jack were lovers for thirty nights. They were nothing more. She wasn't going to ruin this trip, or this time, or her speech by letting emotions cloud her. She was going to finish out this no-strings-attached affair the way it had started—physically. She'd gotten into this to get over Clay, and that had happened. She no longer pined for her friend. She no longer was in love with him. That was all that mattered. She'd taken her medicine; she'd gotten the cure. She didn't need to push forward into something more. She'd keep this affair precisely where it belonged—as an affair.

She was going to make damn sure no one could ever hurt her again.

Not Clay. Not Jack. Not anyone.

She turned on the faucet again, splashed some water on her face, and imagined washing away those words from last night, returning to what she and Jack were. They were a temporary fix to heal each other's hearts. Nothing more.

Besides, she had her work. She was due on stage later today for her keynote. She could immerse herself in what she loved deeply and always. Her work was the great love of her life, and no one could ever take that away from her.

CHAPTER TWENTY-ONE
Turn Around

A fleet of nerves settled down in her belly as she waited in the wings. Julien, the psychologist and editor of the journal that was hosting the event, was on stage introducing her. Taking a few deep breaths, and checking to make sure her shirt was still tucked into her skirt—it was—and that her hair was holding up in its twist—not a strand was out of place—she told those butterflies in her stomach to get the hell out of town.

"And now it is my pleasure to introduce one of our esteemed colleagues from the United States, Michelle Milo, whose research and insight into this topic is at the very forefront. We are delighted to have her here in Paris for our conference," he said, holding out his arm grandly as Michelle walked onto the stage. The audience clapped routinely, the sort of welcoming sound you receive before the crowd knows if they like you.

But forty minutes later, at the end of her talk, the clapping was real, and strong, and it reverberated.

True, the standing ovation didn't happen. Something better did. The whole conference room at the convention hotel in Montparnasse *listened.* They paid attention. They didn't check their phones. They even laughed at the occasional joke she dropped in. She'd brought her A-game, and judging by the crowd gathered at the front of the stage, many had questions ready to ask her. She stayed for them all, listening and answering until it was time to clear out the room for the next speaker.

Julien, ever the gracious host, waited patiently and escorted her off-stage.

"I have one more person for you to meet," he said, then guided her down the hallway to a tall, thin and balding man who extended a hand for her to shake.

"This is Denis Garnier. He runs a practice here in the 6th, and practically begged me to introduce you."

"Thank you so much," she said, as she shook his hand.

"I am so impressed, and we don't have many psychotherapists here in France with your background, so I wanted to talk about your findings. Ask some questions. Do you have a few minutes?"

"Of course," she said, and then found a nearby couch and sat down. She was due to meet Jack soon, but she'd simply have to be a few minutes late. She gave Denis her supreme focus as they chatted. The conversation grounded her. Her work was her anchor; it had kept her going through good times and bad. It was her rock; it had been there for her during the ups and downs of grief and unrequited love.

Men were different. They came, and they went.

* * *

Jack looked relaxed and devilishly handsome in the crowded lobby bar, drinking a scotch, one arm resting on the back of an emerald-green couch. He wore jeans and a button-down white shirt. No tie today, and she missed her favorite accessory on the man, but then he looked good in anything and in nothing. He'd texted her that he'd be waiting at the bar, and to take her time when she said she was running late. When she'd received the text, she was grateful she had her work phone with her, since it was the only one set up to send and receive international text messages.

He watched her the whole time as she walked over, his eyes roaming her from head to toe. Her skin sizzled from the heated way he stared hungrily. This man didn't hold back. He didn't hide his desire. He wasn't afraid to check her out, to stare, to look at her as if he wanted to eat her up. Good—that's what they shared. A deep, and bottomless desire.

The couch he was seated on was next to a marble fireplace, and the plush wine-red carpeting gave the lobby bar a rich, old-money feel to it. It was like a private club. He rose and planted a kiss on one cheek, then the other. Then, a deep, possessive kiss on her mouth. As if he were marking her.

When they pulled apart, she felt dazed. Her head was foggy. The details of the day, of her talk, of her chat with Julien and Denis scattered on the ground. She didn't mind, though; her day had been amazing, and now she was going to take her reward. Jack would be her dessert.

"Did you bring down the house?" he asked, as he gestured for her to sit next to him. She did, crossing her legs. He watched her.

"You're staring at my legs," she said.

"I know. I'm thinking about them draped on my shoulders."

She laughed. "I need a scotch."

He signaled the waiter, and ordered a drink for her as well. "So?" he asked, returning to their conversation.

"It was amazing. I was so energized. I really felt like I was connecting with the audience, and they were responding and learning. It was incredible," she said, and she couldn't wipe the smile from her face if she tried. Professional pride coursed through her. "Days like this remind me that I am so utterly lucky to be able to do what I love for a living."

He held up his glass in toast. "To the smartest, sexiest, most wonderful woman I know. Congrats on a job well done," he said, and a minute later, the waiter brought her drink, so they toasted once more. She took a swallow, then shared more details of her day. The conversation helped keep the focus on the type of relationship she and Jack were having—a temporary one. "I'm not exaggerating when I say I think this day is one of the highlights of my career," she added.

She was tempted to bring up last night, if only to let him know he should simply forget what she'd said, to free him of any sense of obligation. She didn't want him to worry that she'd misunderstood their arrangement. She was a modern woman; she could handle this. She could adhere to the fine details of their verbal agreement. But she'd have to find the right moment for that, because whatever she had to say, she had to say it *lightly*. It had to be believable when she told him to forget she'd ever tried to bring love into the equation. She needed to be able to laugh it off, as if it were in the heat of the moment only—the rain, the perfume, Paris.

"Do you have any idea how unbelievably attractive it is that you love what you do so much?"

"Thank you. I could say the same about you."

He nodded. "I can't imagine not running Joy Delivered. I'm a lucky man to be able to do what I love, and to run it with my sister, who's pretty much my best friend."

"That calls for another toast. Just because," she said, smiling as they clinked glasses once more, keeping their focus on matters of business and pleasure. "Did you approve any fantastic new vibrators today?"

He laughed, shaking his head. "No. I did this instead," he said, reaching into his pocket and handing her a small velvet bag.

"You have a thing for shopping, it seems."

"For you," he said. "Open it."

She tugged at the drawstring and peeked inside. Immediately, her eyes widened, and her cheeks turned a deep shade of crimson.

"Are you embarrassed?"

"No," she whispered, closing the bag. "I've never used one."

"Wear it to dinner," he said in that confident, controlling voice that sent hot tingles racing down her chest, settling between her legs. "It's part of the preparation."

"I'm suddenly very hungry," she said, losing interest for the moment in conversation. Her focus narrowed solely to pleasure. That was Jack's true forte, after all. That was what he was good for. That was the only way he could be in her life for these last few nights.

She wanted to make the most of them. To savor every second of these nights with him.

He knocked back the rest of his drink, and she did the same.

"Let's go upstairs first," he said, and they made their way to the elevator, then to their room.

* * *

In the shower, she washed the day off her, and he did the same. Then he lathered up his hands, and slid them around to her ass, running the soap over her cheeks, then gently near her rear. Her breath hitched as he teased at her.

"Not yet," he murmured, then turned her around, rinsing her thoroughly. Holding her face gently in his hands, he leaned her head back under the hot stream, letting the water wash away the conditioner. After he turned off the shower, he handed her a thick, soft towel and she dried herself. He wrapped his towel around his waist. Then he took the towel from her, hung it up on a hook, and walked her over to the vanity.

"I'm naked and you're not," she said with a pout.

"If it were up to me, you'd be naked all the time with me, so this seems like the way things should be," he said, reaching for her body lotion, pumping some into his palms then dropping down to his knees and smoothing the lotion into her bare legs. She sighed happily, relishing the way he was taking care of her body. That was his specialty, and he knew it so well. He was a master at turning her on, even in the more gentle ways as he moved up to her belly, her hips, then her arms, rubbing lotion into her skin. He cupped her butt in his hands, smoothing lotion across her ass as a groan escaped his throat. Then he spun her around so she was facing the mirror.

He met her reflection in the glass. "Look at how beautiful you are," he said, dropping his mouth to her shoulder, planting a kiss, then gently biting her skin. She felt beautiful as he looked at her. That could only be helpful, feeling beautiful, she reasoned. It could only help her to keep moving on.

He reached for a small clear bottle on the white marble vanity, drizzled some lube onto a few fingers, then returned to her backside once more, all the while keeping his eyes locked on her in the mirror.

"If anything doesn't feel good, just tell me to stop. At any point," he said as he teased at her back entrance. She lifted her ass for him, giving him all the access he needed.

She shook her head. "I know it will feel good," she said, as he pushed a finger into her. She gasped from the pressure, closing her eyes from the quick hit of pleasure that burst through her.

"Just getting you ready," he said, then reached for the bag on the counter, taking out the jeweled butt plug he'd bought for her while she was delivering her keynote. To think, this afternoon she'd been the respected psychologist from New York speaking to a crowd of hundreds of colleagues about serious relationship matters and treatment modalities, and tonight she was Jack's lover, cheeks spread, ready to receive a jeweled pleasure toy in her ass. A Joy Delivered product, of course, the toy was silver, shaped like a rounded bullet and with a sturdy base. On the base, was a deep purple fake gem.

"I chose purple because it's a sophisticated color for a sophisticated woman," he said, holding up the toy in the mirror.

"Nothing says sophisticated like a jeweled butt plug," she said in a playful voice, making him laugh.

But the laughing stopped from both of them as he removed his finger and slowly, carefully inserted the plug into her rear. She tensed briefly as it stretched her. She'd had his fingers in her before, plenty of times, but this was larger and thicker. She exhaled deeply as she adjusted to the size. But then, she needed to get used to it. This toy was tiny compared to him, and she fully intended to have him there later tonight.

"How does it feel?"

"Weird. But good," she said, and he spun her around and dropped to the floor once more, kissing the tops of her feet, then her shins, and up to her knees. He looked up at her, and his eyes blazed darkly with so much heat, so much passion, and so much unbridled lust as he worked his way up the front of her legs, kissing and licking her skin, then her inner thighs. She was hot and wet already, and he lapped up the wetness slipping down her legs.

"How am I going to make it through dinner?" she asked as he flicked his tongue once against her throbbing center, then stood up.

"The same way I am. *Aroused.* Stay right here," he told her, and returned to the bedroom, then was back in seconds with the dress and underwear she'd laid out for herself on the bed. The dress was simple, a red, jersey cotton number that fit softly and well. He handed her the white lace panties, and she stepped into them as he gently lowered the dress over her head, letting it fall down to her knees.

"No bra for me?" she asked, quirking up an eyebrow.

"Don't wear one tonight," he said, smoothing out the dress, then reaching his hands up to cup her bottom through her panties. "But you have to wear panties as much as I'd prefer you naked under the dress," he said, and tapped the jewel.

She gasped from the slightest movement in her rear. "It feels so good," she whispered, like she was telling him a decadent secret.

"All I can think about, Michelle. All I can think about is you, and your perfect ass, and how much I want you."

She eyed his towel, and the way his hard cock was tenting it.

That was her power. The effect she had on him. She wanted some power back. After too many emotions had rattled free from her heart, she needed to *take*. She tugged the towel off him, and his dick saluted her. He was at attention, and a drop glistened on the tip. Using her thumb, she spread that liquid on the head, watching his eyes turn hazy, his breath ragged.

"Can I fuck you with my hand before dinner?" she asked, talking to him as he'd often spoken to her. Controlling. Confident.

"You naughty girl," he said with narrowed eyes, and she took that as a yes.

She was fully dressed, he was completely naked, and she was thoroughly in charge of his pleasure. This beautiful, controlling man was hers to touch and to tease. She reached behind her to the counter, squirted some lube into her hands, and proceeded to stroke his gorgeous cock. She needed this. She desperately needed this right now.

Slowly at first, like it was a luxury, and she wanted to savor every second. "Don't come," she told him sharply.

He shook his head. "I won't," he muttered on an upstroke that had him trying to rock faster into her hand.

"Jack," she warned, thrilling at giving him an order. "I can't have you coming too soon. You need to hold back."

Nodding, his mouth fell open, his breathing intensifying as she upped her pace. He moaned and grunted, and his sexy, masculine sounds of impending pleasure ignited her insides. She used both hands, one to grip his glorious cock that slid in and out of her tight fist, the other to play with his balls.

"You want to come so badly, don't you?" she asked. A spark raced through her body and lit up her mind as she turned the tables on him. This role reversal did wonders for her insides, physically and emotionally. It let her retrieve those dangerous words, and wind them back up inside her, as if the moment from last night had been rewound. As if the messy threat of emotions and feelings and falling too far could be stuffed neatly back into a closed drawer.

It could. Surely, it could, as she used their physical connection to return them to the world they inhabited—thirty nights of pleasure. The end was in sight.

"Yes."

"Tell me you can wait," she said.

"I can wait," he choked out, as if it pained him.

"I'll get you there. But you have to do it my way," she said. He completely gave himself over to her, his eyes pinned on her as he rocked into her hand.

She tugged on his balls, teasing and pulling in just the way he liked, and jacked him harder and rougher. His eyes went glassy; his chest rose and fell quickly. He thickened even more in her grasp. His entire shaft was throbbing against her hand that raced up and down his long, hard length. Watching the expression on his face shift from pleasure to intense concentration, she knew he was reaching the edge. She wanted to send him off in a flurry of white-hot sparks.

"I need you to come now," she said, her voice a command.

He groaned, a primal sound, and she moved her other hand under his balls, rubbing that spot that drove him even crazier, then pressing the tip of her finger against his ass. Not entering, but teasing, hinting.

That was all it took.

He scrunched up his brows, thrust harder and groaned loudly as he came all over her hand.

There was something about this moment that was completely necessary for Michelle's sanity. Without it, she wasn't sure if she could go on with him. But she'd taken back some of the control she'd lost last night.

CHAPTER TWENTY-TWO
New

Visiting the Grand Colbert was like taking a trip back in time to an earlier Paris. Like a scene from the 1920s, the landmark restaurant lived up to its hype from the soft, golden lights to the green leather seats, to the lampposts positioned all throughout the establishment that hearkened to an earlier age. The entire restaurant was bathed in a soft orange-yellow glow.

He'd called ahead that afternoon to secure the very same table made famous in a scene in *Something's Gotta Give*. It was the best table in the restaurant.

They had finished eating, both of them ordering the signature chicken dish, and he poured a third glass of wine for Michelle. She held up a hand when her glass was half full.

"That's all you want?"

"I want to be relaxed and all loosened up, but not drunk," she said, sliding closer to him. They were on the same side of the booth. He couldn't stand to be far away from her, and he'd had his hands on her all throughout dinner. On her shoulder, in her hair, on her leg.

"That gift should have you all loosened up," he teased, pretending to peer at her backside.

Knowing she was wearing one of his toys all throughout the meal had made it nearly impossible to concentrate on anything she said. He'd done his best, though, and they'd chatted about their travels, the places they'd been, the places they wanted to go, and many other topics. The whole time his mind kept drifting downward to her body, and forward to later tonight.

A few times she'd seemed to want to talk more, and had even mentioned last night. She'd seemed so carefree when she said those words, as if all that was said and unsaid was no big deal. Maybe it wasn't a big deal that he hadn't returned her words twenty-four hours ago.

Last night.

Big deal or not, those two words still felt heavy, like a brick weighing him down. He didn't want to fuck up this night, or last night, or any other night. He feared that if he said anything else, if he revealed too much or too little, that he'd simply say the wrong thing.

That fear of fucking up had him in its clutches; it was gripping him, holding him tenaciously in a tight fist. He felt more for this woman next to him than he'd ever felt for Aubrey, which was at once a beautiful realization, and also a cruel punch in the gut. Comparing Michelle to Aubrey made him feel like complete shit. His lack of *enough* feelings for Aubrey had led to the worst thing possible. The fact that he felt anything should be a weight lifting, but it dredged up all the self-loathing that he thought he was finally letting go, thanks to these nights with her.

She was so much more effective than therapy. Being with her was the *only* thing that eased the ache.

And yet he couldn't shake the fear that the more he said, the greater the chance he'd mess up something. Or hurt her. He had a track record, and maybe it was a track record of one, but that was enough to have to protect her from him.

After he paid the check, she dropped her hand on top of his. "Jack," she said, and her voice was serious. "About last night, and the things I said—"

He cut her off. "Last night was amazing. All of it. And tonight will be amazing too. And so will the next night," he said.

"Yes. They will be. The rest of these thirty nights will be amazing, and then we'll move on," she said, flashing him a smile that seemed to exist on the surface only. "Like we planned."

His gut twisted at the thought. He wanted to stay here, in Paris, in this moment in time with her. But they'd made a deal, and they'd never mapped out a contingency plan for more days. Besides, why would they need them? He couldn't give her more than this, even though he hated the thought of the thirty-first day. He didn't want to see that day or the ones that followed it.

"Yes. Like we planned," he echoed, even as he felt something well up in his chest. A desire to say more. To ask for more time. But that wasn't fair, so he kissed her.

Maybe it made him an ass, but the kiss served many purposes. Not only the physical, but it also distracted her, judging from the way goose bumps rose on her bare arms. And it kept his mouth shut. He wanted the night to be perfect for her, so he kept the focus on the one thing he couldn't mess up—sex. He did everything he could to avoid returning to the 'I'm falling in love with you conversation' because that conversation was what had ruined Aubrey, and he didn't want to ruin Michelle.

He wanted to worship her, so after she'd excused herself to stop in the restroom, he took her back to the hotel, his focus solely on the purity of the pleasure he wanted to give her.

He'd spread a small hand towel on the bed and left the lube and some massage oil on it. As the door to the room shut, he dimmed the lights, but didn't turn them all the way off. He couldn't bear not to look at her.

She turned to face him. He couldn't read her expression.

"Are you okay? Are you nervous?"

She shook her head. "No. Not at all."

"Good," he said, grasping her hand and leading her to the bed. He backed her up against it, and when her knees hit the mattress she sank down, her hair spreading across the royal blue bedspread. She looked like a dream to him, her hair in waves, her breasts free under the soft cotton, and her eyes hooked on him the whole time. She propped herself on her elbows and watched as he unknotted the tie he'd worn to dinner and tossed it on a chair somewhere behind him.

It staggered him. Her desire. Her heart. How much she gave of herself. He moved up to her face, cupped her cheeks in his hands, and looked her in the eyes. He didn't say it, wouldn't say—couldn't say it.

But he could say this. "About last night," he began, trying again to fix his mistake.

She placed her finger on his lips. "Don't say a word," she whispered.

He shook his head and kept going. "When I said I can't get enough of you, I meant it. I can't," he whispered, and it wasn't a return of her sentiment, but it was as close as he could possibly come.

"I feel the same about you," she said. Her expression softened more as she ran her fingertips over his jaw. Her touch nailed him in the heart. He grabbed her hand from his face, and clasped it.

His heart beat so hard he swore it was going to fight its way out of his chest, landing in her fucking hands where it belonged. He was aching to tell her how he felt for her. He fought that instinct hard, shoved it away, and returned to the role he could play well.

"Stay like that. I'm going to put on music," he said, and grabbed his phone from the coffee table and called up Ravel's 'Bolero.'

The opening notes were faint, as the composer intended, and Michelle raised an eyebrow in question. "What are you playing?"

"Bolero."

She grinned. "Like you told me you wanted to someday."

"Someday is now," he said, then he stalked over to her, dropped down to his knees and gently spread her legs apart. Her skirt rose up to her mid thighs, and he could only see a sliver of her panties, but the sight of her arousal took his breath away. She must have been wet all through dinner, because she was soaked now. And that delicious wetness was all for him. "I want you so much," he said.

* * *

She'd been lying when she said she wasn't nervous. How could she not be? She might want this, but she'd never done it, and fear was natural. Sure, she'd gotten off to plenty of naughty videos and gifs. She'd seen enough to know she found the possibility of this type of penetration incredibly alluring. The purple jewel had kept her buzzing at a constant state of arousal all through dinner. But that natural born fear of pain still existed. The ass was not designed for a cock, and certainly not one of Jack's size.

Yet, she wanted to feel him, wanted to know if there was more sexual pleasure to be had beyond all the toys and tricks they'd tried so far. When he said he couldn't get enough of her, she knew what he meant. He craved her body, and that hunger of his had been healing her. That desire of his had been restoring her sense of sexiness as he turned her into a wanted woman. The more she took of him, the more she'd felt rebuilt. Ready to conquer the world as a remade woman.

She was choosing to exist in the moment of their arrangement. To let herself live in this sensuality, and this feeling of not ever getting enough. To be happy with what she had, and for a little bit longer, she had him.

He came at her like a ravenous man. His jaw was hard, his eyes were blazing, and his hands were strong as he spread her legs further. In a blur, he was between her thighs, kissing the drenched lace of her panties. She moaned and was tempted to close her eyes, but instead she pushed up further on her elbows, wanting to watch him as he flicked his tongue against the panel, then moved lower, pressing his lips against the jewel. She could barely feel his mouth, but the image of what he was doing was so erotic that more heat pooled between her legs. She'd be gushing soon, and she was sure he would lap up every ounce of her.

She exhaled deeply, unsure of how they were getting from Point A to Point B. But the wine had worked its way through her body, softening her muscles, relaxing her mind, so she let go of the need to know what was coming.

Anticipation was its own elixir.

"Sit up and raise your arms," he told her, and she obeyed. He reached for her dress straps. She lifted the skirt and he tugged the material the rest of the way over her head. His breath hissed when he looked at her breasts. As if he couldn't control himself, he dived in, drawing one pink bud into his mouth and sucking so hard she heard a loud, wet pop when he let go, replacing his mouth with his big hand.

"Perfect tits," he said, then returned his attention to the other breast, licking and sucking her voraciously. She curled her hands around his head, tugging him closer, thrusting her breasts into his face. His soft hair brushed against her chest, and a fresh wave of pleasure tore through her body.

The steady beat of drums and flutes filled the room, the sensual music matching her desire. A build, a tease, a long, kama-sutric piece of music that suited the way Jack loved her body.

"Turn over," he told her.

"Already?"

She'd been expecting a little more foreplay, to be honest.

He laughed as he unbuttoned his shirt. "I'm going to massage you," he said with a smile, and turned her on her stomach, flat on the bed.

She closed her eyes, and with that sense turned off for the moment, her ears trained on the music, and the sound of him pouring massage oil into his palms. His hands came down on her shoulders, and he began kneading. She moaned appreciatively. She hadn't even realized she was sore.

"I'm going to make every single second feel good for you," he whispered, as his thumbs worked the muscles of her shoulders.

"Everything you do to me feels good," she said, and he traveled down her back, the vanilla scent of the massage oil adding to the headiness of the scene that was unfolding here in their Paris hotel room. He rubbed down her back, working his thumbs and fingers along her spine, then out to her sides, then down to her lower back.

"You are so beautiful," he whispered, and his voice sounded different this time. Gone was the commanding, confident tone he usually saved for the bedroom. His voice was full of reverence and something else. Something deeper; something that felt lasting. She tried not to read too much into it. If she did, she'd be lost to him.

She directed her thoughts to her body and the way she felt as he touched her, his hands sending goose bumps across her flesh. His breath ghosted along her spine, as if he were leaving a trail of the faintest kisses down her back all the way to the top of her panties. Then she felt a flick from his tongue along the waistband, and he lowered them perhaps an inch, licking softly across the top of her cheeks.

She wriggled into him as sparks shot through her, straight to her core. "God, I love the way you respond to me," he said, kissing her cheeks more as he continued to rub her back.

"Because you know what to do to me," she said, her breathing growing heavier as his tongue dipped lower, teasing between her cheeks, but never quite dipping down to the jewel that was still safely inside her.

"It's not that I *know* what to do to you. It's that I *love* touching you. I love your skin, and your smell, and everything about you," he said, as he dug his fingers into her hipbones. She tensed at the free and easy way he said *love* in relation to her body and her sexuality. But he hadn't breathed it in relation to her.

Now was not the time to linger on the matters of the heart. That was child's play. This was an adult moment. One she wanted to relish.

"I love everything about you, Michelle," he echoed, and she hated that she wished he were saying those words in a different order. She tried desperately to push her emotions out of the bedroom, to kick them hard into the hallway, and just let herself take his words at face value. At body value. She begged her mind to go blank as best it could; to let her body lead the way back to him. "You are the most sensuous woman I've ever known."

She heard a low growl from his throat, a deep primal sound of approval as he flicked his fingertip against the jewel in her ass. That did the trick. Oh, holy hell, did that do a number on her. Goodbye brain, hello body.

Flipping her over, he tugged off her panties in one fast move, leaving a glistening trail of wetness down the side of her leg. "I need your pussy in my face right now," he said, returning to his rougher ways.

She arched her hips up, ready, so damn ready for him to touch her. But before he did, he tugged gently at the jewel, twisting it once, and then pulling it out, and dropping it onto the towel. The absence of it hit her hard, and even though it had been a low source of pressure, it had kept her humming. Now it was gone, and she found herself wanting to be filled again.

But that was probably the point.

Then, she found herself wanting nothing at all but this very moment as he buried his face between her thighs, and lapped her up. All thought faded, everything in her head disappeared. There was only the exquisiteness of this hungry man devouring her. Licking her pussy, sliding his tongue inside her, flicking the tip against her swollen clit. Heat scorched her veins. She was an inferno, and she was writhing and grinding into his relentless mouth, his hungry lips. She wasn't sure who was louder, him or her, but they were both matching the music as she panted and moaned, and he made the sexiest sounds, as if he'd never been more turned on than he was right now.

She was vaguely aware of the sound of the bottle being opened, then seconds later, he slid his finger into her ass. All the way in, and her hips nearly shot off the bed.

She screamed his name, and he stopped for the briefest of seconds. "You're so fucking ready," he breathed out hard, returning in an instant to his mission.

"I am, oh God, I am," she said, grabbing his head and riding it, fucking his face shamelessly, rocking her hips into him as he consumed her. The pressure from his finger and the intense pleasure from his mouth collided inside her in the perfect storm, and an orgasm blasted through her in a fury.

In seconds, he'd crawled up her and was straddling her. "Unzip my pants," he growled, and she fumbled at the zipper. Somehow in this drugged-out, blissed-out state she was able to work it down, and his beautiful cock sprang free.

"Suck me. Like you did the morning after we met," he told her, guiding his thick erection to her mouth. She remembered exactly what he meant, and grabbed his hips. She opened her mouth wide, and he stroked his dick into her lips, lowering himself into her mouth. She drew him in, licking and loving his cock, and then she reached her hands through his legs, playing with his balls. A deep groan rumbled up through his chest. "Is this how you came alone in bed that morning?"

She nodded as she lapped him up from stem to stern.

"That's how I like it. You know how I like it. But that's all I'm going to take for now," he told her, then moved from the bed to strip off the rest of his clothes.

He returned, and handed her the lube. "Put some on me," he said.

She nodded, and rubbed some onto his thick shaft, thrilling at the way his eyes floated closed and he grunted from her slightest touch. He wanted her as much as she wanted him.

He sighed, a deep satisfied sound. Then he gently laid his body on hers, and kissed her, softly at first, then more deeply, as if he needed to connect with her this way. He pulled apart from her, and moved down her body to her hips, shifting her onto her stomach.

She felt so exposed even though she'd been naked with him countless times. But this time was different. It was a first, and she felt virginal. But not for long. He tugged her up by her hips. "On your elbows," he said, and she did as told.

He ran a hand down her back. "God, you're perfect," he said, stopping at her ass, spreading her cheeks apart. "You're so fucking perfect, and so ready."

She turned her neck to meet his gaze. "I want to watch," she said, surprised at the words that had just come out of her mouth. She hadn't thought about watching. But she found she desperately wanted to. Keeping her eyes open kept her in the moment.

"Watch everything," he told her as he rubbed his thumb on her opening. "So ready," he murmured, lowering his head to flick his tongue against her bottom.

She drew a sharp breath from the sweet intensity of his tongue, then he rubbed the head of his cock against her. Tension rolled through her bones as some deep part of her instinctual nature warned her against the potential pain. But she pushed it out of her mind as he slowly, carefully eased into her.

She curled her shoulders forward in reaction from the pressure inside her rear. Like a deep, far stretching of her whole body, of every muscle and fiber in her being. He was barely in, maybe only an inch, and she had no clue how he was going to fit any more of himself in her.

"Does it hurt?" he asked, stilling.

"Yes," she answered truthfully. "But I still want it."

"Are you sure?"

She nodded, taking a deep breath, and on an exhale, she said, "More."

He pushed in further, and it was like being stretched in directions she didn't know she had. She gritted her teeth. She felt as if she might burst, and she wasn't sure if it felt good or bad. Or just weird. But she didn't look away. She kept her gaze on him the whole time.

"You're so open for me," he murmured, tearing his eyes away from her face to stare at her ass. "So beautiful and so open," he said, and the words were like some kind of ode. Tender and dirty. Just like this man. Maybe that's why she finally was able to relax into this new sensation—because it was him. Because he wanted her in ways no one else ever had. Because he was as possessed by her as she was by him.

At that point it was all mental. Her body was ready to receive him. He'd prepped her well. She raised her ass higher, lowered herself further on her elbows, and invited him in all the way. Her sex throbbed. Her clit ached. She was dying to be touched all over.

He sank in. The sheer pressure spread in waves, radiating across her back, her belly, her breasts, up to her face, even. Like ripples of pleasure, coupled with this sensation of being full as she brought him inside her.

"It's better than I dreamed about," he said, and his voice was the very sound of ecstasy.

"How much did you think about this?"

"So much," he said huskily as he began to move in her, in time to the music, the sexy, seductive music that helped relax her even more. "Since I met you. Since that time on the Met Life Tower when I saw how beautiful you looked with your ass spread for me. I wanted to then," he said, holding onto her hip with one hand, dropping the other between her legs to start rubbing her clit.

She nearly screamed in pleasure from the relief. "I could tell you wanted it then," she managed to say.

"I love being in you," he said on a moan, and began stroking her clit. He thrust deeper, and at one point he was so far inside her she was sure he might rip her in two, but even through all the strange and new sensations, one feeling remained true—it felt absolutely fantastic to give herself to him like this. She wanted him in every way, and she loved how he wanted her. How he never held back. How he demanded every inch of her body, and then commanded every ounce of her pleasure. And now as he drove deeper into the darkest part of her, she felt as if her body was an instrument, being played by a virtuoso who knew what notes to hit and when. He was hitting them all, and he consumed her. He stroked her throbbing clit until she could feel the crest of an orgasm, that delicious build in her belly and between her legs. She lowered herself further, her face hitting the bed now as she cried out her orgasm alert to the sound of the orchestra building towards the towering crescendo.

She shouted his name as the cymbals crashed at the end of the piece, sending her out in a blaze of sensory glory.

Her sounds of pleasure mingled with his as he stroked her clit furiously and fucked her ass lovingly, bringing out a shattering orgasm that made her feel as if the very world around her had been blasted apart and then stitched back together on her cries. It was bliss, it was sweet agony—it was exquisite, soul-shattering fucking.

Even though somewhere in the dark reaches of her mind, the parts that she'd tried to shut down, she hoped that it was love. That even at its dirtiest and basest, it could be love.

The physical didn't lie. Even this kind of sex with Jack felt like love. She wished she could get that notion out of her head, but she didn't want to let go of it, either. She wanted both. She wanted it all. She wanted everything with him. And she couldn't deny that she felt the flicker of hope that he wanted it all too.

"Oh God, I'm going to come, too," he groaned. "Can I come in you?"

"Yes," she told him, loving that he asked her permission before he released himself into a new part of her body.

* * *

Some point later, after he'd cleaned her with the towel, he drew a warm bath. He carried her to the tub, then washed her all over, dried her and brought her back to bed.

"Thank you," he murmured as he kissed her neck.

"Thank you?"

"For giving me all of you," he said, wrapping his arms around her and pulling her close. Then he brushed her hair from her ear.

She wished he were whispering in her ear right now. Telling her he felt the same way she did. God, it was so fucking pathetic to want to be loved this badly.

But there was only silence. A silence she wanted to fill with all she felt for him.

She could taste the words she wanted to say. She could feel them take shape on her tongue. They were longing to escape her lips.

I want you to have all of me. I'm in love with you.

She'd tried. She'd tried so fucking hard to put the genie back into the bottle. She'd worked so hard to treat this only as sex. But it was impossible. The heart wanted what the heart wanted, and that was him. All of him for all of her. She swallowed thickly, trying desperately to get rid of that lump in her throat. But then an errant tear slipped from the corner of her eye, landing on the sheets.

He watched it fall, then kissed her eyelids. "Does it hurt?"

"Yes," she said, because it was true.

She wished she could slide Jack back into the slot she'd reserved for him. But she'd fallen in love with a man who didn't love her back. She had no one to blame but herself.

Fool me once, shame on you. Fool me twice . . .

CHAPTER TWENTY-THREE
Blunt

He was a world-class asshole. He couldn't do this to her. He was a ticking time-bomb, and he could explode at any minute. He didn't trust himself. He didn't trust his instincts.

Awake since four in the morning, he sat parked on the couch, his head in his hands. He'd worked for a few hours, pounding out answers to emails, dealing with business issues with Casey. He'd gone for a walk, leaving behind a note that jet-lag had beaten him and he would be back with bread and croissants. He had them in a bag on the coffee table, and now he was waiting for her to finish her shower. She didn't know he'd returned, and he didn't know what he was going to say. But he had to tell her the truth. She'd opened up to him on everything, and he'd given her nothing.

Soon, he heard the water stop running, then a few minutes later she emerged, her hair sleek and wet. A towel was wrapped around her body.

She smiled the second she saw him, but it didn't reach her eyes. "See? Two mornings in a row. I'm still not a dragon."

He could barely crack a grin in response. But he tried. For her. "And you still have ten toes."

She wiggled them. "Have you been up for a while?" she asked and joined him on the couch, tucking her feet underneath her.

He shook his head, heaved a sigh, and bit the bullet. "Listen, Michelle," he began, and she sat ramrod straight.

"*Listen, Michelle* is never a good way to start a sentence."

"I don't mean it like that," he said quickly, trying to ease her concerns. He reached for her hand, clasping it between his, but she drew hers back. She pressed her lips tight together and motioned for him to keep talking.

He had no choice. This was it. But hell, this was why he came to see her in the first place. He hadn't been able to get the words out with Kana. They'd circled it and danced around it, but he'd never told her about the chain reaction his lack of love had set off. "I need to tell you the truth about Aubrey's death," he said as quickly as he could. This was the only way he could manage. Heave it up. No doubt it wouldn't be the first time she'd heard someone toss his or her distorted emotions at her feet.

Her eyes widened in shock, and her features froze. Oh, shit. She thought he did it? Well, he might as well have. She scooted away from him.

"I didn't kill her," he said, backpedaling faster than he'd expected to.

She jumped up from the couch, one hand clasping the ends of the towel. "I didn't say you did. And I'm honestly not even sure why you would say that."

"Because of how you reacted," he said, pointing at her retreating from him.

"I'm going to get dressed," she said crisply, and he understood the implication loud and clear. She was not going to let herself be vulnerable during this conversation.

She moved to her suitcase and pulled on a bra and panties faster than he'd ever seen a woman slip on clothes.

Fuck this. He wasn't going to mince words. "I broke off the engagement fifteen minutes before she died," he said blurting it out, and he wanted to scream from the pain. It was worse than ripping off a Band-Aid. It was like slamming his hand into a car door. Everything he'd held inside for more than a year was exposed, and it hurt like a motherfucker.

"What?" she asked, blinking.

Even with the ache all over, the open, bleeding wound, he had to keep going. Get it all out. "It was a week before the wedding," he said, each word like gravel in his mouth. "I took her to the mountains for the weekend, thinking that would be the best place to tell her the news that I didn't want to marry her." The bitter sting of regret rose up again. How wrong had he been? He should have told Aubrey in her apartment. He should have told her at a park. Anyplace else.

"You picked the mountains because she was a skier," Michelle said softly, seeming to understand as she tugged on a skirt and a shirt. But even if his choice had made logical sense, it was the wrong choice.

"The mountains were her favorite place," he said, with a scoff directed at himself. "I wanted her to be near something she loved when I delivered the news. After I told her, she got on the slopes, tore down the hill, and hit a tree," he said, getting the last part out as clinically as he could so he wouldn't have to feel the fresh devastation of the moment he learned she died all over again.

She sat down on the edge of the bed, waiting for him to speak more.

"That part is all true," he added, as he stood up and moved closer, but she held up a hand. This was as close as she wanted him to be. Damn. He knew this was how it would go. The second he'd opened his mouth around a woman and voiced the full truth, he'd caused more damage than he'd ever intended.

"Okay. Go on," she said, scrunching her eyebrows together. "What part isn't true then? Why you didn't want to marry her?"

He shoved a hand through his hair, digging hard into his scalp. Is this what it would have been like to tell her in her office? As her patient? Maybe. He couldn't know because he was someone else to her now. He was her lover who couldn't even tell her how he felt. Frustration flowed thick in his veins. What he wouldn't give to rid this guilt from his body. That was too much to ask, though. He sat on the edge of the table, and tore off more of the truth for her. "The image the media paints of me?"

"The widower with the broken heart," she supplied. "That image?"

"Yeah," he said, with the shame that the title brought surely evident in his features. "That image."

"That's not true," she said in a calm, comforting voice. He suspected it was her work voice, and that she'd segued into it. He only hoped she didn't start viewing him as a project, as someone who needed fixing. He didn't want to be that person with her. He wanted to be so much more, but he hardly knew how.

"I cared about Aubrey deeply. I loved her as a friend. But I didn't love her as a man loves a woman," he said in a low voice, one he barely recognized as his own. Because he'd only said these words out loud to his sister, and to Nate. "I wasn't in love with her."

"*Oh,*" she said on a long, loud sigh of understanding. It was all out in the open. She could see him for who he truly was. "But everyone believes you're the person the media portrays you as. The grieving widower." She crossed her arms, protecting herself from the man before her.

A calloused jerk.

He nodded. "Yes. Because that was the least I could do for her."

She tilted her head to the side. "How so?"

"She died," he said, practically shouting as the guilt charged back up through him, rearing its ugly head. "She fucking died, and it was my fault because I didn't love her. I couldn't be anything publicly but the grieving widower. I couldn't go tell the world I didn't love her. I couldn't do that to a dead woman."

"I get that part," she said, nodding several times, taking in what he was saying. Then she was quiet as she stood up, walked over to her purse and rooted around in it until she found a band for her hair. She twisted her wet hair up on her head and moved over to the couch near to him. A dangerous thing called hope dared to make an appearance. Maybe she'd forgive him. "But you think it was your fault she died?" she asked, continuing her questions. He couldn't read her.

"Well, yeah. I told her how I felt. She went for a run down the mountain. She was always incredibly safe, and that was the one time she was out of control. How could it be anything but my fault?"

She didn't speak at first. She steepled her hands together, and there was something about this side of Michelle that scared him. She'd retreated into her work mode, and she was excellent at it, but it wasn't how he knew her and experienced her. She was methodical; she was assessing him. Even though he knew she didn't judge her clients, he felt judged. He felt small. He felt stupid. He was all of those things and more. He deserved to feel this way.

"Jack," she began, her voice distant. "Why did you stay with her for so long if you didn't love her?"

Her question surprised him. He hadn't expected that. He hadn't asked himself that question. *Ever.* He'd only beaten himself up for not loving her. But he'd never delved into why he'd stayed with her so long.

He parted his lips to speak, but no words came.

She spoke for him. "You were together for a few years, and engaged for nearly a year? Why, if you didn't love her?"

He nodded, the hot shame rolling over him again. "I think I just felt as if we were supposed to be together. Everyone expected it. We were high school sweethearts, and then we got back together years later. It just seemed like it should have worked."

"But you knew you didn't love her? How long did you know that?"

"Several months," he admitted, swallowing down a lump. That was the real rub.

"What made you think you should marry someone you didn't love? Why would you stay? That's what I most want to understand," she said gently.

He answered her honestly, feeling completely exposed and naked as he bared the truth to her. That he was a man who was so disconnected from love that he stayed with someone he didn't. "I really don't know."

"Were your parents like that? Like you and Aubrey?" she asked, probing, as if she were on a fearless hunt for his truth.

Her question echoed through the quiet room. It rattled through his head, like a top spinning wildly, then finally settling down. The light bulb went off. The buzzer dinged. And there it was. Something that made sense about his choices. An answer, maybe. A truth he could grasp. Was it that simple?

"They weren't in love either. They stayed together until Casey left for college," he said, then shared more details of his parents' marriage.

"They weren't in love at all?"

"Nope."

"And that just seemed normal to you then," she said, as if she were presenting him with the answer to two plus two. *Gently.* Holding out her hand and offering him *four.*

Could he take it from her? Could he accept such a simple answer? One that had been under his nose his whole life? That he'd simply done all he knew? "I suppose," he said, trying it on for size.

"That was the model you had before you. Even if your relationship was different, the marriage you saw was one not based on love, but on obligation," she said, and he was surely being counseled by her now. He was the patient. She was the shrink. And the shrink understood all that the patient didn't. The shrink guided him through that dark forest to the clearing on the other side. He could see a small sliver of light, and he wanted to grab it, hold onto it. He didn't want to slide back into the darkness. Because maybe, just maybe, he wasn't broken. He just hadn't known anything else.

"So you're saying I stayed with her because of my parents?" he asked, raising his eyebrows, wishing he didn't feel like the guy on the psychiatrist's couch right now. But hell, he wanted to understand what was wrong with him. Or not wrong with him.

"That's why it took you until a week before the wedding to call it off. Because you stayed with her, since you didn't know the alternative. Love looked like obligation, not like some—" she paused, as if hunting for a word, "— incandescent thing." That word hit him hard in the gut. Like a revelation. He'd called her *incandescent* in an email. It wasn't a word you heard often. But it was the fitting adjective to describe the difference between how he'd felt for Aubrey, and how love was supposed to be.

"Yeah," he said, nodding, and he felt just the tiniest bit lighter. With her insight he understood his own motivations. His worries. His fears. He hadn't wanted to wind up like his parents, but he didn't know any other way to be, so he did what they did. "I guess I didn't. But I must have been doing the same thing. I never thought about it like that."

"It's my job to help people see things in a new light. In a light that might help them understand," she said, and she seemed to be returning to the woman he went to Paris with, not the shrink. He wanted to reach out to her, hold her, ask her if they were going to be okay.

But he had to focus on Michelle, not on himself. "You're not mad that I kept this from you? That I didn't tell you right away?" he asked, the worry roaring back into him that once again he'd taken a misstep. A big one.

She shook her head. "No. I understand that it was difficult to process. That you had to tell me in your time, and in your own way."

"And you don't hate me for not loving her?" he asked, his shoulders feeling lighter, his heart freer again. Because of her.

"No. That was your normal. That felt normal to you. It took you a while to realize it, but you did come to that on your own. You did realize that love doesn't have to be based on obligations. That takes a lot of guts to call off a wedding, when you realize you're not in love."

But, but, but. There was still that big overhang. There was still that empty ache in his chest that guilt had set up camp in. He might understand why he'd stayed with Aubrey now, but that didn't exonerate him from the damage he'd done. He inhaled deeply, exhaled, and said the hardest thing of all.

"But it's my fault she died," he muttered.

She shot him a sharp look, as if his statement didn't add up. "I'm going to be blunt with you."

Blunt was good. He could handle blunt. He needed blunt. No more circling around the cold, hard truth. Dive in headfirst. "Please. Be blunt."

"Get over yourself," she said firmly, her eyes fixed on his. She was intensely serious. It was a command. It was an order, and it floored him.

"Whoa," he said, holding up his hands, surprised by the crassness of her comment. "What is that supposed to mean?"

"It means that it's really narcissistic of you to think you caused her death," she continued in the same strong voice that left no confusion about how she felt.

"How is that narcissistic?"

"Jack," she said, as she slid back into full shrink mode again. "You took her to the mountains. You brought her to a safe place for her. You gave her bad news in the most loving way possible, given the circumstances. You did the best you could and no one the whole world over would think an Olympic skier couldn't handle that run," she said, giving voice to his own justifications. That *is* why he'd taken Aubrey to Breckenridge. He'd thought he was giving her a safe landing. Could it be that he was right? That he had? That the rest was simply—

"It's called luck," she continued, filling in the questions that were in his head. "It's called a risk. You didn't cause her death, and you need to get that out of your head right now."

With her words, he felt the heavy weight lift. He didn't know it until now, but he had been seeking absolution. He had wanted to be washed clean of his regret. He'd needed to hear that sometimes, terrible things happen, and you don't cause them because of what you said fifteen minutes before. But that doesn't mean you shouldn't say the hard things.

"So we're okay then?" he asked, the world seeming to come into focus again. The sun dared to shine through the window, the sounds of an early Paris morning floating into the room. They could have their croissants, get a coffee, go to a museum, find a secret nook . . .

She laughed once, then shook her head. "Not so fast."

"Wait. You just said you understood," he said, furrowing his brow. He couldn't lose her. He couldn't bear it. She was his anchor. She was his sanity.

"I do understand. I understand as a therapist. I understand as a professional. But as a woman who loves you? It's a lot harder. I understand in my head, but my heart wants to retreat," she said, placing her hand on her chest, already shielding her own heart from him. From the way he could wield malice without even trying, apparently. "And not simply because of what you told me. Because I don't want to be part of a pattern. I don't want to be the next woman you care for, but don't love. I know you were only doing what you learned. But I've been putting myself on the line for far too long. This isn't separate for me any longer, Jack. I wish it were. I truly wish I didn't feel all that I do for you. But it happened. I fell in love with you, and I need to really think about whether I want to keep putting myself out there when you're not even sure if you know how to love," she said, reaching across the table, and grasping his hands. "I have given you my whole heart, all of my body, and everything in my soul. And I have never felt so wanted. But I need to be loved."

"But Michelle, you are. I swear," he said, wanting desperately to convince her, but failing, judging from the way she winced, as if his words had wounded her. They sounded weak even to him. *You are* was not how you told a woman how you felt. "Let me rephrase that," he said, wishing it wasn't so damn hard just to say it.

She stood up, smoothed out her shirt, and held up a hand. "I'm going out for the day. Just to walk. To be alone."

"Where are you going?" he asked, his heart racing with worry.

"I don't know. But I need some space. And to be frank, you probably do too. Maybe you need to spend some time processing. It's kind of a big deal what you shared with me," she said in a sympathetic voice.

"When will I see you again?" he asked, hating the way he sounded, but needing to know if this was the end.

"I don't know."

"Are you . . . are we still staying together?" he asked tentatively, because it seemed as if the entire trip had been upended now, turned on its head.

"That's a good question. And I don't have the answer to that. This is why I need some time alone right now to think. All I know for certain is we have an expiration date in a week anyway. So, really, what's another week?"

It was a damn good question. They'd already gone further, pushed more, fallen harder than they were supposed to. What would happen in another week? Too much, too little, not enough? Or did she mean what did it matter now if they shared their final days? Maybe they'd done all they could for each other and it was time to move on.

She seemed to be waiting for an answer, but he didn't have one.

She walked away.

CHAPTER TWENTY-FOUR
Closed

She was used to being alone. Had grown more than comfortable with her own company so it was only natural for her to leave, wet hair and all. She hadn't expected the pain though. The ache in her chest from walking away. It felt like a fresh wound, bleeding and tender, seeping crimson tears into the rest of her body, a trail of her unrequited love for him.

She pushed on sunglasses even though the sky was turning gray. Typical Paris weather. But she needed to hide her eyes or everyone could see the sadness. With her arms crossed over her chest, she walked through the mid-morning crowds on rue Royale, past the designer shops, past Cartier and Lanvin, wishing she wasn't sore in her ass. She shook her head, frustrated with herself, and nearly bumped into a woman walking a small Terrier mix.

"Pardon," she mumbled as she kept up her pace.

It seemed an indignity to have gone there with him last night, only to have him decide the next morning to suddenly confess all his goddamn guilt. She'd tried so hard to be rational, to separate herself from all he'd shared, to be the consummate professional. But inside, she'd been reeling, sent back to the starting line. Do not cross go. Do not collect $200. You are once again in love with a man who doesn't love you.

Fine, fine. The situation was vastly different from Clay. He hadn't even known how she felt, and he never reciprocated. With Jack, she *knew* he cared. She knew he wanted her. But was he even capable of love? That's what terrified her. He hadn't returned her words the other night, and he certainly hadn't left her with any reassurances this morning either. He'd only said *You are.*

A slight reassurance, but it didn't cut it.

She understood why he'd left Aubrey, and she didn't fault him for that. But she had to wonder if the man could ever take a big step, and she needed a big step. She'd taken it with him. Not through sex, but by loving him. Loving him desperately. She didn't want *just sex* with him anymore. She wanted it all, and she barely had anything.

But that was her own fault, wasn't it? She'd overstepped the conditions of their deal.

Typical. So damn typical of her. She always fell for the wrong guy. She always felt too much. She needed a straightjacket for her heart. Cage the damn thing up, and wrap chains around it. Stupid organ was working overtime, and she needed it to work less.

She marched past a cafe with a red awning, and peered inside at the plates of eggs and bread being served. Her stomach rumbled. She was hungry, and she was mad for being hungry. Didn't her stomach know that her heart and her head were a terrible mess?

She spotted a couple in the corner, the man happily feeding the woman a slice of potato. The woman rolled her eyes in pleasure. His arm was draped over her shoulder.

Michelle wanted to hiss at them.

She looked away, resuming her walk, but suddenly lovers were everywhere. Around every corner. On every bench. In every cafe. She didn't want to be surrounded by lovers. She wanted to escape from her head, and all these thoughts pounding at her, begging for attention.

At the next taxi stand, she grabbed a cab, and sped off to Gare Saint Lazare. An hour later, the train rattled into Giverny, and she caught another taxi to Monet's Gardens.

She bought a ticket, and crossed into another world, a kaleidoscope of colors with reds, yellows and oranges that blazed under the sun. She wandered through lush fields of purple tulips, red irises, pink poppies and reached the pond where the water lilies floated lazily in the glassy blue waters, under the watchful gaze of a weeping willow.

She walked through the fall morning mist, staring at the endless beauty before her, at the pinwheel of colors—rich purples, pale blues, emerald greens. She wished love were as easy as this garden. As easy as knowing this was as close to perfection as the world would ever get.

But love was not a garden. It was a war zone right now, and she had no notion of whether to retreat or rejoin the battle. She only knew that it would be wise to have her own hotel room. She phoned the Sofitel and booked a second room for the next few nights, biting out the words so she wouldn't break down and sob. This was not how she'd planned to spend five days in Paris with him.

Apart.

* * *

He buried himself in work for the next few hours. He couldn't do anything else. Thinking about her hurt too much.

He put on blinders, and narrowed his focus solely to running his company. Tending to matters. Dealing with suppliers. Even reviewing the plans he'd put together to "change the conversation" when it came to Denkler. The plans were good, solid, strong.

Casey had sent over the marketing strategy. Henry and Eden were fully on board too. But honestly, it wouldn't take much to get the word out. A few well-placed signs outside Henry's Upper East Side store, a few online ads, and some social media mentions. Then word would spread of exactly how Eden and Joy Delivered contributed to the community.

Conroy was winning with a message that appeared positive. Denkler and company would overtake him, with a far, far better one.

The approach would work; he was as sure of that as he was of anything when it came to business. He knew how to navigate the choppy waters of the business world. Show him a problem, he'd show you the solution. That was his specialty. Applying logic. Studying the map and seeing a new route through. Finding the path that others hadn't spotted yet.

With Michelle, he was sure of nothing. He felt so damn much for her. It was like a geyser inside of him, overflowing, and he didn't know what to do with all these thoughts rushing at him. Confessing about Aubrey was like sloughing off the past, shedding all that had held him back.

So why couldn't he take the next step with her?

Michelle vexed him. His feelings for her had thoroughly and completely thrown him off. He had to solve the problem. He had to figure this out. He slammed his laptop shut and paced the room. To the window. To the bathroom door. To the couch again.

The whole damn room smelled of her. He grabbed her red dress from last night; it had been tossed onto a chair by the window. It probably landed there when he tugged it off her. Bringing it to his nose, he inhaled her. She was in him. She filled him. She flooded his nostrils, and permeated every pore of his body.

He dropped the dress on top of her suitcase, missing her, even when she'd only been gone a few hours.

He grabbed his phone, just in case she'd texted him or called. But his screen was quiet, and it pissed him off. He stared at the phone as if it were the phone's fault, then he gunned it at the ground.

It clunked dully on the carpet.

"Fuck," he muttered. He couldn't even throw a phone properly. He couldn't even break a piece of technology. He swiveled around, hunting for a glass, a vase, something. But then he stopped, shoving his hand through his hair. Throwing shit wasn't the solution. He knew better.

He slid the room key into his back pocket, grabbed his phone and wallet, and then left, hoping the distance would mute the longing.

He reached the lobby, and then walked out the revolving doors onto the Paris sidewalk, the sounds of the French language falling on his ears. He invited it in, hoped it would quell the confusion in his head as he walked and walked and walked. He didn't have a plan. He didn't have a destination.

There was only the sidewalk. And the gray sky. And the noises and sights of the city. The clink of espresso cups at cafes, the lush raspberries on a tart in a bakery window, the silvery necklaces on display in a jewelry shop. The beauty for beauty's sake.

Her.

Everywhere.

In front of him.

Behind him.

In his head.

And here, right here, in the perfume bottles in front of him.

Because maybe, somewhere, deep down he'd had a destination. He hadn't known it consciously, but somehow he knew. He'd found himself in the passage with the mosaic floor and the latticework ceiling and all the shops that were now open, including this one where he'd been with her. Where he'd begun his unraveling.

La Belle Vie was the name. A beautiful life. He stopped at the window, pressing his fingertips against it, like a kid staring longingly inside a candy shop. There they were—mirrored shelves upon shelves of perfume bottles like he'd seen the other night. He squinted, and swore that in a far corner of the shop he could see a sapphire-blue bottle.

The one she'd wanted. He ran for the door, and stopped short when a hunched over man in a faded blue sweater was locking the door, then swinging around a sign that said FERMÉ.

CHAPTER TWENTY-FIVE
Consumed

Enough tears were shed. Enough emotions were spent. Enough time was devoted to all this *space*. Space sucked. Feeling sucked. Loving sucked. She left the gardens and walked into the gift shop, desperate for a book to help her get out of her head. Something to numb all these feelings in her chest.

She wandered past calendars and mugs with water lilies on them, and found a tall set of white shelves with books about art history, and coffee table books of Monet's paintings, and a huge tome about the Impressionist masters. She spotted a small sturdy paperback on the gardens themselves. Opening it, she flipped through the pages, bursting with details about all these flowers. How to grow tulips like Monet, climbing roses like Monet, even lilies like Monet. Information, facts, details. Nothing more. It was precisely what she needed. To blot out everything else.

She walked up to the cash register and bought the book, wishing her trip hadn't come down to this moment.

But it had. Oh, it had. It came down to comfort in the form of a book about gardening.

She was the butt of her own joke, only nothing felt funny. Nothing felt right. Nothing felt good.

* * *

"You're closed?" he asked the man in French.

"For lunch. Yes," the man replied.

"But I just want to buy that blue perfume bottle," Jack said, pointing through the window of the shop to the back wall.

"We will be open again in two hours," the man said, tucking a newspaper under his arm, and taking a step away from the door.

"Can you just sell me that blue bottle now? I'll be fast."

The man shook his head. "No. I am meeting my wife for lunch. I have lunch with her every Saturday. Rain or shine."

Jack placed his palms together. Suddenly, it felt vitally important to get her the perfume bottle NOW. "I'll pay you double. *S'il vous plait.*"

The man clapped him on the arm. "You can come back later. I will sell it to you then. Now, if you'll excuse me, I will regret it more if I miss lunch with my wife."

The man turned and walked down the covered arcade and out into the Paris afternoon, that word trailing behind him like the last notes of a song fading out on the radio.

Regret.

This man would regret being late to lunch with his wife. And he'd chosen her over a business transaction.

Jack stumbled into the wall with the realization. It was simple. It was so goddamn simple. He'd let this regret define him. He'd dressed himself in it every day. He'd come to rely on it, like a fucking crutch. He needed to be that man walking away, content with the knowledge that he'd regret *not* seeing his wife for lunch.

Like a cloud rolling away to reveal the sun, Jack knew instantly what he'd regret more. Not telling Michelle everything in his heart. Every single thing he felt for her. Because it was no longer muddled. It was no longer messy. It was as clear as the closed sign on the door. It was as defined as the sapphire-blue bottle he wanted to buy for her. It was as easy as having lunch with your wife on a Saturday.

Distance and muting weren't the solution. They were the essence of the problem. Already, in a few short hours of her being gone, he missed her so much it was driving him mad. Insane with longing. Desperate with the need to see her. If he couldn't get his act together and just tell her how he felt—regardless of the risks, real or imagined—he'd lose her for good.

He couldn't chance that.

He didn't need an elaborate plan or a complicated strategy. He needed to speak from the heart. The thing he was most afraid of doing. His biggest fear was speaking the full truth about his feelings. But he'd lose her for sure if he didn't do more than *try*. Trying was for other men. Trying was not remotely sufficient any more. He needed to *do*.

Fully, completely, without reservation.

He grabbed his phone from his pocket and called Michelle. She answered on the third ring.

"Hi," he said.

"Hi."

"I'm standing in the doorway of the perfume shop, and I need to see you. I need to talk to you. I need to tell you exactly what I should have told you the last time I was here. I need to tell you in a thousand ways," he said, because that's all that mattered. He needed to submerge himself in the words, to drown out all the other things he hadn't said. To start now, and start over, and start better. To stop being so damn terrified of love.

There was silence. Only silence for what felt like an eternity, and in that span of time he simply had to wait for her.

"You do?" she asked carefully.

"I do. Where are you? Are you in your favorite part of Paris that's not in Paris?"

He was rewarded with a small laugh. "I'm predictable."

He shook his head. "No. I just listened. To everything. Will you be there in an hour?"

"If you're coming, yes," she said, and he swore he could see her smiling. He knew he was.

"I am. I'm coming for you."

He doubled back to the hotel, calling the concierge along the way to request a car service stat, and then slid into the backseat of a black sedan that shot him straight out of Paris and along the road to Giverny. Nearly an hour later, the driver pulled up to the gardens, and Jack paid him.

"Do you need a ride back to Paris, sir?"

"Yes, but I don't know when."

"I'm going off-duty, but please call this number and we will send someone for you," the driver said, and handed him a card. Jack slipped it into his back pocket, thanked the man, and bought his ticket to the gardens. He walked through Monet's one-time house, then crossed into the lush landscape that had inspired the painter. In all his time here in Europe, he'd never made it to these gardens. It was a true paradise, an escape from city life, and he understood why this land had inspired so many works of art.

He scanned for her across the flowerbeds, a sea of petals in every color. A central alley was covered by iron arches, roses climbing over the metal. Weeping willows brushed the green ground with their branches. He walked the perimeter, eyes peeled the whole time, and then the Japanese bridge came into view, its green wood slats rising over the lily pond. The most beautiful sight in all the gardens was this bridge, but in his mind it barely compared to her. She was resting her elbows on the bridge, reading a book. He picked up his pace, walking across a path edged by orange and red and gold bursts of petals, then reached the bridge. She looked up when she heard footfalls.

"Did you know this garden displays two hundred thousand annuals, biennials, and perennials each year?" She held up the book. "I read it in here."

"Did you know I started to fall for you when you told me why 'Ode to Joy' was your ringtone?" he asked, stopping in front of her, and gently closing her book.

She shook her head. "No."

"I started to fall for you then because it said something about you. About who you are, and what matters to you. And I fell more the day you came to my office in your librarian outfit, and not because of how you looked or what you did. But when you sat on my lap, and you told me about how you once wanted to be a Broadway star. Except you couldn't sing, dance or act," he said, and he wanted to take her hand, to kiss her palm, to kiss her face. But he had already won her with touch. He hadn't earned her love with words yet.

"Why that?"

"Because it showed your sense of humor. Which is part of what I love about you," he said, and every time he said the word *love* it was as if another small slice of regret sheared away. "And you asked me about Aubrey and if I missed her, and that's part of how I fell in love with you too. Because you *care*. You care about your work, and your clients, and your friends, and your family. And you cared about me long before I could even begin to try to deserve you."

"Don't say that," she said softly, her hands gripping the wood railing behind her.

"It's true. Because you are so good with words and with talking and sharing, and I'm not. But I want to be. Because I want to deserve you. Like the night at the symphony, when you got mad at me."

She looked down at her feet, red coloring her cheeks. Gently, he tipped up her chin.

"I fell for you because of that, too. Because you weren't afraid to tell me the truth. To tell me to stop playing games. To be blatantly honest about something as simple as wanting an orgasm."

She laughed, and glanced away. "You're embarrassing me," she said, but she didn't seem mad. "You make me sound so horny."

"You are. And I fucking love it, Michelle. Like I love you. My God, I have to tell you how much I love you. I wasn't going to sit in that hotel room and wait for you to figure out if you were going to spend the rest of the trip with me. And I had to get my head out of my own ass and out of the past. As soon as I left the hotel, where else did I wind up but the spot where I should have told you in the first place how I felt?"

Her lips curved up, and he was dying to kiss her. But words mattered more.

"I should have told you that night outside the perfume shop. Because I felt it that night. I felt it then, and before, and after, and now. And all the time. And as soon as I realized how monumentally stupid I was for not saying something so simple as *I'm in love with you,* I had to see you. I had to tell you all the things I should have told you a million times already. The things I let myself believe were too hard to say. The things I was afraid of because of the last time I said them to Aubrey. But you're not her. You're you. And I am in love with you, and I couldn't wait for you to come back to the hotel. I didn't come to Paris to *not* be with you," he said, inching closer to the woman he adored.

"Why did you come to Paris?"

"I came here because I can't be without you. And I've held too much back. I've kept it all in here," he said, tapping his chest. "But I was feeling it all along. Denying it, but consumed by it. And I love that you call me out on my bullshit. And I love that you invited me to Paris. And that you let me spend the night with you. You let me into the part of you that you were scared of. The part that made you feel vulnerable. You brought me into all of that," he said, and his heart beat so hard and so furiously, it might leap out of his chest and into her hands. But that's where it belonged. With her.

Her brown eyes were so big, and a tear slid down her cheek. He wiped it away with his thumb, and brought the salty streak to his lips. "Don't cry," he whispered.

She just shook her head, unable to speak.

"I'm not done," he said. "Because I've done a bad job telling you how I feel. I thought if I kept it all inside, I wouldn't hurt you. I thought words were what had ended Aubrey's life. And that if I didn't say them, I could somehow protect you. But you made me realize I was a stupid, fucking selfish idiot for thinking that."

"You're not an idiot."

He nodded several times. "Yes, I am. I'm an idiot for not telling you in the doorway. I'm an idiot for not telling you at dinner last night, or later in the hotel room. Or even this morning. I've been so consumed with regret that I let it dictate everything in my life. And everything with you. And I'm not a shrink, I'm not someone who understands the fine details of emotions, or how people heal or move on. And I know you're worried that I'm not capable of love."

She started to speak, but he silenced her as he held up a finger to signal he had more to say. "It's okay, I'd be worried too. And all I can do is tell you this—I have never felt this way for anyone. I've never wanted anyone the way I want you. You consume my thoughts, you fill my heart, and I want so much more than thirty nights with you. I want the days, too. I want days like this. Good days and bad days. I don't want another week. I want all the weeks. Maybe I'm a work in progress. Maybe I'm like a rough piece of clay. But I can be refined, and shaped, and become better with you. I want to go back to New York and not have an expiration date. I want you to let me keep loving you. The way I feel for you is without question," he said, and now he didn't resist the impulse to touch her. Because he'd done enough resisting. He needed to connect fully with her.

"I want that too," she said in the tiniest voice, full of so much vulnerability.

He cupped her cheeks, holding her face in his hands, looking at her. At the woman he loved madly. Deeply. Truly. Without any regrets, without any reservations. "I'm going to tell you over and over how I feel. Because I need you to know. I always ask you to give yourself to me, and you do, and have in every way. And I want to give myself to you," he said, and she was trembling under his touch. Her shoulders shook and her lips were parted. "If you'll still have me."

"Oh Jack, you know I will. You know I love you. You know I'm crazy in love with you. You're not a work in progress," she said, her voice breaking.

"I kind of am, but I want to be a work in progress with you."

"We can be that for each other," she said, tilting her chin up.

"You want me to kiss you, don't you?" he said, their playfulness coming back.

"Always."

"I will always want to," he said, and kissed her in the garden, on the bridge, the weeping willow the witness to his deep and abiding love for this woman who'd challenged him, who'd changed him, and who'd healed him simply by loving him. That was what had truly washed away the regret. Yes, her words, her insight, her kind understanding of his past had helped him see all that he was clutching unnecessarily. But ultimately, he'd been letting go already. Letting go because she loved him.

* * *

They had a very late lunch at a cafe in town, laughing, talking, touching.

She hadn't expected him to show up. She'd resigned herself to her own hotel room, to a few more lonely days in Paris, and then to a long string of empty nights back in Manhattan, as she immersed herself in another 10K, in more Spanish lessons, in bowling, in whatever she had to do to rid this man from her mind.

She had no doubt the process of erasing Jack would have been even harder than erasing Clay had been.

But she didn't have to, because there was no longer an arrangement or an end. There was only this new beginning.

At lunch, his phone rang. He glanced at the screen, then hit ignore, then silent. "Just a customer. I'll call him later. I will regret it more if I miss this lunch right now," he said, then laced his fingers through hers.

After they ate, they wandered through Giverny, getting lost in the shops, and getting found again. Instead of calling the call service, they simply caught a train back to Paris. Because the train was what they needed and wanted. The last one, and they were all alone in their car. The conductor took their tickets, and then the overhead lights dimmed. She gazed out the window as the train rattled through the countryside at night. The hum of the wheels and the din of the engine made for a relaxing soundtrack at the end of the day.

She felt his hand in her hair, a gentle tug as he pulled her close. He turned her face so she was looking at him. "Make love to me on the train," he whispered.

It was the first time he'd said that. *Make love.* The words were like diamonds to her, and just as valuable. She wanted to be as intimate with him as she could, after he'd said those gorgeous words over and over at the gardens. Besides, they were living in the bubble for a few more days, existing outside the public eye of prying New York City gossip papers. Carla had advised her to be cautious, but as far as she could tell that guidance applied to New York, not to this moment in time.

She kissed him, sweeping her tongue across his lips, savoring the taste of his mouth. His kisses were consuming; they rocketed her to another realm; they turned her on in mere seconds. She felt that sweet ache between her legs, the one only he could soothe, so she straddled him, and unzipped his pants, so grateful to be wearing a skirt. Then, she sank onto him, and gasped silently. He filled her so completely, and held her like she was all he'd ever wanted.

She cupped his cheeks, and he gripped her waist, and she made love to him on the train back to Paris.

"Michelle," he whispered, keeping his eyes locked on hers.

"Yes?"

"I'm so in love with you," he said, holding tight to her, his words better than any dirty ones he'd ever spoken, and those had melted her with heat. But this was something else entirely. This was the deepest connection, her greatest wish. This was everything she'd ever wanted—to love and to be loved back.

"I'm so in love with you."

She looked away once to catch their hazy reflections in the dark of the window. They looked like two people who couldn't get enough of each other. His eyes squeezed shut, his breath came fast and harsh, and he moved deeper into her. She watched for another moment, thrilling inside at all that the window revealed about him, and how he felt for her. She turned back to him, their bodies colliding, their lips connecting, her arms wrapped around him as they came together once more.

Three days later, they boarded the plane for New York, and flew across the ocean. They hadn't even needed thirty nights to know they wanted so many more, and they were going to get to have them.

* * *

But the look on Jack's face when he turned on his phone as they touched down at JFK told her that something had gone terribly wrong.

CHAPTER TWENTY-SIX
Slammed

The tweet bothered her.

Casey's social media manager had alerted her to it this morning. *Not sure if this is anything, but check this out. ConroyforUES: Can't wait for Wednesday's paper. Gonna be a social media field day.*

What was most concerning was the tweet's life. It had lasted for all of thirteen seconds. The social media manager's software scoured Facebook and Twitter regularly, so if a tweet existed at all that they needed to know about, they heard about it. Killing a tweet didn't make it cease to exist. It only made the tweet more worrisome.

Tomorrow's story could be anything. It could be about a new poll revealing Conroy's lead. Or it could be about something else entirely. But given that Casey, and Denkler, hoped to dominate social media with their change-the-conversation news in a few more days, she didn't like the enemy playing in her sandbox, nor preening over it in advance.

That's why she was at the art gallery Rebel on Third and Seventy-Sixth, nibbling on a cracker and pretending to sip wine as Conroy chatted up donors in the corner. He stood next to a pricey piece of abstract art, and she half wondered if some of the wealthy patrons backing him had created the image of two red squares inside a blue one.

She'd infiltrated the event in the simplest way possible. She'd found it online, then bought a ticket under a fake name via Eventbrite. The cocktail party was being thrown to thank the biggest donors to the campaign so far, and Casey hoped she'd be able to pick up a clue, any clue, simply by circulating. She'd figured out the thin, baby-faced man was the press spokesperson, that the blond man was the chief of staff, and that the guy with slick dark hair was the campaign manager. She'd put those pieces together from her earlier digging into Conroy. But she couldn't figure out who the guy in the suit with the short dark hair was. He wore thick, black glasses, and he had the press guy's ear, whispering throughout the event.

She took her phone from her purse, pretended to scroll through photos, and snapped a shot of the two of them.

Casually, as if she were just anyone in attendance, she mingled and circulated, walking past them a few times.

But by the time the event started to wind down, she'd learned nothing more about tomorrow's papers, so she hoped it had simply been a social media slip-up. Surely those happened all the time. Even so, she dumped the photos in a reverse image search when she returned home to her laptop. She found the guy with glasses. He was second-in-command at a strategy firm that specialized in campaigns. She Googled him some more, and found his nickname

The Spin Doctor.

The moniker made her skin crawl. She closed her laptop. She fired off some of the photos to her brother, adding her usual assortment of silly captions.

Good thing she hadn't given up the sex toy business to become a detective, she mused. Besides, it was probably just an errant tweet.

* * *

Michelle looked at Jack as the plane landed.

His eyes were wide. He blinked once, then twice as the jet applied the brakes when the wheels touched the runway. He winced as he stared hard at his phone, scrolling slowly with his thumb. He shut his eyes, squeezed them tight, and it seemed as if he were wishing away what he was reading.

Wrapping a hand around his arm, she asked him if everything was okay. Before he could answer, her phone buzzed, coming alive again now that they were on the ground.

"No," he whispered in a strangled voice.

"What's wrong?" she asked, and her phone buzzed again, then bleated loudly. She snapped her eyes to the screen out of habit. Davis. He never called her work phone.

A chill ran through her bones as she answered.

"Hello?"

"Are you okay?" he asked, and her heart seized up when she heard his voice. This was how he sounded the night he'd told her their parents had died. He was the one who had answered the door when the police officer knocked to deliver the news about the fatal accident on the icy road. He was the one who'd found her in her bedroom upstairs, listening to music, and turned off the radio to tell her. He was the one who had delayed college for a year to help her finish high school because they were suddenly all alone. Just the sound of his voice sent her back to that night, but she couldn't figure out what the hell he could be calling about now. The worst *had* happened. There was no one left but them. Unless something had happened to Jill.

A lump rose up in her throat. "Is Jill okay?"

"Jill's fine. You didn't see the story, did you?"

"No. I just landed," she said, her voice shaky. "What is it? Just tell me."

"I'm waiting at baggage claim for you. It's not good, Michelle."

Shame spilled over in her waves as her mind raced through possibilities. Pictures of her and Jack in the perfume shop doorway, on the train, even at the Grand Colbert. Oh Lord, had her skirt blown up? Had someone seen that jewel in her ass?

But that would have been welcome compared to the story.

Jack handed her his phone, and wrapped an arm around her as she read. "None of it is true. We'll fix it. I promise. I swear," he said, kissing her forehead as the written words sliced through her, like sharp knives, chopping her career to tiny pieces.

Sex Toy Mogul Becomes Sex Therapist for Shrink
By Staff

*Today we learned that a certain prominent psychologist's couch folds out into a bed. And who's the bedfellow for this *cough, cough* intimate relationship therapist? (Intimate indeed!)*

None other than New York City's most eligible bachelor. Jack Sex-Toy-Mogul Sullivan has been providing sex therapy for a sex therapist.

The psychologist, Michelle Milo, who heads up several prominent New York City professional organizations and supposedly counsels patients on all their intimate issues, didn't wait long to pounce on her celebrity patient. (Can't blame you, Dr. Milo, he's a hottie!) They've been playing sexual healing games since he began seeing her to mend his broken heart. Hell, did she ever do a bang-up job! You may recall they were spotted at dinner and at the symphony, and we've learned their relationship didn't start with such innocent dates. It began in the most forbidden way! Scandalous!

Sources tell us their relationship started in her office when he went to see her to cure his woes. Poor guy has been missing his deceased fiancée, the Olympic medalist Aubrey Sheen, and Dr. Milo gave him a little loving between the sheets to make him all better. Evidently, he's done the same for her.

She first treated him at her office in an intake appointment that involved more than just talking. She then bumped him to special patient status, beginning "therapy" sessions, as they referred to them, after hours. "Looking forward to another 'therapy' session with you this evening,' he told her, to which she replied, "Will you be bringing any battery-operated friends?" The answer? When he plays sex therapist for her, he brings along his products. Well, duh. He IS a sex toy mogul. We just want to know which models you use, Jack. You know, so we can try them in our therapy games too.

*Patients of Dr. Milo might want to consider themselves warned. We have it on good authority he gave her the business in her office. Bring hand sanitizer before you bare your soul to the *cough, cough* intimate relationship shrink.*

His phone clattered to the carpet of the plane with a dull thud. Her hands shook. Her chest heaved, and shame flooded her veins from head to toe. Her insides were mangled, like a rusty saw digging through her chest, carving up pieces of her organs. Serving them to the press. She could smell the acrid scent of her career going up in flames as her reputation was burned at the stake.

Someone had clearly hacked her private email with Jack, and twisted their inside jokes and their naughty notes into a sordid story, making public what was supposed to be private, and what was so very personal.

She dropped her head to her knees. The flight attendant stopped and asked if she needed a bag. Michelle waved her off as dry heaves wracked her body. Jack rubbed her back, tried to comfort her, to tell her he'd get to the bottom of this. But even if he did, the damage was done.

CHAPTER TWENTY-SEVEN
Spin

The messages were too much.

They were overwhelming.

All that buzzing on her phone had been a stockpile of voicemails from clients canceling all day long. Clients calling in shock. Leaving messages like, "How can we trust our sanity and therapy to you when you are playing therapy games with him?"

Colleagues ringing her up. Carla wanting to know what the hell had happened.

The last message was the worst. The newspaper called—the real paper, not the gossip tabloid. The reporter wanted to know if she had a comment on the New York Chapter of the Association of Intimate Relationship Psychologists' statement that its ethics division was opening an investigation into whether she slept with a patient and took advantage of him.

She hadn't returned that call yet. That article was slated to run in *The New York Press* tomorrow.

Inside the safety of her own apartment, her brother tried to soothe her, but there was nothing to be done.

"We will figure this out. We will take care of this," he said, echoing Jack's sentiments from the plane. The two men she cared deeply about were here, having met in the most bizarre of circumstances when Davis was waiting at baggage claim. Her brother had wrapped her in a hug, and then shook hands with the man she was sure he'd rather not be meeting. He had known they were together—she told him before she'd left for Paris who she was traveling with—but he didn't know the details that were now being splashed all over the papers.

She curled up in a ball on her dove-gray couch, grabbing a blanket and huddling under it, clutching her phone. As if she could protect herself from more bad news by staying close to it. Making sure she didn't miss a single solitary piece of shit being flung her way.

"Do you have any idea how this happened? How someone got your emails?" Davis asked.

Michelle shook her head, too shell-shocked to even think rationally.

"Who would have a reason to do this?" he said, continuing to prod. "There's always a motivation. Whoever did this had to have motivation."

Michelle managed a humorless laugh. "You're such a director. Always thinking about motivation. Even at a time like this," she said.

"He's right," Jack said, weighing in. "Someone has it out to get you. Is there any chance it could be one of your patients?"

"No," she said emphatically. She wanted to believe they wouldn't skewer her like this. But she knew it would be foolish not to consider the possibility.

"Wait," Jack said, snapping his fingers. "You mentioned something in Paris—"

The phone rang, stopping him and she flinched all over.

"Let me answer," Davis said firmly.

She shook her head. "It might be a client." She put the phone to her ear. "Michelle here."

"On the couch? Is that true?" It was Shayla.

"Hi. And no," she said, because the time in her office was on the chair.

"Oh, thank God," she said with a relieved sigh. "Anyway, I'm so glad you're back. Because my husband is freaking out. When can I see you?"

Michelle was amazed that Shayla was completely focused on herself when the world around her was cratering. But then, at least one client was interested in someone other than Michelle, and she vastly preferred not being the center of other people's attention.

"I just landed. We can set something up for tomorrow. Is that soon enough?"

Shayla agreed, but when the call ended, Michelle latched onto something. *My husband is freaking out.* Could it have been Shayla's husband who did this? Was Clark Shayla's husband after all using a fake name? Was this his way of driving some sort of wedge between his wife, and the shrink he thought was encouraging her to leave him?

"Michelle," Jack said, and she flipped over and looked at him, amazed that mere hours ago she'd been flying home, blissfully unaware that her career was being tanked. "You said in Paris that you had a new client. You thought he was checking you out during a session, and then in the next one he knew too much about you," he said, repeating her words back to her. He'd remembered every single one. "Standard businessman, you said. He had dark hair, dark glasses. He looked like someone you bumped into outside your office."

She nodded. "Yes."

"Could it have been him? Did he take your phone? Did he have access to your phone at all?"

"No," she said, but then she swallowed back the word as the memory unfolded before her eyes. Clark coughing. Michelle leaving him to get water. Was that enough time? "Well, there was this one time right before we went to Paris," she said, and explained what happened during Clark's last session. "But he didn't take the phone. At the end of the session, it was still there in my drawer where I keep it."

Jack shook his head, ran a hand through his hair. "He doesn't have to take it. There's software that can clone a phone like that," he said, snapping his fingers. "All he had to do was have access to your phone for a minute, maybe two. Were you gone long enough?"

Down the hallway. Opened the fridge. Didn't see bottled water. Grabbed a mug. Filled it from the tap. Walked back to the office.

"Yes," she said as the chill seeped from her bones into her skin.

"He had to have done it. He took your personal phone while you were getting water and dropped an app on it that clones it. I bet that's what he did. Then, when he was on his computer watching the cloned phone, he was able to steal your password to your email."

Her brain pounded against her skull. Her mind was swimming, slipping further under water, gulping for air.

"But my personal phone has a screenlock. My work phone does too. How would he have gotten past it that quickly?"

"It's easy to break screenlocks," he said, grabbing his own phone, and showing her the screen. She wasn't sure what she was supposed to be looking for until he tilted it in the light next to her couch. When he had it angled just right, she gasped. The streaks from his fingerprints revealed his own screen lock. "The oils from your fingers. All he had to do was hold it just so to see the pattern you make."

"But why?" Davis asked, pressing once more. "What does someone have against my sister?"

Something caught her eye on his phone. An incoming email flashed across his notifications, and she swore it was from Michelle with two *Ls*. Her veins filled with ice. Before he could answer, Michelle pointed to his phone. "You have a new email from me," she said, in a dead voice.

from: michellewithtwols@gmail.com
to: justjack@gmail.com
date: Oct 1, 6:32 PM
subject: You like it dirty?

Try this for dirty. There's more with this came from. Back off now or else we'll really hit below the belt.

Jack turned to Michelle and her brother and gave them the answer. "They have nothing against her. It's me."

* * *

Her brother was a fighter. He had his fists clenched and was ready to go knock some teeth. Jack understood the impulse. He was ready to go to war for Michelle too. But he knew enough about battle to know this—you don't go to war without understanding the enemy.

Everything you can possibly learn.

That mantra had served his country well during his time in the army. He had to apply restraint now. Casey had sent over a batch of photos from an art show last night, and had captioned them *My lame attempt at playing Nancy Drew.*

But that *lame attempt* might be what they needed.

He showed each one to Michelle. First, a thin, baby-faced man.

She shook her head.

Next, a blond man.

"Not him."

He clicked on a guy with slick dark hair who looked eerily familiar, and the fingers of his memory reached all the way back to the night he'd met Michelle. He'd seen this man at The Pierson. This man had been watching Denkler. And watching Denkler meant watching Jack and Henry. Watching Jack turned into seeing him with Michelle.

She shook her head. He wasn't Michelle's fake client.

"It started with him, though," Jack said, seething. "They've been on us from the start. From the very first time Henry and I met with his brother-in-law. It was the night I met you. Conroy's guys have been watching every move Denkler made from the get-go. They must have been tailing Denkler that night when we met him. Then they stayed on me, and saw me with you."

"What the hell?" Davis said, interjecting, as he held out his hands as if to say *what gives*.

"There's one more picture," Jack said.

He reached the last photo and the quick release of breath, the slow-motion change in her expression, and the way she dropped her head into her hands said it all.

"That's him. Clark Davidson. That's what he said his name was. Oh my God, I feel so stupid," she said, and her brother sat next to her, draping an arm around her to comfort her.

"You're not. He pretended to be someone else. You're not stupid."

She lifted her face. Her eyes were rimmed with red. "I even looked him up. I never do that. But I just got this vibe from him. I tried to track him down online. He said he was a market researcher, but I found nothing, obviously."

Jack stepped away from them, and called Casey. "I need the name of the guy with the glasses," he told her.

Casey answered quickly. "Nick Bradshaw. He's second-in-command at a strategy firm."

"Home address?"

She was quiet for a minute, typing away. "Nope. Private."

"I'll find it," he said, and hopped on the Federal Election Commission page on his phone. This guy was into politics, so chances were good he'd have donated over the years to campaigns, and if he did, his address would be public record. Sure enough, a contribution to the last presidential election revealed that the fucker lived in the Village.

"I need to go," he said to Michelle, then turned to Davis. "Will you stay here with her?"

"Of course," he said protectively, narrowing his eyes. Jack got the meaning behind the stare. Jack was merely the lover who'd brought down a heap of trouble on Davis's sister, his family, his blood. Her brother had been the man in Michelle's life—her steady, her constant, the one person who got her through the shittiest times of all. Seeing that cool stare made Jack even more determined to prove himself. He had to right this ship.

He knelt down by Michelle, took her hand, and looked her in the eyes. It wasn't the sadness that stunned him. It was the defeat. The look of ruin already. This had the potential to destroy her career.

"I love you," he said, because it was all he could say right now that mattered. Anything else was an empty promise. This was the only true thing.

"I know," she said, managing the sliver of a smile.

"And I'm sorry. I'm sorry this is happening. That they're going after you. It's all my fault," he said, clasping her hand tighter.

She shook her head. "It's not your fault."

"I'm going to fix this. I'm going to fix this right now."

"It's okay," she whispered, but he knew it wasn't okay to her. It wouldn't be okay to anyone. She just wasn't the type of person who'd blame him, or anyone.

He left, but her brother followed him into the hallway, letting the door close behind him. "Don't hurt my sister," Davis said, his features stony.

"I won't hurt your sister."

Davis shook his head in frustration. "I mean it. If this is on you, you better make things right. As right as you possibly can."

"I have a sister too. I would do the same, and say the same if I were in your position. Michelle means the world to me, and I'll do everything for her."

Davis gave a curt nod, then turned on his heels.

Jack took off for downtown, hailing a cab, and arriving at Bradshaw's building fifteen minutes later. He buzzed 2C, then waited, muttering *c'mon* under his breath.

"Hello?" It was a man's voice, and Jack was ready to strangle him, so he called upon some extra stores of his best friend—*restraint.*

"It's Just Jack. I believe you wanted to talk about backing off. I'm on your steps."

"I'll be right down."

Jack leaned against the railing of the stoop, watching through the glass panels of the brown front door. Soon, he saw a man descend the stairs, then reach the ground level. He looked exactly as Michelle described. Standard businessman. Gray slacks, button-down shirt, loosened tie. He had dark hair and dark glasses.

He opened the first set of doors, then the second, stepping out onto the stoop.

Jack dug his nails into his palms to refrain from pummeling him, from grabbing this bastard by the throat and shaking the goddamn life out of him. That would do no good.

Instead, he took a different approach. He extended his hand. "Clark Davidson, right?" he asked, and Nick smirked. Jack continued. "Market researcher, I understand?"

Nick smiled wickedly in response. "I see she's been revealing patient-client confidentiality," he said, *tsk, tsking* under his breath.

Jack fumed. "Don't even go there," he said in a hiss.

Nick pretended to bug out his eyes. "Why?" he asked in fake shock. "What are you going to do to me?" Nick's eyes traveled to Jack's clenched hands. "You gonna hit me, Soldier-Turned-Sex-Toy-Mogul? Why don't you try? Why don't you see how I spin that?"

Smoke billowed from Jack's ears. He gritted his teeth.

"Keep it all inside," Nick continued, taunting. "Because they don't call me the Spin Doctor for nothing. You touch me, and I will find a way to make everyone hate you too." Nick laughed, revealing perfect white teeth. "Or maybe, take your chances. Take a punch at me. I turned your girlfriend into garbage. You think I won't find a way to pulverize you?"

Rage coursed through Jack's veins and he grabbed the man by the shirt collar. "You can't touch me. I run a fucking sex toy company. I sell dildos for a living. There is nothing you can do to me. My reputation doesn't matter."

"I know," Nick said with an evil glint in his dark eyes. "You're the fucking Teflon man, Jack. The press loves you. They love the grieving widower story. They love that you run a business with your sister. You're impenetrable. No one gives a shit if you like it dirty. No one cares if you fuck a woman on the Met Life Tower. Same way with Henry. He runs BDSM clubs with his wife, who's a cancer survivor. I can't touch her. But you," Nick said, poking Jack's chest, and he was ready to throttle the man. He'd started this war by going after Henry's business solely to knock down his brother-in-law. He'd already hit below the belt. Now he was firing bullets, by throwing around all the private times he'd learned about from their emails, "you gave us the perfect target."

The anger burned Jack's throat. He gripped Nick's collar harder. "I gave you nothing."

Nick cackled and shook his head. "You're wrong. You gave us everything we needed to take down our opponent. Because you started screwing a shrink. An intimate relationship psychologist, at that. I couldn't have planned it better. It was like taking candy from a baby. It was my easiest job ever. Because she takes herself so goddamn seriously. She's so perfectly above board. She does nothing wrong. Never a professional misstep, until you. We already got to Denkler through his sister. The easiest way to take him all the way down was through you. And now you're going to stop, aren't you?"

"Stop what?"

"Oh, I suspect when you leave my doorstep in twenty seconds, you will go to Denkler's and tell him to resign from the race. Or I will happily share all those emails and texts. My God, the things the two of you did." Nick said, recoiling, as if he were disgusted with Jack. "She's dirty. She likes it dirty, doesn't she?"

The rage spread like wildfire in Jack's blood. He twisted Nick's collar, pushing the man who once called himself Clark against the railing of his stoop.

"Do it. Push me over. Break a bone. And I will find a way to call you a pedophile. You think you're so fucking untouchable? No one is untouchable. For all I know, you might even sell child pornography."

Jack eyes were about to pop out of his head. He wanted to snap this man's neck, to crack every single bone in his body. But he knew he would only hurt Michelle and his sister and everyone at his company if he did that. Instead, he spat on him. It wasn't the least bit satisfying. Then he let go, and backed off.

"That's all you've got?" Nick said, taunting.

"No. That's all you're *getting*. You fucking scum."

Nick held out his hands, like a big-shot boxer gloating in the ring. "Politics, baby. We're the scummiest."

"You did all this to win a councilman race?"

Nick laughed. "I did it because it's my job. My job is to help my client win. By any means necessary. Conroy wants a victory in the Upper East Side, and I'm delivering it to him. Now, you do as I say. You go tell Denkler he needs to step down from the race by the end of next week or I will fucking bury your woman. Maybe I won't leak any more texts. Maybe I'll *escalate*," he said, biting off that word as if it were filthy. "Hell, maybe I'll even go straight to the ethics board and say she tried to seduce poor, vulnerable Clark Davidson in her office, too."

"You have no soul."

"Of course I don't. You should try it some time. It's freeing. Now I need to go wash my face. Because I know where your mouth has been," he said, and Jack broke. He ripped in two. The rational, logical part of him evaporated, and instinct took over. He lunged at Nick, and slammed his fist into the man's jaw.

Hard.

So hard, the man's lip cracked.

Then he did it again.

Nick yowled, and the sound was satisfying for about a second as Jack shook out his hand. He reached into his back pocket, grabbed his cell phone, and showed it to Nick. "By the way, cell phones are such nifty spying devices, don't you think? Feel free to go after me for assault. I've got this entire conversation recorded for posterity."

Then he walked off. When he could speak again without breathing fire, he called his sister and told her it was time for Plan B.

CHAPTER TWENTY-EIGHT
Plan B

Davis wasn't sure if he liked this guy. He wasn't sure if he wanted him anywhere near his sister ever again. But he respected her choices, and if she was in love with him, and was happy, then he'd support her.

Right now, she was asking him what he thought about Jack's Plan B.

Seeing as how his sister had already lost one-third of her clients, and it was only day two of the story from hell, he didn't see how Plan B could hurt. Especially since the *Page Six* story had taken on a life of its own and spawned viral videos on YouTube. Stupid spoofs of patients seducing shrinks, and vice versa. Many were rising up through the social world, his sister's friend Sutton had told him, warning him to keep Michelle off YouTube. That *Page Six* story had the longest legs he'd ever seen.

"Not a problem," Davis had said when Sutton called earlier. "I don't think Michelle even knows YouTube exists."

"Oh, stop it. Your sister is not clueless to the social media world."

"No. She's not. She just prefers to do other things. But I appreciate the heads up, Sutton."

"Is she okay?"

"She's pretty shell-shocked. Her mentor called and told her the workshop she was leading was axed. More clients cancelled. The backlash is pretty bad. They did a number on her with that story. It was like a match that started a whole fire."

Sutton gave a sympathetic sigh. "I'm so sorry. It's awful. Give her my love."

"I will," he said, then returned to his sister, who told him about Jack's plan.

She wanted to know if it could do more damage.

"It's so hard to say," he answered. "But I honestly don't know how it could do *more* damage. Maybe it could deflect the attention to him, where it should be."

"It's fine," she said, her monotone voice an echo of his sister. She was vibrant and sharp, like a high-definition TV. Now, she was playing in black and white as she listlessly opened her fridge, grabbed her water pitcher and poured a small glass.

"It's *not* fine. This should never have happened. It pisses me off that this happened," he said, treading dangerously close to what he wanted to say. *How can I not blame this guy you love?*

She drank the water, then set the glass on her counter. "It's not his fault, Davis. I know that's what you're thinking."

He held up his hands, knowing he'd been caught. "Michelle, you've worked so hard for your career, and I hate that this guy's support of a political campaign is killing you."

She scoffed. "I know. But I don't even care anymore."

"That's not true. You do care. You care about everything."

She shot him a rueful smile. "And look where it got me. Everything I've worked for is going down the drain."

"You'll reinvent yourself," he said, grasping her hand, changing tactics. He had to. His annoyance with Jack wasn't helping. He'd have to let it go. "And I'll be here every step of the way."

"I know. I just want to go away. Maybe I should take the job in Paris," she said in an offhand voice.

Davis straightened his spine. "You were offered a job in Paris?"

"Sort of. Well, almost. After my keynote, Julien introduced me to one of his colleagues, Denis. I talked to Denis for a while. He was impressed with my findings, and he emailed me yesterday to say he wants to talk more to see if I'd be interested in working with him. It was one of the many emails I received when I landed. I haven't had a chance to respond yet. I had a lot going on," she said sarcastically, and the fact that she'd recovered even a modicum of humor gave him a sliver of hope that she'd be okay.

"Do you want to talk more to Denis?" he asked gently.

She waved a hand dismissively. "I'm sure he hasn't seen the reports yet, and when he does, he won't touch me with a ten-foot pole either. You might as well just tell Jack that his Plan B is fine. I'm going to take a shower. I have to see the ethics board in an hour. Why don't you look at the email and tell me what Denis said? I can't bear any more bad news."

When he heard the shower running, Davis scrolled through his sister's work phone. It was the safe phone, as he'd started calling it. Her personal phone was the one that had been hacked. They'd been able to figure that much out since only details from her personal email had been revealed in the story, and she hadn't been emailing Jack while they were in Paris, so at least their time there was untouched, she'd said. She'd smashed her personal phone with a hammer last night.

He'd reset her work phone for her this morning, so they knew that one was clean.

He thumbed through her notes, looking for the one from Denis and read it quickly.

* * *

Michelle didn't think she could take another surprise hit. When she saw Jennifer from her consulting group leave the office of the ethics board on the Upper West Side building, she asked her directly, "What were you doing there?"

Jennifer held up her chin, and flashed a small smile. "I went in on my own. I wanted to tell them how much I admire you. How I know everything being said is wrong. That you're the victim, here, of a smear attack that has nothing to do with you."

A tear of gratitude threatened to escape. "You did that for me?"

The young therapist nodded. "I did. I don't need to know the details. I don't believe the stories."

"Thank you," Michelle said, truly touched. She didn't even know Jennifer that well, which made the effort all the more meaningful.

Jennifer leaned closer and whispered. "I bet it was that client you mentioned who was checking you out. Probably a psycho."

"Probably," Michelle said, then walked through a green door and into the office. She told her colleagues the same story she told Carla, that she told Kana, that she told anyone who'd asked. "He was never my patient."

It was the whole, entire truth, and it was all she had to go on. Kana had been there too, they said. Kana had explained that Michelle had referred Jack to her that very first day. More evidence, but she feared it would never be enough.

When she left, she checked her voicemail, and found more cancellations. She was hemorrhaging faster than a slashed artery. Sometimes the truth wasn't enough to change the reality.

* * *

Jack knocked on the green door. A graying man who looked like a professor invited him in. He was with a woman who had her hair pulled into a tight bun, and another man, who looked to be middle-aged. They were in charge of Michelle's professional fate. They held the power to take her license away.

The graying man went first. "Take a seat."

Jack sat on a hard brown chair. "I know you didn't call me, but I needed to be here."

"We are glad you found us. We treat all these situations seriously. Let's start at the beginning."

"She refused to treat me. It's that simple. Everything else is a lie. Everything is spin. It's the press trying to make it look a certain way."

Later, he joined his sister in midtown, who introduced him to her friend at *The New York Press*. Her name was Caroline, and he sat down with her at the corner table of a quiet cafe. Caroline wore her red hair in a tight braid down her back, and had a pink knit scarf around her neck. She shook his hand. "I'm going to take notes the whole time," Caroline said, diving right into the matter as she began typing on her laptop. "Let's start with the news of the hour, of course."

"The one about me being a guy who happens to be dating a shrink?" he said, doing his best to keep it light.

She laughed. "Yes, that one."

"Here's the story . . ."

He'd expected her question, and he'd answered honestly, as he'd done before the ethics board. He didn't know if this would be enough to save Michelle. But the problems had all started with perception. The media's perception of him. The public's perception of sexuality. Nick's perception of fair targets. If this had all started with warped perceptions, even the ones about him, he could at least set those straight.

After addressing the first question, Caroline dived into a bigger one. "I hope you don't mind me asking, why did you see a psychologist in the first place. Was it because of Aubrey?"

Ah.

The root of his problem. Of his struggles. Of what had sent him down the path and into Michelle's arms in the first place. The last thing he wanted to do was blame a dead woman. The truth of their split was something the deceased didn't need heaped on her.

But he could come clean about his own emotional state.

"You know, it was. But probably not for the reasons everyone thinks. I cared about Aubrey deeply, and I mourned the loss of her as anyone would. But by the time I went to see a therapist, I had a different issue to deal with surrounding her death. We had an argument that same day, a few minutes before her run, and she died shortly after. I'm going to live with that guilt. And I have been living with it for the last year, and I was ready to let it go. That's why I went to a shrink. To start to move past the regret I felt over the things that were said in those final moments. I was able to do that with another therapist, and also with the support of friends, family and people I love."

He wouldn't vilify a dead woman, but he didn't want to be known as the grieving widower anymore. "And that includes the woman I'm in love with. And yes, she happens to be a shrink, and I'm pleased to say she's not my shrink."

Caroline continued typing, then looked up at Jack, pausing over the keys. "I also understand from Casey that you have some new plans in the works related to the political campaign you've been supporting."

Jack nodded. "Yes, we do," he said because he hadn't asked Denkler to withdraw. That was never in the cards.

Denkler was trying to do good for the city, and he'd been forced into a corner. Jack wasn't going to continue to let Michelle, nor his business, his sister, his friends like Henry and Marquita, nor his life be dictated by a bully. Nick "Clark Davidson" Bradshaw might be able to spin a tale to the tabloids and start a viral trend, but that didn't mean everyone would respond to his tactics. "But we'd really rather show you. Do you have a minute to go to Eden?"

Caroline shot him a curious look as she closed her laptop. "I love Eden," she said in a whisper.

"So do a lot of people," Casey said, then dropped her voice too. "Have you tried The Wild One? It's divine."

"God, I know. It's amazing," Caroline said.

Minutes later, they'd reached the store on the Upper East Side. Even from across the street, anyone could tell it was packed. Casey had unleashed the marketing promotional plans on social media that morning, earlier than planned, since they'd switched to Plan B. But the change-the-conversation tactic needed to be moved up. Jack wanted to take all the attention off Michelle and off the BDSM clubs too. He'd gotten into this business in the first place because he believed in pleasure, and all the different routes to it. He believed playing dirty was best reserved for a true war, and for true lovers in the bedroom.

Caroline peered at the large sign in hot pink print on the front of the store.

"All proceeds from any Joy Delivered products bought at Eden in store and online for the rest of the year will be donated to breast cancer research. May your days and nights be filled with pleasure beyond your wildest fantasies."

Caroline's jaw dropped. "Holy shit. That could be a lot of money."

Casey jumped in. "So far today, in the first few hours of the promotion being announced, we've raised several thousand dollars. We planned to wait until the charity gala this week to make the announcement, but now seemed a better time."

Especially when the news of the donation spread throughout the district, to the same people who had once supported Conroy's campaign. Over the next few days, the conversation changed. There was very little talk amongst the residents of shutting down the clubs. In fact, business had never been better at Eden. Jack was pleased that they'd been able to extract themselves from a dirty, muddy race with something positive. That they'd been able to move away from the mudslinging and serve the community in a much more meaningful way.

Just as Jack had suspected, there were more people using battery-operated-friends than not, and they'd simply needed to reach those people with a positive message.

He'd been able to turn things around for business and for Denkler.

Too bad he hadn't been able to turn things around for Michelle. He was responsible for the mess she was in. Maybe not directly, but it was all on him. She was the collateral damage in a bullet aimed at a choice he'd made for his business.

One week after the story hit, she'd been cleared of any ethics violations, but she'd lost more than half her business. She'd lost all her speaking engagements. Her referrals were gone. The court of public opinion didn't offer much leeway for someone in her position. Even though she hadn't crossed any lines, people were only seeing her through one lens now.

The lens of sex.

She was the shrink who was the sex toy mogul's lover.

Even though she was so much more to him. She was everything.

CHAPTER TWENTY-NINE

Seemingly Impossible

"I'm very flattered with the offer, Denis. I truly am. But I want you to know what's been going on here. I don't want you to get into a situation unaware," she said, talking to her French colleague early one morning from the comfort of the small kitchen in her apartment. She was brewing coffee before she headed into the office for one appointment. That's all she had. Shayla. But damn it, she was going to do her best to help a loyal patient. Step one of rebuilding, as Davis had said. In the end, politics was politics. Sometimes the bad guy wins. Sometimes there's nothing you can do to blunt the damage. You take your blows, and you pick yourself back up. That's what she was doing.

"I heard some silly chatter about your private life, and I chose to ignore it. I do not judge people by what they do in private. I don't care what you do behind closed doors," he said, as she watched the coffee drip into the pot. She wished she could reach across the ocean and hug the man for saying the first evolved thing she'd heard in a long while.

"I appreciate it. But I want to make sure it's not going to be a problem," she said, and shared a few more details of all that had gone down.

He paused, and clucked his tongue. She tensed, sure this was the moment when he would rescind his offer. Besides, she didn't even know if she'd take it. "You were cleared by the ethics board?"

"Yes." She had Jack to thank for that. The graying man in charge had called her earlier in the week to tell her Jack's willingness to show up without having been asked, to share all the details, and to take ownership of their relationship had made the decision easy. Even Nick's attempts to discredit her with the board through spurious claims hadn't worked, given his persona as a fake client. She took some small measure of victory that she'd won that battle against Clark Davidson, though she was most decidedly losing the war.

"That is all I need to know on the matter," Denis said. "The offer stands. We would like you to come work with our practice. We need someone like you."

"I will think about it and get back to you."

She hung up, drank her coffee, and met Shayla for a session. But when the session ended, she had nothing to do but twirl in her chair. Twiddle her thumbs. Stare at a blank calendar on her screen.

If this is what reinvention looked liked, it stunk. Ten years of an impeccable reputation, ten years of working her ass off and building relationships with colleagues had led to this—Michelle had nothing to do.

She grabbed her phone and called Sutton.

"I'm bored. Can you get a coffee with me?"

Sutton laughed. "Darling, I have a casting call in an hour. But it's across town. Meet me on the corner of Lexington and Fiftieth and we'll walk together."

At least it was something to occupy the time.

"See you in fifteen minutes," she said. Because she had nothing else to do.

With her dark hair pinned neatly in a French twist, and a pair of brown leather boots for fall, Sutton looked crisp and gorgeous when Michelle spotted her resting against the street sign, tapping away on her phone. Sutton slipped her phone into her shoulder bag and wrapped her in a hug, then pointed to the crosswalk. They began their march across town, and Michelle told her everything about the job offer.

"Should I take it?"

"It does sound like a great job," Sutton said as they walked past noontime crowds scurrying around the city.

"I know," she said with a sigh. "So, tell me the truth. How badly do you miss Reeve when he's on a shoot?"

"Terribly," Sutton said with a pained sound in her voice. But then she softened. "Except, it's lessened because I know he's coming back. If you take the job, it won't just be for a few weeks here and there. You'd be gone. You'd be living there, and he'd be living here."

Michelle nodded. Her heart felt so damn heavy. "That's the issue, isn't it?"

Sutton stopped at the corner, and placed her hands on Michelle's shoulders. "You love your job. You're going through a rough patch right now. But the question is—

which will you regret more? Will you look at him every day and see him as the man who took your career away?"

"No!" Michelle said quickly, taken aback.

Sutton shook her head. "I don't mean like that. I know it's not his fault. But if you don't take this job, what will it do to your relationship with him? Will he simply become the man who got in the way of you taking another step in your career? Will you look at him and see only the lost opportunity?"

Michelle gulped, wishing her words didn't sound so damn insightful. "Are you the shrink now?"

Sutton laughed as they crossed the street at the green light. "I've just spent enough time with you to be able to see all these sides. And hell, I suppose you could try to make it work. Have a go of it. Be a Paris-New York couple. You wouldn't be the first, you won't be the last," she said, then tipped her chin down the street. "I've got to run."

She planted a kiss on Michelle's cheek, and took off for her casting call.

Michelle stood in place on the corner of Fiftieth and Broadway, watching her friend march with a purpose down the street, her silhouette mingling with a sea of other New Yorkers, all coming and going, heading in and out of revolving doors, to work, to meetings, to lunch.

All with purpose. All with a plan.

Except her.

She huffed out a defeated sigh, then shrugged. Maybe Jack was free. Maybe he could come out and play. Entertain her for a spell. She dialed his number, but it rang and rang and rang. Clutching her phone in her hand like a lifeline, she walked towards Times Square. Perhaps she could people-watch for a while. A few minutes later, a text popped up.

J: In a meeting. Thinking of you. I'll call you back soon, OK?

She wanted to kick herself for having been so needy, for having bothered him during the day.

Somewhere in this gigantic beast of a city was Jack, sleeves rolled up, chin down, focused on running his multimillion-dollar business. Meanwhile, she had nothing to do but stare at everyone else, and hope that someone, somewhere would need her.

* * *

"Take ten and then we'll go through the scene one more time," Davis said to the trio of actors on stage at the Belasco Theater on Forty-Fourth. After an hour of wandering, she'd found her way here and was waiting for her brother in the back of the Broadway theater where he rehearsed the play he was directing. As the actors walked off stage, he joined her in the seats.

Row P. Seats 101 and 102.

He ran a hand gently across her shoulder, then asked, "What's wrong?"

"Should I take the job in Paris?" she blurted out.

He didn't need details. He didn't ask for them. He had his answer. "Yes."

"But wouldn't I just be running away, then?"

"You need a breather, Michelle. You need time and space to recover from this. Go to Paris, take the job, and let this all blow over."

"I'll miss him," she said softly.

"I know," he said, his voice soft and kind too. "But you spend your whole life taking care of people, and it's what you love. You'll be unhappy without it."

She flashed back to how she'd felt in Paris. On stage. Delivering the keynote. Talking to her colleagues. She had been energized, alive, and firing on all cylinders. Here, without her anchor of work, she was drifting.

They talked more, and soon Davis gestured to the stage. "I need to get back to work. But join me later. Jill's back in town. We're all going to meet for drinks."

"Sounds good," she said, and as her brother rejoined the cast at the edge of the stage, she returned to a blank day, knowing as hard as it was, and as much as she'd miss Jack, she really ought to say yes to the job in France.

Work had made her happy. Work was her solid, steady, constant. It had never let her down.

* * *

When Jack came over that evening to get ready for his charity event, she didn't know how to tell him she was thinking of leaving. That she'd been offered a job that might have her flying across the ocean in two weeks time. For a woman who trafficked in words, she was floundering with the right ones to say to him. Instead, she focused on the present. She buttoned up his white shirt, tied his bow tie, and helped him slip on his jacket.

"You look so good in a tux," she said, her heart aching because he was so damn handsome, and she'd miss seeing him every day and every night.

"I would look better if you were by my side, but I understand you're not ready," he said, wrapping an arm around her waist and tugging her in for a kiss. She wasn't ready to be his date at the gala, not by a longshot. She wasn't even sure when she'd be ready to have dinner again in a restaurant with him. He didn't seem to mind, though. He understood the wound was still raw, and that it would take a long time to heal.

"Come over when you're done," she said when they broke the kiss. Perhaps, she could break the news then.

"I love that you invited me."

"You're always invited. You're always welcome," she said, even though *always* was being compressed into two more weeks.

"I'll always want to be with you."

"Always is a very long time."

He looked at his watch. "I don't have to be there for thirty minutes."

She rolled her eyes, glad to be playful. "You just got dressed in your tux."

"I'm a very fast dresser," he said, taking her hand and guiding her to the couch onto his lap. He brushed her hair behind her ear, and leaned in to whisper, "Undress me."

"Jack," she said, as if she were chiding him.

He shook his head. "No ifs, ands, or buts. If I can't have you by my side tonight, I want to make love to you now. And again later. And tomorrow, and the next day, and the next. We're together now."

"I know," she said, swallowing back the tears that threatened her. They were together now. But what would happen to being together when she left? For now, though, for this second, she wanted the same thing. She did as he asked, stripping him, then herself, before she sank onto him.

He made the sexiest groan as he filled her, and she nearly cried because it felt so good. Because it felt beyond wonderful. She gripped his shoulders and pulled him on top of her as she lay back on the couch, wanting to take him as deep as she could.

She ran her hands along his strong back, memorizing the feel of his skin, his muscles, *him*.

"See?" he said on a slow and easy thrust that had her gasping. "There's always time for this."

"Always," she echoed, squeezing her eyes shut, letting the sensations carry her away from the possibility of this ending. Of this being one of their last times together. She had so much to say, so much to tell him about all that she felt for him, but she could barely speak. She could only *feel*.

She catalogued the sensations. His bare skin so hot against hers. The sheen of sweat between their bodies. The closeness, the unbelievable closeness, as she wrapped her legs around his hips, inviting him deeper into her. She grappled at his shoulders, digging her nails in. He rocked his hips against her, moving inside her, the delicious friction and the sounds he made sending her close to the brink.

He made love to her passionately, possessively, in a way that blotted out everything but him, her and them.

"Michelle. My Michelle," he whispered reverently against her collarbone, brushing sweet and sinful kisses along the column of her neck.

The sound of his voice saying her name did her in. It set off the chain reaction of tears rolling down her cheeks, and ecstasy racing through her body. Tears and anguish all at once, in her body, in her mind. It was bittersweet, but she didn't want the bitter. She'd had enough bitter.

As she came down from the high of her orgasm, he held her face in his hands and lightly brushed her lips with his own.

"Have I told you today how much I love you?"

Since that day in the gardens he hadn't been able to stop saying it. Even through the mud and the muck and the dirt, he'd kept saying those words. Showing her how he felt. Being the man she wanted, and the man she needed.

After ten years of longing, after all that emptiness inside her, she couldn't give this up. She could reinvent herself in Paris, or she could reinvent herself here.

"And that's why I'm saying no to Denis," she said as they pulled apart.

He gripped her shoulders. "What?"

"He made me an offer today. I told you he'd expressed some interest. He made it official, since I was cleared. He wants me to work in his practice in Paris."

"You said no?"

She nodded. "I'm going to say no. It's past midnight in Paris so I haven't been able to respond to him today."

"Why?" he asked, furrowing his brow. "Why are you saying no?"

She shot him a look like he was crazy. She'd never been more sure of anything other than this—she wanted to be with this man. "Why?"

"Yes, why?"

"Because I'm in love with you, and you're here. Your business is here. You work in New York. I might have lost most of my clients, but I'm good at my job. I'll start over. If he'd made the offer six months ago, I'd have gone in a heartbeat. But everything has changed since I met you. I spent so much of my last decade chasing love with the wrong person. Now I have it with the right person. There are some things worth giving up for love," she said.

"You'd do that for me? Give up a job like that?"

She nodded.

"But that's an impossible choice," he said, hearkening back to their earlier conversation.

She shook her head. "It's not at all. It's what I'd do for love."

He swallowed, and seemed to be processing what she'd just said. "God, I fucking love you, Michelle Milo. More than anything. And I need to go now," he said, quickly dressing again.

She kissed him goodbye at the door.

"I'll see you in a couple hours," she said.

"Yes," he said, then she swore he added *but probably sooner* under his breath as he walked down the hall to the elevator. She waved goodbye and watched him go, feeling content with her choices. All of them—even the seemingly impossible ones.

CHAPTER THIRTY
Incandescent

Jack wasn't worried about Nick's threats to tarnish his reputation. The man had been unsuccessful in his quest to bully Michelle anymore, so Jack didn't have any real fear about being labeled as a pedophile or child pornographer. He also had that handy cell phone conversation filed away safely.

Denkler hadn't pulled out of the race. In fact, Henry's brother-in-law was well ahead in the polls thanks to the rash of money the Upper East Side had raised for breast cancer research. Jack had a hunch that all the orgasms the residents were now having thanks to the Joy Delivered products in their nightstand drawers had made them happier, and they'd be voting from their "pleasure centers" rather than their fear ones. Maybe from their hearts too. Or so he hoped.

But none of that was front and center as he and Casey sat at the head table of the charity gala at the Waldorf-Astoria. He had one thing on his mind. A choice that was not at all impossible.

"You're okay with what I'm about to do and say?" Jack asked his sister quietly.

"You big idiot. I couldn't be happier for you. I'm all set to capture it for posterity," she said, pointing to her phone.

The woman who ran the charity they were supporting took the stage and introduced herself. After speaking for a few minutes, she gestured to the front of the room. The lights were all on Jack and Casey.

"We are so very grateful for our biggest supporters, Jack and Casey Sullivan at Joy Delivered, who deliver so much joy to so many women," she said, stopping to hold up a hand. "Can we just have a show of hands? Who here has used a Joy Delivered vibrator?"

Nearly everyone in the room chuckled and nearly all hands rose.

"Are they the best vibrators in the world or what?"

"The best," someone shouted from the crowd.

"They are," the woman on stage said. "And we are simply overwhelmed and overjoyed with the money this company has raised for breast cancer research, not only tonight but with its tremendous generosity at Eden. I'd like to invite the CEO of Joy Delivered on stage to say a few words."

Jack nodded to his sister, who was poised to hit the record button on her phone. When he reached the stage, he said thank you, and took the microphone.

"It's a pleasure to be here, and an honor to be able to contribute and give back. When my sister and I started this company several years ago, we had a simple mission—bring pleasure to people. Bring happiness to people. Make them feel good. I've learned a lot running it. I've had some amazing times, and I'd like to think we've done some good things, and brought many orgasms to women everywhere. Some men tell me I have the best job in the world. They're right," he said, and took a beat to look out at the sea of faces—employees, donors, charity supporters and many more.

The hall was packed with women in evening dresses and men in tuxes, who stood for the same things, who wanted the same things—a world with more pleasure, less pain. The lights in the ballroom were bright, and he took a moment to imprint this scene in his memory, even though his sister was capturing it all on camera. He'd remember the din of the plates being cleared, the sound of footsteps from the waiters circulating, the rustle of fabric as women crossed and uncrossed their legs, waiting for him to say more.

"I do have the best job in the world. But it's also not everything, and as of now," he said, stopping to look at his watch, "I *did* have the best job in the world. Now I have something else that I want more, so I'm announcing tonight that I'm stepping down as CEO of Joy Delivered. My sister, Casey, will be taking over. She's already the brains and the beauty and the heart behind this company. I trust you'll all be in good hands." He gestured to his sister, who was beaming and crying happily as she held up her phone.

"Come up here and say your first words as CEO," he said.

She walked up the steps, and he walked down, and they stopped to hug along the way.

"I'll send it in fifteen minutes," she whispered.

"Thank you."

He loosened his bow tie, and walked out the back door of the ballroom, quickly racing to the front door to hail a cab. He stopped at his home first to pick up something he needed, then headed back to Murray Hill for Michelle. All the problems she'd encountered had come from his job. All the trouble she'd suffered, the losses, and the collateral damage had been because of him. He could do this one thing for her.

* * *

The flashing light on her phone made her flinch. A knee-jerk reaction, and one she didn't know she'd get over anytime soon. Most messages were friendly, but Michelle didn't know that she'd ever look at email, or texts, or her phone as anything but a potential point of violation again.

Davis raised his eyebrows as if to say, *Is everything okay?* She was at Speakeasy with him and Jill, who was in town for only a few days before she had to return to London for the opening night of her play. Julia was behind the bar, and Clay was here too, chatting with his wife as she poured a drink for Sutton. Nearly all her friends were here, and she was glad to be surrounded by the familiar. They were all part of why she was completely content with her choice to stay. She had friends, she had family, she had love. She was a lucky woman, indeed.

Her wish in this moment was simple—that this note on her phone be from a friend, not a foe. When she saw Jack's sister's name on the email, she felt a sense of relief. She opened the note.

Jack wants you to see this. I think you'll like it.

Her curiosity took over and she clicked on the link for the video, hitting play. It was all of fifty-three seconds, but by the end tears were streaming down her face, and her hand was on her mouth, and her shoulders were shaking. She didn't know what to do next. Was she supposed to find him? Was he going to call her? And was this really, truly all for her?

"What is it?" her brother asked as she wiped a streak of tears from her cheek. He stood up and moved closer. "Are you okay?"

"I'm more than okay," she managed to say, and thrust the phone at him, hitting play on the clip. She watched Jack's speech again, and she watched her brother's reaction, thrilling at the way his blue eyes shifted from inquisitive to delighted.

"I told you, you should take the job," he said playfully, then tapped the screen. "He's calling."

He handed her the phone. With shaky hands, she answered it. "Hello?" she squeaked out.

"It's me. I'm at your apartment, but it doesn't seem that you're here."

"I'm at Speakeasy. It's nearby," she said, giving him the address.

As she waited, her phone was passed around, and then Sutton threw her arms around her in a hug, Jill bestowed a kiss on the cheek, Julia toasted happily, and Clay beamed. But they weren't the ones she was dying to see. She couldn't take her eyes off the door. Every time she heard it open, she swiveled around, hunting for him. These five minutes were the longest of her life.

Soon enough, the most beautiful sight greeted her. Jack, entering Speakeasy, and walking towards her with the biggest grin she'd ever seen on his beautiful face.

He took long strides to reach her, his eyes on her, only her.

"I didn't expect to see you so soon. It's only been an hour," she said.

"It seems I have a lot of free time now," he said. He dipped his hand into the pocket of his jacket and took out a small gift, handing it to her.

She unwrapped it to find a sapphire-blue perfume bottle. She gasped when she saw it.

"You said there was one you wanted, but when you went to get it the shop was closed. It was closed too when I went back that day I found you in the Gardens. But I returned again the next day and bought one for you. I hope it's like the one you had your sights set on."

"It's gorgeous," she said, cradling the small and elegant bottle.

"Beauty for beauty's sake. Love for love's sake," he said. "I was looking for the right time to give it to you. This seemed to be the right time."

"Did you really resign?"

He nodded. "I want you to go to Paris. I want you to take the job." He reached for her hand, clasping it tenderly.

"You do?"

"Yes. More than anything. Well, there is something else I want."

"What is it?" She didn't want to assume anything. She wanted to hear it all from him.

"What would you think about taking me with you? I'm no longer the CEO of a sex toy company. I'm just a man in love with a woman, and willing to go anywhere for her."

Her heart flew out of her chest. It soared on new wings, flying with radiant joy and happiness. She'd never expected to feel this way. She'd never expected a love like this. And she'd never imagined that a man would give up his business to be with her.

"You gave up your business?"

He nodded. "My business caused all the trouble. You could barely do your job here, given the job I had. I want you to have a private life, not just a public one. So I gave up my job to be with you, and you're worth it, because you've given me everything. You've given me love. I didn't even know that I could love, and now I know I can. Because of you. I just hope you don't mind dating an unemployed man."

She laughed, and shook her head. "What are you going to do in Paris?"

"Love you," he said, confidently. "Take me with you. You haven't said yes to me yet. You're toying with me, right?" he asked, the corner of his lips quirking up in a smile.

"I'm not teasing you. I'm just shocked. I didn't think you'd make this kind of choice. Isn't it an impossible choice?"

He shook his head. "It's not an impossible choice. It's the only choice."

She felt as if she were dreaming. As if this moment was going to slip away through her fingers. She wanted to grasp it forever, to hold onto it for the rest of her life so she'd never forget how she felt.

"You still haven't told me if you want me to go with you," he said, reminding her. Then, only then, did she look away from him to take in the scene unfolding before her. All her friends, her family, her brother, the man she once loved, they were all here, and they were all watching her and Jack. Everyone was waiting for her answer. They were all witnesses to her incandescent happiness.

She turned to Jack. She gripped his hand tighter, pulled him closer, never wanting to let go. "Come with me to Paris."

EPILOGUE
Lovely Rain

Life wasn't entirely perfect in Paris.

Some days, for instance, it rained.

Oh, wait. That wasn't a bad thing. Even the rain in Paris was lovely. *Especially* the rain in Paris was lovely.

While Michelle had missed her brother, she'd met him in London a few months ago, when Jill had performed in *A Streetcar Named Desire*. Jack had joined her. His schedule was much lighter these days.

But it was starting to fill up. After a few months enjoying being a man of leisure, drinking espressos, and shopping for lingerie for her while she worked, he'd started up a new business.

He'd begun advising several French companies, some specializing in lingerie, some in sex toys, on entering the American market and the particular challenges and opportunities across the pond. It was a perfect job for his strategic brain.

They lived in the 6th arrondissement, not far from her work, in a flat above a leather handbag store and a macaroon shop. Joy Delivered was thriving back home, thanks in part to its continued business online and in stores with its biggest customer, Eden. The premiere vibrator boutique in New York had remained open and so had the BDSM clubs, thanks to Denkler winning the campaign on the power of a positive message. In some ways, the campaign wasn't even about the candidate.

It was about pleasure being more powerful than politics.

It was about what happened behind closed doors being personal, and private, and not public at all.

It was about doing good for a neighborhood.

The law was a powerful thing too, though, and Michelle had a smart lawyer friend who'd tipped off the federal government about the phone hacking. Nick Bradshaw had been investigated for computer crimes. What he'd done to Michelle was only a misdemeanor, but it wasn't his first time, and it turned out he had quite a sordid history of underhanded tactics in his arsenal as the *Spin Doctor.*

So many that he'd been sent to prison.

Michelle hoped he'd have a hell of a hard time spinning his jail time.

One Tuesday morning in April, after a phone session with Shayla, who'd left her husband and was managing better than she'd thought she would on her own, Michelle caught a train to Giverny. Jack had been working in the countryside today, advising a wealthy client in Rouen, so they were meeting in the middle, and had nothing planned but lunch at a cafe in the quiet village where Monet had painted.

When she arrived, she didn't see him at the entrance. She checked her phone and saw he'd sent a message that he was already inside and to come find him on the bridge.

She meandered through the gardens where ruby red, sky blue, and sun yellow petals were in bloom. Spring had coasted into Giverny, bringing along a blanket of new colors. The lily pond waters were blue and glassy, reflecting the last bit of midday sun before the gray clouds at the edge of the sky blocked it. Soon she spotted Jack on the bridge, one arm resting on the railing, the other in his pocket.

"Fancy meeting you here," she said, and dropped a quick kiss on his lips. She'd never grown tired of kissing him. She never would.

"Thank you for meeting me here. I'm a lucky man to be able to play hooky with you. Do you want to walk around the gardens?"

"I would love to."

"Oh wait," he said, smacking his forehead. "There's something I meant to ask you."

She cocked her head to the side. "What is it?"

He dropped down to one knee, and her mouth fell open. His eyes met hers, blazing with love and passion.

"Michelle, it only seems fitting to ask you this here, since this is your favorite place in Paris that's not in Paris, and it's my favorite place, too. Because it's the place where I was finally able to tell you over and over how much I love you. And ever since that day I haven't been able to stop saying it. Because I feel it everywhere. In every part of me."

Her hand flew to her heart. A tear of joy slid down to her cheek as he reached into his pocket and removed a small black box. "I do too," she whispered.

"I've always asked you to give yourself to me. And you

have. Before I even deserved it. And I hope to keep deserving it, every day for the rest of our lives. And I want to ask you if you can give me one more thing. *You*. Always. Will you be my wife?"

She dropped down to both knees and threw her arms around him, joy flowing through her bloodstream. "Yes. I'm yours. Always."

"Always is a very long time, and it's exactly how long I want you," he said, then slid a beautiful diamond onto her finger, and kissed her endlessly on the bridge. He didn't even stop when it started to rain.

Yes, come to think of it, there wasn't a single thing wrong with Paris, or France. Not even the rain. The rain was wonderful too.

THE END

Check out my contemporary romance novels!

The New York Times and USA Today
Bestselling Seductive Nights series including
Night After Night, After This Night,
and *One More Night*

Caught Up In Us, a New York Times and
USA Today Bestseller! (Kat and Bryan's romance!)

Pretending He's Mine, a Barnes & Noble and
iBooks Bestseller! (Reeve & Sutton's romance)

Trophy Husband, a New York Times and
USA Today Bestseller! (Chris & McKenna's romance)

Playing With Her Heart, a
USA Today bestseller! (Davis and Jill's romance)

Far Too Tempting, an Amazon
romance bestseller! (Matthew and Jane's romance)

Stars in Their Eyes, an iBooks bestseller and
the start of the new adult series Wrapped Up In Love!
(William and Jess' romance)

My USA Today bestselling
No Regrets series that includes

The Thrill of It
(Meet Harley and Trey)

and its sequel

Every Second With You

My New York Times and USA Today
Bestselling Fighting Fire series that includes

Burn For Me,
(Smith and Jamie's romance!)

and *Melt for Him*
(Megan and Becker's romance!)

Coming Soon!

Stay tuned for Sweet, Sinful Nights in the Seductive Nights series in early 2015! Here's a teaser...

"And that's why you should never shave your own balls."

Laughter rang out across the club as Brent Nichols delivered the punchline to one of his final jokes of the evening. There was no better sound than this. Than the crowd unable to stop laughing. Than the pause he had to take as he paced across the stage of the comedy club in Vegas, giving them time to come down from the temporary high of a joke well told.

He lifted the microphone back to his mouth, ready to move into the last few bits in his act, when he zeroed in on a blond at the back table.

At first, he was sure he was seeing things, and conjuring up a far-too familiar face. One who had tripped through his dreams far too many times. One he'd tried to banish over and over. He blinked but she was still here, her hair a wild, wavy tumble, her lips so full and soft, her blue eyes fixed on him with that knowing, naughty stare, her body even better than before.

Curvier, sexier. Wilder.

His breath fled. His heart stopped. He hadn't seen her in years. But here she was, in his club, on his turf.

She was the one that got away.

ACKNOWLEDGEMENTS

Much gratitude and love to my friends and colleagues who helped shape this story. They include Violet Duke, with her impossible choices, Kim Bias with her keen suggestions, and Kelley Jefferson who turned the key in the ignition with the set-up. Big thanks to Tanya Farrell who read every chapter as I wrote and offered tweaks and tune-ups, to Jen McCoy who cheered me on, and to Gale who brainstormed the big gesture.

Thank you to Theresa Stokes Harrell, who is a goddess of sex toy knowledge and served ably as the official sex toy consultant for this book.

Thank you to Sarah Hansen for the gorgeous cover, to Helen Williams for fabulous graphics, to Kelley for the daily grind, and to Kelly P for being my sherpa, coach, cheerleader, mama bear, manager and favorite person to talk to. Lauren McKellar offered her wisdom in fine-tuning details and Kara proved an eagle eye.

I am lucky to have met so many wonderful people in the book community – the talented bloggers, passionate readers, outspoken advocates of books and sexy romance – I adore you all.

Big thanks to my family, my husband, my children and my dogs – they are all my reasons for everything I do, every late night, every early morning. Thank you for being by my side.

Most of all, THANK YOU, the person reading this book. You rock my world and you turn it inside out with joy. Thank you for making dreams come true.

CONTACT

I love hearing from readers! You can find me on Twitter at LaurenBlakely3, or Facebook at LaurenBlakelyBooks, or online at LaurenBlakely.com. You can also email me at laurenblakelybooks@gmail.com.

10609908R00231

Printed in Great Britain
by Amazon.co.uk, Ltd.,
Marston Gate.